He was standing just e bonded witch. She was naked. So was he. They could be joined within moments, hot and sweaty and needful and complete.

Complete. Just like they were destined to be.

Groaning with raw need, T.J. fisted his hands. His birth-right mark glowed. Another wave of yearning swept over him, this time coupled with a vague sweetness that felt completely foreign. And unwanted. He'd be damned if he'd be sweet. He'd be damned if he would *need* this way. He refused now, just like he'd refused three days ago.

But the thought of Dayna standing there, rubbing beads of water from her bare skin, inch by succulent inch, made him feel nothing but need. He closed his eyes to shut it out. That only made the image more vivid. He could almost feel the yielding softness of her skin against his mouth, could hear the breathy gasp she would make when his hands slid over her hips.

He thought of her calling his name—his true name, the one no one knew except his parents, Deuce, and his magus. He wanted that. He thought of her smiling at him. He wanted that, too. He thought of her seeing him—light and dark, warlock and Patayan—and staying with him anyway. He wanted that most of all.

At the intensity of his craving, his knees buckled.

Books by Lisa Plumley

MAKING OVER MIKE

FALLING FOR APRIL

RECONSIDERING RILEY

PERFECT TOGETHER

PERFECT SWITCH

JOSIE DAY IS COMING HOME

ONCE UPON A CHRISTMAS

MAD ABOUT MAX

LET'S MISBEHAVE

HOME FOR THE HOLIDAYS

MY FAVORITE WITCH

SANTA BABY
(anthology with Lisa Jackson,
Elaine Coffman, and Kylie Adams)

Published by Zebra Books

My Favorite Witch

Lisa Plumley

ZEBRA BOOKS
Kensington Publishing Corp.
http://www.kensingtonbooks.com

ZEBRA BOOKS are published by

Kensington Publishing Corp.
119 West 40th Street
New York, NY 10018

All Kensington titles, imprints, and distributed lines are available at special quantity discounts for bulk purchases for sales promotion, premiums, fund-raising, educational, or institutional use.

Special book excerpts or customized printings can also be created to fit specific needs. For details, write or phone the office of the Kensington Special Sales Manager: Attn. Special Sales Department. Kensington Publishing Corp., 119 West 40th Street, New York, NY 10018. Phone: 1-800-221-2647.

ISBN-13: 978-1-4201-0568-1
ISBN-10: 1-4201-0568-X

First Printing: September 2009
10 9 8 7 6 5 4 3 2 1

Printed in the United States of America

To my husband,
John,
who makes me believe in magic every day.
I love you!

Chapter One

By the time T.J. McAllister hit downtown Phoenix, Monday morning rush hour had already begun. Caught in bumper-to-bumper traffic, he stared down Central Avenue, looking for his target. Unfortunately, the buildings nearby were solid. He couldn't see past or through them. Whether stucco or glass and steel—both of which stood side by side in the October sunshine—the structures had been built by human hands and were thus impenetrable.

His InterAllied Bureau partner, Deuce Bailey, wasn't bothered by the impediment. Protected by sunglasses and wielding his usual exuberance, he kept his hands on the wheel of his Mustang.

"Six down and one to go." Deuce nosed the vehicle forward, progressing another block. "I hope this one's expecting us."

"She won't be."

"I mean, after the last one, we could use an easy snare."

"She's a runaway. She won't be easy."

"You don't know that. Maybe we'll get lucky."

"Luck has nothing to do with it." T.J. pulled a pair of dusty handcuffs from the glove compartment. He blew them clean. "Runaways take off for a reason. They don't want to be found."

Deuce looked askance at his handcuffs. "You really think you need those? These cusping witches are unpredictable, but—"

"Better safe than sorry."

"Like hell. When have *you* ever done anything safe?"

"There's a first time for everything." T.J. bundled the cuffs in a tight metallic clump. He closed his hands over them, prayer-style, then focused on their shape. When he spread his palms again, the bonds had transformed into a golden amulet. He lifted it by its thin leather strap, then hung it around his neck. "There it is—Dynamic Research Libraries. Turn here."

Deuce swerved onto a side street. Other vehicles lined its narrow passage. A full parking structure stood to their right; their destination waited to their left, housed in a four-story building with concrete pillars, wide steps, and lots of glass.

Deuce parked. "That glass could be a problem."

"So could your worrywart routine."

Cheerfully, his partner offered an obscene gesture. "Maybe you like being assigned to glorified carpool duty, but I don't. The sooner we finish this job, the better. Let's make it clean this time, too. IAB really chewed my ass after Cobalt."

T.J. frowned, studying their surroundings. On this street, all the buildings were of human construction, but a few of their embellishments were not. The fuchsia bougainvillea trailing up the parking structure, bits of grass and flowers, an SUV with dark windows, custom paint, and elaborate rims . . . all those were of magical origin. To T.J.'s gaze, they appeared pixilated.

The effect owed itself to missing molecules, gaps in the material that had been rearranged. Even witchfolk couldn't create something out of nothing, but they could stretch reality.

"Looks like the landscapers are able."

At his use of the term, Deuce peered at the grass. Then the oleander next to it. Then the bougainvillea. "I don't see it."

"That's why you're staying here."

"I should go. She'll sense you, but if I'm the one—"

"By the time she knows I'm there, I'll have her."

"Damn it, T.J. You should try trusting me sometime."

"Yeah? What would that get me?"

Flatly, he stared at Deuce. His partner, big as an NFL lineman and equally tough, blinked and glanced away first.

Satisfied, T.J. transferred his gaze to the folder lying open on the dashboard. All business now, he stole a final glance at the assembled materials, then flipped the folder closed.

He'd stared at the photo inside for the past hour. He knew Dayna Sterling's wide-set eyes, her aura of open yearning, her attractive but unremarkable features. Unless she'd magiked the arrangement of the bones in her face, he'd recognize her.

"Wait here and be ready to move."

"I thought I'd get an espresso to kill some time." Deuce grinned, obviously recovered from their previous standoff. "Triple shot, fully caffeinated. Sounds good, right?"

"Keep it away from me, or I'll morph you into a gnat."

With no time for further talk, T.J. opened the door and stepped onto the street. Traffic sounds buzzed loudly in his head. The human-built structures, with their solidity and pressure, made his vision burn. His chest ached, an effect of being exposed to so many unfettered human emotions at once.

With steely will, T.J. tamped down his reactions. He couldn't afford to be distracted.

From the Mustang, Deuce whistled a familiar signal.

T.J. turned. His partner had rolled down the window and was leaning out of it elbow-first, sunshine glinting off his shades.

"You forgot to take your bug." He tossed a stoppered vial.

Hell. Reluctantly, T.J. caught it. He turned over the vial, examining the insect within. The brass at IAB were proud of this particular item. They'd lavished plenty of development time on getting the details right. To the untrained eye, it appeared to be an iridescent winged beetle. To T.J., it looked like exactly what it was—the consequence of his recent "noncompliance."

If the agency wanted to monitor him, they'd have to do better than this. He lifted the stopper, then shook out the beetle. It unfurled its purple wings in midair and flew away.

With that done, it was time to get serious. Dayna Sterling was unlinked, unaware, and utterly alone in this world. Wherever she was inside that building, she had no idea what was about to hit her. T.J. would have staked his tracer's license on it.

Dayna Sterling was hip-deep in files, researching the fastest growing varieties of spathiphyllum for a client, when her cell phone rang. Reluctant to lose her place amid the family *Araceae*, she stuck her thumb in the *monocotyledonous flowering plants* section of the desk reference she'd found, then answered.

"Dayna, it's me. Listen, you've got to cover for me."

Recognizing the voice of her best work pal, Jill Mansdale, Dayna stuffed a bookmark in her place. "Sure. What's up?"

"I'm sick." Jill coughed. "I think I have a virus."

"Please. Eighty-six the fake symptoms. It's me, remember? Jane is in a meeting until ten o'clock, so you're in luck. What's really going on?"

Freed from the threat of their boss overhearing their conversation, Jill said, "Thad broke up with me last night."

"Oh, Jill. I'm so sorry."

"He said he couldn't handle the pressure of being with me."

"What? That's crazy! You're wonderful, I swear."

"Also that he'd met someone in his nighttime MBA classes. He thought he and Destiny were a better fit."

"Someone named 'Destiny' is getting her MBA?"

"Yes." A tremendous sniffle. "I hope she chokes on it."

"Me, too. Do you want me to hex her for you?"

Her friend laughed. "I wish you could."

"That makes two of us." Woefully aware of her own short-comings, Dayna put up her feet on her desk. Idly, she examined her black Converses. She focused. *Red red red.* She looked again. Still black. It was a good thing no one here knew exactly how pathetic that was. "I'll cover for you, don't worry. Take all the time you need, okay? Throw darts at Thad's picture, set his stuff on fire . . . whatever you need to do to heal."

"Um, I think the pyro routine might be illegal."

Was it? Even after all these years, Dayna was still shaky on the finer points of her new life. Her knowledge gap—usually compensated for with alphabetized files, an attention to detail that bordered on obsessive, and (when all else failed) a smart-alecky attitude—left her feeling more of an outsider than ever.

With deliberate effort, she shook off the sensation. She was good at what she did. She'd carved out a new beginning for herself. That was what mattered most. "Okay then. Try to stay out of jail. Either way, I'm here for you if you need to talk."

"Thanks, Dayna. I knew I could count on you."

Relishing those words, Dayna smiled. So what if her shoes didn't change color? "Of course you can. What are friends for?"

"Today? Making me feel better."

Just as she heard those words, a peculiar tingle began at the base of Dayna's spine. She stilled as it crept up each vertebra, tiny but insistent. It felt like an electric razor humming harmlessly against her skin . . . except this sensation was anything but harmless. Eleven years of surviving on her own had taught her that. This was a warning signal, plain and simple.

With her senses attuned to the slightest sound or movement, Dayna listened to Jill talk while she scrutinized her cramped office. Stacks of manila file folders waited on her desk. Her laptop computer glowed, displaying an entry from a private botanical research database. Scraps of paper and notes about other clients' assignments adorned her bulletin board.

In the corner, her trusty backpack slumped against the nearest of her four vintage filing cabinets. Photos of friends—her surrogate family—adorned the scarred tops of the wooden cabinets. So did an iPod speaker/dock and a bowl of goldfish. Behind her office door, her ten-speed bike stood propped against the wall, ready for the short ride home to her neighborhood.

Everything appeared normal. But that tingle remained.

"Jill, I'm sorry. I've got to run." With her heart rate kicking into high gear, Dayna gripped her phone more tightly. Her palms felt damp. "I'll see you tonight. Okay if I drop by?"

Her friend answered, but Dayna scarcely registered Jill's reply. She slid her office chair sideways, then unzipped her backpack with her free hand. She fished within, shoving aside papers and books, her wallet, her house keys . . . aha. Score.

She pulled out the item she sought—a child's polka-dotted plastic pencil case. Ending her call with Jill, Dayna put down her phone, then unzipped the case with trembling fingers. Inside, colored pencils, crayon stubs, and fat Magic Markers rolled around. Some of the items were decoys, but others—

"Aha! I *knew* something was up when I saw that rogue log-in."

The voice came from her office doorway.

Startled, Dayna grabbed a Magic Marker. Wildly, she aimed.

Nothing happened. Shana Termagante, her boss's admin, smirked. Her scornful gaze headed straight to the marker.

Feeling ridiculous, Dayna lowered it. The "threat" she'd sensed had been an ordinary, if obnoxious, woman—a colleague armed only with a notepad, a smug expression, and an overdose of nosiness. Even now, Shana sent a suspicious glance toward Dayna's laptop, which displayed an incriminating page from PlantNet, the subscription-only botanical research database.

"I'm sorry, Shana." Dayna stretched her arms, allowing her elbow to "accidentally" close her laptop. "You startled me."

"There's no point trying to hide that screen." Shana's prying gaze didn't swerve from her laptop. "I saw what you were doing. Nobody's authorized to use that access code except Jane." She narrowed her eyes, clearly savoring this opportunity to cause trouble . . . as usual. "I could have you fired for this."

Dayna shook her head. "Jane wouldn't like that."

"Why not? This place is brimming with research assistants. Nobody would mind losing one . . . especially you."

Wounded, Dayna fisted her Magic Marker. A single hurtful comment shouldn't have bothered her. Not after all she'd been through in Covenhaven. She was older now. Tougher. And yet . . .

The marker seemed to grow warmer in her hand.

Surely that was a trick of her imagination.

"Go ahead. Have me fired." Dayna jerked up her chin. "But I hope you have a backup plan for the next time Jane has a report due for a client. Otherwise, there's going to be trouble."

"Really?" Dubiously, Shana crossed her arms over her chest. Her ever-present notebook poked out. "Why is that?"

"Well . . ." Dayna pretended to ponder the question. Her Magic Marker seemed to grow larger and hotter in her grasp, as though fueled by her increasing annoyance. "This might be hard for a nonresearcher to understand, but I'll try to explain it to you."

Another smirk. "Yes, please do."

"Okay. I'll use small words." *Throb* went her marker. "See, one of Jane's favorite tricks is to edit *my* reports, add in a few details from her exclusive sources"—she nodded toward her laptop and the PlantNet database—"then steal *all* the credit."

"That's not true! It can't be true. Jane is brilliant."

"Jane," Dayna said simply, "is a thief."

She couldn't figure out why she'd worked for Jane for so long. Except that she'd miss Jill and her other office buddies if she left. But aside from that . . .

"You're the one who hacked into her database."

Well, that was true. Shana had her there.

"Only to prove my point. Jane can't keep getting away with taking credit for everyone else's work. It's not fair."

"'Not fair'?" Shana arched her brow. "Spoken like a true research wonk. If you people put as much energy into working as you do into complaining, lazing around, and skipping out for coffee together, you might not have to cheat to get ahead."

"I wasn't cheating," Dayna said hotly.

And she didn't drink coffee either. She hated the stuff—for good reason. But when she'd typed in that access code, she'd felt almost heroic. She'd been acting on behalf of all the overlooked researchers who labored behind the scenes to make the brass at the research library look good. No matter how hard Shana tried, she couldn't take away that feeling.

"Let's face it, Dayna. People are either winners or losers. Losers are the ones who get stuck on what's 'fair.' Winners don't care about that, because they're busy succeeding."

Or maybe she could. Uncertainly, Dayna wavered.

Suddenly, she didn't feel very heroic. She felt doubtful. A little angry. And most of all, unjustly judged.

At the realization, Dayna felt her Magic Marker flare with new heat. Curiously, she glanced at it. Children knew the power of a Magic Marker. With a jolt of imagination, they could turn a marker into a rocket ship, a lipstick, a machine gun.

She wished she'd been born with the innate ability of a child—not to mention a child's unshakable belief in herself.

"Even *if* Jane were stealing the researchers' work," Shana

continued, "would it really be that bad? After all, it's the good of the company that matters. That's the bottom line."

"No matter who gets hurt?"

"So melodramatic." Her colleague made a tsk-tsk sound. "If everyone is so bugged by what Jane is supposedly doing, why aren't *they* doing something about it? Why you? All alone?"

"Because—" Abruptly, Dayna stopped. She didn't know. Maybe she *was* alone in trying to do something about Jane. It wouldn't be the first time she'd swum against the tide.

"Anyway . . ." Shana looked her up and down, taking in Dayna's geek-casual ensemble of beat-up Converse, thrift-store painter's pants, and a vintage SAVED BY THE BELL T-shirt. "Good luck with your upcoming job hunt. Believe me, you're going to need it."

Irredeemably pushed, Dayna gritted her teeth. In a flash, she wielded her Magic Marker, brandishing it like a sword.

Shana laughed. "What are you going to do with that?"

Even the score, Dayna thought with a spark of almost-forgotten insight. But things didn't *exactly* work out that way.

Chapter Two

Instead, a weird cracking noise sounded. An instant later, her goldfish bowl exploded in a shower of glass fragments and stinky gushing water. Dayna swiveled, gawking as her two goldfish flopped in the current, streamed over the top of her filing cabinet, then landed in an eddy of water at her feet.

Damn it. That wasn't what she'd intended at all.

But things like this had been happening a lot lately. Especially when she got emotional about something.

With a muttered exclamation, Dayna dropped her malfunctioning Magic Marker and grabbed her desktop pencil cup instead. She shook out all the pencils, then knelt at the spot where poor Buffy and Spike were flopping on the industrial gray carpet. Cautiously, she scooped up the goldfish along with some of their semimurky water, hoping she'd acted quickly enough.

"How did that *happen*?" Wide-eyed, Shana stared at her. "One second that goldfish bowl was fine, and the next . . . pow!"

A shrug. "I guess there was a fault in the glass."

Shana seemed doubtful. "It looked like an explosion to me."

"Accidents happen." It was the same excuse Dayna always

offered. She hadn't had much need for it here . . . until recently. Concerned about her goldfish, she peered into the cup. Buffy and Spike swam listlessly, their glistening bodies expanding and relaxing with their labored breathing. "They look scared."

Shana scoffed. "They were nearly fish shrapnel."

Dayna cast her an appalled look. "Remind me never to ask you to fish-sit. I think they'll be okay in a few minutes."

Also, her feet were getting wet. Suddenly aware of the water squishing into her sneakers, Dayna moved out of the puddle. She frowned downward. "Can you grab a mop, please?"

Shana stepped back. "Mopping is *not* my field of expertise."

"Don't worry. I'll do the actual work." Carefully, Dayna set down her goldfish. She crouched to pick up slimy glass shards, then tossed them in the trash. She brushed her palms together, assessing the job. "I just want you to get the mop."

"No way. I'll call building maintenance."

"By the time they get here, this carpet will be a total loss." Not looking up, Dayna attempted to sop up the worst of the spilled water with leftover deli napkins. "My office will smell like fish bait for months. Come on, Shana. Just help me."

A peculiar silence made her spine tingle again.

Dayna peered over her shoulder.

As she'd suspected, Shana had fled. Her office doorway was vacant. She sincerely doubted the admin had gone for a mop.

Annoyed, Dayna stood. She dropped her final wad of sodden napkins in the trash, then bent to double-check her goldfish.

"Dayna Sterling?"

Startled by the sound of a male voice, she glanced up.

In reaction, a wad of papers flew upward, too. They

billowed as though they'd been shot from a cannon, white and rustling.

Damn it. Not again. She hurried to the corner and batted them down, trying to gather them into a stack on the cabinet.

In the process, she stole a self-conscious glance at her visitor. The man standing in her doorway was big, broad, and curiously intense looking. If he hadn't been frowning so hard, he'd have been breathtaking. As it was, he was merely handsome, with spiky dark blond hair, chiseled features, and eyes that seemed to look right through her. He had one of those cleft chins too—as though the master sculptor who'd created him hadn't been able to resist a final flourish: a mark of special design.

"Dayna Sterling?" he repeated.

Finally corralling all the papers, Dayna made herself quit gawking. Shana must have made good on her offer. If this was the way they built maintenance men these days, Dayna was in the wrong field. Good-bye, research library—hello, mop closet!

His brows lowered, golden and dense. "Dayna Marie Sterling, born in Covenhaven, Arizona, on February 28, 1979?"

Her scalp prickled. That tingling started again, too. His information was close enough to make her wonder . . . and worry.

"What does that have to do with mopping?"

As though consulting an internal data chart, he continued. His voice sounded rough and deep. "Height: five-six, weight—"

"Whoa! That's kind of intrusive, isn't it?"

"It's procedure for the IAB report. Usually I skip it, but today my partner is being a pain in the ass about protocol." His gaze landed on her hips, then skimmed upward in blatant male curiosity. "I decided to play by the book for a change."

"Huh?"

"I knew you the minute I saw you." His attention swerved

to her face. His gaze penetrated her, making her feel both hot and cold at once. He pursed his mouth in apparent thought. "Your field is weak, though. Someone else would have missed it."

"Oookay." Her *field*? Whatever. "I guess that makes you the king of the janitors." He definitely had the machismo for it. Realizing her spine-tingling warning system was on the fritz if it was cautioning her about brawny maintenance men, Dayna pointed to the soggy carpet. "The spill's right there. Go ahead and make janitorial history."

"The reports were right about your smart mouth."

"Really?" She eyed him. "I hope someone's taking notes about your people skills. You could use some work yourself."

"Come with me." He held out his hand, palm up. "You're in danger here. If there's another incident—"

"Geez, it's just a fishbowl spill." Wow, did he take his work seriously. Inquisitively, she scanned the rest of him. His hard-used khaki pants, fine-ribbed tank top, and compact muscles were hard to miss. So were his cryptic tattoos. Men like him didn't normally hang out in research libraries. She was surprised his testosterone level hadn't already drawn a crowd among the mostly female DRL staff. "I did my best to clean it up, but I don't think—hey, where's your mop?"

She looked behind him for one of the wheeled yellow buckets with an attached wringer typically used by the maintenance staff. All she saw was empty hallway—*unusually* empty hallway.

That prickle of unease whooshed all the way to her belly.

"You're placing everyone in danger by staying here." He wiggled his fingers. "You need to learn to control your magic. You must have known you couldn't hide forever. All cusping witches are prone to unmanageable surges as they near—"

Magic? Cusping witches? Whatever further explanation he offered in that sexy, rumbling voice of his was lost to her.

Feeling quivery and sick, Dayna shook her head. She *had* to be hearing things. This could not be happening.

"You know what? I think I'll get that mop myself."

Swamped with denial, she moved to force her way past him. The warmth of his body hit her, followed by an overwhelming impression of authority.

An instant later, she was on the floor. She had no idea how she'd gotten there. Her vision swam. She stared in shock at the ceiling, realizing her ears were ringing, too. Fishy water seeped into the fabric of her T-shirt at her shoulder.

The hunky janitor loomed over her, his mouth set in a harsh line. "If you cooperate, this will be easier for us both."

"I'm not interested in making things easy for you." Panicking, Dayna crab-walked to her chair. She levered upward blindly, then felt along the top of her desk. Her fingers scraped bare wood, metal, her paper calendar . . . her Magic Marker. She clenched it in shaking fingers. "Never mind the mopping."

She stood, then waved her Magic Marker as threateningly as she could. There was always a chance it would work this time.

He stared at it in patent disbelief. "Tell me you've progressed beyond the level of an able child."

Able child. That meant something to her. Something buried. Something . . . that made her embarrassed. She lowered her marker.

"See? That wasn't so hard." He took the marker from her grasp, then set it on her desk. "Come on. Let's go."

He seemed to expect unquestioning compliance. Confused, Dayna shook her head.

Beside her, her cell phone suddenly chattered. It rose and zoomed toward her head, flapping its cover like a clumsy wing. It buzzed just out of reach.

Already formulating an excuse, she lurched upward. Missed.

Her visitor grabbed it, his gaze never leaving her face. Her cell phone, still animated, chirped happily in his grasp.

All her excuses died on her lips. "You're not a janitor."

His mouth quirked—full and finely shaped, possessed of a masculine beauty that almost made Dayna forget her fear of him.

"You're not a research librarian."

"Technically, I am." Her voice shook. "I've been to—"

"Don't waste my time." His expression, both commanding and unforgiving, made her unease return on hasty feet. He dropped her cell phone beside her Magic Marker. The device emitted a low, mournful cry. "Get whatever you need. We're already late."

"Late for what?" she demanded. "Who are you?"

He lifted his gaze to the ceiling, as though he hoped to find a supply of patience waiting there. Disappointed, he exhaled. "I'm the tracer who's assigned to bring you in."

Galvanized by his words, Dayna couldn't move. She'd feared this day. That was why she'd kept the plastic pencil case full of talismans, decoys, and weapons. That was why she'd paid attention to the warning tingles she sometimes felt. That was why—

No. Maybe she was wrong. She *had* to be wrong.

Striving for casualness, she lifted her chin. "In?"

"To Covenhaven." He spoke with the careful slowness some people used to converse with a child. "It's your cusping year. You're required to take mandatory training. I'm here to—"

"No." Shaking her head, she tried to retreat further. She only succeeded in bumping painfully into her filing cabinet. "I'm not going back." How did he know about her? Nobody knew about her—about the *real* her. She'd almost forgotten herself. She lifted her Magic Marker. "You can't make me. I won't do it."

"All right." He regarded her wearily. "Don't say I didn't try this the right way. Be sure to tell them that at the IAB."

"Huh?"

"In other words . . . fuck protocol."

Two seconds later she was in his grasp. He tightened his hold on her arm—heedless of her kicking and wriggling—then slung her backpack over his shoulder as though it weighed nothing. He hauled her out of her office and down the hall.

Obviously, he'd decided on another strategy.

And this one *didn't* include playing by the book.

Chapter Three

Damn. The cusping witches were always the trickiest. For a runaway who was unschooled, unlinked, and unpracticed, Dayna Sterling could still pack a wallop. Most likely, her lack of discipline explained it, but T.J. didn't ponder the matter any further than he had to. He'd been assigned to do one thing: get her back to Covenhaven. Nothing was going to stand in his way.

With his vision disrupted by swirling clouds of office papers and airborne memos, T.J. strode relentlessly down the hall. In his grasp, his target squirmed and kicked. Mostly, she missed him. The hallway's drywall wasn't so lucky. It shattered in chunks, sprinkling the carpet with white powder.

In the bullpen of cubicles they reached next, computer monitors flashed. Overhead fluorescents flickered, transmitting her agitation. A five-gallon jug of water burst as they passed it, sending water splashing onto the break room floor. A tornado of ink erupted from a nearby laser printer, whirling in midair.

Whether Dayna knew it or not, she was causing this mess.

"Calm down." T.J. lowered his mouth to her ear, keeping his voice steady amid the bedlam. Her panic seared into him, twice as strong at close contact. "You're making this worse."

"Let me go!" She wrenched her arm. "I won't go back."

"You have to. It's requisite."

"No. I live here now! You can't make me leave."

"I already am. Keep moving."

With more kicking and dragging, they made it down two flights of stairs. They rounded a corner. At the sight that greeted Dayna there, she stopped.

Wordlessly, she pointed. Dozens of her coworkers stood or sat motionlessly, mannequins in workday poses, still clutching BlackBerrys or telephone receivers or coffee cups. One woman waved at another, her expression frozen in eager interest. Another woman sat with her face contorted, caught with a tissue in midsneeze.

Summarily, T.J. took in the scene. Everything was as it should be. Except for Dayna's uncontrolled magic, of course.

"What did you *do* to them?" she shrieked.

"A harmless entrancement spell." Ruthlessly, he hauled her in motion again. "I'd hoped it wouldn't be necessary."

"A *spell*? Oh God. It's true. You really *are* a tracer." Her words dissolved into mumbling. She tripped over her next step, bumping against him—and inciting a burst of unexpected heat where their bodies touched. "You really have come for me. *Me*. How did you find me? *Why* did—"

"Keep moving. We have to leave." Ignoring the jolt of warmth between them, T.J. strode on. If they didn't get out of the research library soon, she might destroy the place. That *definitely* wouldn't go over well with the IAB. "I'll explain later."

She gawked at her coworkers. "Are they going to be okay?"

Exasperated, T.J. stared at her. "Do you really care?"

That stopped her. For several seconds, Dayna quit struggling. Then, "Of course I care! These are my friends."

"Then you're a bigger fool than I thought. They don't even know you." Not waiting for her to confirm the obvious, he sighted the lobby, with its huge plate glass walls. Given the way she'd reacted so far, he decided to amend his plans. "Wait."

She came to a clumsy halt, her feet stumbling over his.

He cupped her face in his hands, hoping to command her attention. Instead, he ensnared his own. Unable to resist, he marveled at her skin's softness and smoothness. Her features were delicate, her eyes a crystalline blue, her jawline fragile enough to break if only he tightened his hands the smallest bit.

She jerked away, her gaze wary.

Cursing himself, T.J. remembered what had happened the first time their bodies had collided—when she'd tried to evade him in her office. He hadn't realized anything was amiss until she'd landed on her ass at his feet. He didn't want to consider why. Such a reaction wasn't typical for a witch— even a cusping runaway. His tracer's hold should have calmed her. Nothing more.

With that in mind, he tried again. Purposefully, he kept his grasp light, his manner patient, his warlock magic reined in beneath his Patayan control. It was a special gift to meld the two. As a compound, T.J. would have been embarrassed not to have mastered their mingling. As it was, he had, and to great effect.

All the same, Dayna's skin paled beneath his fingers.

Mayhem continued around them, marking the significance of this moment. This uncontainable magic would only hurt her in the end. He had to help her, if he could, before they went further.

"Be calm now," he instructed. "Breathe. Slowly."

He dipped his gaze to her chest, waiting for her to obey.

The action did not endear him to her. Her scathing look said so. He'd recognized her immediately, as he'd said—but he'd underestimated her at the same time. Dayna was quirky and pretty, exactly as predicted in the IAB file, with shoulder-length dark hair and a lanky body hidden beneath boyish clothes. But she was far, far more resistant than he'd anticipated.

"Calm? Ha! Let me go, *then* I'll be calm." Beneath her dark bangs, her frantic gaze searched his, clear and startlingly blue. "Just tell everyone in Covenhaven you couldn't find me."

"Impossible. I find everyone. And I gave my word."

She laughed. "Your *word*? You're kidding, right?"

T.J. frowned. "You've been in this world for too long."

"Not long enough." With new vigor, she wriggled again.

He tightened his grasp, making her cry out. "Cooperate."

Her wounded gaze made him feel ashamed. T.J. couldn't stand it. "You've lost control of your magic. You have to be calm."

"You're crazy. I never had any magic to begin with."

Blandly, he gazed around the research library, with its whirling papers, exploding fluorescents, and sparking PCs.

"Okay, so I had a *teeny* bit of magic once, but I never—"

"Enough. I know your history." Reminded of the way she'd abandoned everyone in her life, he found it easier to harden himself against her. If he'd done the things Dayna Sterling had, he couldn't live with himself. "I'm not a gullible dozer, like these people you've fooled. Save your breath."

He dragged her forward, inciting new chaos.

In the midst of it, an elderly, white-haired researcher wandered out of the ladies' room. She lurched toward them. Her eyes were wide, her face ashen, her steps wobbly. Her sense of alarm whooshed toward T.J., momentarily slowing him.

"Mona!" Worriedly, Dayna tried to rush to her.

Acting on instinct, T.J. nodded at the woman. Her eyes rolled back. Her knees buckled. He released Dayna long enough to catch the woman and prop her up. Elders deserved every respect. If this woman didn't recover, his Patayan magus would never let him hear the end of it.

He crooned a few ancient words in her ear.

"What are you doing to her?" Dayna asked.

"Forgetfulness spell. Keep moving."

Typically, she resisted. "Will she be all right?"

"She was afraid. Now she's not." He shoved Dayna. "Go."

In his arms, the older woman stirred. Color returned to her face. She blinked, instantly alert. "Hello there."

"You'd better get back to your office," he told her.

"I was just thinking that."

She toddled off, happily humming her way down the hall.

Satisfied, T.J. turned to look for Dayna. All he glimpsed was her lithe figure as she slipped through the building's lobby and approached the exit—escaping him into the world beyond.

She'd gotten the jump on him.

Simultaneously relieved and terrified, Dayna reached the research library's exit. Behind her, havoc ruled. Everything she'd known was in chaos—ample evidence of the truth she'd feared but had been unwilling to admit, even to herself.

Her magic was back.

It was back, it was out of control, and it was inexplicably strong. As proof, the moment she touched the door, it flew off its hinges, crashing to the steps outside in a shower of glass. Shielding her face with her arm, Dayna blindly ran past it.

On the steps, she stopped, unsure what to do. People on the sidewalk stared at her. Traffic moved past with its usual stop-and-go rhythm. The businesses nearby went about their everyday routines. Spooked by the surreal ordinariness of it all, Dayna glanced over her shoulder. Had she imagined it all?

Nope. Although the frenzy of papers and flickering lights and flashing computer monitors had stopped with her exit, a few white scraps of paper still hung in the air, drifting with eerie slowness. Lights drooped at crooked angles from the ceiling. Her coworkers still appeared to be locked in place, unable to move.

Utterly panicked, Dayna stared down the street. Her heart raced in her chest. Her awareness felt hypersensitive—the stink of exhaust stung her nose; the autumn sunshine hurt her eyes. It felt as if time had slowed, when she knew it could have been only a few seconds since she'd left the tracer behind.

Where to go? What to do? All she knew was that there *had* to be another way to control her magic—another way besides returning to Covenhaven.

She clenched her fists, trying to reason out her options.

She didn't drive. She'd never trusted herself that far.

Her bike was still in her office.

And the tracer was still after her.

She *felt* his presence before she saw him. His strength of will and irrefutable power hit her, impossible to ignore.

Helplessly, Dayna wheeled around. The tracer strode through the library's exit, his gaze pinned on her with fearful intensity. He moved in the shadows as if he owned them. The hard line of his jaw and the unyielding set of his mouth said it all.

She'd made him mad. Uh-oh.

More afraid than ever, she turned her attention toward the street—toward escape. At the same moment, she felt an onrushing sense of frustration and resolve, undoubtedly coming from him.

She didn't have time to consider what that meant—why she could sense his emotions. A freezing wind whipped through the canyon of buildings, stealing her attention. Next a churning wall of dust rose, bearing down on her before she could blink.

The sandstorm pelted her. She closed her eyes, but it was no use. Coarse grains of sand beat against her eyelids, her face, her arms, scouring her all over. The whispering sound of sand—on concrete, on stucco, on steel and glass, on *her*—was magnified a thousand times, louder than she could have imagined.

Afraid to breathe, Dayna waited. Just when it felt as if her chest would explode from lack of oxygen, the sandstorm stopped. Gratefully, she wiped off her face and dragged in a lungful of dust-filled air. It made her cough. Still wheezing, she opened her eyes . . . then widened them to see a gray sheet of monsoon rain racing down the crowded street.

It moved on a cold gust of wind, headed straight toward her. In disbelief, Dayna gawked. It was bigger than any storm she'd ever seen—any storm she'd ever heard about. Goose bumps rose on her body. Her hair tossed in the wind, blinding her.

In the desert, sudden monsoon storms came sometimes—but usually in summer and never in the morning. Never like this.

Lightning cracked. The sky turned dark just as the rain struck. It bombarded everything in its path with a ferocious torrent, instantly splashing inches of water on the street.

Pedestrians yelled and ran for cover; several slipped on the slick sidewalk. Cars slid, tires squealing. At the intersection, two vehicles collided with an awful crack.

Horrified, Dayna stared down at her drenched body, her helpless arms, her empty hands. This had to be her fault, but she'd never done anything this bad. Not even in the past few months, when her latent magical abilities had seemed to be resurging. Her "accidents" had always been exactly that—mishaps that could be explained, like her exploding goldfish bowl had been, or hidden, like the airborne papers in her office.

The downtown power grid failed next, taking the traffic signals with it. The shutdown turned several city blocks ominously dim—an effect made more noticeable in the sudden gloom. It felt to Dayna as if the darkness might last forever.

What was happening? Why here? Why now? Why *her*?

She didn't have a chance to figure it out.

The tracer grabbed her arm, his fingers digging into her wet flesh. His gaze bored into her. "Take a good look. You did this." He gave her a shake. "And it will only get worse."

Distraught, Dayna blinked at him. She could barely see for the rainwater streaming down her face. Unmindful of the storm, she examined him, taking in the male beneath the rain-plastered hair, chiseled cheekbones, and soaked clothes. He was scary. But he was telling the truth. Somehow she knew that beyond a doubt.

The reality was, staying here and endangering everyone around her felt scarier still. She could not maintain her life here—her peaceful, *ordinary* life with her friends, the life she'd fought so hard for—if this continued. That much was clear.

Out of options, Dayna nodded. "What do I have to do?"

"Take this." The tracer fisted the dripping, leather-corded amulet he wore around his neck. He pulled it over his head, then held it out to her, his expression enigmatic. "All you have to do is put it on."

Chapter Four

"Just put it on?" Suspiciously, Dayna stared at it, blinking to clear her gaze of rainwater. The amulet swung beneath the downpour, held in the tracer's certain grasp. Even in the rain, its gold charm stood in bright contrast to its rough leather thong. She shivered. "That's it?"

"It's the first step to making all this right again."

He nodded toward the storm, the frightened pedestrians and skidding cars . . . the life she'd been living until today. Dayna cherished that life. But now her reawakened magic threatened it all. If the tracer could help her learn to control it . . .

"How do I know you're telling the truth?" she asked.

"I can't lie to you." His dark gaze met hers. "You'd know."

She scoffed. "That's impossible."

"Not much is impossible for us."

Despite the rain coursing down his face, the tracer didn't waver. Another two vehicles collided down the street, sending an awful screech into the air. He didn't so much as flinch. It was as though he'd expected mayhem and disaster to follow her.

He wouldn't have been the first.

When she didn't instantly grab the amulet, he exhaled. "All the other cusping witches were much easier to snare."

Somehow, Dayna knew. Her eyes widened. "You're lying!"

His curt nod confirmed it. "Witches are able to detect deception. They've used that skill to survive centuries of persecution." Rainwater ran down his temple. It curved along his cheekbone, doing nothing to soften his hard face and unforgiving demeanor. He raised the amulet. "Take this. I could put it on you myself, but it's stronger if you accept it willingly."

She had no choice but to trust him. Still, she hesitated.

"Do it," he urged. "We're already late."

He kept saying that. "Late for what?"

"For your last chance to redeem yourself."

She laughed . . . then realized he was serious.

Frowning, Dayna grabbed the amulet. It felt heavier than she'd expected. Smoother. Slicker. That was the rain, she guessed. Then . . . the golden charm *moved*.

Opening her palm, she gaped at the amulet. Even as she watched it, the thing somehow came to life before her eyes.

Still golden, still charmed, it grew reptilian arms and legs. It formed a head, a mouth, and eyes. It looked up at her through those eyes, then snaked its way up her bare arm.

She shrieked. Rainwater gushed into her mouth, choking her. Sputtering, she stood with her arm outstretched, trying to keep that *thing* away from her. Undaunted, it skittered across her wet skin on clawed feet, then wound its body around her upper arm.

It squeezed her. "It's trying to get under my skin!"

"Calm down." Seeming perplexed, the tracer took a step nearer. "Hold still. I don't think it will hurt you."

The thing prickled. "You don't *think* it will hurt me?"

"No." He stared at it, his expression shuttered.

There was a definite chink in his imperturbable cool, though. Whatever was happening to her, he hadn't expected it.

"It's . . . so cold." She shivered more violently.

"Just hold still. It'll be over soon."

"*Over*? What will be over?" She should have known better than to trust a good-looking man bearing gifts. "Tell me!"

Before he could, the thing quit moving. It began to glow, making the raindrops sparkle all around it. In a final heated flash, it warmed to just above her body temperature.

Then it was finished.

The rain quit. The skies cleared. The amulet stopped transforming. The only sounds were liquid ones, formed as rainwater sluiced from every surface in minute rivers. Shaken, overwhelmed by the sudden peacefulness, Dayna looked down.

A band of golden scrollwork, inanimate now but no less remarkable, wound around her upper arm. With beautiful curves and an intrinsic grace, it fit as if it had been made for her. The tracer stared at it, too, looking as dumbfounded as she felt.

Hmmm. "What was it *supposed* to do?" she asked.

His frown returned. "Bind you. And it has. Let's go."

With his mind racing, T.J. ran for the Mustang with Dayna in tow. The streets were still glossy with rain, but now oily rainbows sparked in the puddles, instigated by the return of the sun. The storm was over. The last of his assigned snares was in his grasp. He was on his way back to Covenhaven. T.J. should have been satisfied. Instead he felt raw with uncertainty.

"Bind me? What does that mean?" Dayna yelled.

He didn't answer. But her golden armlet winked at him all the same, seeming to mock his usual assurance. He'd expected handcuffs—the same handcuffs he'd enchanted himself. He'd gotten something entirely different. Dayna might not realize the significance of what had happened between them, but he did.

Yes, Dayna was bound. But now *he* was, too.

He was bound to *her* by an unbreakable witching bond. She'd taken the amulet from his hand, and the transference had somehow transformed them both. Now they were a lifepair—or would be, once a consummation formalized their union. Until then, they were marked by their symbols. Promised to one another.

Bonded.

"Look, I did what you wanted. I put this thing on!" She waved her arm, showing him her damned armlet. "So how about giving me a few details? Showing me a little faith in return?"

"Faith? You're asking the wrong guy for that." T.J. stopped beside the Mustang, shoving Dayna ahead of him. This grab should have been simple enough for a greenie. Instead, it had just turned a thousand times more complicated. "I'm the one who asks the questions. What the hell was up with that rainstorm?"

She clenched her jaw, stubbornly not answering.

Most likely, she didn't have an answer. The unschooled witches never did. But this one was especially infuriating.

She shook her wet hair, a visible shiver coursing through her. It sparked a reactionary shudder in him, too—one T.J. could neither stop nor deny. He didn't like it.

Worse, he could swear her emotions were blocked to him now. The elder researcher's alarm had walloped him, partly because it had caught him off guard. Dayna's reactions were observable, but he could not intuit them anymore.

Just when he needed that ability the most.

"Are you part Patayan?" he demanded.

It wasn't in her file, but Patayan blood was the only explanation for what he'd seen when he'd stepped outside the research library—and maybe for the bonding magic between them, too. As descendants of ancient indigenous peoples, Patayan were gifted with varieties of enchantments that ordinary Anglo-Saxon witchfolk were not. They could control sun, wind, rain—and usually, unless they were part warlock like him, their emotions.

"You never said I had to answer your questions." She glowered at him, a die-hard rebel with her hands fisted. "Aren't you supposed to read me my rights first or something?"

"This isn't a human issue." He slung her backpack to the puddle-dotted sidewalk, then crouched to unfasten the zipper. Raindrops scattered from the metal track. An instant later, he had the access he wanted. "Human rules don't apply."

"Hey! That's my stuff." In protest, Dayna grabbed his arm.

Immediately her touch made ripples of pleasure race along his skin. Recoiling, T.J. stared at her. If this was an effect of their bond, he didn't like it. He needed to focus.

He *didn't* need to imagine a runaway witch beneath him, naked and smooth and willing. He didn't need to want her.

"I have to search for contraband." He ducked his head and riffled through the backpack. The items inside jabbed at his fingers, wholly unpleasant to touch. He made a face. "Human origin." The only soft and pleasurable things of human origin were humans themselves. "You deserve better than this."

"Better is subjective. Will those people inside be okay?"

He glanced up. She bit her lip, gazing anxiously toward the Dynamic Research Libraries building. On the verge of affirming that her "friends" would be unharmed, T.J. shook his head.

"You answer my questions, I'll answer yours."

"No, I'm not Patayan. I don't even remember what that is."

That meant the rainstorm was twice as inexplicable.

Unhappy with that realization, T.J. went on examining her belongings. None of them revealed who she truly was— a legacy witch on the verge of her most potent magic. The discovery disappointed him. "You've left your real life altogether."

"*This* is my real life. Right here."

Her indignant tone made him look up again. His gaze skimmed her sneakers. They were ratty and comfortable looking; good if they had to run. Her pants, similar to his own, clung wetly to her legs, emphasizing their slender length. Her T-shirt, faded and adorned with a kitschy logo, stuck to her drenched skin. The fabric had turned transparent, revealing her skimpy white bra, the outline of her breasts, the pink jab of her nipples.

Heat surged to his groin. The warlock part of him, so attuned to pleasure and so able to attain it, made itself felt.

With a firm denial, T.J. rose and shoved her backpack at her. "Keep this away from me. I don't want to see you using any of that worthless shit. If I do, I'll hex it into next week."

"Ooh, big man. Scared of a little hairbrush? A wallet?"

He had to be hearing things. "Are you *taunting* me?"

"Maybe."

"That's stupid of you. Get in the car."

"Not until you promise me everyone at work will be okay."

He stared at her in incredulity. She'd straightened to her full height. Even though hers was a puny stature, T.J. found himself bizarrely impressed. He refused to dwell on the feeling.

He suppressed a growl. "Fine. I promise."

"Good." She nodded. "Where are we going first?"

In reply, T.J. opened the car door. He flipped up the bucket seat, then crammed Dayna in the backseat. "Your place."

"Hey! Watch it." Almost upside down, Dayna scrambled to sit upright. She grunted with exertion, her vision righting itself to reveal the interior of an ordinary-looking sports car—with a few special touches. A pair of official *InterAllied Bureau* tracer licenses filled the plastic holders clipped to the visors. A two-way radio hummed with a report she couldn't interpret in a dialect she couldn't recall. A peculiar-looking vial swung from the rearview mirror, Scotch-taped together and containing what looked like . . . a beetle?

"I don't know exactly what tracers are supposed to do," she shouted, "but I doubt it's manhandle the goods!"

"Don't bother. He can't hear you. The car has a protective charm on it to keep our conversations private. IAB regulations." The man in the driver's seat swiveled. Handsome and dark-haired, he extended his hand, his gaze hidden behind a pair of sunglasses. "Sorry for the rough handling. I'm Deuce Bailey."

Guardedly, Dayna looked at him. To her relief, she wasn't instantly attuned to his feelings. That was a phenomenon she didn't crave a repeat of. She accepted his handshake. "Dayna Sterling."

"I know. You're a record. Fourteen minutes and counting." Deuce tapped his watch. "Usually it's half that. You must be one tough customer. That probably explains the manhandling."

His gaze dipped over her, examining her with friendly interest. Feeling awkward and cold, Dayna rubbed her arms. The gesture made Deuce's gaze flick to her armband . . . then hold.

She jabbed her chin outside. "Who's he?"

Startled, Deuce lifted his gaze. "He didn't tell you?"

"He mostly grabbed me and ran."

"Typical. Again . . . sorry." Deuce's attention wandered back to her golden armband. "That's not protocol."

They both looked through the car's window. Dayna's tracer could be seen near the passenger door, staring bleakly into the distance. His distress reached out to her, a tendril of feeling she didn't want to be aware of. What difference did it make to her if *he* was upset? She was surprised he had feelings at all.

Aside from his face, he appeared to be made of stone.

"He's T.J. McAllister," Deuce said. "T stands for—"

The door opened. "Shut up, Deuce," T.J. snarled. His face,

clean shaven when they'd met, now looked raspy with beard stubble. Those whiskery hairs glowed golden in the autumn sunlight. "Quit yapping and drive. You know where to go."

The car remained parked at the curb. Deuce put both hands on the wheel, humming quietly as he tapped his fingers.

T.J. frowned at him. "Fine. *Please* quit yapping and drive."

"Not until everyone's ready."

T.J. darted a glance at Dayna. "We're ready."

Deuce cleared his throat. He shot T.J. a meaningful look.

"Oh Christ." With jerky motions, T.J. fastened his seat belt. He gestured for Dayna to do the same. "Deuce is a stickler for details. You won't get anywhere with him by bending rules."

Dayna buckled up. "We have a lot in common, Deuce."

Deuce's gaze met hers in the mirror. "I like you already."

"God help me." T.J. scrubbed his palm over his mysterious new beard stubble. "Stop the damn love fest and get moving. It's a long way to Covenhaven."

Covenhaven. Remembrance of where they were ultimately headed chilled Dayna all the way through. She hadn't thought she'd ever return to her hometown—the site of so many mistakes. If she had, she might have left things differently.

Unfortunately, changing her past was impossible now.

Deuce pulled out. The Mustang's tires squealed. The force of their departure threw Dayna against her seatback. Up front, the stoppered vial swung crazily from the rearview mirror.

T.J. grabbed it. "What the hell is *this* doing here?"

"You, uh, abandoned it in the street by mistake."

"I don't make mistakes."

"The poor little guy was lost without his mission. He crashed just a few yards away from where you freed him." Deuce cast a pleading glance at his partner. "I had to rescue him."

"It's. A. Bug. A bug set on *us*. Don't you get it?"

"If you paid more attention to the rules, the honchos at the IAB wouldn't need to use a monitor. After the Cobalt witch—"

T.J. cut him off with an obscene suggestion.

Driving one-handed, Deuce snatched the vial. He murmured a few words of reassurance to its winged occupant, then hung it on the rearview again. Clearly, Deuce was the softy in this team.

"I'll take care of it," he told T.J. as he cornered, then zoomed toward Dayna's street. "You've got enough to deal with."

T.J.'s jaw tightened. He didn't turn around. He didn't look at her. He didn't even acknowledge her presence. But Dayna knew his tense demeanor owed itself to her. For once, she was glad to have a few inches of vinyl and padding between them.

With cautious interest, she examined T.J.'s rigid posture and strong profile. His nose looked sharp enough to cut glass; his jaw held a similarly hard edge. Only his mouth appeared gentle. He wore tattoos—none of which were decipherable—on both brawny arms and on his neck. In vast contrast to her own SPF-protected pastiness, his skin appeared burnished with sunshine. She felt as if she might singe her fingers if she touched him.

She wanted to do it, all the same.

Dimly, she remembered hearing warnings during her teenage years about warlocks—about their charisma and pleasure-loving natures. Every nonhuman mother in Covenhaven had cautioned her daughter to be wary of warlocks. The human mothers would have issued warnings, too, had they known such beings existed; with a few exceptions, humans were oblivious to witchkind. It was better for them that way. Now, confronted with a warlock for the first time in years, Dayna wondered if those old cautionary tales were justified.

As though he sensed her scrutiny, the tracer looked over his shoulder. At the same time, the Mustang stopped abruptly.

"We're here," Deuce announced.

Surprised, Dayna looked out the window. Her apartment—

one half of an older duplex unit—squatted in its usual place, with a scraggly ocotillo near the sidewalk and a batch of prickly pear cactus by the front door. The rest of the landscaping consisted of decorative rocks, all of them gray and dark with rainfall.

The tracer continued to watch her. Ominously.

Deuce unbuckled. "You're allowed to bring a few personal items. It's procedure." Aiming a significant glance at his unmoving partner, he palmed his car keys. "I'll help you."

"No, thanks." Hastily, Dayna unbuckled. "I travel light. What do I need? Enough for a day? A week? What's the plan?"

Her question was met with stony silence.

"A little help here?" she prodded. "Now that I'm committed, I'd just as soon get this over with. How long will I be gone?"

Uncomfortably, Deuce shifted. "We don't know. We're assigned to track you and bring you in. Nothing more."

Irritably, T.J. wrenched his gaze from her armband. "Can't you magik whatever you need when you get there?"

To him, it was an obvious solution. But Dayna knew better. She *didn't* have magic enough to do that. She never had. That was part of the reason she'd left Covenhaven in the first place.

Bereft of words, she jabbed his seatback. "I can't do anything if you don't let me out of here, Sasquatch."

T.J. touched his jaw, then scowled. Threateningly.

"I'll need time to change, too," she added, pushing her luck. "My clothes are completely soaked. Shoes, too."

"Fine. Don't dawdle." T.J. got out, adept and formidable. He moved the bucket seat to make way for her, then fastened his gaze on hers. "I'll take you naked if I have to."

He looked as though he meant it. God help her.

"Hmmm." With a what-the-hell shrug, Dayna climbed out from the backseat. She accepted the hand T.J. gave her, crossing the final few inches that separated them. "Well, that would be one way to go. Too bad your warlock mojo doesn't work on me."

His eyebrows rose. "It doesn't?"

"Nope. Maybe I've lived in the human world for too long."

"You're lying." T.J. gave her a long look. "Not that it matters. If I want you naked, I'll have you naked."

"Right." She withdrew her hand. "With a spell. *Maybe.*"

"With these." He showed her his palms, then flexed them with a wolfish grin. "*And* your willing participation."

His gaze lengthened. Dayna felt herself weaken. She swayed toward him, suddenly fascinated with his mouth.

T.J.'s husky laughter snapped her out of her daze.

Damn it. She'd have to be on guard against the pull of his warlock appeal. His skills seemed especially powerful, too—maybe that's why T.J. was marked by the cleft in his chin. "That one's a gimme," she snapped. "Next time I'll be ready."

"Mm-hmmm. I've heard that before."

"Maybe," she agreed. "But not from me."

Leaving him behind, Dayna scampered up the sidewalk, acutely aware that she was about to leave her hard-won human-style life behind . . . maybe for a very long time. And that she was about to face her problematic past at long last . . . whether she was ready to confront her demons or not.

Chapter Five

With his shoulders painfully taut, T.J. stared at the desolate yard that bordered Dayna Sterling's apartment. The runaway witch had no sense of the natural world. Her ocotillo had been pruned to fit the human aesthetic; now it was dying. Her prickly pear cactus drooped, too, planted thoughtlessly in a shady patch that deprived it of essential sunlight.

"If we don't get her out of here," T.J. said, "she'll die."

Deuce laughed. "It's an up-and-coming neighborhood; I'll agree with you there. But come on—it's not deadly."

Unsatisfied, T.J. clenched his jaw. A moment passed.

He looked out the window to gauge the passage of time.

The sun had scarcely moved. T.J. frowned more deeply.

"It's only been three minutes." Deuce shot him an amused look. "Give her a chance, why don't you?"

"She said she travels light. She should be ready by now."

His partner laughed. "You don't take your dates on overnighters, do you?"

"My dates aren't bound by human convention. Neither is she, as much as she pretends to be." T.J. glimpsed a flicker of movement at one of the apartment's windows. His whole body snapped into alertness. "That's it. Here she comes."

For the space of four breaths, he waited.

When Dayna didn't emerge, he frowned.

Deuce noticed. "Hey—what's going on with you?"

I need her to come out. No. T.J. couldn't say that.

He didn't even want to admit it to himself. If this was what it felt like to be bonded—out of control, compelled by need, fascinated against his will—he hated it already.

"I have more important things to do. Back in Covenhaven." *Like free myself of this unwanted bond.* Alive with the need to move, T.J. squinted at Dayna Sterling's front door. "I want this grab over with. Now."

"You Patayan are famous for your patience." Deuce's gaze dropped to the birthright symbol on T.J.'s arm. With interest, he examined the golden Gila monster tattooed there. "Waiting another two minutes for this snare won't kill you."

"I'm only half Patayan. The rest of me is warlock. And all of me is sick of waiting." He grabbed an item from Dayna's backpack, then opened the Mustang's door. "I'm going in."

Dayna was still packing, shoving items willy-nilly into a duffel bag, when she sensed the tracer's presence.

First, the warning tingle she'd felt before prickled the nape of her neck. Then it swept along her shoulders and both arms, making her drop her clothes. Finally the charge swept to her jaw, making it ache with the same sweet-sour sensation she'd gotten as a child when sampling Pixy Stix. T.J. McAllister wasn't sweet, and his attitude toward her was decidedly sour.

She turned to face him anyway.

Instantly, he made her bedroom feel small. Not just because of his size and strength, but because of his . . . aura. That was the only way she could describe it. T.J. pulled all the light in the room to him. Sunbeams seemed happy to glide along his skin. They pursued him as he moved closer to her, turning his hair a leonine gold and revealing the renewed stubble on his jaw.

T.J. held up something. "You forgot these."

Dayna's gaze arrowed to the thing in his hand. At first she didn't understand what she was seeing. Then she spied the two small objects inside the translucent, balloon-shaped container.

"Buffy and Spike! How did you . . . ?"

"They bear the imprint of your breath. I thought you'd want them." T.J. shrugged. "It was a simple pinch."

She squinted in disbelief. "*That's* my pencil cup?"

"Like I said, a simple pinch."

"Of course." For him, everything seemed easy. Amazed, Dayna accepted the magiked container. She peered inside. Both her goldfish swam contentedly. "It was nice of you to rescue my fish. You don't seem the type to bother with pets."

"The Patayan are guardians. We believe all living beings should be protected." His gaze lowered, taking in her wet clothes and bare feet. "You should put down your goldfish."

"Why?"

Before he could tell her, she knew. A rush of emotion moved from him to her with the same unstoppable force it had before. Longing. Curiosity. Need. Hunger. Even a rough tenderness, all snarled together in a torrent of feeling. The subtleties of the tracer's mood added up to one undeniable message—a message that made Dayna stand motionless before him.

I want you.

The rawness of his emotions buffeted her, making her quaver. She set down Buffy and Spike, her fingers clumsy with imminent loss of control. The magiked bowl plunked to the bureau with a slosh of liquid. Water drops slid along the slick surface, sparkling in a shaft of sunlight as they raced to the floor, compelled by gravity to move toward a single purpose.

Similarly driven, T.J. stepped nearer. The warmth of his body reached her; the rain-washed scent of his skin made her dizzy. Only inches away, he fisted his hands and looked at her, his eyes dark with a need he didn't have to voice.

Dayna's heart pounded. He was new and unknowable and *here*. Even as she told herself this was probably just warlock spell casting—just some macho ruse to demonstrate his dominance over her, both in the witching world and right here in her own bedroom—she knew there was more between them than that.

"I only came in here to give you your goldfish."

She smiled. "Do you always lie to yourself this way?"

"Only when I have something to hide." His gaze lifted to her face, then lowered, with obvious intent, to her mouth. He gave her a grin filled with self-mockery. "And I *always* have something to hide. But that's pointless with you, isn't it?"

"You mean because I can tell when you're lying?"

"Because you can feel how much I want you." He kept his solemn gaze locked on hers. "Right here. Right now."

Involuntarily, Dayna nodded. She *could* feel it. She could feel his desire, his needfulness . . . even his darker impulses.

At those, she widened her eyes. Images of the two of them, coupled in a naked embrace, filled her mind. She didn't know if T.J. had put them there or if they were her own unfulfilled wishes. Either way, they were too powerful to deny.

"I don't usually—" she began in a faltering tone. "I—"

"Me either," he said, and kissed her.

The first meeting of their mouths was incredible, hot and wet and urgent and necessary . . . everything but sweet. With a hoarse inhalation, T.J. buried his hands in the damp ropes of her hair and dragged her to him, inciting all her nerve endings to a frenzy. Crowding closer, Dayna knew she could never get enough of his mouth, his hands, his heat and need and power.

Primitively, his emotions swamped her, coming faster and faster as their lips lingered, slid, parted. Their breath met and mingled; their bodies pushed nearer, impatient with the barriers of space and clothes. All that mattered was feeling. All that lasted was hunger. All that satisfied was *more*. More of their kissing, more of their touching, more of their arms and legs tangling together, leaving her weak and potent at once.

She'd never felt freer. With the tracer, there was no need to wonder if he wanted her. She *knew* he did, and that knowledge felt incredibly seductive. She clenched her fingers in his tank top, encountering not only the luxurious web of witch-made fabric, but also the hard ridges of muscle beneath it. Her hands shook as she held on, arching herself to get closer.

His violent groan encouraged her. So did his roving hands, his talented mouth, his fearlessness in tipping her off her feet and onto the bed, squashing unpacked clothes beneath them.

Her bed frame protested with a crack. The whole thing lurched. Faintly, Dayna heard her duffel bag drop to the floor.

She didn't care. Driven by pure wanting, she splayed her fingers over T.J.'s back, then lifted them to his head. His hair felt close-cropped and unusually silky, the way she remembered witchfolk hair always did. But it also felt *dry*, even after the rainstorm they'd just endured.

That should have been no surprise. Her whole body felt dry now too—dry and overheated—licked by the sunshine that seemed to follow T.J.'s every move. More than likely, his body was as hot as hers . . . all over. Wanting to find out, Dayna grabbed his muscle-corded biceps for leverage and pushed nearer.

Her nipples brushed the huge wall of his chest, abraded by their writhing motions. Panting and giddy, Dayna gave herself over to the sensation. It was all she could think about. They rolled over, blinded by tangled sheets and forgotten clothing. They lurched sideways, unable to get enough, groaning between kisses, biting and taking, learning the sleek textures of wet mouths . . . the resiliency of arms, legs, and rocking hips.

"Touch me," she urged. She wanted more, and T.J. gave it to her. His big palm took possession of her breast; his knee wedged between her thighs. Fueled by that point of contact, Dayna gasped and ground against him, awestruck by his strength—by his understanding of what she needed . . . what she yearned for.

Liquid heat flowed through her, deep and immediate. Pleasure rolled along every inch of her skin, creating a craving for more. She might be headed for a day of reckoning with her past, but right now she meant to indulge every ounce of wickedness she'd ever denied herself. She meant to take from T.J. everything he'd give her . . . and then some.

Greedily, she opened her eyes wider. She drank in the sight of her tracer, balanced over her with his tattoos gilded by sunlight and his mouth drawn in a pouty line. He would have hexed her if he'd heard her describe him that way, but his lips' fullness defied any other description. Spurred on by his next kiss, she moaned and arched higher, her whole body aflame with a hunger only T.J. could gratify.

"Yes. *More*." She grabbed at his tank top and yanked. The fabric resisted her efforts, so she shoved it out of her way, forcing it to bunch at his ribs. Her fingers made contact with bare skin, new and unexplored. She glided over his torso, encountering ridged muscle, silken hair, and remarkable warmth. Eager and determined, Dayna captured his lips with hers.

Compelled by an urge she refused to examine, she writhed and shoved her hand lower. She felt the sturdy barrier of T.J.'s canvas pants, the metallic kiss of the button at his waist, the hopelessly intricate hurdle of his zippered fly. Impatiently, she wrestled with it, utterly mindless of the room, the bed, their place in the world.

Ah. For the briefest instant, she made contact with the stiffest and most unyielding part of him. Just as she realized it, T.J. caught her wrist in his hand. He forced her away.

Disappointed, Dayna wriggled closer. "Please. I need—"

"Stop." His face appeared drawn with effort. "Deuce is—"

A series of thumping footsteps canceled out whatever he'd meant to say. Deuce appeared in the doorway, burly and jovial.

"Look, I know I'm just the driver on this gig, but—"

Dayna froze. At the same instant, several of her bedroom furnishings—a lamp, a lacquered jewelry box, a digital alarm clock—crashed to the floor. She gaped at them in disbelief. Then she realized that she and T.J. had managed to levitate half her belongings, all of them human-built and thus twice as resistant to magic. The bed had collapsed, too; she and her tracer had burrowed into the very center of it, with the mattress jutting to both sides of their incriminating position.

"Uh. Sorry." Awkwardly, Deuce thrust his forearm over his face. "You two . . . go right ahead. I'll just wait in the car."

He bolted, leaving Dayna heaped atop T.J. in the middle of her bed. She couldn't feel . . . *sorry* for her position, exactly. Her body still thrummed with T.J.'s touch, sensitized to savor his callused hands and wandering mouth. Breathlessly, she looked down at him, wondering how she'd wound up straddling him.

Sensibly, she knew she ought to follow Deuce and try to regain some semblance of dignity. Emotionally, she knew she wouldn't. Not while T.J. still lay within reach, packed with all that intriguing muscle and those mysterious eyes.

Not while she still wasn't satisfied.

She *definitely* wasn't satisfied.

But she meant to be. Soon.

"I know it's wrong," she panted, "but I still want you."

"This was a mistake." With movements so fast she might have imagined them, the tracer set her aside from him. He stood and grabbed her scattered clothes. In seconds, her duffel bag was haphazardly packed. "We're leaving. *Right now.*"

T.J. was as good as his word. For the third time that day, Dayna found herself in the grasp of a steely-eyed tracer, headed for a future she couldn't begin to anticipate and destined to revisit a past she didn't want to remember. This time, though, there might be perks involved, she decided as she followed T.J. to the Mustang and allowed him to slam her into the backseat.

This time, she just might enjoy being in Covenhaven.

Especially if T.J. was in Covenhaven, too.

At five-thirty that evening, the Mustang skidded to a stop at the center of Covenhaven. T.J. opened the passenger door. He stepped out, then grabbed Dayna's duffel bag from the backseat.

He threw it on the ground. He added her backpack.

Stone-faced, he reached in for her. But the moment T.J. touched her bare arm, he remembered the soft feel of her skin, the alluring scent of her body, the hungry, breathy way she'd moaned for him to keep touching her. All during the gritty, two-hour drive across the desert, he'd avoided her. Now, lost in an unintended reverie, he tightened his grasp. He wanted to pull her to him—to strip her bare of those scratchy human-made clothes and learn exactly what she liked . . . and how she liked it.

Searching for control, T.J. lifted his gaze to her face. The maneuver didn't help. In the afternoon shadows of the car's interior, Dayna looked lost. Innocent. Unreasonably seductive.

Feeling himself weaken, he slid his hand slowly up her arm. Instead of tugging her out of the car, he enjoyed the sensation of his fingers sliding over her warm, smooth skin. He did it again. Again. Again. Dayna squirmed and shivered in his grasp, leaning toward him with a wanting he recognized and shared.

Time slowed. All that existed was the connection between them—a connection that demanded to be made complete. T.J. felt destined to touch her. He felt driven to kiss her. He *needed* to be with her. That was all that mattered.

"I need you, too." Dreamy-eyed, Dayna leaned nearer.

She pressed her thighs together in unconscious yearning—a yearning he knew he could satisfy. T.J.'s hot-blooded warlock ancestors wouldn't have hesitated even this long, he knew. But they would not have had an IAB mission to complete either.

With great force of will, T.J. turned his mind toward the task at hand. He hauled Dayna out of the car. He told himself he was only finishing his mission—making sure his final cusping witch was delivered at last. That was all. But as soon as Dayna swayed and leaned against him, he knew it was a lie. All he wanted was to feel her—to know the pressure of her arms and hips and breasts and belly, all meeting his body in perfect rhythm.

He lowered his head. A single kiss wouldn't hurt . . .

"Hey, I'm double-parked here. So if you two don't mind—"

"Shut up, Deuce." Almost there. Just a few more inches, and he'd have possession of her mouth. He'd hear that tiny intake of breath she made, feel the wet slick of her tongue against his. Driven beyond all reason, T.J. stood beside the heap of Dayna's belongings. He cupped her jaw in his hand, tilting her face to his. He inhaled. "Hold on to me. This is going to be good."

Obediently, she did. Her hands tightened. "I'm ready."

"Well done." He almost wanted to smile. Instead, he nodded in approval. "If you're this diligent about learning to control your magic, those cusping-witch classes should be easy for you."

With a roar, Deuce revved the Mustang's engine.

Irritated by the mind-clearing stink of the car's exhaust, T.J. glanced in his partner's direction. All edgy impatience, Deuce leaned across the passenger's seat and stared up at him, his hand fixed on the wheel. His warning expression made something stir inside T.J.—something besides desire for Dayna.

"Don't you have someplace to be?" Deuce asked.

With a muttered oath, T.J. remembered.

He looked at Dayna, then hastily brushed her aside. He kept his tone harsh, his manner impersonal. "Check in with the InterAllied Bureau first. They'll give you instructions."

He turned, then got in the car and slammed the door.

Dayna stood motionless with surprise . . . but not for long. She pursued him to the Mustang and tried to open the door. Defeated by the lock, she rapped on the passenger-side window.

"Holy shit." Deuce flinched. "She looks pissed."

"That's not my problem. Drive."

Dayna yelled something, but he couldn't hear it.

"Wow. That protective sound charm works both ways."

T.J. gritted his teeth. "Will you get moving?"

His partner shot a dubious glance toward Dayna. "I dunno—her file said she hasn't been back in Covenhaven for more than ten years. Maybe you should take her in yourself."

Picturing the scene, T.J. shook his head. Given the way he'd reacted to her so far, they'd probably drop to the hood of the nearest car and start peeling off each other's clothes.

"We'd never make it inside the building." Uncomfortably aware of how much he liked that idea, T.J. made himself roll down the window. "Just get to the IAB," he told Dayna tersely.

"Fine." Her whole body looked uptight. "Where is it?"

"You can't see it?"

"All I see is the usual Covenhaven kitsch. New Age-y stuff. Adobe buildings. Cowboy hats. Native American hand-crafts. Unless the IAB is located inside that shop selling cactus jelly . . ."

As she yammered away, T.J. turned his face to the front, automatically scanning Covenhaven's touristy main street. Everything seemed as it should be. Visitors to the desert resort town walked side by side—however unknowingly—with witches and warlocks. Legacy witches coexisted with

Followers. Gifted Patayan gardeners made sure the town's succulents, palo verde trees, and gnarled mesquite thrived in the waning sunshine.

"The IAB entrance is hidden from human eyes," he told Dayna, cutting her off. "You'll need your magic to find it."

"Awesome." Her frustrated gaze collided with his. "Exactly how am I supposed to do that? In case you haven't noticed, whatever magic I have has been pretty unpredictable lately."

"That's not my problem."

"You're the one who brought me here!"

"Good luck."

"Hey!" Dayna smacked her hand on the car. "Aren't you supposed to help me? You said you're a guardian. Don't you have some kind of Patayan code that covers this situation?"

"You got here safely, didn't you?"

Mutely, she nodded.

"Then I've done what I have to do."

"*That's* your 'code'? Getting me here safely?" She scoffed. "A *bus* could do that much. A taxi, a train, a '67 Chevy—"

"You left Phoenix without a scratch. That's more than I can say for the people whose cars skidded through the intersection during your rainstorm."

"People were *hurt*?"

"Yes." T.J. gave her a hard look, forcing himself to be unmoved by her horrified expression. "Do what you have to do to master your magic. In the meantime, don't come to me."

"But I—"

"*Don't come to me*, and don't expect me to come to you."

He looked at her face, mobile with unexpressed emotion, and cursed whatever impediment had blocked his ability to intuit Dayna's feelings. Blaming their bonding, he shot an irate glance at her golden armlet. His birthright mark throbbed in response.

"Don't wait for the IAB to find you," he told her.

"Why not?"

"You're already late. Get moving." T.J. nodded at Deuce. Without looking at Dayna, he rolled up the window. "Let's go."

His partner revved the Mustang's engine. The vehicle peeled out from Covenhaven's peaceful town square in a haze of burning rubber, leaving Dayna with her luggage at her feet. T.J. didn't need to look back to know how lost she'd look . . . how alone.

Deuce flicked a glance at the rearview. He frowned. "You sure about this? She looks pretty helpless back there."

"She's a witch." T.J. stared straight ahead, his mouth flat and his body fraught with resistance. "She'll survive."

"Maybe so." Deuce took a corner with his customary finesse. Unlike T.J., he relished human-made vehicles. He had yet to encounter the engine he couldn't improve or the chassis he didn't feel compelled to take apart and reassemble. "But *she's* not the one I'm worried about."

Pushed to the edge of his limits, T.J. exhaled. "If she complains, I'll take the hit from IAB. Don't worry about it. None of the fallout will land on you."

"That's not it either." Deuce bared his teeth, not quite smiling as he reached the town limits and increased speed. "I'm tough. I can take it. What I'm worried about is—"

Like the sun breaking through the clouds, T.J. could intuit Deuce's feelings again. One emotion came through much more strongly than the others. "You're worried about *me*."

Dourly, his partner nodded. "I'm not blind. I saw how you—"

"You're human. You'll always be blind."

"Hey, fuck you, too, buddy. Just because somebody cares enough to watch out for your sorry ass—"

"You should know better than to talk to me about caring." Wearing his most stoic expression, T.J. stared toward the sun as it sank below the horizon. "Don't pretend you've got any compassion for witchfolk. Not after what Anya did to you."

His partner glowered, his hands taut on the wheel. "You don't know what happened. Don't pretend you do."

"I know what it did to you."

"Yeah. So try to avoid the same fate, why don't you?"

T.J. shook his head. "It's not a problem. I'll probably never see Dayna again. She's delivered. That's it. Case closed."

Deuce shook his head. "It's not going to be that easy. I saw the way you looked at her. And did you notice? Her armband matches your Gila monster tattoo. *That's* one weird coincidence."

It wasn't a coincidence. T.J. refused to admit it. His bond with Dayna Sterling didn't matter, because it would never be completed. As long as he stayed away, everything would be fine.

Do you always lie to yourself this way?

Swearing under his breath, T.J. contemplated hearing that witch's voice—sexy, vaguely husky, and all too knowing—in his head for the rest of his days. Either Dayna had sized him up completely after one encounter . . . or he was losing his touch.

Either outcome was unacceptable.

With a frustrated groan, T.J. lolled his head against the Mustang's seatback. He turned his face toward his longtime partner. "You'll keep track of her for me, right?"

Deuce grinned. "I'm already on it, asshole. You never had to ask."

Chapter Six

Stuck on her own in the middle of the hometown she'd thought she'd left behind forever, Dayna stared at the horizon. There, dust still hung in a choking line; closer to her, the smell of singed rubber lingered in the air, making her wrinkle her nose. Overlying all of it were the ordinary goings-on of Covenhaven, lending an unreal quality to the problem she faced.

Where in the world were the IAB headquarters?

All she saw were false-front buildings, adobe-spackled art galleries, and gift shops promising crystals and other New Age items. In Covenhaven, free spirits reigned. Auras were cleansed, incense was burned, and counterculture types found solace with others who wanted to escape conventional lives. No one here looked askance at creative differences—unless the people doing the looking were witches . . . and one of them was an outcast witch who'd never mastered her magic and had run away because of it.

According to T.J., the InterAllied Bureau entrance was in plain sight—if a person looked for it through witching eyes. With residents giving her curious glances and tourists strolling blithely along in their overly crisp Stetsons and elaborate hammered-silver belt buckles, Dayna slung her backpack over her shoulder and she picked up her duffel bag. She stepped onto the sidewalk and turned in a circle, squinting as she tried to identify the entrance she needed.

Don't wait for the IAB to find you.

Anxiously, she sighted a gas station, a shuttered shop selling turquoise jewelry, and a café with dreamcatchers hung colorfully in its windows. None of them seemed right. Tightening her grasp on her belongings, Dayna swiveled one more time.

But all she saw was T.J.'s face, infuriatingly impassive as he dumped her and left her behind. Filled with new frustration, Dayna frowned. She should have known better than to trust a hard-fisted tracer, especially one who could practice magic.

Everyone in the witching community had let her down. There was no reason T.J. should be different—and every reason he should be eager to get away from her.

You left Phoenix without a scratch. That's more than I can say for the people whose cars skidded through the intersection during your rainstorm.

Still chilled by his words, Dayna closed her eyes and gathered her focus. She *had* to succeed at this. She didn't want anyone else to be hurt because of her. She didn't want to be outed as a witch among her friends back home either. It was true that some witches felt free to live openly among humans, whether as pierced and pale Goths or practicing Wiccans, but those lifestyles weren't for her. She wanted to live her life as she had been—unobtrusively and *un*magically.

It had been tough to start over, more than a decade ago now. But it had been worth it.

In Phoenix, no one knew she was a witch. No one pitied her because she couldn't summon a hex or cast a spell. No one made fun of her because she'd never maintained a familiar. For her, Buffy and Spike were enough. Her friendships were enough. Her work at the research library was enough. As soon as she settled her "cusping witch" issues in Covenhaven, she intended to go back home and forget she'd ever met T.J. *or* practiced witchery again. But first she had to find the IAB entrance.

Focus. *Focus* . . .

With a surge of emotion, Dayna opened her eyes. As though she'd willed it, all the bean pods blew off a nearby mesquite tree. They rattled to the ground in a clatter of dried husks.

The landscaper frowned at her.

No sign of the IAB headquarters. But at least nobody had been injured by her efforts.

Counting that as progress, Dayna reassembled her focus. She tried a few half-forgotten incantations from childhood, spells that required not much more than memorization and aptitude.

She failed on both counts. Worse, a man nearby had stopped to watch her—a warlock, if she didn't miss her guess. His sexy posture and obvious self-confidence gave away his abilities.

Feeling sweat seep into the armpits of her T-shirt, she pressed on. *Reveal, reveal, reveal,* she thought. *Please.*

The café's front door blew open with a bang.

Surely *that* wasn't the IAB headquarters? As far as Dayna knew, the InterAllied Bureau was responsible for policing the witching world—for making sure that witchfolk didn't get out of hand. They were the magical realm's FBI, for lack of a better description. They *had* to demand better stomping grounds than a roadside restaurant peddling ostrich burgers and slices of pie.

A chuckle nearby broke her concentration.

She turned, surprised to find herself surrounded by three people in dark suits. One was the warlock she'd already glimpsed; another was an amused-looking witch. The third was an imposing warlock with a shaved head and clear blue eyes. He was the obvious leader . . . and the one who'd laughed at her, too.

Probably at her lame attempts to enact magic again.

Damn, she hated being back among practicing witchfolk.

"You're right," he said. "But we *do* like the pie."

Nervously, Dayna slid into a seat in a space no bigger than the cramped copier room at the research library. To make it here, she'd traveled a warren of hallways and offices, cubicles and conference rooms. It was hard to believe that the Inter-Allied Bureau had magiked all this into existence behind the false fronts of Covenhaven's downtown tourist traps. But they had. Apparently, around here, false fronts were all too real . . . if you knew where—and how—to look.

As she tried to get her bearings, the warlock and witch who'd found her took up positions near the door. The laughing warlock—the leader—scraped out a chair across the table from her. With easy equanimity, he steepled his hands.

Music issued from between his joined fingertips.

Startled, Dayna blinked at his hands.

"Ah. You *are* green, aren't you?" He traded an insider's glance with his cohorts, then addressed her again. "It's a charm. The music calms people down. You look a little rattled."

"Something to drink?" asked the witch in the corner.

Curtly, Dayna nodded. A silver carafe and two glasses whooshed into existence. They clattered into place with a tinkling sound, perfectly centered on the table.

Unfazed by the objects' abrupt materialization, the warlock across from her poured her a glass of water. With a polite word of offering, he set it near Dayna. His fingers were deft, the way warlocks' often were. His whole being exuded composure.

So did his companions. And why shouldn't they? Dayna realized as she studied their lanyarded silver talismans—

devices similar to the ID badges she and her coworkers wore at DRL. They hadn't been kidnapped from their ordinary lives and transported to Covenhaven. They hadn't wrecked their workplaces, whole city blocks, and—potentially—their friends' lives.

This was business as usual for them. The IAB agents *belonged* here in the magical world. The blond witch—Emme, according to her talisman—had probably never known a moment's failure in her life. The warlock, Luis, probably didn't know what it was like to feel ostracized, just for being himself.

Clutching the arms of her chair, Dayna frowned. At one end of the room, conjured sunlight filtered past a pair of captive green plants; their leaves and stems gleamed with good health. Water flowed from an invisible source into a tabletop fountain, then vanished harmlessly into the stone floor. A fresh-air charm sweetened the artificial breeze, and an array of silver styluses stood at the ready in a bamboo cup. Not a detail had been spared in an effort to put visitors at ease.

With an audible sigh, her chair settled beneath her.

Alarmed, Dayna jerked. Her chair did, too, bucking in eager readiness. Rocking sideways, she tightened her grasp.

The lead warlock gestured. "Your chair is charmed to react sympathetically. It can tell when you feel comfortable—and when you're startled. If you relax, your chair will, too."

"Sure." Leave it to witchkind to devise a seat that revealed everything its occupants tried not to. "No problem."

Clenching her jaw, Dayna forced herself to be still.

It wasn't easy. An outwardly sentient chair was even more disconcerting than advanced water-carafe conjuring. She wasn't used to being around magic anymore. And she was a perennial outsider here in Covenhaven, too. Her ineptness with magic seemed tattooed on her skin, as easy to see as the symbols she'd noticed on T.J.'s brawny arms and neck.

The three agents watched her, doubtless sensing her need

to move, to fidget, to do *something*. In unison, they crossed their arms. Beneath their serene gazes, Dayna felt like a wayward kid called into the principal's office, then made to watch a magician perform tricks before learning what she was in trouble for. She didn't care about flashy magic. All she wanted were facts about the cusping-witch training she was supposed to complete. More than anything else, she needed a way to prevent more accidents from occurring when she returned home to Phoenix.

Clearly, she wasn't going to get it by letting these three run the show. Mimicking them, Dayna crossed her arms over her chest. She propped her Converse-covered foot on her knee and studied them all.

"Look, it's been a pretty awful day." Ignoring her glass of water, she examined her tablemate's talisman. LEO GARMIN. "So I'd like to cut to the chase, Mr. Garmin. What do I have to do to fulfill this 'cusping witch' requirement and get back home?"

He appeared surprised. "For a witch who was late getting here, you're all business now, Ms. Sterling."

"I don't commit to much. But when I do, it's all the way."

"Interesting. That's a very unwitchlike attitude. Your time among humans shows." Garmin poured a glass of water for himself, then drank. He gave her a friendly smile. "Let's start with some background information then, shall we? I'm not sure how aware you are of the goings-on in the witching world . . . ?"

He hesitated, obviously offering her an opening. Dayna had nothing to contribute. She'd been estranged from the witching world for over a decade now. Her parents traveled to the Valley for visits. Otherwise, they would seldom see one another.

"All right then." Meditatively, Garmin pressed his palms together. He tapped his fingertips against his lips, then appeared to come to a decision. "The capsule version is this: All witches come into their most powerful magic during their thirtieth year—their cusping year. It's a bit like human puberty, only delayed in onset and much more powerful. Warlocks don't experience it." Ruefully, he twisted his mouth. "Unlike witches, we peak in ability when young, then decline as we age—much as we'd all prefer to ignore that fact."

"Haven't you guys conjured some warlock Viagra yet?"

Sobering, he unsteepled his hands. "Sadly, no."

"I was kidding."

"Warlock sloping is not a laughing matter."

"Of course not." Putting on a solemn face, Dayna thought about what he'd told her. Delayed-onset witch puberty went a long way toward explaining the things she'd been experiencing lately. Her escalating magic, her inability to control it . . . her frustration, moodiness, and overall horniness when the tracer had come to get her. Those effects could be due to overactive witching hormones—or whatever the witchfolk equivalent was.

If she hadn't been so distant from her coven, maybe she would have already known about cusping. But escaping Covenhaven and its witchy ways had been a matter of survival eleven years ago. Dayna felt convinced it still was. That's why she'd remained unlinked—a decidedly unnatural state, even for a failed witch.

Garmin cleared his throat. "Until recently, the official IAB position on cusping has been to leave those witches to the support of their families and the elders in their covens until the process is complete. But in our modern age, with unprecedented witch migration and integration occurring, many witches forsake their home communities. This leaves them alone during cusping, without the support and instruction they need."

That much Dayna could believe. She'd migrated. She'd definitely integrated. And she'd had no support at all.

"Allowing so many unschooled witches to remain alone in

the world while they underwent cusping was causing tremendous problems. Not only because of unintended . . . *events*"—here, Garmin tactfully averted his gaze—"but also because it became increasingly difficult to hide the existence of those witches. Despite our shared pasts, humans aren't ready to admit our presence among them. They force us to live in hiding."

Dayna shrugged. "Living in hiding isn't that bad."

"Some disagree." With an easy move, Garmin loosened his necktie. His chunky platinum ring glinted in the conjured sunlight. "In any case, it became clear that the traditional ways would have to be amended to cope with this new reality."

"That's where *we* came in, here at the bureau. With the cusping-witch training program." The flawlessly groomed witch, Emme, brightened with pride as she spoke. "Nothing like it has ever been tried before. We're making witchstory."

"It's only year one, of course." Garmin studied his pristine shirt cuffs with apparent modesty, drawing Dayna's gaze to his powerful hands. "And there are some kinks to work out in the process. A few witches fell through the cracks. It's been a scramble to locate all the eligible cusping witches in time."

"Is that why you sent out tracers?"

A nod. "But even with those issues accounted for, our IAB taskforce has been instrumental in creating the change we need. If all goes as planned, we'll finally be able to educate and train our cusping witches as they should have been educated and trained all along: with systemic procedures instead of old superstition and outmoded sentimentality."

"Right. Who needs emotion when you can have efficiency?"

The lead agent glanced up from his cuffs. He squinted at Dayna, then gave a pleasant nod. "Something like that."

She pulled a sardonic face. "Sounds cozy."

"It's actually a very big deal. A major coup." This from Emme again, who appeared bulletproof when it came to sarcasm. "We even work closely with representatives from the League of Covens. It's a consultancy that's totally new."

"It's groundbreaking," Luis added. "An important pact."

"It sounds like a power grab to me." Dayna leaned back in her chair. For the first time, it held her placidly in place, sensing her ease with witchy mutiny . . . however minor. She swerved her gaze to Garmin. "How do the covens feel about having your taskforce usurp their positions with the cusping witches?"

The lead agent gave her a quelling look—one she recognized from years of school-age rebellion. "Cusping witches like you need help, Ms. Sterling. The InterAllied Bureau recognizes that. That's why we've replaced the old model of inconsistent personal support with IAB-managed public classes. In those classes, witches like you can learn to perfect your burgeoning magic."

He paused, undoubtedly waiting for Dayna to *ooh* and *ah* the way Emme had. Characteristically hardheaded, Dayna did neither. In pointed silence, she frowned at the sandblasted and rain-soaked cargo pants she hadn't had time to change out of, unhappy with this whole scheme—and her required participation in it.

Garmin's smooth voice pursued her all the same. "Some of our most admirable leaders are fully formed witches who've made it well past cusping," he said. "Their mastery of magic has increased their connection to the community. It's enriched their lives enormously. Yours can, too, with a little effort."

At last Dayna glanced up. Although Garmin possessed the usual warlock charisma, his encouraging smile left her unmoved.

"You can skip the hard sell. I'm not interested in learning anything more about magic than I have to. All I want is to control it. Or better yet, to get rid of it. Is that possible?"

In unison, Emme and Luis stepped back. Eyes wide, they

shook their heads. Even Garmin appeared disturbed by her remark.

"No? Hey, a girl's got to ask." Undaunted by their stunned expressions, Dayna leaned forward. She rested her elbows on her knees. The agents' gazes dipped to her human-made clothing with evident disdain. "And you can keep your witch-folk 'community' for yourself, too. It's not for me. It never was."

"Nonsense," Emme said. "The community is for everyone!"

"Spare me." Dayna rounded on her. The witch's rah-rah attitude and smug smile reminded her of all the reasons she'd left Covenhaven in the first place. "If that were true, you wouldn't have had to drag me back here by force, now would you?"

The conversation lapsed, leaving only the trickle of the fountain's waters in its wake. Garmin lowered his gaze to Dayna's golden armlet. He studied it, then exhaled deeply.

"We understand you've been unlinked for some time now, Ms. Sterling, but there's always hope that—"

"I won't take a class. Give me a tutor instead."

At least private lessons would spare her the embarrassment of public failure. And if someone like T.J. could train her . . .

"I'm afraid that's impossible. No one is allowed to receive solitary instruction." Garmin shook his head, his mouth a firm line. "We wouldn't want to give the impression of favoritism. This new taskforce is strictly nonsectarian in nature. We pride ourselves in working equally with all witch factions."

"Except the ones who don't want to be worked with."

Garmin's genial efficiency never wavered. "With our help, you'll be registered for classes today. After you finish your lessons, you'll be tested, then licensed. Really, all we're asking you to do is take one continuing education class—"

"Adult ed?" Dayna laughed. "*Night school* for witches?"

"—followed by an accreditation exam and a lavish graduation ceremony to recognize your transition. Your family and friends will be invited, of course. This year the graduation rites will be conducted at Janus, the finest spa-resort in Covenhaven."

"I'm not much for mud wraps and seaweed smoothies."

"That isn't the point." Garmin glanced at the other warlock, Luis, with bland forbearance. "Her file was accurate in at least one aspect. She does have a smart mouth."

"So I've been told." Dayna arrowed her gaze to Garmin's face. "What if I *don't* go to remedial witch school? What then?"

"This training is important, for your own safety and the safety of those around you." Emme's tone was somber. "If your magic remains uncontrolled, it poses a danger to everyone."

Like the people who were hurt today. Guiltily, Dayna shifted. So did her chair. It scrunched in on itself until she had to jab an elbow in her seatback to force it upright again.

Garmin's shrewd expression met hers. He nodded—a gesture so slight, Dayna thought she might have imagined it. She found herself nodding in return. Her commitment to cusping-witch classes suddenly felt like a foregone conclusion. Why argue?

"We've already assigned you to a witch class according to your place and date of birth." Garmin directed a pointed look at Emme, who magiked a clipboard. She ticked off an item with one of the silver styluses. When Garmin returned his attention to Dayna, his smile was a benediction. "For an intelligent witch like you, classes will be easy. We've designed the classes to be very much like high school—"

"High school?"

"—except with an all-magic curriculum. You'll probably see several familiar faces there." His smile broadened. "Our research shows that most witchfolk have fond memories of—"

"No way. You have *got* to be kidding me."

Garmin gave her a perplexed look. "Is there a problem?"

"For me? Yes. You're damn right there's a problem."

Luis came forward. In whispered tones, he conferred with Garmin. The two warlocks glanced up at her. Luis returned to his post by the door. Garmin gave her a contemplative frown.

"Whatever . . . issues . . . you've experienced in the past, there's no need to react emotionally now. I'm sure that you—"

The rest of his assurances were lost to her. Dayna felt too distraught to listen. She stared at the lead agent in disbelief, shaking her head. She wanted to learn to control her magic, but the IAB could not have devised a more disagreeable training method for her if they'd tried.

High school redux? She'd suffered enough in high school the first time around. The last thing she wanted now was an impromptu class reunion with all the mean witches who'd ruined her teenage years. It was enough to make her queasy.

Dayna became aware that Garmin had quit speaking. All eyes were on her—and on her undoubtedly dread-filled expression.

In the silence, Emme piped up. "I can't *wait* until I'm old enough for my cusping-witch classes." She flicked a hank of blond hair over her shoulder. "It's going to be incredible!"

No. No no no no. Feeling trapped, Dayna put up her palms in a universal *stop* sign. She cast Garmin a pleading look. "Are you *sure* I can't opt for a tutor? I'll pay extra."

"The cusping-witch class is an IAB program. Since it's a nonnegotiable obligation, it's offered without fees to qualifying witches. We do take care of our own. We witchfolk have endured humankind's biases and maltreatment for ages. Our strength of community is paramount. You must remember that much?"

She didn't. "How about a volunteer tutor? If I can find—"

"I applaud your initiative." Actually, Garmin seemed to find it entertaining—the same way Albert Einstein might have found a toddler's attempts at logic entertaining. "But it wouldn't be fair to give you an advantage over the other students. Especially since you'll all be vying for the position of *juweel*—teacher's favorite. It's a mark of distinction, much like human valedictorian or *summa cum laude* status."

"It sounds like a nightmare."

Luis stiffened. "It is a *very* high status position."

Right. And Dayna had about as much chance of scoring it as she did morphing herself into a toad and hopping out of there.

She decided to sidestep the issue. "Exactly how long does this witch school last? And when does it begin?"

Maybe she could find a tutor on her own. It wouldn't be the first time she'd ignored the rules. Dayna had no problem with that. If she could get a head start on the curriculum . . .

Emme glanced up from her clipboard. "It started yesterday."

Terrific. She was already behind.

"It's a three-week commitment," Garmin explained. "Mostly during the evenings and weekends. We've made it easy for even the most time-pressed witch to fit classes into her schedule."

The three of them beamed, obviously pleased with the IAB's efficiency. Dayna hated to throw a monkey wrench into their bureaucratic bliss, but she had to. The research librarian in her demanded she take care of the dangling details.

"That's super, but I don't live in Covenhaven anymore." She could arrange a temporary leave from DRL. She had the tenure. But in Covenhaven, the only people she'd remained in touch with were her parents. There was no way she could impose on them for almost a month. Although she *did* hope, Dayna realized in a burst of unstoppable wistfulness, that they'd be happy to have her in town again . . . the prodigal daughter returned. "Where am I supposed to stay while all this is going on?"

"Housing is available for transitory witches." Emme

consulted her clipboard. "We've anticipated your needs in that regard and arranged for a place for you to live while you're here. You will have to contend with roommates, however. And all cusping witches have been assigned IAB chaperones, too."

Dayna opened her mouth to object. Garmin spoke first.

"The chaperones are strictly precautionary." He took in Dayna's fisted hands. A faint line creased his otherwise perfect forehead. "For your protection and the good of the community. Well-behaved witches will have nothing to worry about."

"That leaves me out then."

"Not as much as you might think." With evident certainty, Leo Garmin gave her a smile. "You might enjoy yourself."

Ha. Dayna stifled a derisive snort. "So . . . I move into IAB student housing, I go to cusping-witch night school, I get tested and licensed in three weeks." She performed a few mental calculations. "The graduation ceremony is on Hallowe'en?"

"We prefer Samhain," Luis told her. "In keeping with the ancient traditions. Everyone in town is gearing up for the festivities. You must have seen the banners? The flyers?"

Distractedly, Dayna shook her head. She didn't care what they called it. It was still the holiday she avoided most.

Humans made observing All Hallows' Eve a ridiculous affair, with their costumes standing in for transmogrifications and their trick-or-treat candies serving as crude charms. Besides, coming face to face with a wart-nosed, cackling "witch" dressed all in black with an ugly pointy hat was just awkward. Humans had seriously missed the boat with that cliché.

More than likely, warlocks had floated the rumor that witches were hideous in order to keep them all to themselves.

Selfish, sexy, irresistible bastards.

"What if I don't pass the licensing test?" she asked.

"That's not an option."

"For other witches, maybe not. But when it comes to me and magic? Trust me . . . failing to pass is definitely a possibility."

The trio of agents smiled tranquilly at her, secure in their own magic and—evidently—in hers.

Dayna still had her doubts.

"What if I don't finish classes?" she asked.

"You're thinking of running away again." Garmin gave her a hard look—one that reminded her *he* was in charge here. The InterAllied Bureau was his domain. "I don't recommend it."

"What's the matter?" She raised her eyebrow. "Don't want to pay for another witchfolk bounty hunter to come after me?"

"Cost is not the issue. Keeping tabs on our own kind is part of the IAB mission. It's a necessary evil, I'm afraid. At least until humankind wakes up to our existence." Garmin transferred his gaze to Luis. The other warlock agent had magiked a stack of paperwork and what appeared to be the witching equivalent of an iPhone. "When someone goes a little farther afield than usual"—Garmin's gaze returned meaningfully to Dayna—"our tracers can be very helpful."

"Helpful." She scoffed. "Is that what you're calling it?"

"What would you call it?"

"Intrusive. Invasive. Scary."

"Really?" Appearing mildly surprised, Garmin pulled out his own pocket-size electronic device. He swirled his finger over its smooth black surface, making notes. "Anything else?"

Yes. Exciting. Intense. Hot. "No, that about sums it up."

"Thank you for your input, Ms. Sterling. We'll keep your comments in mind for future tracer deployments. We value our constituents' input here at the IAB." With an efficient air, Garmin put away his device, then gave her an interested look. "Are you ready to get started?"

With a rush of relief—now that she'd fully committed herself—Dayna straightened. Her chair perked up, too, almost chirping. "Is there any way I could have done this yesterday?"

Garmin frowned. "Actually, according to The Old Ways, with the proper spells we could reverse time. But here at the IAB—"

"You disapprove of time reversal." Evidently, Emme wasn't the only one who was immune to sarcasm. "It's inconvenient and messy, and it leaves gaps in your employee time sheets. Right?"

He gave her a long look. Then a trace of real humor sparked in his eyes. Leo Garmin was, it occurred to Dayna, a very attractive warlock—virile, smart, and skilled at magic. It was too bad his talents were wasted here in witchy civil service.

"For the first time, I actually feel sorry for Agent McAllister. It couldn't have been easy to bring you in."

"They tell me it wasn't."

"Also, for the record, time reversal *is* messy."

Dayna laughed. "What do I have to do first?"

At Garmin's nod, Luis stepped forward. He took the time to give Dayna a flirtatious wink, then dropped a stack of paperwork heavy enough to make the table shudder beneath its impact.

"First, you'll need to complete these forms in triplicate."

"Wow." She'd left Covenhaven at nineteen, barely old enough to register her dubious magical "abilities." Since then, she hadn't given much thought to how things worked among witchfolk. "I guess policy and procedures have invaded the witching world."

"Remedial magic training is a grave business." Leaning back in his chair, Garmin folded his hands across his lean middle. His gaze followed Dayna's movements as she sorted through the paperwork, giving it a preliminary examination. "It's important for our agents and teachers to adhere to protocol. We wouldn't want to, say, accidentally train a human by mistake."

"Oh, I don't know about that." Reluctant to tackle the pile,

Dayna searched her backpack for a pen. Luis conjured one and handed it to her, blowing her excuse for procrastinating. "It might be handy if humans recognized their fundamental natures."

"As witches, you mean?"

She nodded. She might be terrible at practicing magic, but she still remembered a little witchfolk theory and witchstory. "We were all magical beings once, right? I mean, humans might be stuck with lowly vestigial magic like intuition, déjà vu, and good luck charms, but they *could* have been witches, too, if they hadn't been scared out of it eons ago."

An eerie silence fell in the room. Not even the leaves on the captive green plants rustled. Frowning, Dayna glanced up.

"There's no pleasing you people, is there? First you think it's hilarious that I can't find this place, then you lecture me almost nonstop about how awesome remedial witch school is going to be, then you clam up when I show a little cultural insight. What does it take to—"

Garmin lifted his hand, cutting her off in midsentence. "Yours is an interesting perspective, Ms. Sterling. But I'll thank you to keep it to yourself. Witchfolk are witchfolk. Humans are humans. I think you'll see that we're getting farther apart from one another, not closer."

Perplexed, Dayna stared at him. She didn't remember it being particularly taboo to discuss humans' magical origins.

"I think it's time you left us," the lead agent added.

The impulse to disagree nagged at Dayna. So did a yearning to get the hell out of there. Getting out won.

"All right. Later. If you're ever in Phoenix, look me up." Dayna stuffed her paperwork in her backpack, shouldered her duffel bag, then aimed her most acerbic glance at Emme. She flicked her hair over her shoulder—not easy when her dark locks were still lank from the rainstorm. The intent was there. That was what mattered. "No wait. *Don't*."

Without looking back, Dayna headed for the door.

Chapter Seven

Caught in the stark glare of a single outdoor floodlight, T.J. examined the target before him.

Many times he'd struck that target; a few times he'd missed. Tonight, with the desert cicadas stirring around him and his mind crowded with thoughts of his unwelcome bonding with the runaway witch Dayna Sterling, T.J. lifted his arms to shoot . . . and missed. His basketball struck the rim and bounced into the darkness outside the floodlight's reach.

"Yeah! I win!" Jesse Obijuwa, the fifteen-year-old son of his good—and deeply missed—friend Henry, bounded off the court. His long dark legs flashed as he chased the basketball. When he returned to the light, his face shone. "Thanks for the game, old man. You can come back and let me beat you anytime."

"You got lucky." Unbothered by his defeat, T.J. slung his arm around Jesse's shoulders. "Next time I'll whup you good."

The boy crowed. "I'd like to see you try."

"Same time next week?"

"I guess." Not looking at him, Jesse flung the ball from hand to hand with practiced ease. He sniffed. "If you've got nothing better to do than hang out here on the res, I mean."

"Hey." T.J. shot him a stern look. "Don't badmouth this place. I was born here, remember?"

T.J. had been happy living on the reservation, too—at least until his parents had died, and everything had fallen apart. He still liked being there. Unlike humans, Covenhaven's Native American population understood the importance of their magical counterparts. They lived in harmony with the Patayan, both groups benefitting from and sharing their unique abilities.

Such peaceful coexistence was important, especially in a world fraught with dangers. Even the traditional legacy witches understood that. Long ago, they'd enacted a truce with the Patayan, partly to keep their ancient battles from endangering humankind and partly to preserve their own dwindling numbers.

But the legacy witches had never found the same accord with their human complements. They still lived apart from each other. Some traditional witches—*myrmidon*, or Followers of The Old Ways—resented humankind's freedom. They worked against integration and everything it stood for, preferring to preserve their witchy purity. Their purposeful detachment was almost as bad as humankind's constant competition and self-interest.

Those were attitudes T.J. didn't understand. As a compound—born of a warlock father and a Patayan wise-woman mother—he'd been caught between worlds from the start. But he'd never felt apart from either one. Instead, he'd kept footholds in each.

He hadn't sensed the same ease in Dayna Sterling. Despite running away to live among humans, she'd seemed distant from their world—hindered, like the ocotillo and cactus in her apartment's front yard, from the growth and connectedness that all beings needed. He wished, for her sake, that—

No. He refused to think about her. He turned to Jesse.

"Yeah. What I don't get is why you keep coming back."

Jesse flashed him a rare grin. "Probably you like a girl out here."

"I like women everywhere."

"Me, too." Jesse aimed a shy glance in his direction. "So, uh, do girls like it when you do magic? I'll bet that totally reels 'em in. Or maybe you don't have to show off for them at all. You can just look at them and they go crazy for you."

Technically that was true. As a warlock, T.J. did possess certain . . . *aptitudes* where the opposite sex was concerned. A talent for seduction was ingrained in him. So was a hunger for pleasure. More often than not, though, T.J.'s inborn skills only got him into trouble. Or at least they had, during his wilder days—before he'd discovered the IAB and the discipline it conferred.

That discipline had probably saved his life . . . or at least his soul. Without it, T.J. didn't know how dark his life might have become, as he searched for release in all the wrong places.

"Women who are that easy aren't worth the effort," he told Jesse. "There's more magic to be found between equals."

"Right. Equal *witchfolk*, you mean. Doing magic must be totally sweet." The boy spun the basketball on his fingers, slapping it with his opposite hand to make it spin. His young face showed the effort of concentration. "My pops was doing magic. You know . . . before he . . . ." He cleared his throat and tried again. "He was doing *tons* of magic."

T.J. frowned at him. All kinds of emotions caromed from the boy—anger, hopefulness, pride. None of those were easy to deal with, especially alone. T.J. had been the same vulnerable age when his parents had been killed. He hadn't handled it well. He didn't want Jesse to go down the same shadowy paths he had.

"Jesse, you know humans can't practice magic." He was careful to keep his tone gentle, his expression matter of fact.

He remained steadfastly beside the boy. "I know you want that to be true, but as great as your father was, he couldn't—"

"He *could*! He did. I saw it." Stubbornly, Jesse thrust out his chest. His jaw tightened, hinting at the manliness that had begun to emerge in his face. "I saw my pops do magic. Not that earth-sun-water-wind Patayan bullshit either, but *real* magic."

"Legacy magic? Like the witches and warlocks practice?"

"Yeah. He didn't show my mom, because he knew she'd yell at him. But he showed me." Pride filled Jesse's voice. "He magiked a stone into a dollar coin. He transformed a rabbit to look just like our dog. You should have seen the look on Jumper's face when he saw that rabbit dog. He started barking like crazy."

Animals held intuitive insight. Troubled even further by that telling detail, T.J. deepened his frown. "Jumper could sense the existence of your father's magic?"

"When it came to that freaky rabbit, he sure could." Jesse caught a glimpse of T.J.'s face and laughed. "Don't worry, he changed that rabbit back. It was like the magic couldn't stick or something. Rabbit parts kept popping out of the dog bits, like bunny ears on top of its head. I was trippin' to see that shit." He spun the basketball faster, then shrugged. "I found that rabbit a few days later. Dead. I guess maybe it wasn't the same one. Or maybe it was. I don't know."

"Did your father do any more magic tricks?"

"They weren't tricks!" With an abrupt motion, Jesse stopped the basketball from spinning. He gave T.J. a fierce glare. "It was real magic he was doing. Just like all those witches and warlocks in town. They might have looked down on him sometimes, but if they knew about his magic, they wouldn't have."

"Your father was a talented gardener. There's no shame in doing the work he did, no matter what anybody says."

"Hell, I know that." Jesse twisted his mouth in a disgusted

frown. "It's everybody else who needs to learn that lesson, bro. Look, I've got to go."

The boy slammed the basketball onto the court in a savage imitation of dribbling. With a halfhearted wave—more of a *fuck you* that used his whole hand than anything else—he trotted toward the edge of the court. He vanished into the darkness that lay beyond the scope of the floodlight.

Left behind, T.J. swore under his breath. His heart still clenched with the impact of the emotions he'd absorbed from Jesse. Pain and loss were especially difficult to take in. Minds and bodies wanted to resist it, but T.J. was determined not to.

Henry Obijuwa had been a good friend of his. His death—from a brain aneurysm little more than two weeks ago—had been sudden and unexpected. His loss had been a blow to everyone. One day Henry had left for work . . . and had never returned. It was no wonder Jesse wanted to make up stories about his dad. He wanted to remember his pops as a hero—as a man who was extraordinary.

A man who was magical.

In time, Jesse would learn acceptance. Until then, T.J. would be there for him. It was what Henry would have wanted.

Squaring his shoulders, T.J. waited another few minutes to see if Jesse would return. When he didn't, T.J. gritted his teeth and headed for his car. He hated driving the damned thing. It left him feeling out of control—at the mercy of machinery that refused to acknowledge his magic. But it was the only way to travel between Covenhaven and the reservation without spending an hour on the task—or recruiting Deuce to help him.

Fifteen fist-clenching minutes later, T.J. parked in front of what appeared to be an enormous dirt mound. Guided by the rising moon, he picked his way between spires of red rocks and the ruts of a dry wash, keeping his gaze fixed on his destination. As he neared it, the dirt mound arched higher. Its breath became audible. Its respiration became perceptible. The mound rhythmically rose and fell, as alive as he was.

A colony of bats winged its way overhead. A saguaro leaned nearer, its centuries-old vigilance evident in its many long arms. With a nod for its watchfulness, T.J. stopped. He waited.

Gradually, he became aware of the light emanating from within the mound. It splintered through minute cracks in the dirt and gaps in the crimson rock, casting a welcoming glow into the night.

T.J. smiled. She was here.

Chapter Eight

Inside the mound, T.J. sat across from his magus. As the spiritual leader of the Patayan people, she was both wise and patient. She was learned and articulate. She was hospitable.

She was not, however, a skilled baker.

T.J. accepted the slice of pie she offered him all the same. His magus had become almost like a mother to him. He refused to offend her by doing any less than forking up a big bite. The leathery piecrust resisted his chewing; the orangey filling inside tasted a little like pumpkin, but wasn't.

"It's butternut squash." The magus curled into her favorite chair, surrounded by modernistic furnishings. A newcomer would not have expected to find them inside the "earth ship" she called home—an ecologically sound dwelling dug partway into the desert floor. Its interior felt both snug and protected. Above the magus's head, skylights revealed slivers of stars and sky. To her side sat a gray wolfhound, her companion for many years. She stroked the creature as she went on talking. "Baking appeals to me. Its scientific aspects are a constant challenge."

With effort, T.J. swallowed his first bite of pie. "I never thought I'd say this, but I miss your cookies."

"When I served you cookies, you missed my cake."

"I've been told I'm hard to please."

"*You* are hard to *know*." The magus smiled. "You like it that way. You think that if you stay hard, like the rocks outside my door, that nothing will penetrate you. Nothing will hurt you."

T.J.'s next bite of pie turned sour in his mouth. His jaw ached with it. He swallowed again, then set aside his plate.

"But a rock is not unbreakable." The magus pulled her attention from her wolfhound to T.J. Her demeanor was calm and sure, her posture alert. "A strong rock can withstand a great deal. But the smallest trickle can work its way inside. Given enough time, a meager stream can split apart a huge boulder."

"Maybe. But I have something a huge boulder does not."

"What is that?"

"Legs." Grinning, T.J. put his hands on his thighs. "I can walk away from that trickle of water, and I damn well would."

The magus, her aristocratic face lined with the cares of a thousand Patayan, did not smile in return. "I think you already are walking away. Running, almost." Her gaze dipped to the birthright mark on his biceps. "I sense a difference in you."

His Gila monster tattoo prickled in response. Irritably, T.J. rubbed it. "What you sense in me is impatience. I want to fulfill my promise to our circle. Instead, I was delayed again today with a greenie's mission to trace a runaway witch."

"Your work for the InterAllied Bureau is important, too."

"Not as important as my promise to the Patayan."

"You are of both worlds. You do an admirable job of balancing them. As far as your promise is concerned, I'm not worried. You have never failed me or your people."

T.J. grunted. He poked his pie with his fork, then lifted his gaze to the magus's walls. Here in the main living space, where his magus accepted visitors, the walls were lined with totems and photographs and historical artifacts. Each piece fit in its niche as though made for it. They were spotlit like museum pieces, clean and venerable. He felt a million miles from them.

"I haven't earned anyone's praise. Especially yours."

"You deserve praise without action. Love without measure."

With a cynical snort, T.J. stood. A swift current of wind followed him, stolen from the night and shaped by his restless mood. It ruffled his hair and scoured his skin, much the way Dayna's rainstorm had. Reminded of her, he frowned.

"You appear angry," his magus observed. "But you *feel*—"

"As though I want to have this mission done," T.J. interrupted. His voice sounded harsh, even to his own ears. "I want this danger settled. You still sense a threat looming?"

A pause. A grudging nod. "I do. The confrontation we've feared feels closer than ever. I've had signs. Spirit visions. Evidence from EnchantNet. Hateful traditions are returning, building to a new and destructive force."

T.J. exhaled. He'd hoped to hear differently. He'd been gone for a few days while tracing cusping witches for the IAB's inaugural remedial magic classes. He and Deuce had been assigned the stragglers—the cusping witches no one else could bring in.

"This force's dark energy is centered on Covenhaven," his magus said. "Maybe because of all the cusping witches who've gathered there. Maybe because Samhain is almost here. I still don't know the reason, but the danger is real." She broke off, studying him through curious eyes. "But talk of divisive witchfolk is not what you came here for, is it?"

She was right. T.J. refused to admit it.

Instead, he strode to her avant-garde bookshelf and picked up an ancient Patayan lifewheel, a gift from a neighboring Patayan circle. He turned it in his hands. He could confide in his magus. But confidences—like closeness—led to betrayals.

T.J. refused to be vulnerable again. Like the lifewheel, he was closed now. Like the lifewheel, he was unbreakable.

Unbreakable . . . like his bond with that witch.

In a whir of movement, he put down the lifewheel and paced instead. The wind he'd conjured swirled around him, revealing more than he wanted with its restive nature. When his magic conspired against him this way, he couldn't hide a damned thing.

As proof, his magus's soft voice chased him from across the room. "Why did you come here, T.J.?"

Because I'm beginning to feel lost again.

The truth burbled inside him, wanting to be told. Striding across the dwelling's polished floors, T.J. ruthlessly squashed it. He could deal with these feelings the way he always did—by refusing them. Other people's emotions kept him busy enough. From the moment he awakened, he absorbed feelings that were not his own, the way all Patayan intuitively did.

It was no wonder a few Patayan typically entered the human world, where their powers of insight and compassion earned them natural work as therapists, psychologists, and psychiatrists. Listening and hearing and *feeling* were unavoidable for them. In T.J., those elements were especially strong. He accepted that.

"The signs you've seen . . . this threat comes from witches?" he asked. "You weren't specific about the danger until now."

"I didn't have specifics until now. I only knew that The Old Ways would return. That they would divide us again. That they would pit us against one another—legacy witch versus human, human versus *myrmidon, myrmidon* versus Patayan. I knew that, like the last time, one vixen witch would—"

"—rise up fearlessly and end the conflict for everyone." With a derisive sound, T.J. dropped into his chair again. His trailing current followed him, blowing past the chair's clean lines before dissipating into mist. "I know the vixen legend is cherished. But most witchfolk don't even believe—"

"*I believe.*" His magus gave him a warning look. "So did you, when you made your promise."

Beneath that look, T.J. relented. She was right. According to The Old Ways, vixen witches—those witches born on the same day and in the same year—were especially powerful. When joined to form a vixen "pact" of two or more witches, they were capable of all kinds of potent and unusual magic.

Rumor held that the last time a vixen pact had formed, it had ended badly—with the infamous Salem witch trials. What had been lost in human telling of that story was that the members of that particular vixen pact had sacrificed themselves to free other witchfolk; they'd saved countless witches from fiery deaths in the process. As devastating as the Salem trials had been, they had cemented vixens' mythological status, turning them into the larger-than-life heroes of the witching world.

"Your belief guided you to accept your mission. To give your promise." His magus turned her considerable authority in his direction. "Have you found her yet? The *juweel*?"

Unhappily, T.J. shook his head. According to his magus's prophesy, one vixen witch, the *juweel*, would help the Patayan defeat the dark forces in the conflict to come. Even though it wasn't known how or why, the Patayan had learned that no proof was needed to accept a magus's vision; magian prescience was accurate without fail. His magus's tocsin had to be heeded.

"I've identified the vixen witches in Covenhaven. That was simple enough, given Deuce's skills with the IAB database." Even turned, his partner was better with human-built machines than anyone in the witching world. "But I've been busy tracing for the IAB. My last target was . . . complex. I've had no time to—"

"You must make time. The *juweel* is key." His magus's grave tone allowed no dissension. "Right now she is lost—hidden among her own kind. But she will awaken. And her struggle to come into her own—to choose an allegiance among the witch factions—will mean the difference between good and evil for us all."

T.J. eyed his magus. "You've had new information."

"Yes, but still not enough. I fear it comes too late."

Too late. Sobered by the details she'd shared, T.J. considered the situation. His magus's visions were becoming more vivid. More complete. That could only mean that the threat facing them was also completing itself. "If the *juweel* exists, I'll find her. In a few days, this crisis will be averted."

The juweel. The term—in the old tongue, "the one who is tested"—had lost its original associations long ago. In the years since its inception, it had been co-opted for other uses and other meanings—including "the prize" and "the favorite." Even the IAB had selected it as a mark of distinction for the participants in their cusping-witch classes. T.J. doubted Leo Garmin and his associates knew or cared about the true connotation of the word. They trampled witchfolk traditions with impunity, all the while bragging about creating "efficiency."

"But there must be a missing piece to your prophesy. Only legacy witches can be vixens." T.J. turned over the problem, considering his half-forgotten culture lessons. "If the legacy witches want to battle with The Followers—with a subset of their own kind—there's no reason we should become involved."

"Their division will endanger the human world."

"It can't. The human and witching worlds are more separate than ever."

"It will. I've seen it." She paused. "I fear it."

T.J. swore. He knew better than to doubt his magus's view. She'd always been right, for as long as anyone remembered. She and their Patayan circle had discussed this matter already.

"As guardians of the magical world, we Patayan are bound to maintain peace," his magus reminded him. "Whatever the cost."

At times, that cost had been great. The Patayan's role as

protectors was both fated and elemental. In the same way witches could detect deception after eons of persecution, Patayan could detect impending conflict after ages of battles. Resolving those conflicts sometimes got dirty. Dark magic and lethal spells were used. Neither could be employed without hurting the Patayan who wielded them. Every instance of magic came at a price.

T.J. knew that price all too well. Caught by that reality, he examined his hands. They were scarred with the remnants of old spells—fraught with evidence of everything he'd done in the years before he'd found salvation at the IAB.

He didn't want to become that man again, without scruples or trust or lasting satisfaction. But if the old darkness kept tugging at him the way it had today . . .

"Maybe this time," he said bleakly, "we should let the dozers fight their own battles."

"Never." His magus gave him an unyielding look. "And I will not have that slur spoken in my house."

Dozers. The term was crude, but it fit the humans he'd encountered—people separated from their natural world, oblivious to the interconnectedness they all shared, moving with a tunnel vision that narrowed their options and their happiness.

But it didn't pay to debate his magus. Like most women, she could outlast a man in an argument. She could always win.

"I'm sorry. It won't happen again."

"No, it won't. Especially from you."

He knew what she meant. Contemplatively, T.J. scraped his knuckles over the cleft in his chin—a sign of his compound birth. As a child, he'd been taunted for that telltale marker. As an adult, he'd become proud of it.

But the dozers couldn't be proud. They'd never awakened to their magical natures. They didn't know what they were missing.

That was probably just as well. Even the Patayan's Native

American counterparts—enlightened and strong people—weren't immune to wanting what they didn't have. Jesse, with his dreams of his father's impossible "magic," was proof of that.

Everyone wanted more. Even T.J., today, with Dayna.

Haunted by the memory of the runaway witch beneath him on her flimsy human-made bed, he slid his hand to his jaw. A quarter inch of beard stubble met his fingertips—evidence of all he'd endured. When confronted with emotion—theirs or other people's—Patayan sometimes couldn't contain it all. T.J. had never met anyone who'd overwhelmed him more than Dayna.

He'd been bulldozed by the strength of his need for her. His body had reacted with bristly stubble—a visible *keep away* sign that would have been laughable . . . if it hadn't hurt so much.

His magus saw his gesture. "Are you ready to tell me?"

T.J. jerked away his hand. "Tell you what?"

"About the surge in your magic." Her eyes sparkled. "I sensed it the moment you arrived. I've been waiting for you to—"

"It's nothing." He rose, pulling a swath of darkness through the skylights along with him. Barely noticing its sleek shape churning around him, T.J. paced. "A bond. With a runaway witch. I didn't mean for it to happen. I was trying to cuff her. *That's it.*" He broke off, clenching his fist at the memory. "After all this time, I thought I had better control."

"It's not your control that's in question. Some magic is still beyond our understanding." His magus watched him pace. "But all magic recognizes its like. Your birthright mark must have found its mate and enacted a bond for you both."

"Without *me* knowing it? That's fucked up."

"Your birthright mark *is* you." His magus gave him a censorious look. "It's you at your most elemental self, forged when your identity first becomes your own." She nodded at his Gila monster tattoo. Her mouth quirked. "Have you forgotten how much you complained when yours emerged?"

"Not with you around to remind me, I haven't."

"'Ow, it hurts! Put a charm on it to make it better.'" His magus put a teasing face on her mimicry. Unfortunately, that didn't remove its sting—or its accuracy. She sighed. "Even as teenagers, you men have no tolerance for pain."

"The damn thing *burned itself* onto my skin!"

"Gradually." She waved away his complaint. "It took its time. It happens to everyone, remember? All Patayan, at least. And now look at you. You've almost brought your birthright mark to its fruition." She beamed at him like the proud mother she nearly was. "Soon you'll be fulfilled, with the kind of loving, whole-hearted, lifepair union that most can only dream of."

With a sarcastic guffaw, T.J. kept walking. The darkness he'd pulled engulfed him, leaving him safe and cool in its midst. As a child on the res, he'd dragged the shade of the mesquite trees with him on his walks to school, trying to temper his intrinsic Patayan reaction to the sun. His people didn't burn under the UV rays. In their presence, Patayan became stronger and more magical. Like junkies for sunshine, they were laughably eager to strip naked at the first opportunity and soak up more of that magic-giving heat and light.

That reality was not easily understood by fifth-graders. Fifth-graders liked to laugh, point, and occasionally use the slide T.J. had chosen as a sunbathing platform. A parent-teacher conference the next day had made T.J. realize, for the first time, that he would have to control himself around other people.

It was a lesson he'd never forgotten.

"You *have* consummated the bond, haven't you?"

Ignoring the question, he continued walking.

"You haven't!" His magus gave a tsk-tsk sound. "Oh,

T.J. I'm disappointed in you. You should have consummated your bond."

Even the freaking wolfhound whined a complaint at him.

"I was tracing for the IAB! It was complicated." It was . . . *hot*. Seduced by Dayna's nearness, he'd wanted to make her his with no questions asked. She'd made him drunk with need. Rock hard. As urgent and unschooled as a warlock still coming into his own. Roughly, T.J. stopped moving. "It doesn't matter. I'm not consummating the bond. If I don't make it complete—"

"It will still haunt you." His magus made a gentle gesture. Magically, her motion cleared away the darkness surrounding him. The gloom he'd cultivated fell to his shoes and seeped through the floorboards. "And it will haunt the one whose magic has bonded itself with yours. This witch, your bonded witch—"

"Dayna." Even saying her name made him feel breathless.

Disgusted with the realization, T.J. frowned harder. He felt like a damn riser. The epithet was usually given to insatiable young warlocks who hadn't yet mastered their skills, but today it fit him like a shadow. He didn't like it. He refused to be led around by his cock—or worse, by his need to see one particular witch smile at him. He refused to *want*.

"Dayna is important." His magus gave him a solemn look. "She's important to you. You were fated to find her."

"And now I've lost her, so it's done."

"Lost her?"

"I left her at IAB headquarters. I told her not to come to me. I told her not to expect me to come to her."

A perceptive frown. "How did that feel?"

T.J. gave a bitter laugh. "Worse than my birthright mark searing onto my arm. So what? It's done now."

"Nothing is ever done." His magus smiled gently. "Everything is a journey. This is a rare opportunity. Your bond could still become a source of great joy to you."

"Or it could be a big pile of trouble. Even the stupidest greenie knows that being bonded with a witch is irresistible."

He glanced at his magus, hoping she'd disagree.

She did not. More alarmed than ever, T.J. paced faster. As a teenager, he'd been enamored with the legends about witching bonds. A lifetime of mind-blowing sex had sounded pretty good to a horny rising warlock. But now, faced with the reality of an all-consuming connection, T.J. wanted no part of it.

He shook his head. "A bond is seductive. A bonded *partner* is seductive, without even knowing it. The last thing I need is to let my warlock side run wild with that kind of temptation."

"Ah." The magus nodded. "That's true. Most Patayan don't also have witchy blood in them. That complicates things."

Spurred on by her agreement, T.J. continued. "Being with Dayna is a dangerous distraction. I'm glad to be free of her."

"*Are* you free of her?"

He turned away. "How about another piece of pie?"

"Very funny. You haven't finished your first." His magus murmured softly to her wolfhound, then cast T.J. an empathetic look. "The truth is, you don't trust yourself around this witch. You don't trust what a union with her would create."

He snorted. "If you mean a fairytale ending . . . hell no."

"All right. That's understandable."

"Oh hell. Don't give me that soothing tone of yours either. It won't work." Cynically, he eyed his magus's easy smile and relaxed position. He dragged his fingers through his hair, unable to withhold a frustrated sigh. "You haven't read her file. I have. This witch is trouble. She's intelligent, I'll give you that. She's amazing to look at." He lapsed for one shameful second, remembering her transparently wet shirt. "But she's also impulsive, stubborn, and rebellious."

"She sounds perfect for you."

"She ran at the first sign of difficulty in her life."

"You've done your share of running."

"But *she* didn't just run." He felt his shoulders stiffen as he admitted the worst of it. "She turned her back on everyone she knew. She left her family behind without a thought."

A pause. "You think she betrayed them."

It wasn't really a question. He knew his magus could read his jaded expression. "Of course she betrayed them."

It was the worst charge he could have leveled. His magus appeared suitably troubled by it. All Patayan were irredeemably wounded by betrayal. As an interconnected people, they needed trust as much as they needed breath. Being deprived of that trust hurt them deeply . . . but only for those stupid enough to be vulnerable. T.J. knew better than to go down that road.

"She'll probably do it again, given half a chance."

"No one is without flaws, T.J. Witchfolk, humans, Patayan . . . we all make mistakes. Dayna must have had a reason."

"There's no reason good enough."

"You can't say that for certain."

"I'm pretty sure I just did."

His magus appeared amused. "Is there anything more?"

"She refuses to use her magic, but it escapes her all the same. She's a menace to everyone around her." T.J. accidentally stirred up the soil in his magus's potted plants. It lurched upward in moist clumps, ready to race toward him and perform whatever action he needed next. With an impatient gesture, he tamped it down again. "She shuns enchantments in favor of filing cabinets and computers. She uses human-made things!"

"You're reaching at straws now."

"She made my magic malfunction." He glowered, newly pissed at the memory. "I charmed those damned handcuffs myself. They should have been impervious to trickery."

"Your bond was not a trick. It was fate."

"Oh yeah? Well, this time fate screwed with the wrong warlock." He'd come here for solace—for wisdom and instruction. Instead, he'd found more confusion. In the space of one day, his life had become a million times more complicated. "I'll be damned if I'll be fate's bitch, to kick around at will."

"T.J." His magus pursed her lips sorrowfully. "Falling in love is not the same as being kicked around."

"If they both hurt, what's the difference?"

With a muttered good-bye, he made ready to leave.

"That's it?" his magus asked. Her wolfhound scrambled to its feet. "You really won't complete your bond with Dayna?"

The mournful tone in her voice got to him. Against his better judgment, T.J. released the starlight he'd just plucked. He needed it to light his way back to his hated car, but he could always capture more when he stepped outside.

"I have work to do." At the thought of failing his people, T.J. felt his usual steeliness crack—just for a heartbeat, but even that long was intolerable. He blamed Dayna; her witchy influence had already affected him. It had already softened him. "I have to prepare for the conflict that's coming. I gave my word that I'd find the *juweel,* and I will. Before it's too late. If this disaster can be averted—"

"It must be. I can't argue with that."

T.J. stood silently. They both knew that an event, once prophesied, was unlikely to be altered. Still, it was comforting to behave as though it could be. Even magical folk needed hope.

"But I still would have liked to see you happy with someone. I would have liked grandchildren someday."

With a laughing shake of his head, T.J. headed for the door. He pet the wolfhound, then snatched more starlight.

"Someday *soon,*" his magus persisted.

Smiling, T.J. grabbed the door. "I won't promise that."

Almost there . . . but his magus spoke again.

"Ahem. Aren't you forgetting something?"

She couldn't be serious. Yet T.J. knew she was. He pocketed his starlight and doubled back, then shoveled in his last bite of butternut squash pie and chewed furiously.

He swallowed. "Thanks for the pie."

Her smile was beatific. "You're very welcome, T.J."

She rose, her flowing garments whispering their witch-made enchantments as she moved. Knowing what would come next, T.J. stiffened. He visited often but was never prepared for this part. Trying not to wince, he took a single step nearer. That was his duty. He was not a man who shirked responsibility.

As he'd expected, his magus hugged him. Her embrace was as warm, as caring, and as inclusive as ever. She smelled of squash and sugar and arthritis ointment. She smelled almost like home.

Almost . . . but not quite. He'd lost his home at fifteen and had never found a place to belong to since. That didn't stop his magus from acting as though she could heal him somehow.

Uncomfortably, T.J. shifted. "Are we done yet?"

"Yes." Her smiled appeared all too knowing.

"I'll be back when I have news."

Or when I need you.

Damn it. He blocked the thought as rapidly as he could.

"All right. Be well, T.J." With a confidently maternal gesture, his magus put her thumb on his chin and tilted his face downward. She studied his keep-away beard stubble and surly expression, then sighed. "Be happy. And be very cautious when you're searching for the *juweel*. The magical elements in Covenhaven are in flux now. That makes them unstable."

"I'm a rock, remember? Nothing can get to me."

"You seem to truly believe that." At his assured smile, she arched her brow. "And yet a single witch scares you silly?"

T.J. couldn't help laughing. "You never quit, I'll give you that. Nice try, but I'm still not giving you grandchildren."

"Someday?"

"Hell. I was right, wasn't I?" He shook his head. "A woman *can* win any argument, just by persisting long enough."

"Thank you." His magus smiled. "And? Grandchildren?"

Without a word, T.J. leaned forward. He kissed his magus on the crown of her head, lingering a moment longer than he meant to.

"That arthritis ointment is fucking hypnotic," he said. "I don't know how you keep the geezers from swarming this place."

Then he pulled out his starlight and headed alone into the night, feeling no more reassured than when he'd arrived . . . but feeling a little less empty, all the same.

Chapter Nine

Stepping onto the grounds of Covenhaven Academy for the first time in eleven years, Dayna held her breath. She didn't know what to expect, how to feel . . . or where to go. As usual, she'd wound up on the outside of things, clueless where other witches were magically adept. But after a restless night spent at the curiously roommate- and chaperone-free apartment she'd been assigned by the IAB, she'd finally made her way to her first (and everyone else's third) cusping-witch class.

Gathering her nerve before going inside, she examined the school. Like most of Covenhaven, the academy looked about the same as it ever had. Cast in the glow of an autumn sunset, its redbrick buildings rose two stories high. Patches of graveled landscaping surrounded it. Both areas were prefaced by a walkway and a tarnished sign announcing the site's establishment in 1879. New solar lighting lined the walk; a banner announcing the Samhain Festival stretched across the double entryway.

GET A TASTE OF THE OLD WAYS AT THE COVENHAVEN HALLOW-E'EN FESTIVAL! MAGICAL FUN FOR THE WHOLE FAMILY! OCTOBER 31ST AT JANUS RESORT AND SPA.

Taken aback, Dayna stared at it. Any humans glimpsing the banner would have thought nothing of it. But to witchfolk, it contained the same coded message she'd seen on posters and signs and bumper stickers all over downtown: THE OLD WAYS ARE BACK.

And they were meant to be enjoyed by "the whole family."

She didn't remember there being any special enthusiasm for The Old Ways in Covenhaven. Her parents, for instance, had never been especially traditional or culturally aware. Neither had her friends' families. But since she'd been away, witchy nostalgia seemed to have swept through the town like a fever, filling its residents with a new pride in their witch-folk heritage.

Somehow, all that pride had gotten attached to the Hallowe'en Festival. It made sense, in a way. Samhain was important to witches; parties were important to humans. The festival filled both niches—and kept Covenhaven's local economy hopping.

Here in the red rocks country, the annual festival was a major tourist draw. It was visited by thousands over the course of a single autumn weekend. Each year, the *Arizona Republic* devoted a special newspaper supplement to it; state TV news stations sent satellite vans and on-air reporters to cover the event in gushing detail (and usually in costume). So while the Hallowe'en Festival wasn't new, its emphasis on The Old Ways was. And their incorporation into the festival made Dayna uneasy.

A revival of witchy purism probably didn't bode well for someone like her—a lapsed witch who'd spent the last decade living among humans—and *not* practicing magic . . . at least not on purpose. Any Follower would have thought she was crazy for abandoning her "gifts." But she didn't have time to worry about that now. To her, the Samhain Festival meant graduation day from cusping-witch classes . . . and graduation day meant being tested.

She'd never felt less ready for a test in her life.

Too bad her readiness didn't matter.

Because her magic was here, stronger than ever.

Which meant she'd done enough procrastinating. It wasn't like her to hesitate. Sucking in a deep breath, Dayna strode straight to the school's looming double doors. At her approach, they crashed open with a resounding bang. Yikes. Her renewed magic appeared eager for this training program.

Hoping that was a positive sign, Dayna entered the school. Instantly, she felt catapulted into her past and her future at the same time. The academy, with its labyrinth of classrooms and ever-shifting magical room numbers, looked the same as it ever had . . . yet it *felt* strangely different. Stuck in a real-life walk-through of that nightmare she'd had so often—the one where she was late for school, hadn't studied all semester, and now faced a final exam—Dayna searched for the correct classroom.

Typically, she couldn't find it.

Walking faster, Dayna grabbed her backpack. With her free hand, she dug out the map she'd received with her IAB paperwork. It didn't help. She passed several empty classrooms, casting frustrated glances inside each one. Damn it. More than likely her inability to see through witching eyes had failed her again.

This was one area where devising a new filing system, developing an original coding rationale, or creating an analytical research database—all the detail-oriented work that was her specialty at DRL—could not help her. Damn it again.

All at once, Dayna just wanted to go home. Home to Buffy and Spike (whom she'd left in the temporary care of her kindly landlady). Home to Jill and the rest of her friends. Home to discipline instead of magic, reliable systems instead of tricky talismans, and certainty instead of The Old Ways, with all their pro-magic, pro-witch, antihuman, anti-Dayna rhetoric.

But the stakes were too high to bail out now. If she didn't

succeed, she might never be able to return to the human-style life she treasured. So stubbornly, Dayna kept moving.

Finally a handwritten sign directed her to CONTINUING EDUCATION: NEW AGE STUDIES down the next hall. Decrypted for witchfolk, that meant cusping-witch classes. Even an outsider like her recognized that much. Maybe she was getting the hang of this after all, Dayna told herself with a sigh of relief. Maybe being back in Covenhaven was helping already.

Tugging her backpack higher on her shoulder, she turned the corner. She sighted a beam of light coming from beneath a closed door, then headed straight for it.

Barefoot and chilled to the bone, T.J. scrunched his toes. The tiny motion solidified his position atop a second-floor ledge outside the Covenhaven Academy. Framed by the window behind him, he flattened his palm against the glass for leverage. With his free hand, he shook out a hearing charm, grateful for his Patayan ability to cloak himself in stolen shadows.

A flick of his wrist sent the charm sailing across the academy's now-deserted quad. It coasted in midair, then landed on a lighted window opposite T.J.'s position.

With a barely audible *snick*, it attached itself. Satisfied with its connection, he nodded. Until now, he'd been able to hear everything that went on in the room. A few minutes ago, though, the last of the sunlight had faded from his sheltered position. Since then, he'd felt his magic diminishing . . . just when he needed it most to hide his surveillance.

That had never happened to him before. But he didn't have time to worry about magical fuckups now. He had work to do.

With effort, T.J. turned his mind away from thoughts of his erratic magic—and the seductive witch who'd caused it. He inhaled deeply. He closed his eyes—precarious on the high ledge, but necessary. Just when he was nearly centered, his mind wandered again . . . offering up an image of Dayna as she'd looked while straddling him. With a hoarse oath, T.J. gave up on prudent preparation. Centeredness was not coming to him tonight.

He used a warlock spell to activate the hearing charm.

The noise struck him at once. Recoiling, he jerked himself out of position. His toes scraped the ledge. One foot dangled in midair. Wide-eyed, he struggled for balance. Then he swore. He should have known that two dozen chattering witches would blow his ears off. Sloppiness like this could get him killed.

With renewed concentration, he regained his position, arranging his hands and heels against the window glass. Its cold surface made him wince. He was made for sun and sand. But there was no help for that now. He needed to find the *juweel*. The three likeliest vixens were in the cusping-witch class about to begin across the quad. If he was to have any hope of making contact, he needed to gather more information first.

Through the space and thin-paned glass dividing him from the classroom, T.J. listened. He watched as the witches milled around. A few tossed off spells to fix their hair or makeup. Others talked nonstop while they whirled their fingers in the air to conjure memory flickers—enchanted moving pictures—for one another. Some practiced minor spells, most likely homework assignments, then laughed uproariously as their friends sprouted quickly vanishing tails or wings. One witch had brought a ferret, probably her familiar, in a pink sequined pet carrier. She cooed in baby talk to the creature, who wore a flashy rhinestone collar and had the same watery gaze a trout did.

Flattening his mouth, T.J. removed his palm from the cold glass. Without taking his attention from the distant classroom, he tucked his hand inside his shirt. Blissful warmth flooded his skin, returning sensation to his fingers. He groaned with relief, then switched hands. This grunt work was necessary, but it pulled on his warlock abilities and his Patayan instincts alike. It divided his energies in a way he didn't trust or enjoy. Fortunately, that division was nothing a restorative session of nude sunbathing wouldn't cure.

Promising himself exactly that after sunrise tomorrow, T.J. sharpened his focus. The remedial magic instructor had arrived, making all the witches snap to attention. The warlock, assigned by the IAB, was unfamiliar to T.J. But he could tell at a glance that he was a typical, by-the-numbers witchfolk academic: good-looking, solidly built, and arrogant to the point of irritation.

But his class was T.J.'s key to getting close to the *juweel*— at least if all went well. With that fact in mind, T.J. melted farther into the shadows he'd pulled. Mindless now of the cold infiltrating his skin and muscles, he began his study.

Dayna opened the door with a thud, revealing a classroom full of witches seated primly at rows of individual desks— a blur of faces she didn't have time to register. Out of breath and defiantly late, she took a quick survey of her surroundings, then marched toward an empty seat with her head held high.

Detecting the lingering smell of magic in the air, she wrinkled her nose. Usually that faint sulfurous odor wasn't noticeable; over the centuries, witches had devised incense, candles, a variety of flowery aerosol sprays, and (more recently) plug-in air fresheners to disguise it. But when many witches practiced their craft at once, even the most powerful spray or gel couldn't completely contain the aftereffects.

After being so long in the human world, Dayna had forgotten that smell. Experiencing it now made her instantly regret the microwavable burrito she'd made for dinner before leaving for class. Sulfur made her queasy; it always had. But she was a witch who believed in preparation—who lived to research and loved to organize. The logical side of her had insisted that she'd need sustenance to get her through her first night of remedial witch school . . . and she'd been right. At the moment, she was so nervous that she could scarcely think—or see—straight.

No, wait. That was caused by a blindingly bright light, shining right over her head. Confused, Dayna stopped and looked around.

At least two dozen witches stared back at her, some of them surreptitiously, others with open curiosity. Nearby, two witches in matching cashmere sweaters and pencil skirts leaned across the aisle between desks. They exchanged whispered comments.

A burble of witchy laughter floated toward her.

In that moment, it became obvious to Dayna that she was *way* underdressed for this experience. All around her, the gossipy witches wore cute cropped jackets, skinny black pants, sleek shirts or sweaters, and skirts with high-heeled boots. Some of their clothes were probably from well-known designers' collections; that didn't mean they weren't witch-made, as Dayna well knew. Either way, one thing was clear: Their fashionable wardrobes stood in stark contrast to her vintage T-shirt, wrecked jeans, Converse sneakers, and corduroy jacket.

From the front of the class, the instructor droned on with his lecture, probably thinking that Dayna would take her seat quickly. Like most warlocks, he possessed the face of a movie star and the body of an Adonis. Unlike them, he was lacking in the charisma usually afforded to a warlock college professor.

That didn't seem to matter to the witches, who paid him rapt attention. After all, the notion of teacher's pet had not been devised by humans, but by witches . . . witches who craved the approval of their (mostly male) instructors the way the spathiphyllum she'd researched craved fresh air and sunlight.

"It's important," he was telling his avid students, "to begin training at exactly the right moment. As you'll see—"

He broke off. Pointedly, he cleared his throat.

As though the light surrounding Dayna were related somehow, it suddenly grew even brighter. Annoyed, she squinted, now unable to see the desk she'd been headed for at all.

More whispers rose around her. The cashmere witches nudged the witches near them. One pointed. A few witches giggled.

Hot with embarrassment, Dayna moved blindly. She bumped into a desk, making another witch's purse slide off.

"Ahem." The instructor cast her a reproachful look, his handsome face unsmiling. "Please be seated. I'd rather not waste energy on this guidance beam if you're not going to use it."

Aha. That explained the insanely intense light. Now that she felt slightly less frazzled, Dayna realized it was aimed at the desk she'd chosen—the only desk that was still free. Did the instructor think she was an idiot? She didn't need a guidance beam to find the *only* available desk in the entire classroom.

"Turn it off then." She jerked up her chin. "All you're doing is blinding me with the damn thing anyway."

A chorus of witchy gasps whooshed through the room.

The warlock instructor was silent. Then, "Fine."

Peevishly, he released a blanket of cold darkness. It shrouded everything, including Dayna, in impenetrable, sticky-feeling black. She couldn't see her hand in front of her face—or the purse she'd accidentally knocked off the desk.

"Very funny," she groused, crouching to pat her free hand in the vicinity of the fallen bag. "Overkill, much?"

With a whoosh, the lighting returned to normal.

"Good. At least you're not a total tool," she muttered.

Even as the instructor took up his droning again, Dayna

closed her shaky fingers on the purse. With a murmured apology, she set it back on the desk . . . and was astonished to see someone familiar behind it. It was Camille Levy, her best friend from high school, all grown up and sporting . . . a pastel twinset?

Back in the day, neither of them had ever worn anything pastel to school. Or anything that matched, for that matter. She and Camille had been rebels in everything, refusing to conform as a matter of principle. Now Camille, formerly of the pierced nose, hennaed hair, and ripped flannel, was wearing something that would have been right at home on Perky Suburban Barbie.

What the hell had happened around here?

An awkward moment passed, during which Dayna realized that she hadn't seen Camille since she'd left Covenhaven. She hadn't told anyone she was leaving, and she hadn't been in touch with anyone besides her parents since. It had felt easier that way—easier for *her*, it occurred to her. Not for anyone else. There was every possibility her former best friend hated her now.

Camille leaned forward. "Still kneeing authority in the nuts, I see." She winked. "It's good to have you back, Dayna."

Awash in relief, Dayna smiled. "I missed you, too."

"AS I WAS SAYING." The instructor's voice boomed loudly enough to overcome the disruption Dayna had presented. "If we begin training too soon, cusping witches don't yet possess the power that they'll eventually need to harness. If we begin training too late, *unintended consequences* can result."

His scholarly gaze swept the room again.

Dayna bit her lip. Under the instructor's gaze, she beat a hasty retreat to the desk he'd highlighted for her. Even as she settled in, dragging a few necessities from her backpack and then dropping the whole thing to the floor beside her, she felt as though the evidence of her earlier magical incidents was imprinted on her skin—just like her failures were.

Unintended consequences could result.

He could say that again.

She hoped the people who'd been hurt during her storm were all right. She hoped everyone at DRL had unfrozen themselves and gotten back to business. She hoped her many magical screwups were known only to her—and to her hunky tracer, T.J. But it was completely possible, Dayna realized uncomfortably as she flipped open her trusty Moleskine notebook, that everyone in Covenhaven knew about her disastrous magical accidents. Along with the resurgence of The Old Ways, they might have implemented a gossipy, witchy version of *Us Weekly* for the locals. Who knew?

This wasn't just any old desert resort town, after all.

Covenhaven was exclusive, exclusionary, and always aware of its special significance. No other Southwestern town was like it. Covenhaven was redolent of sage and creosote, nestled on a canyon's edge, ringed by enchanted red rocks. It was sheltered by freakishly blue skies and endowed with special magic. The tourists who flocked here to see the rocks and creeks believed it. The witches and humans who'd been born here lived it . . . and they sometimes had the privileged attitudes to prove it.

"Psst." The hissing sound came from beside her. "Psst."

Trying to take notes, Dayna ignored it.

"Hey." A poke to her shoulder. "Is that *human made*?"

Startled, Dayna looked up. One of the cashmere witches was staring at her notebook, her expression filled with curiosity.

It *was* a nice notebook, modified with Dayna's most useful divider tabs and bound with a custom laser-engraved cover. It had been a gift from her friend Jill at DRL. Drawn in by the cashmere witch's apparent friendliness, Dayna relented.

She nodded. After all, if she was going to get through this, she'd have to be a little less guarded. Otherwise, she'd slow her own progress. Everyone knew that successful witches depended on one another. Cooperation was the witchy way.

"Yes, it's human made," she whispered. "So is my pen."

In demonstration, she held it up.

"Oh. That explains why they're both so hideous." The cashmere witch sent her gaze downward, then fluffed her hair. "At least they match your . . . um, *outfit*. Such as it is."

A cascade of giggles greeted her comment. Too late, Dayna realized that all the witches surrounding her had been listening. Some of them had craned fully around in their seats to enjoy the spectacle; others had cast personal charms to record memory flickers. By tomorrow, images of Dayna's first ignoble day of witch school would be all over EnchantNet.

Frowning, Dayna studied her classmates. Evidently, none of the other witches needed to take notes to master their magic. Their hands and desks were empty—except for one witch, who'd set out a bottle of Revlon Red and was magically painting her nails in between casting adoring glances at the instructor.

Defiantly, Dayna gazed back at the cashmere witch. Then she wielded her pen and made a deliberate note in her Moleskine.

Learn ugliness hexes. Starting now.

The cashmere witch blanched.

Pasting on a sweet smile, Dayna raised her hand.

The instructor paused in midsentence. Appearing exasperated, he sent a brief nod in Dayna's direction. "Yes?"

"Will we be learning about hexes?"

"Of course. In due time. Once we've finished covering the basics and establishing safe boundaries, then I'll—"

"Can we learn about them tonight?"

A minor hubbub swept through the room. A few desks ahead, Camille swiveled in her seat. A suspicious frown made her perfectly lipglossed mouth turn down at the corners.

"Tonight?" The instructor frowned. "There is a curriculum

to be considered. More than one thousand witches are taking classes in Covenhaven right now. This training is a complex endeavor, filled with—"

"Can we learn about hexes *tonight*?" Dayna persisted.

"Well . . ." The instructor shrugged. "I don't see why not."

Pleased, Dayna raised her brows at her cashmere rival.

"It's not on my schedule for today, but hexology is part of my IAB syllabus," the instructor mused. "And since you are so eager to tackle the subject, Ms. Sterling—"

With a prickle of warning, Dayna stilled.

"—*you* may be the first volunteer. Please come to the front of the classroom, so everyone can see, and we'll begin." The handsome instructor paused, clearly relishing the moment. "Is there any particular hex you had in mind?"

When T.J. had felt the initial surge of heat in his birthright tattoo, he'd reasoned the warmth was just another magical malfunction, like his fading sharpness as the sun set. Or his forgetting to consider the amplified effect of two dozen witch voices over his hearing charm. Or his unwanted bond.

But then Dayna Sterling had entered the classroom, and he'd realized the truth. This was no malfunction. This was fate screwing with him again. This was fate grabbing hold of his unbending heart and knocking it around in his chest. This was fate trying to make him face the future it wanted for him.

Well, fuck fate. T.J. didn't like the way it played.

With his frown deepening, he kept his bare feet pressed to the window ledge for balance, then dropped to his haunches in a protective stance. His cold-stiffened muscles protested the movement. During the time he'd been perched two stories above the ground, the temperature had dropped a good fifteen degrees. The wind had risen, cutting between the redbrick buildings and rustling the dried mesquite pods on the trees below. But he hadn't yet gathered enough information, so he'd stayed.

Now he'd had enough. The shadows he'd pulled to hide himself had thinned the air beside him, making his perch feel twice as unstable as the wind kicked up in rowdy gusts.

Spooling his left hand, T.J. gathered up impressions and images, vocalizations and gestures. They streamed from the distant classroom to his fingertips like a river of disrupted moonlight. He watched their progress with an absorbed air. It was more important to monitor the stream than to heed the insistent sting of his birthright mark. *Much* more important.

And yet . . . even as T.J. watched the information he'd collected, even as he studied its muted colors and churning shapes, he felt himself drawn elsewhere. Without his awareness, his body aligned itself with Dayna. Without his permission, his gaze lifted from the data stream to the window beyond . . . to the bonded witch who called to him without even knowing it.

He caught a glimpse of her standing at the front of the class. Instantly, his muscles clenched with remembrance. His chest ached with . . . something. His mind took in all the details of her appearance, registering the fact that her raggedy jeans showed her shape more than her khaki pants had. He liked them.

He'd like to take them off her. Thanks to their encounter on Dayna's scratchy, poorly constructed human-made bed, he knew the curve of her backside, the yielding softness of her hips, the insistent jab of her elbows. He knew the need in her heart. He wanted to know more. Like the scent of her skin. The pulse of her heartbeat. The slick, tight feel of her body as he slid inside her and made her his own.

Hell. With unyielding effort, T.J. directed his attention back to his data stream. Deuce would have found it incredible, he told himself in a bid for distraction. As a human, Deuce was used to information being shared and stored in clumsier ways. The dozers' wireless technologies hinted, ironically, at their true birthright and their inherent abilities to manipulate their surroundings . . . but ultimately were just another example of their stumbling toward enlightenment without realizing it.

Feeling his frown deepen, T.J. cut off the data stream with a practiced gesture. He processed the information with an IAB spell, simultaneously encrypting and shrinking it. He'd have liked to have more time to study the three vixens in the cusping class, but with Dayna's unexpected appearance . . .

As though called to her, he glanced up again. She'd closed her eyes in an effort to conjure a spell. It was the perfect opportunity to look his fill. Prodded by yearning, he did.

Dayna's eyes opened. She gazed directly at him.

What the hell? She shouldn't be able to see him at all, not through the darkness he'd pulled to cover himself.

And yet she did. Her eyes widened, appearing eerily blue. Her mouth opened. A jolt of recognition passed between them.

Shaken by it, T.J. jerked backward against the window.

His whole body wobbled on the narrow ledge.

Swearing, he righted himself, then made sure his shadows still surrounded him. At his feet, the information he'd gathered fluttered down, disappearing through the thinned air and falling into the night. Now he'd have to retrieve it. But first . . .

He sneaked a final glance at Dayna. Her hunched shoulders and defiant chin were at odds with one another, as usual. But what caught his eye was her magic. It hovered *outside* her, an aurora borealis of shimmering shapes and possibilities.

He'd never seen anything like it, either witch or Patayan.

As though gathering strength, the particles surrounding her ballooned outward. They hovered. Silence fell, broadcasting like an indrawn breath through his hearing charm. Then a crack seamed its way through her magic . . . and the whole endeavor split apart.

Shit. That had never happened before. With all his senses on the alert, T.J. leaned dangerously far from his ledge, trying to see Dayna amid the iridescent pieces of her broken aurora.

He couldn't. Her magic was too uneven.

He hesitated, on the verge of conjuring an airstream strong enough to sweep him to the other side. Helping her would be a risky move, impossible to perform without rearranging the darkness and revealing himself. But if Dayna needed him . . .

Before he could act, the reflexive movement ended.

Dayna stood in its center, no longer surrounded by magic. Her hair stuck out, snarled and broken. Her clothes drooped, newly ripped and stained. Her cheeks were scarred; her nose was adorned with a huge red zit. It seemed to grow even as T.J. gawked at it. Another popped up beside it, nearly pulsing.

"That's disgusting!" one of the witches shrieked.

With her eyes widening, Dayna clapped her hands over her face. From above her fingertips, she stared at the assembled witches in dawning horror. Clearly, her spell had gone wrong.

With a hoarse exhalation, Dayna did what T.J. should have known she'd do—she fled. She turned her back and ran.

The classroom door slammed, punctuating the witchy laughter flowing over his hearing charm. With a savage yank, T.J. pulled it free of the window. In growing disgust, he considered what he'd seen. Running was a way of life for his bonded witch. He doubted she'd return to finish her cusping-witch classes.

She'd run before. She'd run now. She'd always run.

The realization slowed his stupid fluttering heartbeat like nothing else. Frowning, T.J. studied the wind as it eddied past his window ledge. As a Patayan, he could see the swirling currents. As a warlock, he could ride them. Not far, and not with a damned broomstick the way the human legends falsely claimed, but far enough. At the correct moment, he jumped.

He drifted. A few seconds later, his feet landed on the artificially nurtured turf. The chemically treated soil stung his soles. The sharp, nonindigenous grass razored his feet.

Surprised, T.J. levitated a few inches. He peered downward. Usually the gardeners, talented Patayan and their Native

American counterparts—like his friend, Henry Obijuwa—didn't plant species that weren't native to the area. They didn't thrive. They usually didn't even survive. It was curious that someone had ignored those conventions here at the academy.

The aberration puzzled him.

Whatever the reason for it, T.J. would have to bring shoes next time. He didn't need them while perched two stories in the air; his grip on the building's ledge was better barefoot. And he preferred being naked whenever possible, even if only from the ankles down. But another prickly landing like this one would leave him with chemical burns for days.

Feeling dark and discontent—about his aborted mission, T.J. assured himself, *not* his runaway bonded witch—he sighted his bundle of magically encrypted data. He headed toward it.

At the same moment, a whoosh of emotion reached him. Impatience. Eagerness. Anger. All in multiples, and all moving with special speed, directly toward him.

"Hell," he muttered. "Not this again."

An instant later, he was surrounded.

Chapter Ten

In the hallway outside the classroom assigned to cusping-witch classes, Dayna glowered. She shot an impatient glance at the light emitting from under the door, then tapped her foot.

She was lucky her toes didn't fall off. The epic case of magical athlete's foot she'd accidentally hexed herself into hadn't been pretty. Maybe that was why running away from class had felt so excruciating. Usually, running felt liberating.

At least to her.

Wanting to run even farther, Dayna contented herself with pacing down the hall. Floor tiles pinged upward at her approach; strips of fluorescent lights flickered overhead with an audible buzz of malcontent. If the classroom door didn't open soon, she'd wear a freaking groove in the academy's ancient flooring.

A part of her liked the idea, she realized as she yanked off her ruined corduroy jacket and slung it over her arm. Tearing up the academy was destructive enough to suit her mood.

Why had she believed she could actually do this?

She should have known better than to try again.

For the umpteenth time, she cursed herself for forgetting her backpack in the classroom. Leaving an important item behind really put the kibosh on storming out of someplace.

But she couldn't leave without it. So now she waited. And waited.

And wondered if she'd *really* glimpsed that hard-bodied IAB tracer, T.J. McAllister, standing outside—*on the window ledge* of all places—or if she was losing her mind completely.

At this point, her money was on *losing her mind completely.*

But maybe T.J. was still supposed to be tracking her. She *had* felt something special pass between them. Something that went way beyond, *Don't come to me, and don't expect me to come to you.* Obviously, he had come to her. And she'd known it somehow.

She'd *felt* it, the same way she'd felt his emotions.

And the strongest of those emotions had been undeniable longing . . . for her. The realization made her shiver.

When the door finally opened, pastel-wearing Camille was first through. She shouldered her way past the other witches with an air of concern, then beelined straight toward Dayna.

"Oh my God. I'm so glad you're still here! Are you okay?" Wide-eyed, she took in Dayna's face and clothes and hair. She touched the sleeve of her ruined corduroy jacket—the only item that had yet to drop its hex. Everything else had returned to normal several minutes earlier. "You *look* okay, but that couldn't have been fun in there. For a second I thought you were really going to show those bitchy witches their places!"

"Me? Not hardly. All I wanted to do was make up for lost time." The lie slipped from Dayna's lips easily, its path greased by all the half-truths she'd told to fit in among her human colleagues at the research library. "And I definitely did that. You've all been living without Dayna Sterling fuck-upery for a long time. Now it's just like back in the day, right?"

Pretending not to care about her disastrous hex attempt, she watched as two of the cashmere witches exited the class-room for what appeared to be a short break. They wandered a few feet away, then leaned against the academy's wall like models posing in *Vogue*. They lit up cigarettes—the sweet-smelling clove variety favored by witches, even in the human world. Through tendrils of hazy smoke, they examined the torn-up floor tiles near Dayna. Their eyes narrowed with speculation.

"Hey, your ugliness hex might have gotten misdirected, but at least it didn't last all night." In a cheery voice, Camille pointed out the obvious. "That's a relief, right?"

"Right. I misdirected that hex *and* I couldn't make it stick." With effort, Dayna dragged her gaze from those mean witches. She didn't know what they had that she didn't. "I shouldn't be surprised. Everything I touch falls apart lately."

"What do you mean?" Her friend appeared surprised—maybe even concerned. "I see your folks down at the shopping center sometimes, and they say you've been really happy living in Phoenix. They say you've done really well on your own."

On your own.

The words shouldn't have hurt. They still did.

Everyone knew it wasn't natural for a witch to be alone.

Dayna tried to focus on the fact that her parents had also said she'd done "really well" in Phoenix. She didn't get far with the effort.

"Yeah, well . . ." She shrugged. "I could be living on the sidewalk and wearing Parkay tubs stolen from a Dumpster for shoes, and my parents would find a positive spin for it."

She's always been innovative, they'd say. Or, *Waste not, want not. That's our Dayna.* Or, *Look, she's recycling!* Even in the face of their daughter's repeated failures, Sam and Margo Sterling had always been unfailingly supportive.

"They must be *so* psyched to have you back in town."

"I haven't seen them yet." Dayna couldn't explain why. "I'll probably head over there soon. Maybe tomorrow."

It felt like another lie. But Camille only smiled again.

Gamely, Dayna smiled back. But their conversation lapsed anyway. She and her former best friend had spent too many years apart, she realized, for their usual camaraderie to spring back to life so easily. Feeling responsible for that rift, she frowned. She had no idea how to bridge the gap between them.

In the silence, sweet clove smoke drifted closer, helping to hide the sulfurous smell of magic in the air. Maybe she should take up the habit, Dayna mused. She'd need cover for the many hours of magic practice in her future. And witches weren't prone to addiction . . . unless they were stupid enough to try caffeine. Most weren't. Especially her. She'd always had too much to lose if the effects of caffeine took hold while she was among humans.

With a rueful shake of her head, Dayna considered the times she'd been tempted. If only humans knew the real reason some of their friends and neighbors drank decaf coffee. It sure as hell wasn't to avoid caffeine "jitters" or sleep more soundly.

"So . . ." With forced joviality, Camille spoke up. "You've been gone awhile now. I'm dying to know . . . What's it like?"

She could mean only one thing. "In the human world?"

An avid nod.

Dayna looked away. "Different from here."

"I'll bet you're *so* happy to be back, though, right?"

Dayna gave a wry grin. "'Happy' doesn't quite cover it."

"Thrilled is more like it, I'll bet." Camille put her hands on her hips, her upbeat demeanor never faltering. "This is where you belong, after all. I hope you'll be staying awhile."

Reluctant to answer, Dayna hunched her shoulders. She wanted to keep her conversation with Camille going, but she refused to offer false hope. And the truth was, there was *no way* she belonged here. She watched discontentedly as two nearby witches rewound a memory flicker of her backfiring ugliness hex. The witches laughed as her magical split ends blossomed.

"It's been years since I've seen a memory flicker," Dayna blurted out. Surprised at the nostalgic tone in her voice, she covered her gaffe with a fierce frown. "I mean, not that I've missed them or anything. I sure as hell didn't want to star in one again. Already. Or ever. Stupid memory flickers."

Those things had haunted her teenage years, replaying all her many magical foibles—her unsuccessful transmogrifications, botched hexes, and garbled spells—and archiving them forever. Memory flickers were like instant, on-the-spot YouTube. Fun . . . unless *you* were the subject of the day's hilarious video.

"Come on. Human movies and TV *cannot* be nearly as good."

They weren't. But Dayna refused to be lulled into admiring any part of the world she'd failed so spectacularly in. "And seriously—everyone here couldn't *be* any witchier, could they?"

"Well, duh." Camille gave her a friendly shove. "They're all witches. How else would they be, besides witchy?"

Welcoming. Helpful. Nonsabotaging. But how likely was that?

Dayna shifted, wishing she didn't need help. Or to be welcomed. Or anything else from the magical world. She'd thought she'd escaped it years ago. Glumly, she stared toward the classroom. "I can't believe I have to endure almost three more weeks of this."

Camille laughed. "The time will fly by, believe me." She rummaged in her handbag, a retro model with a rigid handle and a jeweled clasp. She pulled out a business card and handed it to Dayna. "Here's my card, so we can be *sure* to stay in touch while you're here. You can't *believe* how excited I was to see you in class, Dayna! Finally. I mean, all of us are supposed to be here, and that means you, too, but I kept looking at that empty desk these past few days, wondering where you were. And I *know* how you live for breaking the rules, so—"

"Wait. You work at a *children's activity gym*?" Dayna gawked at the card in her hand. Its face depicted a cozy cartoon house with cartoon children beside it. Camille's contact information was displayed in crisp letters. "*You?* But you hate kids!"

"What? Of course I don't hate kids!" Blushing, her friend looked around to make sure no one had overheard them. "At least not since I had a few of my own." She smiled. "And working at Toddler Time was only practical. I already knew everyone there, because we spent so much time at Tumbling Tuesdays classes."

Dubiously, Dayna frowned. Apparently, the pastel twinset had been just the beginning. Maybe the only person who *hadn't* changed over the past decade was *her*. "You have children?"

"Three children, one husband, and a corgi."

"A what?"

"A dog. His name is Spencer."

"Spencer?" That did it. Despite her disastrous night so far, Dayna laughed. "Oh, thank God. I thought you were serious."

On the day she and Camille had graduated from Covenhaven Academy, they'd both vowed to remain independent, single, and fabulous. Dayna hadn't exactly nailed the *fabulous* part, but she'd done pretty well otherwise . . . even if she was a fugitive from her former witchy life. She'd liked the idea, she realized now, that she'd been sharing a small dose of solidarity with her best friend, even if they'd been separated all these years.

Camille looked puzzled. "I'm not joking."

"Right. Next you'll tell me you're in the PTO."

Her friend tilted her head. "Well . . . of course I am." A tiny frown line appeared between her groomed brows. She drew in a deep breath. "You must have known some things would be different around here. People change. They grow. They move on."

"Yeah. Well, you know me. I'm only familiar with the

'move on' part." Suddenly distraught for reasons she couldn't explain, Dayna looked away. "Speaking of which, I've got to run."

Camille grabbed her arm. "You're not leaving, are you?"

Dayna had considered it—leaving class, leaving town, leaving witchy life altogether. If only that were possible.

Not that Camille would understand those impulses. She'd obviously mastered small-town witchy life and everything that went with it. How else could she look so perfect? So serene?

Even with her own best friend, Dayna felt like an outsider.

"Nah." Mustering a smile, Dayna shook her head. "I'm not leaving yet. I'm just going to get my backpack."

Without it, she felt inescapably vulnerable. She needed it—needed to have the illusion (at least) of being able to run at will. She needed to have her things nearby—in particular, her plastic pencil case of decoys, talismans, and weapons. T.J. might have compared her defenses to the playthings of an able child (a humiliating memory she still winced at), but Dayna had to have them. Now more than ever, she felt antsy without them.

Not that she intended to admit it.

"And to clear my head for a minute," she continued, putting on a straight face. "You know, so I can be ready when you tell me you're a die-hard Follower now."

Camille gave her a solemn look. "Actually . . ."

Oh God. Stricken by the thought of her former best friend siding with all those self-righteous "purifiers" of witchkind, Dayna stopped in her tracks. "You mean you're—"

"Kidding. Gotcha!" Camille laughed.

Her laughter was the same inelegant honk that Dayna remembered. When she heard it, her heart—usually so guarded—gave an unashamed squeeze. For an instant, her old rabble-rousing friend reappeared, shining through her newly polished clothes, flawless makeup, and expertly highlighted blond hair.

Hearing that laugh, Dayna suddenly felt much less alone.

"Okay. I can deal with the kids and the husband. And the dog." She smiled. "But I can't deal with *this*"—she aimed a meaningful nod toward the nearby classroom—"without you. What do you say we rearrange the seating chart after the break?"

"Rearrange it? Let's throw it out the window!" Camille threw her arms in the air like a woman just freed from etiquette prison. "Let's sit on the floor! Let's conjure Barcaloungers for everyone! Let's sit on Professor Reynolds's lap!"

"Woohoo!" a witch cried from a few feet away.

The three of them shared scandalous smiles.

"You're on," Dayna said. "Hang on. I'll be right back."

Feeling lightened in a way she'd never expected, she headed for the classroom. With a wave to Camille, Dayna stepped inside . . . and stopped dead at the sight that greeted her.

T.J. had only seconds to hide his encrypted packet of data. Still shrouded in darkness, he sent a burst of magic straight toward it. As instructed, the data packet nudged its corner into the ground. Using its rigid edge as a shovel, it made a hole. It shouldered its way inside, then burrowed deeper. T.J. sent dirt to tamp down over its top. It was a shitty hiding job, but it would have to do until he could retrieve the packet later.

The information it contained was too valuable to leave buried in the academy's quad for long. But for now he had other problems. Like his eager, angry, impatient pursuers.

They were almost on him. He could hear their ragged breath.

Light on his feet, he cast off his shadows and turned to face them. There were four, all warlocks, all perfectly placed to cut off potential areas of retreat—except the dark sky above.

T.J. knew as well as they did—that was no good either. All five of them could ride the currents and take this battle to the skies. But doing so was risky and unpredictable. Winds failed. Currents died. As a Patayan, T.J. could summon an airstream on command—an airstream that might sweep him to safety. As coached by the IAB, he considered it . . . then mentally shook his head.

He was having a bad day. It might feel good to smack a few heads together.

With a blur of movement, he unleashed a clod of turf. It smashed the first warlock in the face, temporarily blinding him. T.J. followed up with his fist, then a fast kick to the knee.

The warlock crumpled, grunting in pain.

T.J. gave a fierce grin. Witchfolk were always caught flat footed by human fighting techniques. Not stopping, he rounded on the second warlock, landing punches to his jaw and gut. The warlock doubled over, grunting out a transmogrification spell.

T.J. dodged it. He wasn't as lucky in sidestepping the two remaining warlocks' magic. One hit him with an immobility spell. It glanced off his left knee, leaving him wavering but upright.

Barely grounded, T.J. punched and kicked. His blows found targets. Satisfying targets. This was what he'd needed tonight. Aided by magical targeting and ancient Patayan martial arts, he kept moving. He liked fighting—liked pitting his skills against an opponent and winning. In his younger days, he'd used his abilities for darker purposes. Now he used them to stay alive.

And to do battle for the good guys at the IAB. Of course.

The fourth warlock conjured a net. Witchmade, it shimmered in the scanty glow of the academy's landscape lighting, moving with its own intelligence and purpose. Its end snaked around T.J.'s bare ankle. He jerked and shook it off, then aimed a hit of Patayan earth magic at his pursuer. It sucked the air from the warlock's position, leaving him gasping for breath.

Enveloped in an oxygen-free space, he collapsed.

T.J. returned the atmosphere to normal. He swiveled to confront another warlock, his immobilized knee making his motions jerky. He took a blow to the chest. A wallop to the chin. The gleaming witchy net twisted around his feet again, determined to capture him. He knew better than to kick it.

One of the warlocks on the ground stirred. T.J. kicked him into silence. The whole world narrowed to bursts of magic and hoarsely spoken spells. Conjuring a fistblade from the toxin-soaked grass, T.J. swung his arm in a wide arc. His blade caught one of the warlocks in the neck. With precision, it skidded away, leaving a gash that would be painful but not deadly.

T.J. nodded, satisfied. He wanted to find out who'd sent these foragers, not kill them. Not if he could help it.

These days—unless the darkness took hold—he could help it.

The witchmade net tangled around his feet again. Grunting with annoyance, T.J. aimed his fistblade downward. It sliced through the net with a sharp *thwack*, then embedded itself in the turf. Beside it, the remaining warlock wavered as he clutched his wounded neck. His eyes glittered in the net's fading glow.

"You're outmatched," T.J. told him. His muscles thrummed with exertion. Eager for more in a way he'd almost forgotten under the IAB's strictures, he motioned to the other warlock. "You should have brought eight foragers with you."

"What makes you think I didn't?"

With an eerie smile, the warlock signaled. His body moved like a bundle of underwater seaweed, jerking to and fro with an invisible current. An instant later, he appeared to divide.

T.J. eyed the newly formed doppelgängers surrounding him. They appeared as real as the warlock did, but T.J. knew better. He sighed. "You know it's easier to hurt fractionals, right?"

The magical pieces of a divided warlock or witch were more vulnerable to attack. Everyone knew that. Creating fractionals was an effective way to share magical strength with wounded partners—the IAB employed that tactic among its agents—or more commonly, to befuddle dozers. But T.J. was no fearful, superstitious human, easier cowed by his own fears than by reality. He created his own reality. He knew others did, too.

"Easier? Maybe," one of the fractionals said in its uncanny echoing voice. "It's also easier to capture a half-breed compound when he's distracted by a fucking parlor trick."

Oh hell. Too late, T.J. felt the witchmade net climb his body. Its deceptively soft coils clamped across his chest, as sturdy as iron bands. The net trapped his arms at his sides and muzzled his voice. It answered his mumbled counterspells—his efforts to free himself—with an eerily sentient binding caress.

Beneath its touch, T.J. squirmed, filled with disbelief.

In front of him, the fractionals coalesced, merging into one smirking, dark-suited warlock. "You must have forgotten, half-breed. Witchmade nets, once knit into loyalty by a knowing warlock, are resistant to other magic." He tilted his head, examining the situation. He appeared pleased with T.J.'s capture. "Oh . . . and while we're on the subject of witchstory and other trivia, you do know that cutting a witchmade net—"

Makes it divide. Christ. T.J. couldn't believe he'd forgotten that. He'd been duped by a trick so simple, even the greenest IAB agent was capable of dodging it.

He blamed Dayna. It was a good thing his bonded witch had run again. Otherwise, if T.J. found her alone, he'd . . .

"—makes it separate and grow stronger. That's right." The warlock approached, smiling at T.J.'s bared teeth and surly expression. "Just like the dozers are separating from us and growing stronger as they hump their way into oblivion, squirting out ignorant babies and pretending their so-called technology is going to save them in the end." He sneered. "The only thing that could possibly save them is an awakening. And the only thing that could possibly save you—"

With an explosion of effort, T.J. jerked forward. Using his rigid, net-encased body as a battering ram, he head-butted the warlock. His opponent howled and stumbled backward. T.J. nearly followed him to the ground. At the last instant, he conjured an airstream to keep him on his feet. Still, he faltered.

There was definitely something wrong with his magic.

All the same, his maneuver was sufficient to break the charm the forager had placed on his witchmade net. It slackened just enough. Groaning with relief, T.J. wriggled free of it.

With a dark look, the other warlock stood. He raised his hand to his forehead. A purplish lump already rose on his skin.

"I forgot to tell you," T.J. said. "I don't like lectures."

"Fuck you, McAllister. I don't care what Garmin said—"

Garmin? What did Leo have to do with this?

"—you're not worth all this trouble."

The warlock gathered his strength. A flare of magic caromed toward T.J., fast and lethal.

T.J. ducked. The other warlock snarled. He rose in the air with his arms outstretched. His suit swirled against the blackness as the wind he'd conjured intensified, harsh and cold.

Too cold. Clenching his jaw against it, T.J. reached upward. He assembled his scattered focus, then caught hold of the trailing current, capturing it the same way he'd captured the surveillance information he'd gathered from the cuspingwitch class. With a Patayan incantation, he yanked.

Deprived of wind, the forager plummeted.

He hit the ground with a sickening thud. At the same instant, his emotions went blank. With his face impassive, T.J. leaned over him. He flipped open the warlock's jacket and searched his pockets. His fingers closed on a steely lump.

He withdrew a familiar lanyarded silver talisman.

Son of a bitch. It still wasn't over with yet.

Chapter Eleven

Standing in the classroom doorway, Dayna couldn't help gawking. One of the cashmere witches rose from a kneeling position in front of their rumpled-looking instructor. With her back three-quarters to Dayna, the other witch said something to Professor Reynolds. Her husky tone carried. Her exact words didn't. Still, the implication was plain. Dayna had interrupted a private moment . . . one no one had been intended to witness.

With a lithe grace, the other witch turned her head. Her profile—beautiful, subtly exotic, and unplaceably familiar—faced Dayna. In an unhurried gesture, she touched her index finger to the corner of her mouth. She offered Professor Reynolds an intimate smile and another murmured comment. The instructor nodded, pinned to his chair with a blissed-out expression.

Or maybe that was an uncomfortably . . . *eager* expression on his face. Dayna couldn't tell for sure. Her gaze slipped lower. She wished it hadn't when she glimpsed the bulge in his pants.

Hmmm. Despite Camille's plans, Professor Reynolds's lap appeared too busy for anyone else to be sitting on it right now.

Intending to tell her friend exactly that, Dayna turned to

leave. In her haste, she accidentally unleashed a dose of mis-aligned magic. A stack of books took flight from a nearby shelf, arrowing straight toward her professor and his . . . prodigy.

Uh-oh. "Look out!" she yelled, trying to remember the spell used for steadying wayward items. Despite her tendencies toward organization, it wasn't one she'd had much practice with.

Professor Reynolds froze, unable to move. Dayna wondered if tomorrow's EnchantNet news headlines would read: CUSPING-WITCH CLASS INSTRUCTOR KILLED BY FLYING BOOKS— ALL BLOOD TRAGICALLY CONGREGATED IN GROIN. Even for a warlock, death by hard-on seemed an ignoble way to go. Urgently, she tried another spell.

The other witch rolled her eyes. She sighed, then aimed an unhurried glance at the flying books. As though in slow motion, her mouth formed the words of an incantation that Dayna wasn't familiar with. She spoke its magic too low to be heard clearly—especially above the crash of the books falling to the floor.

Whew. Feeling her face flush with embarrassment, Dayna set aside her wrecked corduroy jacket and rushed to scoop them up. With jerky and uncoordinated movements, she piled the books back on their shelf. At last she faced the instructor— and his companion, a witch she suddenly recognized.

Francesca Woodberry.

Her sleek presence made Dayna feel twice as gawky—and hugely aware of her own magical shortcomings, too. Francesca had been queen bee of Covenhaven Academy during Dayna's time there. Indisputably popular, adept with magic, and occasionally cruel, Francesca had been the girl everyone wanted to be friends with—and no one wanted to cross. Her clique of popular girls had ruled the school. Whatever Francesca had wanted, she'd gotten.

Ten years later, it appeared nothing much had changed.

Apparently, witches born of privilege never lost their aura of specialness. Francesca certainly hadn't. The moonlight hurried through the windows to gild her famous dark hair. The oxygen molecules leaped over themselves to allow her to glide by. The evening silence held steady, waiting for her to speak.

Instead, Professor Reynolds snapped out of his daze.

"Careful, Ms. Sterling." Appearing much more alert now, he gave Dayna a censorious glare. "That could have been dangerous. You're fortunate Francesca was here to help out this time. Your next mistake might not be repaired as quickly . . . or as easily."

"Oh, don't be so hard on her, Professor." With an indulgent air, Francesca smiled. In a barely perceptible gesture, she flicked her fingertips over his knee, her caress both flirty and authoritative. "She's probably doing her best, poor thing."

Her gaze dipped to Dayna's clothes, swerved to her ornately shaped golden armband, then lifted again. Francesca offered a cursory smile. No sign of recognition stirred among her perfect features. It was just as though she and Dayna *hadn't* shared classes, hallways, and several years of their lives together.

Unfortunately, they had.

Beneath that dismissive look, Dayna couldn't help but slump. She was a successful research librarian, a good friend, and a kickass presence at the annual Southwest Salsa Challenge hosted by her human neighbors in Phoenix. But in that moment, she might as well have had PERSONA NON GRATA stamped on her chest in foot-high Day-Glo letters. That reminder of exactly how little she mattered here in the magical world didn't feel good.

Then again, being in Covenhaven had never felt good. If she'd actually belonged here, Dayna never would have left.

"You're right, Francesca. Of course." Reynolds aimed an owlish glance at Dayna. "I'm sorry, Ms. Sterling. I'll try to keep your . . . limitations in mind. Did you need something else?"

"Just my backpack." Awkwardly, Dayna hustled to it. She slung it over her shoulder, feeling comforted by its familiar weight and its promise of easy escape. She paused, prodded by a force she couldn't describe. "And an application. For class *juweel*."

Professor Reynolds blinked in apparent surprise.

Francesca laughed openly. "*You?* For *juweel?*"

With languorous movements, she left the instructor behind and approached Dayna. Her nearness felt . . . threatening. That made no sense at all, even given Dayna's latent inferiority complex.

Defiantly, Dayna lifted her chin. She nodded.

Francesca pursed her lips. "But . . . Are you even in the right class, Darla? You don't seem to belong here."

"It's Dayna. And I'm in the right class."

"Really? Because you don't *look* like you're cusping at your full magical powers." Her gaze slipped dismissively to Dayna's modest cleavage and jeans-covered hips, then rose to her face again. She gave a derisive cluck of her tongue. "And you seem awfully outmatched compared to everyone else's abilities—at least their abilities to throw a hex." Francesca leaned nearer and lowered her voice. "Speaking of which, I think your ugliness hex is still in full force." With overt commiseration, she frowned. "I'm seeing a few split ends. Well, more than a few. I thought you'd want to know, so you can touch up before—"

Dayna fought an urge to smooth her hair. "I'm in the right class. Everyone is allowed to compete for *juweel*, aren't they?"

"Well, technically that's true." Francesca chuckled. "But you shouldn't worry about that, Delilah." Confidingly, she leaned closer. "You see, the position is already filled."

The backward glance she cast at their instructor made her intimation obvious. *She* intended to be *juweel*. If the pup tent she'd pitched in Professor Reynolds's pants was anything to go by, she was well on her way to cementing that prize, too.

"The position can't be filled already," Dayna argued. "The *juweel* isn't announced until graduation day. It's traditional." Silently, she thanked Leo Garmin for sharing that useful detail with her. She straightened her spine and directed her gaze at Professor Reynolds. "I'd still like an application, please."

He looked intrigued. Francesca looked irked. Dayna felt almost triumphant. Also, stupid. Because she didn't have a rat's chance in a witch's brew of making *juweel*. She was getting in way over her head again. But in that moment, she didn't care.

Ignore me now, *snooty Francesca Woodberry*.

Her moment of ersatz victory was cut short by Professor Reynolds's world-weary sigh. "Ms. Sterling, if you hadn't been away from Covenhaven for so long, you would already know this, but . . . there is no application for *juweel*. It's awarded solely at the instructor's discretion on graduation day. The truth is, witchfolk are not overly fond of paperwork, so—"

"Really? You should tell that to the folks down at the IAB. They've got mounds and mounds of paperwork."

"Is that so?" Professor Reynolds paused. "Still, I'd be careful if I were you. There's a great deal you don't know about Covenhaven." He gestured vaguely. "About . . . the new Covenhaven."

"You mean the Covenhaven that's obsessed with The Old Ways? The Covenhaven that's run by the IAB and filled with pastels and cashmere? Yeah, I'm becoming pretty familiar with that. I don't like it much, but I'm here for now, so if you don't mind—"

"Whoops! Debbie, your pants are on fire."

"Really, Francesca?" She rounded on the other witch, who smirked at her in return. "My *pants* are on fire? That's the best you could come up with? That's pretty juvenile, even for you."

"I'm being serious. Your pants are on fire."

She motioned downward. At the same moment, Dayna felt the first surge of heat, like blowback from the preheated gas barbecue on her neighbor's porch when someone opened it to start grilling hot dogs. The hems of her jeans sparked, making an ineffectual sound like a faulty Bic lighter.

An instant later, the flames ignited in earnest.

In a blur of motion, T.J. strode through the offices of the InterAllied Bureau. At this hour, the place was almost deserted. The computers were quiet. The lights were low. The usual hum of witchy busyness was gone, replaced by the glimmer and click of the agency's newly installed autoshadowing memory flickers.

The smell of stale decaf coffee hung in the motionless air, underlaid by the sulfurous stink that had haunted his first years here. He'd never gotten used to that smell. Growing up on the res, he'd mostly been exposed to Patayan magic.

Patayan magic was clean. It imbued natural materials with directed energy. It didn't strong-arm other elements—or people—into magical cooperation, the way legacy magic often did. It didn't leverage weakness and exploit humans the way *myrmidon* magic almost always did. Instead, Patayan magic just . . . arose, called into being by its user's inborn skill and training.

But the truth was, T.J.'s Patayan side couldn't deconstruct legacy magic the way his warlock side could. So at times like these, being of compound birth came in handy. Scowling with fierce intent, T.J. peered through the IAB's witchmade walls. In contrast to the human-constructed buildings in Phoenix, they were pixilated by magic. He was able to see through them easily. That flaw was something the IAB had inexplicably failed to address when they'd placed their headquarters in the magical spaces above Covenhaven's false-fronted Main Street buildings. On the other hand, when you were mostly hiding from unaware humans, pixilation wasn't much of a tell.

An admin witch called out a greeting. T.J. gave her a brief nod, then kept moving. He reached the agency's private interior. Here the lighting was better, the sulfur stink was muted by air filters, and the carpet was more luxurious than in the common areas where agents and their constituents spent their time. His steps depressed the cushy pile uncaringly beneath his feet; his hand squashed the lanyarded talisman he'd found in one tight fist.

Moving faster, T.J. let his gaze rove from office to conference room to bullpen. He didn't find what he was looking for. At the end of the hall, one door remained impenetrable. Knowing that barrier stood intentionally, T.J. headed toward it. He bared his teeth as he eyed the name on the placard outside, then shoved open the door to reveal a luxe executive suite.

Inside, Leo Garmin glanced up from his desk. His features looked handsome and implacable, his expression a trademark mix of caring and undisguised arrogance. Garmin was happy to show concern for others, T.J. knew. He might genuinely have felt it, at least some of the time. But he made sure everyone knew he was the better, kinder warlock for having done so. In Garmin's world, keeping score mattered. Winning mattered most of all.

"Ah, Agent McAllister. I'm glad you're still with us."

"Bite me, you bastard." Filled with cold irritation, T.J. dropped the lanyarded silver talisman on Garmin's desk. It landed with a clatter, its IAB logo glittering in the artificial witchy light. "If you wanted me to report in, you could have asked. *Foragers?* What the fuck is the matter with you?"

A shrug. "Nothing a little obedience wouldn't cure."

"You want obedience? Get a dog."

His boss offered a small smile. "You were supposed to be here yesterday, to drop off your last assignment, that runaway witch. Steerling . . . Starling . . . oh, that's right. Dayna Sterling."

"You know damn well who I've been tracing."

"I know you were supposed to deliver her personally."

Things had gotten *plenty* personal between him and Dayna. Shutting out the memory, T.J. crossed his arms. "You might have some complaints coming from those foragers in your shadow army. You should tell them not to try jumping me by surprise."

Garmin steepled his hands. "Is anyone dead?"

"You tell me. You must have been watching."

"If I could watch you, I wouldn't need special agents."

T.J. couldn't help grinning. During his dark years, he'd developed a few special tricks to keep his whereabouts unknown. Even after recruiting him, the IAB hadn't been able to weasel those tricks from him. "Old habits are hard to break."

"Unfortunately, protocol isn't. Not for you."

"You knew that going in." T.J. nodded at the talisman on Garmin's desk. "Consider that a polite request. Call off your foragers. Next time I won't go so easy on them."

"They're IAB agents. You can't just—"

"Watch me." With grim anticipation, T.J. inhaled a raspy breath. He rotated his arm to examine a bloody scrape just below his shoulder—evidence of his earlier fight. "My loyalties last only as long as yours do. You knew that going in, too."

Garmin muttered an obscenity. "You're a Patayan. You're supposed to eat, sleep, and breathe loyalty." He gave a cocksure grin. "Hell, you people probably shit loyalty."

"I'm only half Patayan." T.J. stood unyieldingly. "The rest of me is suspicious of everyone, all the time."

With a sigh, his boss shuffled a few papers. He loosened his tie to show off the ten-year-service pin the IAB gave its veteran kiss-ass executives. Its crested logo shone brightly, evidence of Garmin's ability to be loyal to at least one entity.

T.J. was part of that entity; that was true. But if push came to shove, he had no doubt his boss would put the IAB first and his agents last. It was just the way things were.

"Why were you at Covenhaven Academy tonight?" Garmin asked.

"It's personal." T.J.'s mission to find the *juweel*—like his promise to his magus—had nothing to do with the IAB. The bureau may have saved his ass once, but his life as a Patayan guardian had little to do with his work for the witching agency that employed him. He crossed his arms and frowned at his boss. "All I want is your word. Don't send any more foragers after me."

"You know I can't promise that."

"Then we have a problem. I have a commitment I can't break. Your foragers are getting in my way."

"Foragers wouldn't be necessary if you would report in."

"I'm hardly a greenie. I don't need to punch a clock."

"Maybe *I* say you do." His boss eyed him. Then he ran his hand over his bald head, a move that typically—in Garmin's easy-to-read world—signaled a change of topic. "We've had a complaint about your services, by the way. According to one of your recent snares, you were 'intrusive, invasive, and scary.'"

"Yeah." T.J. nodded. That was probably true. "So what?"

"So we're trying to run a civilized agency."

"Save the PR campaign for the media." Annoyed, T.J. fixed Garmin with an impatient look. Then curiosity got the better of him. "It was one of the cusping witches who complained, wasn't it?" He shook his head. "I knew it. Those tracing jobs were bureaucratic busywork. You should have sent a nice, compliant greenie on those grabs—someone with a clipboard and an IAB-approved bedside manner."

"A junior agent would not have succeeded."

T.J. scoffed.

"*You* almost didn't succeed." Leo Garmin gave him a penetrating look. "You almost lost the Sterling witch during that storm of hers. You're still pissed about it. I can tell."

"Oh yeah?" T.J. flipped him his middle finger. "How?"

His boss only laughed. "You might not have had so much trouble if you hadn't left your partner behind." He gave an affable smile. "Why did you go for that snare unaided, Agent McAllister? You know it's against procedure to work alone."

Jesus. Here it was. The real reason Garmin had sent those foragers after him. Garmin wanted to reprimand T.J., and he couldn't wait a single goddamn day—until T.J.'s next scheduled shift at the IAB—to ream him. He knew how this had happened, too.

"Freaking bug." He'd thought he'd disabled it.

"You *did* disable it." With that annoying semiclairvoyance sometimes displayed by legacy witches who were in full command of their magical capacities, his boss raised his eyebrows. "You just didn't disable it fast enough. Deuce Bailey might not be able, McAllister, but his capabilities as a turned human are valued by this agency. You should try trusting him sometime."

T.J. flexed his jaw. It ached where one of the foragers had punched him. Experimentally, he worked it from side to side.

"Don't make this into another Cobalt," Garmin warned.

Stubbornly, T.J. remained silent. He didn't want to talk about Cobalt. That grab had gone disastrously wrong. At least his turned human partner hadn't been implicated in the problems they'd encountered. Deuce's record with the agency was clean.

That mattered more to T.J. than covering his own ass. He could take the heat. He wasn't as sure about Deuce's capacities.

Deuce was tough; there was no question about that. But he was still adjusting to being turned. Sometimes, when Deuce wasn't putting on his aw-shucks, easygoing human act, he seemed downright dangerous—hell-bent on getting even with the magical world and the duplicitous witch who'd upended his life.

"And don't stonewall me either." With a weary sigh, Garmin leaned back in his office chair. He gestured for T.J. to take a seat as well. T.J. refused. His boss seemed amused. "All right, have it your way. You know I have the authority to make you talk, if I decide it's necessary to the organization."

"Yeah, thanks for the reminder." T.J. frowned. He wiped a smear of blood from his forearm, then glanced up. "I'll watch myself . . . in case you ever develop the nerve to try."

A long moment stretched between them, fraught with the tension that had existed ever since Garmin had recruited T.J. to the IAB . . . from a dank jail cell in the middle of the night.

T.J. broke the silence first. "In the meantime, while we wait for you to grow a pair, try to keep your foragers in line."

He turned, stirring the air around him into restless currents, feeling more than ready to put this night behind him.

His footsteps carried him silently across Garmin's office, taking him past awards of merit, tokens of civic appreciation, and a row of confiscated elixir bottles that Garmin kept on display as reminders that disobedience would not be tolerated.

It wasn't the elixir bottles that spooked visitors as much as the former drug peddlers themselves, trapped in the bottles by a form of dark magic not many legacy witches knew.

"Wait," came his supervisor's voice from behind him.

Reluctantly, T.J. stopped. Fists clenched, he turned.

Garmin glanced up from his coffee cup, his expression genial. "Fine. You've got it. I won't send any more foragers."

Skeptically, T.J. raised his eyebrows.

"I promise. Okay? But you'll have to meet me halfway."

T.J. laughed. "With you, there's always a catch."

"That's why *I'm* the boss." Garmin grinned. "Now that we have a deal . . ." He pinned T.J. with a look. "Explain your use of illegal bonding magic during the Sterling grab yesterday."

At first, T.J. was too shocked to react. By the time he'd

recovered enough to enact a concealment spell, it was too late.

His birthright mark already pulsed with guilty awareness.

"It was a mistake." He ignored the telltale warmth in his biceps. "I've taken measures to ensure it won't happen again."

His supervisor nodded. "I appreciate your candor. However, that doesn't change the fact that your actions were careless."

T.J. remained silent, knowing there was no point trying to figure out how Garmin had learned about his bonding magic or defending himself against an action he'd already taken. It was not the Patayan way. He'd examined his part in the situation, considered possible recovery scenarios, and acted on one. Period. The incident with his bonded witch was over with.

As long as he stayed away from her.

"Ancient magic—including bonding rituals—is banned for good reason," Garmin went on. "By using prohibited magic, no matter your motive in doing so, you endangered yourself, your snare, your partner, and any vulnerable humans who were nearby."

"No one was nearby." T.J. gritted his teeth. "My snare was safe, already in custody. Deuce was unaware of the situation until afterward. I was—" *Most at risk*, he started to say, then stopped himself. "I contained the situation. It's done."

"Nevertheless, such recklessness is a warning sign." Garmin appeared troubled. "It's not what I'd expect from an agent of your experience and dedication. And it's directly counter to our mission here at the IAB. Frankly, that's what bothers me most. Have your loyalties to the agency changed, Agent McAllister?"

"Have my—" T.J. broke off. "Screw you. I'm leaving."

"Is that a yes? Because these are dark times in Covenhaven. The Followers are rising in influence. Humans have died—"

"Watch yourself. Henry Obijuwa was my friend."

"—and we can't afford to take anything for granted."
Garmin pressed on relentlessly. "This 'other' mission of
yours—"

"Is none of your goddamn business." Again, T.J. turned to
leave. Light on his feet, he headed for the unpixilated door.

Its knob came off in his hands. It melted away, falling to
the carpet like the dried pods on the mesquite trees outside.

"Oh *come on*." T.J. smacked the door. It shuddered and
turned even more opaque with self-protective magic. From
the first, Garmin had been fond of sentient furnishings.
Sometimes T.J. wondered if his supervisor's attentive cradling
chairs and solicitously self-moving tables were really trans-
mogrified agents who had crossed him sometime during his
rise at the IAB.

"I wasn't finished." Garmin shrugged. "I have no choice
but to put you on forced leave, Agent McAllister. You are
stripped of your magic, forbidden to use it until further
review."

"You can't do that." T.J. shoved the door. When it held
steady, he turned to face his supervisor. "You wouldn't."

"I just did. As of this moment, you are unlicensed."

Unlicensed. When word got out that he was stripped of
magic, every miscreant he'd ever taken down for the IAB
would want a piece of him. And he wouldn't be able to legally
defend himself, whether with Patayan skills or warlock defenses.

Incredulously, T.J. stared at Garmin. Of everyone he knew,
Garmin understood best how important the InterAllied
Bureau was to him. He understood how the IAB had changed
his life and pulled him from the shadows he'd fallen into.
T.J. couldn't afford to be cut loose from the agency's discipline, its strictures . . . its sense of good purpose. Especially
now, in the wake of his unwanted bonding and all its tempta-
tions.

Faced with this suspension, T.J.'s only choice would be to

go against his better nature. To use magic without the IAB's approval, as his Patayan instincts and his promise to his magus demanded. If he did that, he'd be one step away from giving in to his bonded witch, too, as his warlock instincts compelled him so strongly to do.

Once he started rebelling, who knew where it would lead? Once he lost control, would he be able to find his way back?

T.J. wasn't sure. But he was sure that *his* instincts were not to be trusted. Not with innocents like Dayna Sterling, and not without the constraints he'd purposely leashed himself with.

Somehow, he'd have to walk the line between illegally using magic . . . and surrendering to his compound nature completely.

Unless he could change Garmin's mind.

"Christ, Leo." T.J. forced a laugh. "I know you can be kind of an asshole these days, but come on. You know how important—"

"Leave your talisman with me."

Disbelievingly, T.J. stared at Garmin's outstretched palm. All at once, T.J.'s lanyarded silver talisman, identical to the one he'd snatched from the forager, felt like a dead weight around his neck. With a savage motion, he yanked it over his head.

Or at least he tried to. Instead, it tangled with his leather-corded traditional Patayan amulets. The whole lot jerked against his skin, strangling him. A more fanciful warlock would have imagined they conspired to retain his magic for themselves.

T.J. was more pragmatic than that.

He freed his IAB talisman, then fisted it as he crossed Garmin's office. With a wrenching motion, he released it. It fell to Garmin's desk and landed beneath his uneasy gaze.

The moment the separation was complete, a searing pain cut across T.J.'s chest. Caught by surprise, he doubled over.

"T.J.?" Garmin hurried to his side. "Hey, what's the—"

Racked with pain, T.J. muttered the most vicious swearword that came to mind. Then his brain fogged. His whole body shook. Trying to stop it, he braced his hands on his thighs and panted.

Nothing helped. He hadn't experienced anything like this since he was a teenager—since the days after his parents had been killed. Was this part of his bond? If so, the legends had given him a truly fucked-up view of the wonder of being bonded.

Maybe this was what he got for rejecting his bond.

Or maybe this was just a brutal reminder—a reminder of how dangerous it would be to give over to his shadowed nature again.

Dimly he heard Garmin pick up his phone. In a voice filled with concern, his supervisor called for emergency aid.

Muffled voices came over the phone's speaker, washing over T.J. in garbled waves. The whole world was coming in waves now, searing waves that threatened to tear him apart from the inside.

"I don't care what else is going on in the building," Garmin snapped, swearing at the unlucky IAB agent on the other end of the line. "I want medical help in here *right now.*"

Chapter Twelve

Safely inside the apartment she'd been assigned by the IAB, Dayna threw down her backpack. "Honey? I'm home."

Nothing but silence met her greeting. With a shrug, she flicked on another light, examining the small space as she walked to the nearest of the two bedrooms. Apparently her roomies and their IAB chaperone were still no-shows. Everything appeared exactly as she'd left it before heading to cusping-witch class tonight.

The sparsely furnished living room was still dominated by a huge flat-screen TV and a videogame console. In the kitchen, the refrigerator hummed, busily chilling the frozen burritos and lonely carton of vanilla soymilk inside it. Dayna remembered the box of Cap'n Crunch she'd spotted in the cupboards and promised herself a bowl after she took care of one minor detail.

Her scorched jeans.

The smell of burned fabric trailed her steps. With a disgusted sigh, Dayna reached the bedroom and peeled off her now-soggy jeans. Relieved, she threw them on the bed. They landed in an incongruously mocking pose, both legs akimbo as though ready to take flight. She was fortunate the situation hadn't been worse.

Clad now in her T-shirt and underwear, she lifted one bare leg. She peered cautiously at her shin. It looked fine. She checked the other leg. It appeared unharmed, too.

She couldn't say the same thing for her ego. At the sight of those flames, she'd thoroughly freaked out, flapping her arms in a mindless panic. The one thing Dayna feared most was fire. As a witch, she'd been born with an inherent dread of flames. Even Professor Reynolds, who should have been implacable in the face of any emergency, had turned white-faced and immobile when he'd glimpsed the sparks shooting up from her jeans hems.

The witch who'd come to her rescue had, ironically, been Camille. Sweet, gentle, PTO-loving Camille was a dynamo in a crisis. Dayna's former best friend had cut loose with a five-gallon bucket's worth of water. Then with a conjured fire extinguisher. Then with a series of cold towels, wrung out in the privacy of the Covenhaven Academy's girls' bathroom and applied with placid thoroughness to forestall serious burns.

"At least they weren't brand-new jeans!" she'd assured Dayna with one of her Pollyanna smiles. "That's a plus, right?"

"Right," Dayna had replied with a grimace. "I'm *so* lucky."

It had taken all her best assurances to convince Camille that she was really unhurt. It had taken all her courage to return to that classroom afterward. And it had leached away all her pride to endure Francesca Woodberry's mocking whispers to her cadre of trendy cronies throughout the rest of the class.

"I don't know how she managed to set herself *on fire*," the snobby witch had confided in a stage whisper to her friends, Lily and Sumner. "It was just . . . poof! Up in flames. I think she did it on purpose. Some people just can't get enough attention, and when you're not *naturally* gifted with magic . . ."

Cutting short the humiliating memory, Dayna glanced

down at her wrecked jeans. It occurred to her that she could probably fix them . . . and redeem herself in the process. Surely it wouldn't be too difficult to conjure some new denim or enchant the existing fibers to weave a repair job on the burned fabric.

Newly encouraged by the fact that she'd thought of a magical remedy at all, she sucked in a deep breath. She held out her hands—not because it would help, necessarily, but because it made her feel slightly more witchy. She focused on the blackened fabric, then closed her eyes and recited an approximate spell.

The air went still—but crackly, the way it did before a thunderstorm. A whiff of sulfur drifted toward Dayna's nostrils. Buoyed by that sign of progress, she repeated the spell.

A sudden sighing sound made her snap open her eyes.

Her formerly favorite jeans had dissolved on the bed.

Which meant her spell hadn't worked. Her ruined jeans weren't repaired. And her magic was still useless.

Dayna slumped. Even in private, her spells went awry. So much for the hope that it had only been the pressure that had made her hex boomerang onto her. But just when she was about to give up, the remnants of her jeans wavered. They lurched atop the coverlet, then split into hundreds of fluffy white pieces. In disbelief, Dayna identified them as . . . raw balls of cotton?

Before she could congratulate herself on making partial progress, each piece popped. Or rather, each piece imploded. Shrunken but weirdly united, they levitated over the mattress, still roughly in the shape of a pair of jeans.

Except they weren't jeans anymore. They were seeds. Thousands of tiny brown seeds, all spinning in a vortex and getting faster all the time. The blowback from their spinning actually made her squint as her hair blew away from her face. A few of the seeds pinged outward. One caught her on the cheek.

It stung. Dayna slapped her hand over the tiny wound, staring in bewilderment. The vortex of jeans seeds paused. They seemed to realize they'd found a target. They spun faster.

Too late, Dayna realized the truth: She'd created the world's first killer pair of deconstructed jeans.

Could she do *nothing* right? Shrieking, she covered her head with her arms as the jeans seeds revved up, obviously ready for a bigger attack. They were probably vitalized by her cowering, imbued—as all magical things were—with a bit of her emotions.

They charged straight at her. Dayna ducked. They missed, whooshing past her head with an angry buzz.

Whew. She was safe. The seeds were gone.

Embarrassed to have recoiled from a bunch of tiny *seeds*, Dayna straightened. She would have liked to have been a little braver. Over these past few days, though, she'd used up a lot of her courage. Being dragged out of the research library by that scary tracer, causing that horrific rainstorm, finding herself in Covenhaven again, trying to practice magic at cusping-witch class . . . It was all too much for one witch to take, at least without losing a few degrees of cool.

Down the hall, a scraping sound caught her attention. The seeds! They were still enchanted. She couldn't let them get away.

Turning, Dayna stared down the apartment's short hallway. The jeans seeds careened down the center, then coalesced. They struck the brief ninety-degree turn that marked the bathroom and appeared to stop in blind confusion. This was her chance.

Shouting out a new spell, Dayna chased them. The seeds appeared to gather strength from her incantation. They formed a new volcano of cottonseeds and veered sideways, hitting the wall. The paint scraped from it in wispy shards. Yikes.

"Stop!" Dayna shouted. "Stop!"

All she'd wanted to do was salvage her pride. Not sandblast

the walls, peel the hallway paint, or give herself an unwanted microdermabrasion treatment. She doubted this was what *Cosmo* had in mind when it recommended regular exfoliation to its readers.

She raised her arms and chanted a different spell. The seeds merged, ballooned upward, then hovered. As a unit, they swiveled. They split again and tried once more. Chilled, Dayna recognized their behavior. They were searching. For her.

Holy shit. Somehow, she'd gathered all the disappointment she'd felt over her disastrous first day at cusping-witch school and channeled it into a pack of killer cottonseeds.

In a way, *they* were *her* . . . and they were out to get her.

With another shriek, Dayna ran in the bathroom. She yelled out every spell she could think of, but still the seeds pursued her. She heard them scour the door, the walls, the tiled floor. She yelped and jumped into the bathtub, then pulled the curtain.

A shower of seeds hit it. They fell to the floor, then surged upward again. In disbelief, Dayna stared at their shadows on the semitransparent shower curtain as they surged against it.

An instant later, another shadow loomed. It was big. It was broad-shouldered. It was unmistakably male. Against all reason, Dayna begged with fate to let it be that tough-as-nails tracer, T.J. McAllister, come to her rescue. But another worried glance told her it wasn't T.J. This man possessed spiky hair, a menacing growl . . . and a thousand-watt vacuum cleaner.

It roared into service upon his command and slurped up cottonseeds like a hungry desert rattler went after field mice.

Soon, the coast was clear. Gratefully, Dayna scraped back the shower curtain. Her gaze fell on Deuce Bailey's affable smile, then his steady grasp on the neck of a vacuum hose.

The last few cottonseeds pinged into the canister.

Surprised to see the IAB agent there, Dayna could only

stare at him for a second. Deuce's attention lifted from his heroic handling of the vacuum to the witch he'd rescued.

They must have trained all IAB agents to remain calm in a crisis, Dayna realized shakily, because this particular agent appeared downright happy-go-lucky as he switched off the vacuum.

The motor subsided. Deuce grinned and put his hands on his hips. "How's it going, Ms. Sterling? Everything all right now?"

She nodded. "I can't believe you recognized me."

"Why not?" He held out his hand to her, palm up.

The entire situation felt engulfed in surreality. But then, that was her life these days. Ever since T.J. had found her.

"Because your gaze never traveled any higher than my underwear." With dignity, she snatched a towel from the nearby towel bar. She wrapped it around her waist, sarong-style, then accepted Deuce's hand out of the tub. "Thanks for the rescue."

"Anytime." With the implacable calm of a man who could handle anything, he watched to make sure she landed with both feet planted safely on the bathroom floor tiles. "Haven't you heard? I'm a regular IAB hero these days. Rescuing is my job."

"I thought policing and punishing was the IAB's job. With time off for teaching runaway cusping witches, of course."

"Yeah. All those things, too." For an instant, Deuce's rugged face grew taut with an emotion Dayna couldn't identify. His voice lowered menacingly. "Especially punishing."

His intense demeanor spooked her. Deuce Bailey was big, strong, and undoubtedly tough. If he wanted to punish someone, she had no doubt he could do it. Thoroughly. And memorably.

Worried anew, Dayna took a step backward. Her heel nudged the bathtub. Something tiny and sharp bit into her ankle.

She slapped it. Another cottonseed. "Damn it!"

Deuce hunkered down. He pinched the seed between his fingers, then showed it to her. "So . . . you want to explain?"

"You go first." Dayna eyed him, then pushed past him, eager to put distance between them. "You can start by telling me exactly what you're doing here in *my* apartment."

Watery-eyed, T.J. peered up past Garmin's desk.

His supervisor was still on the phone, his aura of authority shot to hell by whatever was happening to T.J. Seeing Leo that way only made things worse. Was he dying? At the thought, T.J. felt his chest spasm again, harder this time.

"Then do it," Garmin barked. Realizing T.J. was looking at him, he put his hand over the receiver. His eyes were wide with alarm. "It was protocol, T.J. It's my job. That's it. I swear, I never wanted you to have a freaking heart attack over it."

T.J.'s heart constricted again . . . which made him realize, foggily and disbelievingly, what must have happened.

Garmin's demand for his IAB badge must have activated his Patayan instincts against betrayal. His stupid, outmoded, inbred need for loyalty had hit him where it hurt—in the heart—making him feel physical pain over his supervisor's lack of trust.

Simultaneously relieved, irritated, and embarrassed by his own weakness, T.J. straightened. His chest still hurt, but he could take it. He could take it because he knew it was a fault to be overcome. He pressed his mouth together, then held up his hand to halt Garmin's phoned-in harassment of the other agent.

His supervisor raised his eyebrows. But he got the message.

"Never mind," he barked into the receiver. He hung up, then suspiciously eyed T.J. "You're trying to tell me you're all right now? Hell, T.J.! You looked at death's door a minute ago. You're still pale." With an urgent gesture, Garmin sent his office chair scuttling sideways to offer support. "What the—"

"I'm fine," T.J. rasped. With a tremendous effort, he grasped the sentient chair. It helpfully rose higher, allowing him to stand straight. Mostly. His chest still felt as though someone had opened it up with a buzz saw and rooted around awhile, rearranging things. He raised his palm. "I'm out."

He trod across the carpet, more slowly this time. He felt a million years old, vulnerable in a way he hated. Every instinct told him to get away. Now. But when Garmin's voice rang out behind him, he was forced to stop. The IAB had awakened a sense of duty in him. Whether stripped of his magic or not, he could not ignore his training—or his supervisor's sorrowful tone.

"Hey. Next time you sense foragers," Garmin said in a low voice, "it would be in your best interest not to kick their asses. They might be trying to clear your name with the bureau."

"They'll never get a chance. They'll never catch me again."

"I'm saying, *let them* catch you. Let them watch you," Garmin urged. The sentient chair wheeled itself along beside T.J., squeaking as it tried to assist him. "If we can't find any proof that you're being disloyal, I'll reinstate your license to practice magic. We'll go back to the way things were."

"My own agency plans to spy on me. *You* suspect me of disloyalty." T.J. fixed Garmin with a jaded look, his chest still aching. "We can never go back to the way things were."

That was why it was past time to go. With a weary motion, T.J. raised his hand. He drew an arch in midair, then focused on its shape. After a few seconds, the pixilated wall of the deluxe office suite lurched sideways. Then it vanished altogether, creating a new exit beside the impenetrable door.

From outside, a rising clamor could be heard. Voices shouted. Equipment clattered in a distant room, chased by the sulfurous odor that meant magic was under way.

"Hey, don't leave like this. All you have to do is cooperate," Garmin said. "It doesn't have to be this way."

"It didn't. But now it does." T.J. felt the loss of his IAB talisman keenly. Without it, his Patayan amulets swung too freely, deprived—as he was—of the IAB's controlling influence. "Congratulations, Leo. You just created the rogue agent you were afraid you already had. Nice work for a Tuesday."

"T.J. Wait."

Shaking his head, T.J. stepped into the hall. He almost collided with a witch agent. She was on full IAB alert, her talisman glowing with a magically transmitted amber warning as she ran toward Garmin's office. She stopped short, looked curiously at the opening T.J. had made, then peered through it at Garmin.

"Sir, there's been another death. A human. We—" She faltered, gasping for breath with one hand over her talisman. Its amber color brightened. "We know legacy magic was involved."

"I see." Garmin's gaze shifted to T.J. And held.

T.J. could take the hint. Frowning, he headed down the hall—possibly for the last time. As though trying to drag him backward, snatches of the witch's conversation with Garmin pursued him. Their voices sounded clear and urgent.

"Legacy magic?" Garmin asked. "Are you sure?"

"Yes," the witch agent said. "The signs were apparent."

"Someone's magic has gotten out of control then."

"Not quite, sir. This wasn't a case of magic misuse," the witch argued crisply. "At least not a typical one. This was another gardener. Another brain aneurysm, like Obijuwa."

Halfway down the hall, T.J. slowed. In front of him, corralled by the nearest row of cubicles, agents rushed to and fro. They herded witnesses toward enclosed areas where truth spells could safely be cast without affecting IAB personnel. They whirled paperwork in the air, examining it with anxious eyes.

They hustled by with cell phones to their ears. The activity was proof that something important had just happened.

"The weird thing is . . ." Behind T.J., the witch agent paused, possibly waiting for him to move out of earshot. "There were certain . . . artifacts near the body. We have reason to believe the victim was trying to practice legacy magic himself."

In the hallway, T.J. stopped dead.

My pops was doing magic, he heard Jesse Obijuwa say again. *He was doing tons of magic. Just like all those witches and warlocks in town.*

At the time, T.J. had told the boy what he knew to be true—that humans couldn't practice magic.

Now, suddenly, he had his doubts.

Ignoring the frenzy of activity, T.J. headed for the IAB's exit. This latest human death was a tocsin to be heeded. If it meant what he thought it did, his magus's prophesies were coming true faster than either of them had expected. There was no time to waste.

In the kitchen, Dayna and Deuce sat companionably at the minuscule peninsula with bowls of Cap'n Crunch at their elbows. Fortified by the sweetness of Crunch Berries, Dayna gazed at the IAB agent opposite her, still perplexed by all he'd told her.

"So you hacked into the IAB database and had my housing assignment changed. I get that. But why?"

"Never ask a hacker why. It's like asking a mountain climber why. Because it's there. Because I can."

In the subdued glow of the overhead pendant lamp, all the ambiguity she'd sensed in him earlier was gone. Deuce appeared to be exactly what he was—an oversize kid with a yen for sugary cereal and an openness that made her want to be around him. He was, at best, an unlikely IAB enforcement agent. He seemed far too easygoing to be any good at official magical peacekeeping.

On the other hand, there *was* that dangerous enthusiasm he had for the punishment phase of IAB business . . .

"I was a programmer before I was turned," Deuce went on, naming a well-known technology company, "but after that—"

"Wait. Turned?"

"It's what witchfolk call humans who can sense the presence of magic." Deuce spooned up more cereal, crunched thoughtfully, then swallowed. "Turned humans can't practice magic themselves, but they're aware of it. Unlike dozers, we recognize witches at a glance. But they can't tell we're turned."

"Aha. So if a bunch of witchfolk are up to no good—"

"They don't have any problem practicing illegal magic around a supposedly ignorant human." Deuce grinned. "Like me."

"And then you nab them. Whammo!"

"That's right."

"So you're like the IAB's supersecret double agent."

"Something like that." Deuce shook the box of Cap'n Crunch, peered inside, then frowned in apparent disappointment. "The bureau started using turned humans as agents in the past year or so. The program is still in the trial phase. Some of the witchfolk agents don't trust us."

"Are there a lot of you? A lot of turned humans?"

A distant look came into his eyes. "I hope not."

Against all reason, Dayna felt sorry for him. She considered reaching out in commiseration . . . then took one look at Deuce's burly, muscle-corded forearm and changed her mind.

"But I've never even heard of turned humans before. I didn't think I was *that* out of touch with the magical world."

"It's not something that's talked about much. Turning happens through *myrmidon* magic. The magic of The Old Ways.

And it's only recently that The Old Ways have made a resurgence," Deuce said. "I'm not up on all the witchstory, but I get the impression that witch-human contact used to be frowned upon."

"Only by the most bigoted witchfolk," Dayna assured him. "The truth is, we should have planned our futures better. The magical population retreated to tiny, closed-off communities like Covenhaven centuries ago. I mean, the Extraction was understandable. Witchfolk were under siege. But closing yourself off that way doesn't exactly lead to tolerance."

Deuce frowned. "Is that why you left here?"

Dayna wished she could say it had been. She wished she could tell him that idealism had led her to bail out of the town she'd grown up in. But the truth was . . .

"I think there's another box of cereal in the cupboard." She headed for the kitchen. "I'll get more soymilk, too."

"Hey, it's cool with me if you don't want to talk about it. You've probably got enough on your mind, what with being bonded with T.J. and going to witch school. It's a lot to take in."

With one hand on the open cupboard door, Dayna stilled. She swiveled her head. "Being what?"

"Bonded. With T.J. He didn't—" With a creative swearword, Deuce broke off. "He didn't tell you, did he?"

"No. 'Bonded'? What does that mean? It sounds positively medieval." Dayna raised her arm and pointed to her golden armband—now decently paired with pajama pants, a tank top, and bunny slippers. "Does it have something to do with this?"

"I thought you'd know already. You're the witch here."

Dayna snorted. "So far? In name only. So tell me."

"I shouldn't say." He shook his head. "All I promised was that I'd keep an eye on you for T.J. That's it. That's why I—"

That's why I altered your housing assignment.

Deuce broke off with another swearword. His expression

made it easy to fill in the blanks, though, with no complicated research theories necessary.

That's why I placed you here, in my apartment.

No wonder he'd been so evasive when she'd questioned him earlier. He hadn't wanted to admit the truth.

"Keep 'an eye' on me?" Dayna stalked toward Deuce, all thoughts of cereal gone now, hating that she felt simultaneously intrigued, flattered, and annoyed by the machismo inherent in those words. "I'm not T.J.'s property," she informed Deuce with a lift of her chin. "Nobody has to 'keep an eye on me' for him."

"That's not what I meant! It's more of a favor. Friend to friend. Your bond makes you special to T.J., but he—"

Clearly catching himself in the nick of time, Deuce quit talking. He pressed his mouth together. "How about that cereal?"

Dayna crossed her arms over her chest. She shook her head. "Maybe you don't care if I spill my guts, but I care if you spill yours. Tell me what it means to be bonded."

Deuce's gaze skittered to her armband.

"It *does* have something to do with this new metalwork tattoo of mine, doesn't it?" With a fierce gesture, Dayna indicated her armband. She'd kept it on because she'd liked it. It was cool, in a baroque, darkly Goth kind of way. It made her feel witchier—something with which she needed all the help she could get. "Tell me, Deuce. Tell me the truth, right now."

"I've already said too much." He stood. "Good night."

"Good night? You're kidding, right?" With her mouth open in disbelief, she followed the tracer to the sink. He deposited his cereal bowl and spoon, his shoulders tense. "Come on, Deuce."

He turned to face her, his expression filled with equal measures of obstinacy and regret. "No way. T.J. will kill me."

"Why? Is it that important?"

His silence told her it was. More alarmed than ever, Dayna stared at him. Then an idea occurred to her.

"Fine. Don't tell me. I'll just take off this armband, and whatever that 'bonded' thing is, it'll be over."

With as much bravado as she could muster, Dayna grabbed her golden armband. She tugged. It didn't budge. She tried again.

Deuce looked on with unhappy eyes.

Irritated now, Dayna resorted to the tactic she usually used to remove stuck-on jewelry. She pumped some soap from the sink dispenser, then slathered it sloppily over her arm. With a defiant look at Deuce, she pulled the armband again. Hard.

It actually seemed to *tighten*. "Ouch! What the hell?"

"It won't come off. Not unless something really drastic happens. T.J. told me that much." Deuce put his hand on hers, then offered a hesitant smile. "Hey, at least you don't have it as bad as T.J. does. He's bonded with you through his birthright mark tattoo—the one on his arm. When I told him he should get unbonded with you by removing his birthright tattoo—"

"You wanted him to get unbonded?"

Why did she feel hurt by that? It was ridiculous.

"Well, no," Deuce admitted. "*He* wanted to get unbonded."

Dayna snorted. "Typical. Jerk."

"I was cool with it. I still am." Deuce regrouped. "But the point is, T.J. told me that removing his birthright mark tattoo would be like removing a piece of his soul. He said it wasn't impossible, just . . . costly. Especially to a Patayan."

Aghast, Dayna gawked at him. "His *soul*?"

"Shit. I've said too much again." Appearing panicky—at least as much as a two-hundred-pound tough guy could—Deuce backed off. "Just believe me, okay? You might get hurt if you try taking off that thing." He nodded at her soapy armband.

For a second, silence fell between them.

Then, "If they made wedding rings this way, fifty percent

of all humans would be seriously bummed right now," Dayna said.

At her joke, Deuce didn't smile. He only averted his eyes.

That could only mean one thing.

"Oh my God. I'm *married* to that tracer?"

"No! No. Not yet," Deuce rushed to assure her. "I've been reading up on it." He seemed proud of himself for having learned some new cultural witchstory. "For that to happen, the two of you have to complete your bond before the next full moon."

Rapidly, Dayna calculated. That gave them about two weeks.

"And 'complete your bond' means . . . ?" She raised her brows.

Deuce's seductive look made the situation plain. If she got a little down and dirty with T.J., it was as good as pledging her troth to him. Nookie equaled commitment in the witching world.

"I'm engaged then," Dayna concluded. "I'm promised to T.J."

"Well, in witching terms . . ." Deuce shrugged. "Kind of."

This could not be happening. "I think I'm losing my mind."

"No you're not," Deuce said in a soothing tone. "No."

"Yes. Yes, I am," Dayna insisted. Just to be clear, she laid it all out for him. "Two days ago, I was knee-deep in botanical research. I was hanging out with my friend Jill. I was biking to work and taking care of my goldfish. My biggest problem was fending off my credit-stealing piranha of a boss and her toady of an assistant." She inhaled, frowning. "Now I'm going to witchy night school, I'm failing at magic all over again, and you're telling me I'm somehow *bonded* to a know-it-all hard-bodied tracer who's considering chewing off his own arm, coyote style, instead of sticking with me?"

"Umm . . ."

"Don't bother making excuses." Feeling overwhelmed, she

snatched up the kitchen towel hanging nearby. She scrubbed the soapsuds from her arm with unnecessary vigor. "I don't want to put you in an awkward spot. I know he's your partner."

"He's my friend, too," Deuce told her earnestly. "When everyone in the department was hassling me as a new recruit, T.J. stepped up to partner with me. He volunteered."

Dayna groaned. "Great. Now he's a nice guy, too?"

"I wouldn't go that far." With a consoling grin, Deuce moved nearer, then enveloped her in an almost-hug. He patted her on the back. Gruffly. And briefly. For whatever reason, Deuce was clearly gun-shy with witches. "But look on the bright side! From what I read, there are definite perks to being bonded. For one thing, it turns out that you're irresistible to your bonded partner."

He waggled his eyebrows with devilish intimation.

She perked up. "Irresistible?"

"Yeah." Eagerly, the tracer pressed on, apparently sensing that he'd stumbled on a potential game-changer. "And the sex is supposed to be mind blowing, too. The *best* in all the witch-world. Ordinary humans can't even aspire to it. It's legendary."

"Legendary sex." Mulling over the idea, Dayna found that she liked it. Granted, it was a little bizarre to be discussing it with someone like Deuce, but . . . why *shouldn't* there be some magical compensation for all the difficult times she was going through right now? Besides, it wasn't as though she and T.J. hadn't already gotten pretty close during that encounter in her bedroom before they'd left for Covenhaven. "You don't say?"

Appearing wary, Deuce stepped back. He held up both hands in a keep-away gesture. "No. No, I *don't* say. And if you tell T.J. that I told you *any* of this, I'll deny it, straight out."

"Why would I tell him anything?"

"I don't know. But I don't like the look in your eyes."

Dayna gave him a playful nudge. "You can trust me, Deuce."

At that, the tracer's expression hardened. Every evidence of camaraderie vanished. "I trust myself these days. Period."

"Hang on. I'm sorry. I didn't mean to—"

"I'm out of here. Good luck at witch school tomorrow."

With that, Deuce turned his back on her and left the apartment. The door slammed soundly behind him, leaving Dayna with the unmistakable feeling that she'd just kicked a puppy.

A big, menacing puppy with deadly sharp teeth . . . and every intention of using them on the very next witch who wronged him.

Chapter Thirteen

Shortly after sunrise, Dayna jolted awake. With her heart pounding, she lay alert in bed, straining to figure out what had awakened her. She was alone. Her bedroom—Deuce's guest bedroom, decorated with Ikea insta-furniture, a comfortable double bed, and extra pillows—seemed still. Sunlight poked through the blinds in hazy shafts, illuminating her backpack and her zipped-up duffel bag. If she hadn't known better, she'd have sworn they were waiting patiently for her inevitable escape.

Judging by the angle of the sun, it was still early—maybe seven o'clock or so. Or even earlier. Squinting as she tried to gauge the time, Dayna gazed at the blinds covering the glass-paneled door that led to the patio outside her bedroom window.

Something moved outside.

The motion was silhouetted against the blinds. Clutching the coverlet, Dayna stared at it. It moved again in a bobbing shift. Then a side-to-side whoosh. The outline of the thing looked like arms, reaching . . . reaching for the doorknob?

Newly watchful, she sat up in bed. She scanned the room for a potential weapon. *Her backpack!* It still contained her plastic pencil case full of talismans and decoys and weapons.

Keeping her eyes trained on that movement outside, Dayna slipped stealthily from under the coverlet. She dropped to the wood-plank floor and started crawling, hoping to stay out of sight. The hard, cold floor struck her bare palms and pajama-covered knees, making her wince. She kept going.

Whatever was out there scraped against the window again. Jarred by the sound, Dayna halted. Balancing awkwardly on her hands and knees, she looked over her shoulder. The shadow was still visible, but it had quit moving. For now.

Not that she could do the same thing. Desperately, she wished she had enough magic to summon her backpack straight to her, rather than having to crawl to it herself. All it would take would be a simple spell—she grumbled the closest approximation she could think of under her breath—and then . . .

Whoosh. Right on cue, her backpack scuttled to her side.

Astonished, Dayna stared at it. Huh. That might have been the first truly successful spell she'd cast in months.

"Thanks." Cynically, she eyed her backpack. It quivered on the floor beside her like an eager-to-please Labrador retriever waiting for a treat. "Why don't you just unzip yourself and hand over my pencil case while you're at it, smarty-pants?"

The zipper split itself open. Her pencil case shot out.

Truly awestruck now, Dayna gawked. It was true that spells weren't necessarily needed to practice magic. Enchantments, hexes, charms, and the like were only amplifications of magical power. A witch's true magical power came from her brain, with its many connections and extrasensory activity zones. But witchfolk, like everyone else, liked to feel they had a sure thing at the ready, just in case. Over the centuries, the theory and practice of magic had expanded to include several different forms of helping agents—like spoken incantations.

At one time, she knew, all beings had possessed the capacity to use their minds the way witchfolk did. Even humans had possessed the neural pathways and intuition necessary to practice magic. But they'd feared those things. They'd allowed their abilities to erode and had exulted in science instead, until their magical natures had been lost to them forever.

Just like, it had seemed, Dayna's magic had been lost to her. But now . . . maybe things were starting to change.

With no time to waste, she grabbed a fat Magic Marker from her pencil case. Armed and confident with her newly awakened witchy sensibilities, she fisted her marker-weapon, then slowly got to her feet. Doing her best to remain out of sight of whoever—or whatever—was out there, she edged closer to the glass-paneled door. Keeping her gaze fixed on the shadow beyond it, she crouched with her marker at the ready. She held her breath, then used her finger to nudge one of the slats upward.

Through the slice of the outdoors she'd revealed, Dayna glimpsed blue sky, the concrete patio slab that spanned both her bedroom and Deuce's, and the fuchsia bougainvillea that were planted along the patio's edge and on a trellis near her door. One of the trailing bougainvillea vines bobbed gently in the autumn breeze, reaching from the trellis toward the sunshine.

And scraping against her door.

And causing a suspiciously moving shadow.

Ugh. She was an idiot. Sagging with relief, Dayna slumped against the door frame. She leaned her head on the cool wood and closed her eyes. She didn't know who she'd thought would be lurking on her patio, waiting to . . . to what, exactly?

She didn't know. All she knew was that Covenhaven felt *dangerous* to her—now more than ever. She couldn't explain it. Still, as she stood there clutching her Magic Marker, the sense of menace she'd been so sure of a few seconds ago slowly ebbed.

It was a good thing Deuce wasn't here to see this. Or Professor Reynolds. Or Francesca Woodberry and her ultrapopular friends. All through her teenage years, Dayna had yearned to belong to a clique like theirs. She'd yearned to be accepted and admired and *proven,* the way they were. To *not* jump at shadows, but to wield magic like a trueborn witch. She wasn't proud of it, but it was the truth—the truth she'd never admitted to anyone. Now, it seemed, she would never be any of those things.

Unless she got moving and started training.

With a surge of determination, Dayna yanked the pull cord on the blinds. She was ready to greet the day. She was ready to get started. She was ready to take names and kick magical ass.

She was *not* ready to see the IAB tracer, T.J. McAllister, lying outside on one of Deuce's patio lounge chairs, naked as the day he'd been born. But when the blinds zipped upward with a dusty snap, that was exactly what they revealed.

Startled, Dayna took a step backward. Her heartbeat surged all over again. Her breath turned shallow, too. This was wrong. This was weird. This was . . . what *was* the tracer doing out there?

Well. The only way to find out was to examine the situation in greater detail. After all, it was what the researcher in her demanded. Biting her lip, Dayna took another peek.

T.J. appeared to be sleeping. Soundly. And again, nakedly.

Intrigued despite herself, she sucked in a breath. She should not be seeing him this way. Especially when he wasn't even awake to be aware of it. It was intrusive. It was . . .

Irresistible. Insanely curious, Dayna stepped back to the glass-paneled door. Mindlessly, she dropped her Magic Marker weapon and brought both hands to the glass. She splayed her fingers. Her mouth opened as she stole a more thorough look at T.J., just to be sure of what she was seeing.

After all, proper research required verification.

From here, she noted with an attempt at clinical detachment, most of him was visible. His streaky blond hair, angular jawline, and cleft chin. His pouty mouth, even more luscious when it wasn't locked in a frown. His long, muscular torso, his myriad tattoos—she'd glimpsed only a few of them, it seemed, during his capture of her—and his multiple charms and amulets, all strung on cords around his neck. His bare arms and strong biceps, his powerful legs, his curiously vulnerable feet.

Swerving her gaze back to his biceps, Dayna frowned at his tattoos—the same tattoos that, according to Deuce, bound him to her with magical force. Would it really hurt his *soul* if T.J. removed them to end his bond? Would he really do it, if it did?

Probably, she concluded with a dour twist of her lips. T.J. McAllister was nothing if not contrary. But he was also damn *fine*, sprawling on that lounge chair like a sun-kissed lion, too tough to care if anyone saw him and too impervious to normal warlock concerns to bother with so much as a shielding charm. She might not have been able to conjure something like that herself, but she knew they existed. She knew most witchfolk were not so immodest—despite the undeservedly wanton reputations given to them by jealous humans—that they spent most of their time completely nude. Outdoors. Where anyone could see them.

Feeling a little . . . well, *overheated*, Dayna nudged closer to the glass dividing her from T.J. She could practically feel the warmth rising from his skin, could almost inhale the musky, manly scent she imagined emanated from him. And okay, so he wasn't *really* out there bare-assed for the whole world to see. The border of bougainvillea shielded the patio from passersby.

In fact, it created a nicely private area. An intimate zone where almost anything could happen. Anything at all. *Anything*.

But still . . . did he do this *often*? she wondered. And what did Deuce think when he looked outside his patio door and spotted his IAB partner in the nude on his lounge chair?

Dayna didn't care. Deuce was gone. She was here. And if what Deuce had told her was right, she was irresistible, too.

Contemplatively, she let her gaze rove over T.J. again. She got stuck on his beautifully wide shoulders, then made herself move on to his burly chest. Like the rest of him, it was nicked by scars. She wondered about them. She wondered about *him*, then moved her attention lower. Much lower. Naughtily lower.

Disappointed, Dayna let loose an obscenity under her breath. If only T.J. hadn't brought out that stupid blanket with him! So what if the desert nights got cool in autumn? If not for that blanket's cottony weave, she'd have been able to take the true measure of the man . . . warlock . . . Patayan. As it was, that blanket shielded his groin, revealing only an intriguing glimpse of finely honed abs and the indented hollow above his hipbone.

Mmmm. Her imagination filled in the rest, supplying her with an arresting image of T.J.'s . . . assets. If it was true what they said about warlocks, they were probably considerable. It had been a long time since Dayna had experienced a witchy union.

Probably too long, she decided just then. And if she was going to change that statistic, she had some preparation to do.

Leaving the blinds as they were, Dayna grabbed the towel she'd dropped before putting on her pajama pants last night, then headed for the shower to make herself *truly* irresistible.

On the patio, T.J. opened his eyes. He groaned, then reflexively reached under his blanket and grabbed his cock. It surged upward to meet his palm, huge and hard and ready.

What the hell had he been dreaming? This went beyond the usual morning hard-on. He hadn't felt this urgent since . . .

Since meeting up with his bonded witch in her human world.

Muttering a swearword, he released himself with a final inadvertent stroke that made him shudder. Jesus. He'd hoped a dose of sunshine would heal his battered spirit, the way it always did for Patayan. He'd definitely needed something restorative after last night—and after the past few days. But this went beyond restorative . . . all the way to pornographic.

It was a good thing he knew Deuce had already gone. His partner had spied him on the patio and thrown him a blanket at some point early this morning, cursing T.J.'s "exhibitionist fetish" in no uncertain terms. But since Deuce was accustomed to T.J.'s occasional midnight visits, he'd left without further comment to continue his volunteer mission: shadowing Lily Abbot.

Along with Francesca Woodberry and Sumner Jacobs, Lily was one of the cusping witches who might be his magus's prophesized *juweel*. And even though finding the *juweel* was a Patayan duty and not an IAB one, Deuce had still agreed to help T.J. during his off hours. T.J. had filled in Deuce about everything he knew—everything his magus had told him.

It still wasn't enough, but it was all they had.

Knowing that was all the more reason to get on with his mission, T.J. threw off his blanket and stood. His muscles ached with reminders of yesterday's encounter with Garmin's foragers. His chest hurt, too, making it plain that the loss of trust he'd suffered was not without lasting consequences.

Last night, that pain had lingered long after he'd visited the res, checked up on the dead gardener's family, then slipped past Deuce's neighbors and taken refuge here. He had a feeling it would be with him for a while.

Unless he could repair it. Unless he could heal that damage and emerge stronger than before.

He'd hoped sunbathing would be enough. Judging by his lingering pain, it wouldn't be. At least not soon. Stymied by that realization, T.J. frowned. He needed to be strong enough to complete his promises to his magus. He needed to be tough enough to find the *juweel* and enlist her help. He needed . . .

He needed connectedness.

Swearing, T.J. resisted. The truth was, all witchfolk needed connectedness. In that regard, they stood in stark contrast to independence-prizing humans. Usually T.J. denied himself that necessary union with other witchfolk. Today, he couldn't afford the luxury of solitude. Not when he'd already been wounded by his break with Leo Garmin and his lost alliance with the IAB.

Considering the problem, T.J. stretched. Then, with interest, he spied the upraised blinds on the glass-paneled door leading to Deuce's guest room. Beyond it, a duffel bag and the outside edge of a rumpled bed were clearly visible.

Most likely, Deuce's human sister was in town to visit him again. The last time Avery had come to Covenhaven, she and T.J. had struck up a flirtation that he—as a warlock—hadn't been able to avoid, and she—as a human—hadn't been able to resist. If not for Deuce's staunch insistence that T.J. "lay off with the warlock routine," things might have gone further between them.

It wasn't as though Avery wasn't willing. She was. Ever since learning about Deuce's turning—and being sworn to secrecy about it—she'd been fascinated with witchfolk . . . with the magical world and all its inhabitants.

T.J. knew she was curious about warlocks. Especially about him. And with Deuce gone from the apartment—and T.J. in need of the connection and healing he craved—maybe it was time to satisfy that curiosity of hers, once and for all. A connection with a human wasn't as powerful as a witchfolk connection. But that couldn't be helped now. It would be better than nothing.

And all right, so using Deuce's sister to forge the healing connection that T.J. needed wasn't exactly honorable. Right now, he didn't care. The Patayan part of him craved a warm touch. And warlocks had earned their bad reputations honestly. *His* bad reputation included—especially after his suspension from the IAB last night. It wasn't as though Avery wouldn't enjoy their encounter . . . thoroughly and completely. He'd make sure of it.

Decisively, T.J. opened the door.

At once, a sensation of yearning swept over him. His heart, still weakened, ached with it. Confused, he stopped in the open doorway. The breeze played over his bare skin. His feet lodged on the threshold. His scarred fingers clenched the door frame as he considered the new pain in his chest. It felt different from the pain he'd experienced after Garmin's disloyalty last night.

It felt . . . bittersweet.

Dismissing it with a frown, T.J. moved forward. Avery wasn't in the bed, as he'd hoped, but he could hear the shower running in the bathroom. With easy warlock devilishness, he pictured her, wet and curvaceous beneath the shower's spray, her arms outstretched in an invitation to join her.

His brain offered up an image of Dayna Sterling in that pose instead, identically welcoming . . . and identically naked.

That sense of yearning increased. He almost shook with it.

Swearing, T.J. moved on. He had to focus. The room was dim and quiet, its atmosphere hushed with secrecy. Expectation. Desire. Reasoning that those emotions were moving from him to Deuce's sister in anticipation of their meeting, T.J. edged past the bureau. He stepped on something hard and tubular.

A Magic Marker. A short distance from it lay a plastic pencil case. More markers. Spilled crayons. And a backpack.

Too late, T.J. realized who had slept in this room.

And why he'd kept picturing Dayna, eager and ready for him.

Fuck. He was going to pound Deuce for this. When he'd asked him to keep an eye on Dayna for him, he'd meant from a safe distance. Not from a few feet away, near the sunny patio where T.J. routinely slept. What had Deuce been thinking? With T.J. and his bonded witch in close proximity like this, it was only a matter of time before one of them yielded to the power of their bond.

The shower shut off, stealing his attention. Holding his breath, T.J. listened. Water sluiced over the tiles. The tub drained with a guttural swirl. Bare feet squeaked against the rubberized petals Deuce had glued in for safety. More than anything else, realization of that mundane detail brought T.J. to full awareness of what was happening.

He was standing just a few feet away from his seductive bonded witch. She was naked. So was he. They could be joined within moments, hot and sweaty and needful and complete.

Complete. Just like they were destined to be.

Groaning with raw need, T.J. fisted his hands. His birthright mark glowed, warming as rapidly as his cock. Another wave of yearning swept over him, this time coupled with a vague sweetness that felt completely foreign. And unwanted. He'd be damned if he'd be sweet. He'd be damned if he would *need* this way. He refused now, just like he'd refused three days ago.

But the thought of Dayna standing there, rubbing beads of water from her bare skin, inch by succulent inch, made him feel nothing but need. He closed his eyes to shut it out. That only made the image more vivid. He could almost feel the yielding softness of her skin against his mouth, could hear the breathy gasp she would make when his hands slid over her hips.

He thought of her calling his name—his true name, the one no one knew except his parents, Deuce, and his magus. He wanted that. He thought of her smiling at him. He wanted that, too. He thought of her seeing him—light and dark, warlock and Patayan—and staying with him anyway. He wanted that most of all.

At the intensity of his craving, his knees buckled.

What the fu—? Wide-eyed, T.J. righted himself with a hasty warlock spell. He had to get out of here.

He started to move, heading for the glass-paneled patio door he'd entered the bedroom through. It wasn't until he'd made it halfway there that he realized he'd already broken the IAB's suspension. He'd already practiced unlicensed magic with the spell he'd used to keep himself upright. The dam he'd constructed between his old self and his agent self had broken at last . . . and he had no idea if he could rebuild it.

Just when T.J. stood on the brink of a future he could no longer be sure of, Dayna rounded the corner and saw him.

Chapter Fourteen

The tracer looked even better, Dayna decided with a shiver of anticipation, when he was awake.

Even though he was standing motionless, obviously caught unaware by her appearance in the hallway, T.J. still emanated a certain sense of power. Authority. Unmistakable vigor. Every cell in his warlock-Patayan body seemed to pulse with vitality, ready to meet any challenge, defeat any enemy . . . or simply sweep a curious runaway witch off her feet.

Intrigued by the notion, Dayna stepped nearer. T.J.'s eyes widened, his gaze dark and magnetic beneath his furrowed brows.

Helplessly, she smiled. At the sight of him, her heart simply . . . opened a little wider. She couldn't explain it. The plain truth was, she loved everything about him. She loved his tousled hair, his agile fingers, his crookedly worn amulets on their leather strings. She loved his cleft chin. She loved his full lips, his magnificent arched cheekbones, his acres of golden, sun-kissed skin. She wanted to be closer to all of them.

She *needed* to be closer to all of them.

"I was hoping to surprise you," she said. "And yet, before I could, here you are. I guess I'll have to amend my plans."

My plans to seduce you . . . exactly the way a bonded witch should. She didn't know how she knew that; she just did. She knew it the same way she knew T.J. could read her plans in her eyes, in her expression, in her parted lips. Dayna had never felt witchier than she did in that moment. She'd never felt more seductive either. She knew T.J. could tell that, too.

"No. I was just—" He hooked his thumb toward the patio. *Leaving* hung in the air between them. *I was just leaving.*

"You've got a way of turning up unexpectedly." The gap between them diminished with every footstep Dayna took. Feeling herself quiver with expectancy, she adjusted her damp towel and then kept going. "I didn't like that at first. But today—"

"I was just leaving," T.J. said with more force.

His deepening frown should have lent credibility to his threat. And yet he only stood there, like a classical statue come to life, not moving one way or the other. Dayna dropped her gaze from his face to his torso. This close, his muscles seemed even more defined, compacted with strength and hard use. A primal need gripped her—a need to touch him that felt so strong, she could scarcely keep talking. Somehow, she did.

"Today I do like that. Later we can talk about why you were camped out there, outside my bedroom." Privately, she thought it was because T.J. was still assigned to her. He'd shadowed her to class last night, then he'd followed her home. It was obvious. "But right now, I'd rather test a theory I have."

His gaze narrowed. His posture hardened. His shoulders turned partly away from her in a forbidding stance. "I don't care about your theories. I'm leaving."

She smiled. "So you keep saying. Yet you're still here."

It was because he wanted her. Dayna knew it as plainly as she knew she wanted him. She could feel the emotions rippling from him to her, the same way she had in the shower a few minutes ago. The same way she had on the day they'd met.

Desire. Need. Curiosity and . . . resistance?

That wouldn't do. Not when her own body felt hotter

already with the need to join with him. Not when her heart-beat raced and her breath caught in her throat. Not when the core of her—so recently beaten down by failures and mistakes, with more of the same to come for sure—desperately needed to feel whole.

Needed to feel wanted and strengthened and warm.

T.J. could give her that, Dayna knew. Somehow she knew. But she might have to take it from him. She was prepared to do that. Especially now, when she felt infused with magical allure.

Maybe there *were* perks, she decided, to being a witch.

"You're not leaving." She stopped at arm's length from T.J. He smelled delicious. The combination of fresh air, sunshine, and magical practice had imbued his skin with an intoxicating aura. It was indescribably appealing. "Not until I say so."

T.J. raised his arm. Upon his command, the shafts of sunshine she'd noticed earlier swept across the room. They fell in her path like bars on a prison cell, either keeping her out . . . or keeping the tracer in. She couldn't tell which.

Magically, transparently, they prevented her from coming closer. And this time, fear was the emotion she sensed from him.

It seemed impossible. T.J. McAllister was practiced, commanding, and gifted with a presence that most magical males would have killed for. His body was chiseled, his demeanor calm, his appeal unavoidable. Why was he keeping himself from her?

Impulsively, Dayna swept her arm sideways.

The barrier of sunshine fell away.

Astonished, she could only stand there for an instant. Dropping that barrier hadn't required a charm or an incantation. She hadn't had to conjure a familiar or call upon some obscure spell. All she'd had to do was think of what she wanted and it had happened. Just the way it did for trueborn legacy witches.

"You shouldn't seem so amazed. You're a witch, first and

last." T.J. gazed at her, unabashed in his nudity. "Practicing magic is your birthright. It's what you were born to do."

He was wrong; last night had demonstrated, all over again, how little magical ability she really had. Publicly. It was plain to Dayna that she was still stuck between worlds—not human, but not a practicing witch either. It was equally plain that the tracer hadn't had to ease her feelings about that.

He still had. His kindness meant a lot to her.

"Thank you for saying that."

His frown eased a fraction. "I believe it."

"Thank you for that, too."

A shared amity rose between them, subtle and new, fueled by his unexpected generosity and by her welcoming of it. It shifted all of Dayna's perceptions. Suddenly, what she was about to do felt even more momentous. What had begun as a lark—as a treat to herself after two long, tough days of witch-world reentry—became something much deeper. Something fated and real.

"Do you feel that?" she asked him. "Between us?"

With his jaw clenched, T.J. shook his head. It was obvious he was fighting . . . something. "No. I don't feel a thing."

"Liar," she teased, coming a few steps closer.

"Stop." T.J.'s voice sounded hoarse, rough with a dark warning that matched his battle-scarred body. "I'm not leaving. I . . . can't. So you should. Go right now, before it's too late."

"Nope." Dayna stepped nearer. "I'm not leaving either."

Why should she? This was inevitable between them. The proof of it was in the way she felt, in the way he looked, in the way the tracer's body heat pulled her even closer. Enveloped by it, she gazed up, beginning at his chest and moving in a slow arc to his face. His breath feathered across her forehead, as soft and gentle as a caress. She felt blessed by it, crazy as it seemed.

"This is a bad idea." He closed his eyes. "I need—"

"You need *me*," Dayna said, and brought her mouth to his.

Their breath mingled, intimately. Their lips touched, provocatively. Before she could think of a single coherent thought, all her thoughts fled. The whole world shifted. Dizzy and needful, Dayna grabbed T.J.'s shoulders and held on tightly.

She needed this. She needed him. Now. *Now.* Acting on that need, Dayna nudged her tongue at the seam of his mouth, urging him to open to her—to open to what *had* to happen between them.

Instead, T.J. ended their kiss. Filled with dismay, Dayna cried out as he reared back, his expression somber.

A sense of warning rolled from him like waves, coupled with the merest inkling of release. She knew he would give in to her soon. His resolve was crumbling, inch by tight-fisted inch.

"Now." His face, beautiful and rugged, hovered above hers. "Go now. I didn't know it was you. Otherwise, I never would have come in here. I never would have started—"

"Go?" Dayna couldn't help laughing. "Not on your life."

"On yours," T.J. said seriously. "Go on yours. Leave now."

"Hmmm. That's some kind of sweet talk you've got there." She brought her hand to his head, touched his spun-silk witchfolk hair, and nearly purred with eagerness. "I'm beginning to think you warlocks are overrated in the romance department."

"Are you *taunting* a warlock?" He jerked his head, ending her caress. He frowned. "Don't ever taunt a warlock."

"How about a Patayan guardian? Can I taunt him?"

"Not advised."

"Oh? Your body tells me differently." Coyly, Dayna swiveled her hips against him. They could both feel him, rising hard and ready against her towel-covered hip. "I think you like it."

"Oh yeah?" He growled. "I'll tell you what I like."

As proof, T.J. lowered his head. On another harsh indrawn

breath, he brought his mouth to hers. His raw need bordered on roughness, thrilling her with its intensity. Yes. *Yes.*

"I like your mouth, opening to me. Give me more."

She did. His beard stubble scraped across her cheek. Dayna didn't care. Because an instant later, his tongue swept against hers, soft and erotic and unbelievably skilled.

"I like your eyes, watching me. Watch me now."

He flattened his palm against her back, arching her spine. Eagerly, Dayna bowed herself upward in his arms. She watched, transfixed, as T.J. brought his mouth to the modest cleavage above her wrapped towel. With his gaze fixed on hers, he kissed her there. Softly, then with heated intent. Ripples of goose bumps rose on her skin, following his mouth like a wave.

"I like your breath, catching in your throat as you feel me against you. Feel this. *All* of this."

With a purposeful move, T.J. brought his pelvis against hers. The fullness of him crowded the apex of her thighs, making Dayna catch her breath exactly as instructed. Barely shielded by her bath towel, her body pulsed against the tracer's in an insistent hidden heartbeat that demanded more. More more more.

"I like your voice, telling me what you want. Tell me now."

"I want you." Moaning, she flexed her thighs. The movement only made her more aware of how hot she felt. How wet, how ready, how close to the edge. "I want *you*. Please. Now. I—"

"More." Arching his brow with a confidence she knew was wholly deserved, the tracer slid his thumb across her cleavage. With full absorption, T.J. studied her chest as she panted for breath. "Tell me more. I want everything."

"*I* want everything. You. Me. Now—"

"Soon."

He sealed his promise with a kiss—a greedy, openmouthed kiss that made Dayna sway in his arms. She moaned, desperate for more of him. She couldn't get close enough, couldn't taste enough, couldn't touch enough. If she could have, she would have climbed his body, absorbed him into her, merged with him, skin to skin. Instead she squeezed his shoulders, feeling his sleek muscles bunch beneath her palms. She panted and rose on tiptoes. Higher. Higher. The only thing that mattered was having more of them, together, exactly as they were meant to be.

But T.J. wasn't going to dictate all the terms.

"Not 'soon,'" Dayna said. *"Now."* With a power she hadn't known she possessed, she focused, then nodded at the tracer.

At her command, he rose from the floor, lifted by the force of her desires. For an instant, he lingered there in midair with an expression of utter surprise on his face. Probably, Dayna knew, her expression matched his. She could scarcely believe her magic worked so well—especially on a powerful warlock like him.

Then he fell backward on the unmade bed, and she quit wondering about her magic and its vagaries altogether. T.J. was just too distracting. And now she had him—almost— where she wanted him. In her bed. Waiting for her. Against the whiteness of the sheets, his skin looked twice as sun kissed, his muscular body a long, lean lure that only she could take advantage of.

"Yum. That's more like it," she told him.

A new sense of alarm rushed from him to her. It was combined, this time, with an even stronger anticipation. In evident denial of it, the tracer pushed up on his elbows. He frowned, clearly intending to get to his feet again.

Dayna shook her head. "You're not the only one who finds something to like around here. Let me tell you *my* favorites."

"No. You don't know what you're doing. We can't—"

She leaned over and silenced him with a kiss. She meant it to be authoritative, wanted it to be *hers*, with exactly as much control as T.J. had shown her. But when her mouth touched his again, all her plans scattered. All she could do was savor the slow glide of their lips, their tongues, their mouths. With a sound that was almost pain-filled, T.J. grabbed her shoulders.

He broke off their contact. His face seemed stippled with beard stubble, coarser and longer than just a few seconds ago. It reminded her of the instant shadow beard that had appeared on his face in Deuce's car on the day they'd met. Dayna didn't know what that meant, but she didn't have time to wonder. She felt mesmerized as his dark-eyed gaze bored into hers, filled with regret and longing . . . and something with a harder edge to it.

She didn't want to know what that was.

Before he could speak, Dayna did. Stubbornly and softly, she said, "I like your voice. I like the way it goes all rough when you talk . . . but only when you're talking to me."

"Dayna—"

"Yes." She smiled in approval. "Exactly like that, husky and sweet. I like it. I like your strength. I like the way you want to protect me with it . . . whether I need you to or not."

"Oh." A telling smile quirked his mouth. "You need me to."

She inhaled, barely begun and definitely not finished. "I like your eyes. I like the way you look at me. I know you can't believe I'm really here with you . . . but you're so happy I am."

T.J. snorted. "Me? Happy? No one would believe that."

"But I do. And I'm right." Feeling an inexpressible tenderness toward him, Dayna smiled. The tracer looked away, directing his gaze deliberately toward the empty bedroom, but she wasn't fooled. She *felt* the need in him. It matched her own.

With steady fingers, she untucked the trailing end of her bath towel. Like the most teasing of burlesque dancers, Dayna toyed with that corner of terry cloth. "Look at me now, T.J."

He turned his head in silent refusal, his jaw tight.

Then, grudgingly, he brought his gaze around to her.

Triumphantly, Dayna dropped her towel. It fell to her feet

in a clump of cotton, baring her skin to the cool air. Her nipples puckered at the exposure; her thighs quivered.

At his first look, T.J. groaned aloud. His fingers clenched the sheets. The sound of rent fabric drew Dayna's attention.

Beneath his hands, the sheet came away in tatters. The tracer stared at his fingers, bewilderment plain on his face.

Clearly, he was not used to his self-control failing.

"Get used to it," Dayna told him with a wicked, witchy smile. "This is only the beginning between us."

Then she raised her hand, sent him straight onto his back with her newfound magical abilities, and made her next move.

T.J. was still wondering how the hell he had flopped onto his back when Dayna straddled him. She flattened her palms on his chest, found his erratic heartbeat, then climbed on the mattress . . . and buried him inside her with one swift stroke.

Hot. Slick. Tight. *Yes.* Filled with disbelief, T.J. gave a single hoarse yell. His whole body bucked upward in utter need. This time, no sheets were at hand. Empty fists were all he had.

Gripped with pleasure, he gazed at Dayna. She straddled him with grace and insistence, smooth-skinned and proudly bare. Her hips flared, begging his touch. Her breasts jutted outward, swaying with her movements. She was beautiful and wild, raw and urgent, pure and tough. She was everything. She was *his*.

He had to slow down. He knew it. But his bonded witch's next low moan made that almost impossible. Naked and eager, Dayna swiveled her hips in a move that almost made him lose his mind. Her thrusts were hard and deliberate. Seeming lost to everything but their point of connection, Dayna rode him with seductive strength. Her thighs flexed with feminine power as she rose . . . rose . . . slipped almost tantalizingly away . . . then plunged downward again, sending them both into spasms of ecstasy.

Shuddering, T.J. grabbed her hips. "Wait." Breathlessly, he peered up at her. "Wait. There's more to this. There's more."

"*More.* Yes. Ah." With her hair tossing around her head, Dayna nodded. She clutched his chest, her fingers tangled in his Patayan amulets. She closed her eyes and slid more slowly, torturing them both with exquisite friction. Up. Down. More. "Oh my God. You're . . . so . . ." She broke off, panting. "Mmmm. *Yes.*"

Mindlessly, T.J. reared up to meet her. He cradled her with his arms. His fingers closed on her hips. Determined to meet her equally, he held her in place and met her thrusts with savage movements of his own. Harder. Harder. The air filled with their cries; the mattress rocked beneath them, driven to its edge of stability by their coming together. Yes. *Yes.* He'd never felt anything so good. So right. So necessary, in all his life.

Shaken by his need to claim his bonded witch, to mark Dayna as his, to please her, T.J. almost didn't notice the affection that welled inside him. But his fevered thrusts brought more than pleasure; they brought a true union. There was no denying it. Even as he savored the seductive glide of their bodies, even as he lifted Dayna with a warlock strength he scarcely used—all the better to satisfy *her*—he felt his heart opening.

No. Not that. Frantic and divided, he rolled them both over on the bed. He needed control. He needed *this*, needed her, but if that meant being vulnerable . . . In defiance of the very concept, T.J. growled, then levered himself above Dayna. She was more than willing to meet him there. Her smile looked warmhearted and wicked, both at once. Her face looked beautiful, framed by wild dark hair and illuminated with . . . caring?

Fuck. Closing his eyes, T.J. took her again. He surged inside her blindly, his whole being enveloped by her heat, her slickness, her softness. His Patayan amulets jangled; he looked down to see them jouncing on Dayna's breasts, another point of connection in a world turned incomprehensible with desire.

Against his will, he liked that. He liked that the two of them fit so well together. Improbably, even his Patayan symbols of manliness and courage and truth sought her out.

Groaning with an urge to resist any more wayward thoughts like those sappy ones, T.J. brought his mouth to hers again.

He could stifle this yearning. He would. Soon. But first . . .

Ah. Dayna's mouth stretched wide beneath his, welcoming him in every way. Her tongue played with his. Her hips collided with his in a timeless rhythm. Her breath fluttered over him. She was pulling him, draining him, driving him closer to the edge—closer to a place where it would be impossible to be alone.

Filled with unease at the depth of their connection, T.J. froze. But his inaction seemed only to push Dayna forward. Her thighs trembled against his, straining as she kept thrusting. Her hips pounded against him. Grinding, moaning, she clutched at his back. With her eyes wide, she stilled. "Oh, *yes*. Ah!"

Her body pulsed around him. The sensation was exquisite. Blindsided by it, T.J. felt himself tilt toward the inevitable.

Gripped by a force he couldn't resist, he plunged harder, deeper. Dayna moaned and urged him onward, but T.J. was lost to everything except reaching that peak of sensation. He moved faster. Faster. Not caring, he told himself fiercely, about anything except finding release, he pinned his bonded witch to the bed with his hands and rammed himself fully inside her.

Still meeting him in every way, Dayna urged him on. With breathy cries, she begged him not to stop. T.J. didn't. His reward was a brilliant smile from his bonded witch. It arrested his attention in a way nothing else could have. His heart softened all the way in that moment, making his desire complete.

An instant later, everything went hazy. Locked in violent pleasure, T.J. tipped over the edge. He couldn't think. He could only feel as his muscles seized, clenching with spasmodic release. He shouted in hoarse approval. Yes. Yes, *yes*.

For a moment he slumped, his face buried in Dayna's neck. She smelled sweet. She felt soft and warm and misted with sweat. Despite all his resolve not to allow it, T.J. felt a smile steal across his face. His chest heaved with his indrawn breath.

His heart pounded with an intensity that wouldn't have been sustainable for anyone but a Patayan. Thrilled with everyone and everything—especially with Dayna—T.J. sighed with contentment.

Beneath him, Dayna sighed, too. She trailed her hand over his shoulder blade, then moved downward in a leisurely path.

She squeezed his ass. Her witchy laughter applauded them both. She began another slow stroke upward to his shoulder, clearly determined to savor the connectedness between them.

Lulled by her touch, sensitized by her nearness, T.J. shivered. He loved this. Loved *her*. Feeling on the verge of another smile, he lifted his head and pressed his mouth to hers. This kiss was gentle, tender . . . everything their other kisses hadn't been. Roused by it, T.J. kissed her again. And again.

He cupped her face in his hand, examined her for a long while, and found her irredeemably perfect. He kissed her again.

Her answering smile was everything he needed.

His chest felt good. His heart felt full. His body felt rejuvenated, as though he'd lain beneath a thousand suns.

As though sensing that, Dayna stretched in his arms. Her nipples dragged across his chest, inciting a new round of dangerous thoughts. Lazily, she traced her fingers over the birthright mark on his biceps . . . then she glanced at her arm with apparent surprise. Her gaze focused on her golden armlet.

"Hey." Her voice sounded sleepy, drunk with pleasure. "Your tattoo is glowing. And so is my armband." She touched them both, her pretty face scrunched with thought. "They feel hot, too."

Growing instantly still, T.J. stared at the items that bonded him with his inadvertently chosen witch. He realized what had happened immediately. No wonder his chest felt better, his body stronger, his mind more aware. No wonder his heart felt overflowing with goodness and light.

He'd never had time for that bullshit before.

"Hell." Disgusted by his own susceptibility, T.J. frowned at Dayna. Her mystified expression met his, then grew sharper with growing comprehension. "We've completed our bond."

With another, harsher swearword, he got out of bed. Then he stalked away before things could get worse . . . or he could weaken even further and lose himself in Dayna all over again.

If he did that, there'd be no hope left for him at all.

Chapter Fifteen

Okay. So T.J. wasn't exactly the pillow-talk type.

She could deal with that, Dayna decided a little more than an hour later as she headed downtown. Because thanks to T.J., she felt so good that nothing could get her down. She felt energized, awake, *invigorated* in a way she'd never experienced. It was as though T.J. had shared more than his body with her—he'd shared his vitality. And it was intoxicating.

Smiling, she bounced down from the trolley that passed for a public transit system in Covenhaven. It rolled away behind her, occupied by two tourists and a few city workers, sporting another banner advertising the Hallow-e'en Festival.

GET A TASTE OF THE OLD WAYS AT THE COVENHAVEN HALLOW-E'EN FESTIVAL! MAGICAL FUN FOR THE WHOLE FAMILY! OCTOBER 31ST AT JANUS RESORT AND SPA.

Hmmm. Looking at that banner with new interest, Dayna thought about what Camille had told her last night. Apparently, the Janus Resort and Spa was Francesca Woodberry's baby—she was owner and proprietress. Her two best friends since high school, Lily Abbot and Sumner Jacobs, both worked with her—Lily as a pastry chef and Sumner as the manager of the Janus gift shop.

It figured. Privileged Francesca was still at the center of

everything in town—including the biggest event of them all, the Hallow-e'en Festival—and her chosen friends still had it made.

Being selected by Francesca—and treated to the benefits of her extrapowerful magic—definitely had its rewards. Snooty Lily had looked broomstick thin last night, showing no signs of indulging in the supercaloric enchanted desserts she created. And spoiled Sumner was curvaceous and drop-dead sexy in a way that Dayna—with her athletic build and nonmagically augmented hair and face—could never hope to be. Sumner had been the mean witch who'd sneered at Dayna's human-made Moleskine notebook in class last night, too . . . although given the kinds of useless baubles and artsy Covenhaven souvenirs that Sumner probably stocked for the wealthy tourists in Janus's gift shop, Dayna seriously doubted she had room to diss her taste in accessories.

Not that anyone would dare say so. Judging by the way all the other cusping witches had fawned over Francesca and her cohorts last night, she had grown up to become queen bee of all of Covenhaven, ruling from her ultrachic roost at Janus. Lily and Sumner were still her chosen court. And no one else mattered unless anointed by Francesca. It was just like high school all over again, with Dayna playing the part of the outsider witch who could never fit in . . . and everyone else standing on the periphery, waiting to conjure memory flickers of her failures.

But today she had a plan to change all that. She still wanted to learn to control her magic well enough to go home again, of course. That was essential. But she also meant to compete for the prize of Professor Reynolds's *juweel* on graduation day, and she wanted to redeem herself in the eyes of her cusping-witch classmates, too. After her public humiliation last night, that felt more important than ever. With her new plan in mind, Dayna looked around, trying to get her bearings.

Here on the southern end of Main Street, the faux-authentic

Southwestern ambiance that was so prevalent in the tourist zone eased. The buildings here were made of real adobe with red-tiled roofs. The sidewalks were paved with redbrick and lined with indigenous Palo Verde trees. In the distance, the red-rock mountains pierced the skyline, leaving no doubt of the town's scenic appeal. It was idyllic, in an autumnal sort of way.

And for once, despite the realization that her high school rivals had grown up to rule the town, Dayna almost felt a part of it all. All thanks to T.J. and his invigorating . . . presence.

Feeling giddy with remembrance of the way he'd looked at her after they'd come together, she smiled. Yes, her assigned tracer looked tough. Yes, he made her senses clamor with a mixture of alarm and eagerness whenever he was near. Yes, he seemed as though he would rather shave with barbed wire than actually *say* something sappy to her. But the truth of his feelings was in his eyes and in his touch. It was in the way he said her name. It was the way they fit together. Perfectly.

T.J. McAllister was not romantic. But for now he was *hers*. And that mattered more than hearts and flowers and pillow talk.

Catching sight of her destination, Dayna headed toward a distant adobe building. Constructed in traditional Southwestern style, it contained two arched sections, each connected by an open-air zaguan that allowed natural breezes to cool the interior. As she reached it, the flowers blooming in the beds alongside the entryway sent up their rich fragrances.

Happily, Dayna breathed deeply. She'd never seen any place with as much abundant landscaping as Covenhaven. Plants and flowers of all descriptions flourished here. Obviously, the mild weather had something to do with that. But so did the talented gardeners—one of whom tipped his wide-brimmed sun hat at her as she skipped up the steps. His handsome features and burnished skin reminded her of T.J. . . . and made her smile all over again.

"Nice work on the flowers!" She waved as she opened the building's antique arched door. "They're really beautiful."

The gardener smiled and waved at her, then went back to work. An instant later, Dayna stepped into the cool darkness of the Covenhaven Public Library. The dusty, tangy smell of ancient papers and books struck her; so did a familiar sense of peacefulness. She inhaled, savoring it . . . and remembering.

She'd spent countless hours here in the town's tiny library. This place had helped foster her love of reading and discovery. Ultimately, the time she'd spent here had led her to her job at Dynamic Research Library. More importantly, being here had helped her discover her best skill—organizing data.

In the magical world, organizational ability was an afterthought. No one needed human-style systems to remember things; they could conjure up memory flickers. No one needed individual books to show the way; they could consult EnchantNet, which had existed in various—and hidden—forms for centuries.

But Dayna, lacking in natural witchy talent and anxious to fit in, had needed more than EnchantNet's wiki-like communal knowledge. She'd needed to know things that other witches hadn't. Like proper spell-repair techniques. Methods for tracking runaway familiars. And strategies for escaping to the world beyond Covenhaven . . . and existing there without being outed as a witch or persecuted for magic she couldn't even practice properly.

Quite accidentally, Dayna had found more than answers in the town's overlooked public library stacks. She'd found a natural gift for sorting through information and categorizing it, for streamlining systems and crosschecking data. She'd found *herself*. And then she'd taken herself someplace where she fit better.

In the human world, her attention to detail was seen as a skill . . . not a compensation for magical failures. Her hunger to know more was viewed as admirable curiosity . . . not a second-rate substitute for natural magical talent. So while it was true that Dayna was still an outsider in her human life, at least there she was an outsider by choice. That made all the difference.

And that was why she intended to return there. Just as soon as she completed her cusping-witch training and got her magic under control. And maybe . . . okay, *definitely* . . . after she used her burgeoning magic skills to nail down some grade-A warlock while she was in town. Especially now that she knew exactly how enthralling being bonded with someone like T.J. could be.

It was a witch's right to go after the partner she wanted, after all. Witchfolk were different from humans in that regard. When it came to courtship, witches ran the show. Warlocks were only along for the ride, hoping to be chosen. That was why they'd developed such dangerous skills of seduction over the ages. Warlocks needed those abilities to get as much witchy action as they could before warlock sloping took hold.

When she'd come to Phoenix, it had taken Dayna time to adjust to human dating rituals. She'd scared off more than one partner by being too aggressive. But T.J. had met her on equal terms, she remembered with a tingle. He had countered every move she made with an aggressive one of his own. His intensity had driven her crazy. Straddling him had almost sent her over the top immediately. If not for the way he'd suddenly flipped her over and taken a dominant position, she would have—inevitably—come right away. It was the witchy way. As it was, the switch to being subordinate had slowed her down just enough.

Just enough that she'd been able to savor T.J.'s husky groans, adroit hands, and masterful cock. Just enough that she'd felt his heartbeat, tasted his skin. Just enough that she'd felt uncommonly close to him. Just enough that she craved more of him, right now, and felt aggrieved that she didn't know when she would have a chance to sample more. It was definitely true what they said about warlocks' skills in the bedroom, Dayna decided. And once you added some Patayan to the mix . . . *whoa.*

Feeling herself flush, she shook herself from her reverie. She hadn't come here to have a sexy flashback about T.J. She'd come here to tackle the next phase of her cusping-witch training in true Dayna Sterling fashion: by checking out a pile of library books on the subject.

Shouldering her backpack, she headed past the library's seasonal display of carved jack-o'-lanterns, Indian corn, and sheaves of wheat. She passed a rack of colorful brochures for the canyon and other tourist attractions. She skirted a table occupied by an elderly warlock who was surreptitiously watching a memory flicker from behind an open newspaper, then approached the card catalog. It was a relic from her first visits to the library, but it was clearly still in use. Dayna scanned the rows of neatly labeled drawers. She focused on one. *Open.*

Nothing happened. Hmm. Disappointed, Dayna tried again.

The drawer remained stubbornly shut. So much for her revitalized magic. Evidently it was still on the balky side.

Well, that was to be expected. Rome wasn't built in a day. Her magical abilities probably wouldn't be reinvigorated in a day—or three—either, despite her unprecedented successes this morning. She would need to concentrate harder. Or access the information the traditional way.

Deciding efficiency trumped magical acumen, Dayna frowned at her formerly magical backpack. She slung it to the floor.

"Thanks for nothing. And after that showoff move at the apartment this morning, too," she grumbled. "Sliding across the floor. Shooting out my pencil case. Being all magic-y. Admit it. You're just messing with me now, aren't you?"

"I hope you're not expecting an answer."

At the sound of that familiar voice, Dayna turned. "Mom!"

Margo Sterling stood behind her, dressed in the gauzy

tunic, flowy pants, and flat leather sandals that were all the rage among the fashionably bohemian midlife residents of Covenhaven. A squash blossom necklace hung in showy turquoise around her neck. Above that, her face beamed, clean-scrubbed except for its signature embellishment of bright lipstick.

"I was wondering when you'd get around to visiting."

"Well, wonder no further. Here I am!" Filled with a sense of homecoming at last, Dayna hugged her. Her mother felt delicate but strong in her arms, her slender figure shaped by daily yoga practice and probably a few witchy enhancements. "I'm sorry I didn't come to the house sooner. It's been crazy."

"I imagine." After a final tight squeeze, Margo released her. "Your father and I heard about the cusping-witch program. If I'd known all it would take to make you come back to town for a visit was an official IAB ruling and an armed agency tracer to drag you here, I'd have started a petition years ago."

"Very funny." Feeling guilty for having avoided her parents over the past two days, Dayna held her mother at arm's length. She didn't know now why she'd waited. She clasped her mother's hand. Margo's hair was entirely white now, curling around her head in disorderly ringlets. "You look great! I love your hair."

"Oh this?" Her mother tossed her head with a girlish smile. "Just a little magical touchup to make the white sparkle."

"Well, it suits you. I'll bet Dad loves it."

"He does. And your new aura suits you, too." Giving Dayna the kind of knowing look only a mother could, Margo leaned her shoulder against the card catalog. She crossed her arms and raised her brows. "Is there something you want to tell me?"

"Tell you? I don't know what you mean."

Her mother's smile wavered. Her expression lost a fraction of its lightness. Her eyes were still the same bright blue that matched Dayna's, but all of a sudden Margo looked . . . troubled.

"Do you mean about why I'm in town?" Dayna pressed. "You know it's because of the cusping-witch training. We just—"

"Not that. Your aura." Her mother gave her a penetrating look. "Are you seriously going to stand there and deny what I can see with my own eyes? Please, Dayna. I thought we got past the pants-on-fire stage when you were a teenager."

Ha. If her mother only knew how prescient that was.

"Mom—" Hardly knowing what to say, Dayna frowned. "I'm not trying to bluff my way past anything. I seriously don't know anything about my aura." She lifted her arm, trying to see it.

Her mother's gaze swerved to her golden armband. "It's especially strong there. Where did you get that?"

"It's a gift from someone I'm seeing. It's—he's—it's not important." If she mentioned the bonding thing with T.J., her mother might misunderstand its implications. It wasn't as though Dayna meant to *stay* with T.J. forever. But Margo was a trained witchstorical archivist. She would undoubtedly know exactly what it meant to be bonded. Besides, there was still the issue of Dayna's apparent aura to consider. Frowning, she stared at her other arm. Then her torso and legs. They looked unchanged. "Are you saying I have a visible aura? I never have before."

"I know." Now Margo seemed downright spooked. "It's probably nothing. A trick of the light, maybe. I'm sorry I said anything." She gave Dayna a reassuring squeeze. "I just thought that if you had an aura so strong and the magic to emit it, you would *feel* that magic, too. You would see it, like I can."

Right. Because both her parents were perfectly adept at magic. That was why everyone—their friends and relatives—

had been so baffled when they'd spawned a witchy washout like Dayna.

Her mother examined her further. A crease appeared between her brows, stealing attention from her trademark lipstick. Her expression grew even graver. She lowered her hand.

"Mom! You're freaking me out. Stop looking at me that way."

Margo blinked. Her expression eased. "What way?"

"As though I'm some kind of—" *Freak*, her ever-helpful brain supplied. Dayna ignored it. "As though you're worried about me." She offered her mother an unsteady smile, wishing she possessed a fraction of T.J.'s charisma or Deuce's easygoing charm. "I promise, your days of worrying about me are over with."

"Humph. I see." Her mother's gaze swept over her human-made jeans and T-shirt, settled on her Converse sneakers, then lifted. "Then you're happy living with all those humans?"

Here we go. "They're not 'those humans,' Mom. They're my friends. You met Jill. She's wonderful! And my neighbors are—"

"No, we don't need to go there again. I'm happy if you're happy." Her mother gave her a suspicious once-over that didn't exactly jibe with her statement. And her smile looked all weird again, too. There was definitely something going on here. "I've just . . . never seen you with an aura. Especially one like that."

Feeling doubly self-conscious, Dayna turned around. She felt ridiculous the moment she did it. Did she seriously think she could catch her aura unaware by sneaking up on it?

But still . . . "What does it look like?"

Her mother gave her a long look. "Oh, Dayna. I don't . . ."

She trailed off, then offered a compensatory smile. But her sorrowful tone said it all. *I don't think you should hope again.*

"I don't think we should put ourselves through all that again, do you?" Margo asked brightly. "Maybe your IAB training has sparked something. Something *temporary*. I wouldn't put too much stock in it. You can never tell with cusping."

"Professor Reynolds says cusping *can* be unpredictable."

"Especially in a group like yours. Did you know this is the largest generation of cusping witches *ever*? Over a thousand strong. No wonder the IAB had to step in and help."

"Yes, they're very efficient." Struggling not to show how much it hurt that she had—once again—disappointed her mother with her lack of magical acumen, Dayna seized on the change of topic. "So . . . How was your cusping, Mom?"

"Crazy. Are you kidding me? Your father barely survived. The moods, the magical seductions, the nonstop sex. You know, we broke so much furniture, we had to start doing it on the floor."

"Mom!"

"His back got thrown completely out of whack. I didn't even have the magic to fix it. My own coven advisor couldn't help either. Eventually we wound up going to a Patayan magus—"

"I don't want to hear this."

"—who gave us a healing potion that worked wonders." Lost in a daydream, Margo smiled fondly. "Of course, it was a topical potion. And your father couldn't reach his own back, you see. So I had to rub it on. And wouldn't you know it? One thing typically led to another, and we'd find ourselves on the floor again." Her eyes sparkled. "I loved my cusping years."

"Thanks. But a play-by-play of your love life with Dad isn't quite what I had in mind." Dayna leaned nearer. "What about your cusping magic? Did it ever . . . malfunction?"

"Did yours?"

"I asked you first."

"What exactly has been happening to you?" Margo narrowed her eyes, making Dayna remember where she'd learned a few of her prized analytical skills. It was because of Margo that Dayna had spent so much time in libraries at all. "Be straight with me, Dayna. Are you having trouble with your magic again? Tell me."

This was a conversation Dayna *really* didn't want to have. She'd spent enough years disappointing her parents with her inability to master even the simplest of spells. They'd always stuck by her, that was true. But that was no reason to confide her latest problems—like her disastrous rainstorm before leaving Phoenix, her boomerang ugliness hex, her inexplicable pants-on-fire incident and the resulting showdown with the cottonseed vortex . . . The hits just kept coming. Or not.

Too bad there was only one public library in Covenhaven. Otherwise, Dayna might have avoided this talk with her mother altogether. She was happy to see her mom. But she would have been even happier to sneak into the stacks, extract the books and information she needed, then visit her parents later. On neutral ground. When she was better prepared for a Q&A session.

When she *wasn't* (apparently) sporting a tell-all aura.

What did her aura mean, anyway? Did it have something to do with her recharged magic? With T.J.? With their bond?

He hadn't exactly seemed psyched about making their bond complete this morning. But Dayna felt more sanguine. There was no way the coven elders had created a system where one witch would be bonded to one warlock (or Patayan) *forever*. It would be unnatural. No matter how in sync she and T.J. were, Dayna knew things were temporary between them. They had to be. Surely when it came time for her to return to her real life in Phoenix, it would be possible for them to get an official witchfolk separation—one that would end their bond without soul damage.

There had to be. Otherwise, she'd done something awful to T.J. by jumping him and having her way with him—however mind-blowing the experience had been for her. Dayna bit her lip, suddenly concerned that she might have damaged T.J. with sex.

With shuddering, hot, sexy, screaming, *amazing* . . .

"Well, you don't *look* bothered by your cusping, whatever has been going on to prompt all these questions." Her mother's voice intruded on her thoughts, hauling her back to the present—to the library, the card catalog, and Margo Sterling's newly cheerful expression. "So I guess you're doing fine?"

"Yes, Mom. I'm doing fine," Dayna reported. "I'm eating well, I'm making progress at work, I'm avoiding caffeine—"

"Don't even joke about that!"

"—and I'm planning to ace cusping-witch class, too, just as soon as I get some more information." Intending to get started, Dayna turned to the card catalog again. "Any hints on finding a magical cheat sheet? I can use all the help I can get."

"I will not help you cheat, young lady."

"All right then. Just tell me if it's possible to cheat."

"No."

"No, it's not possible? Or no, you won't tell me?"

Silence. Still wearing a lighthearted smile, Dayna glanced at her mother. Margo appeared more worried than ever.

"Hey, I'm only kidding." Dayna nudged her, hoping to cheer her up. It was probably a bummer when your only daughter was an embarrassment in the magical accomplishments department. Still joking, she said, "You don't have to help me cheat. I'll do it on my own. You won't be implicated at all."

She turned back to the catalog. As though she'd commanded it—and maybe she had, Dayna realized—it flipped open to the section on rudimentary magic. Of course, those cards were disguised as information on New Age philosophy, but still—that was an encouraging sign. All she needed now were a few primers on the skills she'd missed as a teenager—an accelerated study course to help her meet the likes of

Francesca and her buddies on equal footing. Or at least on less *un*equal footing.

Drawing in a deep breath, Dayna placed her hand an inch or so above the cards. After glancing around to make sure no nosy tourists were watching, she muttered a charm. One by one, her selected cards rose from the catalog. She scanned them, pinched a few between her thumb and forefinger to mark them with her identity, then set them free. Like a flock of papery birds, they raced to the ceiling, then whisked themselves into the stacks.

Beside her, her mother gasped.

Finally! She'd done it. She'd made Margo proud. All she'd needed was the same mastery of magic an able second-grader had.

Cheerfully, Dayna glanced sideways. "See? I'm not so—"

Hopeless, she meant to say. But the word died in her throat. Her mother wasn't staring in awe at Dayna's use of minor magic. She was staring at Dayna—specifically, at an area about four inches away from her body—with a revelatory expression that could *not* bode well.

"I've got it!" Margo said. "You've *connected* with someone!"

Connected. Oh God. There was nothing quite so embarrassing as having your mother pinpoint your AM booty call with a hot warlock. Instantly, Dayna went on the offensive. She was trying to turn over a new leaf, magic-wise, but she wasn't *that* strong.

"What? That's crazy. You can't possibly see something like that. It's personal. It's—it's crazy, that's all. Just crazy."

Wow. Brilliant. *Way to go, genius.* That wouldn't throw her mother off the trail at all. As predicted, it didn't.

Margo shook her head. "Nope. I'm not crazy. I'm right. I've been racking my brain, trying to figure out where I've seen an image of an aura like yours. It's *very* unusual. All this time, I'd figured you'd simply mangled yours somehow—"

"Gee, Mom. Thanks for the vote of confidence."

"—but I just remembered. It was from a very old memory flicker. It may have been based on a legend. I'm not sure about that part." Margo squinted, plainly trying to recall the details. "But it was definitely about witchfolk connectedness. It was a sign of a deep lifepair, an enduring union that—"

"Hang on. Before you go all voodoo with this, this is *me*, remember? The original loner from Toad Croak Lane. I seriously doubt I'm sporting the mark of a big-time joiner who has a lifelong connection with someone. If that kind of sentimental aura got near me, it would bounce right off again."

Her mother gave her a dubious look. Whatever she saw in Dayna's face made her relent. "Well, yours *is* a slightly deeper color than the one I remember seeing," she admitted with a studious frown. "It's a different, distinctive shape, too."

"See? Whatever you see"—and Dayna was still irked that she couldn't see it herself—"it's probably perfectly normal. Maybe it's a holdover from cusping-witch class last night."

"Well . . . Maybe you're right. Speaking of that, did you have a nice time?" Just like that, the witchstory archivist vanished. Motherly Margo stood in her place. "Did you reconnect with some of your old classmates? Your father and I saw Camille Levy a few days ago. She was *so* excited at the thought of seeing you again."

At the memory of last night's class, a palpable sense of dread washed over Dayna. She didn't have much time to lose, it occurred to her. In just a few hours, she'd be back there again, revisiting the failures of her past. She had to get busy.

"Yes, I saw Camille, and that was great. But actually, Mom, I've got to get going." Dayna leaned sideways. Several of her chosen cards from the catalog hovered dutifully between bookshelves, waiting to show her where to find the items she needed. "I have a lot of, um, homework to do before tonight's class."

"All right. No more of that cheating talk, though, you hear? After all, there are more important things in life—"

"—than being good with magic," Dayna repeated for what had to be the millionth time. That exhortation had been a popular refrain in her household. "I know. All I'm trying to do is get good enough to be licensed, so I can go back to Phoenix."

Her mother leaped on that. "You're going back? When?"

"After the graduation ceremony." At the eager tone in Margo's voice, Dayna frowned. Did her mother *want* her to leave earlier? That hurt. "The day after Samhain, I guess. DRL won't let me take an indefinite leave. It was tricky enough explaining to Jane why I needed time off on such short notice."

Her mother's eyebrows drew together. She glanced around the nearly deserted library as though making sure no one was watching them. Or listening to them. Or connecting them to the same gene pool. Her behavior was downright crushing.

"Mom? You and Dad are coming to my graduation, right?"

"Of course." Margo squeezed her hand, still appearing distracted. "Of course we're coming," she said in a stronger voice. Her preoccupied gaze returned to Dayna. She smiled unevenly. "It's your graduation! Why wouldn't we be there?"

Because you think I'm liable to wash out of cusping-witch school before then. Because you don't want to be seen with me. Because you obviously wish I would leave town and never return.

"Oh, I don't know. Maybe you're both busy that night. Or something." Then a more optimistic scenario occurred to Dayna.

"You weren't . . . hoping I'd stay here in Covenhaven, were you?" She gave her mother an apprehensive look. "Tell me this isn't all a giant conspiracy between lonely parents and the IAB, designed to bring all the prodigal daughters back home."

"Of course not. Don't be ridiculous."

"Well, you seem a little . . . distracted. What's the matter?"

"I'm fine."

"No you're not." But Dayna didn't have the fortitude to

push further, only to be told that *she* was what was the matter. Repentantly, she hugged her mother. "Geez. I'm only asking because I love you. You're getting cranky in your dotage."

"I'll show you dotage. I'll bust your butt with my dotage."

"Something is definitely going on with you," Dayna said. "You don't usually talk like Evander Holyfield before a fight."

"Mmm-hmmm." Leaning closer, Margo gave her another hug.

"Mom, you just trash talked me. *You*."

"Mmm. Good luck with your research." Her mother gave her an abstracted wave. "I have things to do. Bye!"

Dayna stared as Margo hustled across the library. Without a backward glance, her mother disappeared into one of the offices.

Hmmm. That was weird. Except for the intrigue—and short-lived hopefulness—engendered by her new aura, it was almost as though her return to Covenhaven had thrown a monkey wrench into . . . something. Something mysterious. But what? And how?

Worried and a little dejected that Margo hadn't been completely thrilled to see her, Dayna picked up her backpack.

She waited. After a few minutes, it was plain that her mother wouldn't return. Frowning, Dayna headed for the stacks.

If the new IAB program was as big a deal as Leo Garmin claimed, it was possible that everyone in town was following its progress closely—including her parents and all their witchfolk friends. It was possible that Margo was simply worried about being the mother of Covenhaven's biggest screwup. Again.

Miserably, Dayna realized that the pressure had just ratcheted up a notch. Somehow, she had to succeed. She *had* to.

The first step was getting those witchcraft books. And the next?

She had no idea. Because if learning from books couldn't help her, she was well and truly stuck . . . all over again.

Chapter Sixteen

It was hard to conduct an undercover operation when every step reminded you of your . . . off-duty activities.

Suppressing a groan, T.J. prowled the perimeter of the Covenhaven farmers' market. He passed tented stalls filled with homegrown winter squash and crisp apples, vendors selling hand-dipped chocolates and homemade cactus jelly, and merchants hawking everything from soy candles to heirloom beans to Native American handicrafts. He wanted to focus on his surroundings. He needed to be alert to the arrival of his target. Instead, his body ached with vivid reminders of his encounter with Dayna this morning, and his mind offered up possibilities for the future.

For their future—the one they would share as bonded partners. He and Dayna. Together, as they were meant to be.

Ruthlessly, T.J. quashed that line of thought. Then he ordered his body to quit feeling so hard used and tingly, too.

This was why being bonded was disastrous for him. This distraction. This yearning. They could get him killed.

And yet . . .

As he spied a fat pumpkin, T.J. imagined himself laughing with Dayna as they carved it into a fanciful, witchy shape. As he spotted a cache of beads, he pictured Dayna wearing them—and giving him one of her irrepressible, smart-alecky smiles. As he stopped at one of the stalls—the better to sell his presence at the market—he found himself standing beside a gray-haired couple in their seventies. They were holding hands. He decided that he and Dayna would do that, too, in their golden years together.

Their golden years? Christ. Appalled with himself, T.J. turned away—and nearly ran into his target, Sumner Jacobs.

She was wearing an impractical all-white outfit, a lot of jewelry, and a hairstyle that could only be the result of a time-consuming appearance charm. Flirtatiousness moved from her to him in a rush; the force of her emotions nearly bowled him over. Her interest would make things easier for him today.

Flexing his best warlock charm, he took a step closer.

Sumner did, too. "Hey! We meet again." She smiled, then juggled her tote bag and offered her hand. "It's Neal, right?"

"Neal Michaels." T.J. nodded, acknowledging the alias he'd given himself for this part of his mission to find the *juweel*. He'd used an appearance enchantment the last time he'd met Sumner. Despite the IAB's ban on his magic, he'd exercised it again today—just one more brick in the wall of his dissolution. Ignoring the dangers of that ethics breach for now, he enclosed Sumner's hand in his own. Subtly, he cast an endearment spell. "I was hoping I'd see you here again."

"Every Wednesday, like clockwork. There's no better place than the farmers' market to find unique items for my shop."

"Clever farmers, growing necklaces and knickknacks."

"Oh. Well, they don't actually grow those." With an earnestness his joke didn't warrant, Sumner withdrew her hand. She let her gaze rove over him, taking in his tank top, his utilitarian cargo pants, his birthright mark, and his Patayan amulets. Sexual interest zoomed from her to him, fervent and obvious. "But I do like to support local artisans."

"Me, too." T.J. smiled. "That's something we have in

common. But then, these people are my family. I love their work as though it's my own. I love to see their creativity on display."

"Wow." She admired him more openly, offering him a smile that was heavy on the lip gloss. "That's so passionate of you."

With a modest shrug, he started walking to the next market stall. As though they'd planned to tour the place together, Sumner fell in step beside him. Her perfume's fragrance trailed them both. Her hips swayed with deliberately provocative movements. Warlocks and other males watched her hungrily as they walked by, drawn by Sumner's confidence and sexual heat.

Unmoved by either of those things, T.J. embellished his cover story with anecdotes involving his fabricated history as an artist who worked in metals. Sumner's eyes widened as she soaked up every detail. Her laughter rang out. She touched his bare arm as he made a point. She lingered, then stroked upward.

Instantly, her hand flew violently away from him.

Frowning in confusion, Sumner stared at her wayward arm. She covered the incident with a smile, then tried again. This time her hand moved straight to his birthright mark tattoo.

Then it bounced away again.

It was almost as though his birthright mark was protected by . . . something. In a way, T.J. realized in surprise, it probably was. Now that his bond with Dayna was complete, his birthright mark had magically branded him as off-limits to other witches.

In essence, he was hexed into fidelity.

Perversely, he liked the idea. It made him think about Dayna. He wondered where his bonded witch was now. Was she thinking about him, too? Did she feel a lingering soreness where they'd come together? Did she want more, the way he did?

Would she seek him out again? He hoped so.

Oblivious to T.J.'s internal battles, Sumner kept flirting. With all the subtlety of a petite blond tigress in heat, she let their hips touch as they walked side by side between stalls. She tossed her hair. She gave him erotically charged looks. She licked her lips as she watched him, ostensibly hanging on his every word—and obviously not listening to a single one.

T.J. had the uncomfortable sensation that Sumner wanted to devour him like one of the Indian fry breads they sold at the other end of the market. He'd underestimated her voraciousness. Judging by the emotions he sensed moving from her to him, she liked to be desired. She liked to be dominated. She also liked to belong, and that was what interested T.J. the most.

That was what he could use the most in this operation.

After all, he already knew Sumner was a vixen witch. The public records Deuce had uncovered had told him that much. What he didn't know was whether Sumner planned to join a vixen pact. Or whether she already had. Or whether she might forgo her pact to help the Patayan avert the crisis that loomed on the horizon.

A fully formed vixen pact could offer Sumner the validation and belonging she craved. But so could T.J.'s people—if Sumner allowed them to. If she were truly destined to be the *juweel* his magus had identified, he had to appeal to her for help.

Observing Sumner now, it seemed likely that she was the vixen he sought. His magus had warned T.J. that the *juweel* would be a witch who felt alone. Judging by the emotions he sensed coming from Sumner, she did feel isolated . . . and had for some time. His magus had warned that the *juweel*'s struggle to choose an allegiance among the witch factions would mean the difference between good and evil for everyone. If Sumner's difficulty in selecting items for her gift shop from among the offerings for sale at the market was indicative of her personality, she would struggle with every decision, large and small.

Keeping those factors in mind, T.J. wound up his patter. With a final "passionate" story about his connection to the artisans in Covenhaven, he stopped in the feathery shade of a mesquite tree. Beside him, Sumner stopped, too. She waved a market map in front of her sweat-dappled cleavage.

"Whew! It's so hot today, isn't it?" she asked. "And it's almost Samhain, too. I guess that's the desert for you, though, right? Totally sunny and eighty degrees in October."

T.J. agreed. "Some people like it hot."

"Mmm. I sure do." Sumner turned to him, her purchases hanging forgotten from her arm. She raised her hand as though to touch him again. After a glance at his darkly drawn birthright mark, she appeared to think better of it. She pursed her lips at him instead. "How about you? Do you like things . . . hot?"

She waggled her eyebrows, her innuendo about as subtle as a Mardi Gras flash to earn a necklace of beads. T.J. began to have doubts that she could be the vixen witch he sought. Yes, Sumner was isolated and indecisive, as foreseen. But she was also naïve. And she seemed to have no special grasp of her magic.

Then again, her naiveté could be a sham. Vixen witches were the most powerful of all witchfolk. It was possible Sumner had so much magic that she outpaced even a compound like T.J. Magical skills at that level could cloud the judgment of any warlock.

Deliberating the issue, T.J. bantered with her again. All around them, market-goers traipsed past with canvas bags full of purchases. Children ran by with agua fresco—cold drinks in fruit flavors—in their eager hands. A trio of musicians played an acoustic set beneath a shaded awning, adding to the festival ambiance that always prevailed at the Covenhaven market.

That ambiance was one reason the farmers' market was so popular with tourists. The other reason was that it employed magic to bewitch the tourists into spending far more on trinkets than they'd planned. They didn't remember being bewitched; they remembered only that, at the time, that Ironwood carving or turquoise bracelet or beeswax candle had seemed essential.

Feeling less than proud of his magical heritage upon remembering that, T.J. abandoned all subtlety. It was time to have this done. He moved closer to Sumner, then looked directly into her eyes. She gazed back with dopey adoration. A single drop of sweat slipped from her neck to her witchily augmented breasts, then disappeared between them. He'd have sworn the maneuver was magically designed to draw his attention there.

"It's not often I feel so free with someone I've just met," Sumner confided. She pressed her breasts against his arm. "But when I saw you here last week, I just felt drawn to you, Neal. I'm so glad you were here again today." She offered up a flirty smile. "If I didn't know better, I'd swear you came here just to see me. Tell me you did, Neal. Even if it's not true. Tell me—"

"I did come here to see you."

"Really?" A whoosh of gratification moved from her to him, mixed with very childlike delight. "That's so sweet of you!"

"We could be very important to one another," T.J. went on. "I could give you what you need. You could give me what I need. If we join together, starting right now, we can—"

"Whoa. Hold on a second." Making a face, Sumner raised her palm at him. "I don't want anything, like, serious. You know?"

She thought he was trying to pin her down too soon—to rush things between them, the way human females sometimes did with the men they were interested in. The notion was laughable.

But T.J. didn't laugh. Soberly, he said, "What I want from you is serious. I came here—for you—for a very special reason." T.J. kept his tone gentle. It was better to approach a vixen cautiously. If a vixen witch became upset, her payback could be cruel. "I need a vixen. A very special vixen . . . like you."

"Oh God." Sumner's flirtatiousness vanished. She gave him a disgusted look. "You're trying to sell me something, aren't you?"

T.J. frowned. He shook his head.

"Then you want me to help you sell something. I knew it!"

"No." Another frown. "I want you to help me, but—"

"Ha. I get it." Her gaze swept over him—derisively this time. "This happens to me all the time. You don't look old enough to be sloping already. Or to need a spell from me to fix it. But . . . whatever. I guess you do." She broke off, giving a sound of utter aggravation. "I knew no good would come of it when Francesca made such a big deal out of us being vixens. Now everyone in town knows about Francesca and Lily and me, and I'm the one who always gets dunned for favors." She broke off, hands on her hips. "Do I look like a soft touch or something?"

Angry emotions cascaded from her to him. T.J. fisted his hands, shielding himself from their force. "You look," he made himself say, "like a vixen witch who wants to do better."

"Right. Let me guess—'do better' for you, right?" Sumner exhaled, shaking her head. "Not a chance. You're the second warlock this month who decided I was the solution to his sloping problems. You guys are as bad as those human males who use younger females to ward off their own pathetic midlife decline." Considering him, she pursed her lips in thought. "You do look better than most slopers do, though. What did you do, use an appearance enchantment to look younger? It's good. Really good. I've got to say, I would almost go for helping you, Neal. You look pretty damn hot for a guy who can't get it up anymore."

"You look pretty damn dense for a witch who could rule

the world, if she wanted to. What's the matter? Are you too afraid to seize your true power? If you are, I can help you."

"I'm not afraid! And you're clearly not from around here, if you think you can talk to me that way." Sumner's aura glowed purple, emitting a low-level vibration that hurt T.J.'s ears. Humans thought their ears "popped" in response to elevation changes. Witchfolk knew that reaction was a warning—a response to angry vixens nearby. "You're a real jerk, you know that?"

"If you're not afraid, then let me help you." T.J. had to focus on what was important here. He moderated his tone. "I can show you a way to use your power together with the Patayan to—"

"The Patayan?" Sumner barked out a laugh. "Why would I help a bunch of irritating do-gooders like the Patayan?"

Taken aback, T.J. stared at her. "Because they need you."

"Ha. They need a lot of things. Like a life, for instance."

"You don't understand." T.J. had encountered this prejudice before. It was no less ugly coming from a beautiful woman. Still, he hadn't expected it from his magus's potential *juweel*. "A conflict is coming. No witch faction will be unscathed."

"Really? Good. If that means the Patayan get some of the smugness knocked out of them, then we'll all be better off. There's nobody in the world more annoying than a Patayan."

In truth, there was no one more annoying than a person who embraced ignorance and fear. But telling his targeted vixen witch that would not advance his cause. T.J. shook his head. "The Patayan are guardians. If you join us, you'll be a rescuer to millions. You'll end this conflict before it begins."

Sumner's mouth dropped open. For a second, she seemed almost intrigued. Then her usual cynicism returned.

"Nice try, Neal. Does this come-on line really work for you? Ever?" With her arms akimbo in WWF style, she affected a macho demeanor. She lowered her voice to a baritone. "You'll be a rescuer to millions." Her tone changed to its usual pitch. "That's me. Sumner Jacobs, swooping in to save the world. Not."

She laughed again. Bitterly. In that moment, T.J. truly felt sorry for her. But he didn't have time to waste on pity. If he couldn't convince this vixen to help him, witchfolk—and likely, humankind—were both doomed by the threat facing them.

His magus had said it. He believed it.

"You can do this," he said. "You can save the world, if that's your destiny." *And if you believe you can.*

According to his magus, the *juweel* would require unshakable confidence in her magic in order to succeed. But T.J. didn't need to tell Sumner that. Like all vixens, she had the potential for extraordinary power—and she knew it. Growing up with that knowledge had given her an aura of self-assurance that witches envied . . . and that warlocks sensed—and desired—on an intrinsic level. He could see it in passersby's responses to her.

"Help me," T.J. urged. He touched her arm, adding a dose of endearment spell to emphasize his appeal. "Join me."

But this time, his warlock charisma failed him.

"Yeah, I don't think so." Sumner shook off his touch. Resistance surrounded her like a wall, barricading some of her emotions from him. "I mean, really—Patayan?"

"They need you."

"Do they? Is that why they're always prattling on about how they descended from ancient indigenous peoples—as if that makes them better than the rest of us somehow—and boring everyone at cocktail parties with a bunch of woo-woo talk about elemental earth magic? That's not even the useful kind of magic, you know. Everybody knows legacy magic is the best." Sumner rolled her eyes. "I mean, come on. What Patayan ever came up with a good money-multiplying charm? Huh? What jilted Patayan ever cast a good spell to make their ex-boyfriend fat, bald, and warty?"

"Patayan don't get jilted. They mate for life."

"Mate?" Sumner's eyebrows rose as a dawning horror crept from her to him. "Ugh. Neal, don't tell me you're a Patayan."

Lifting his head, T.J. stared at her. He knew exactly the moment when the truth struck her. Her gaze traveled over his face, slipped to his cleft chin . . . then held. She froze.

Disdain rolled from her in waves. It battered him the way it had when he'd been a boy on the res, before he'd learned to control himself and his magic. As a child, he'd been wounded by scorn like hers. Now, he scarcely felt a prick of pain. He was hardened, just like his magus had said. He was a rock—impervious to hurt.

Except when it came to betrayal. But he didn't care enough about Sumner to let her inside him. No one had come that close to him in years. Except maybe his bonded witch . . .

"You're a compound." Sumner sneered at him, her voice filled with contempt. "I can't believe I didn't notice."

T.J. could. His appearance charm was impenetrable. He'd worked a long time to make it so. The only reason Sumner could discern his compound status at all was because he hadn't bothered to disguise it. It would have required too much magic to conceal something so fundamentally a part of him.

Trying another tactic, he smiled. Remembering her interest in him earlier, he touched her again. "You were . . . distracted."

"Maybe. But not anymore. This was a waste of time." With a jerk of her head, Sumner gathered up her overflowing shopping bags. "Have fun acting all superior to the rest of us, half-breed. Because acting is all you'll ever have. Losers."

"Ouch." T.J. grabbed his chest. "Now that hurt."

With typical indecisiveness, Sumner paused.

At that moment, T.J. knew he might still have her.

Somewhere inside Sumner Jacobs, a sensitive witch still lived—a witch who didn't want to trample over everyone else, no matter how much she tried to sound as though she did. No matter how much her friends did. No matter how much Covenhaven expected her to. T.J. didn't want to make the mistake of underestimating her—or letting her leave. Especially if she was the vixen witch he'd been searching for. As of right now, he believed she was.

Stiffly, Sumner glanced backward. "I'm . . . sorry. I guess. Whatever. Just don't follow me around the market, okay? Someone might see us together and come to the wrong conclusion."

She glanced around, as though making sure that disaster hadn't already occurred.

"I'll try to stay a safe distance away," T.J. assured her.

In response, her posture relaxed a fraction.

Determined not to smile at his own outrageous piety, T.J. waited a beat. His next move was risky. Especially if he'd misjudged her. He'd done that before—with the Cobalt witch and with Deuce. "You know, if you feel that bad about it, you can always make it up to me."

Sumner examined her manicure . . . but stayed where she was.

In a deeply bored voice, she asked, "Oh yeah? How?"

Heartened by that evidence of her hidden softheartedness, T.J. strode forward. "If you're the vixen witch I think you are, you're important, Sumner. Vitally important."

A smile played around the corners of her mouth. He could tell that Sumner enjoyed feeling special. She enjoyed feeling chosen. T.J. intended to make that work to his advantage.

"You're important," he repeated. "And you can prove it to everyone. Everyone in Covenhaven will remember your name."

She bit her lip, then glanced around the market again. This time her expression looked more furtive—and more hopeful—than ever. "Even more than they'll remember Francesca?"

Bingo. "Compared to you, Francesca will be a footnote. You're the one who can make witchstory, Sumner."

She stared him down. "I'm not sure I believe you."

T.J. shrugged. "When you do, I'll be here." He conjured a business card, breathed on it to imprint it with his identity, then handed it to her, fully loaded with magical identifiers. "You can reach me anytime, day or night. When you decide to help me, I'll come for you."

Then, without waiting for her answer, he turned and left the market. In his wake, tiny Patayan flowers bloomed on every cactus he passed . . . evidence of the hopefulness T.J. suddenly felt and could no longer hide.

He had his *juweel*. It had begun.

Chapter Seventeen

Stepping out of the Covenhaven Library with a loaded backpack and an armful of witchcraft books she could scarcely carry, Dayna stared at her surroundings with surprise.

Sometime while she'd been inside, the Covenhaven farmers' market had sprung up in the parking lot across the street. It appeared to be in full swing, too. Town residents came and went in tandem with tourists, all of them carrying canvas bags full of purchases. Fruits and vegetables and handcrafted wares were piled at every tented stall. Sunshine glinted off an array of turquoise and opal jewelry. Dried leaves from the town's single oak tree skittered across the street, and the mingled scents of burnt sugar and apples traveled enticingly on the crisp air.

Mmm. Caramel-dipped apples. Their fragrance transported Dayna instantly to her childhood, making her feel a tiny bit nostalgic for Covenhaven and its traditions. For an outsider like her, that felt like a minor miracle.

But it was no wonder, she realized as she inhaled deeply. As a little girl, she'd visited the Covenhaven market with her parents whenever the event had been held on the weekend. Back then, she'd savored those delectable apples and spent her allowance on pretty but inexpensive jewelry, while her parents had visited with their neighbors and practiced reining in their magic so they wouldn't be exposed as witchfolk.

Escaping detection had been a game with Sam and Margo Sterling, and with their friends. Even though Dayna hadn't needed to cast shielding charms to keep her magic from giving away her status as a witch, those weekends had been good times for her, too. Unfortunately, she didn't have time for a trip down memory lane now. She had to get back to Deuce's apartment and hole up with her books for a serious crash course in witchery.

Feeling determined to do exactly that, Dayna retraced her steps to the trolley stop she'd arrived from. But she'd only traveled half a block before she reached an obstacle. The street adjacent to the trolley stop also led directly to the farmers' market, and it had been cordoned off with yellow tape, orange traffic cones, and a police cruiser to prevent gate crashers.

There would be no trolley arriving at that stop soon.

With a sigh, Dayna stared up the street, searching for an alternate route. The sound of acoustic guitar music drifted her way from the market, along with children's laughter. She shaded her eyes with her free hand, then turned in the other direction.

A lone stop stood there, marked by a trolley sign and occupied by two tourists wearing brand-new cowboy boots.

She would just have to look at the trolley map and figure out a new route to Deuce's when she got there. Still hoping for another, closer trolley stop, Dayna readjusted her books and then took one last look around, gazing past the market's exit.

Wait a minute. Someone familiar was in that crowd! Filled with curiosity, Dayna looked more closely. She squinted at the people leaving the market, searching for a recognizable face.

Was it her father? Camille? One of her fellow students

from witch class? Professor Reynolds, out for a hit of jalapeño jam?

Nope. It was *T.J.*

It was definitely him. She glimpsed his familiar rugged features, his aquiline nose, his hard jawline. His hair looked tousled, his muscles sleek and strong, his demeanor . . .

No way. T.J. actually appeared *pleased*.

He strode through a clump of Covenhaven residents with an actual swagger, his shoulders relaxed and confident. A series of cactus flowers bloomed in his wake—unnoticed by most people and utterly out of season—on the succulents he passed. That was weird. Dayna had no idea what those flowers meant . . . but she hoped, with a jolt of feminine pride, that it had something to do with *her* and what they'd shared together this morning.

Then, as though Dayna were watching T.J. through water, his features . . . shifted. They rippled, blurred, then realigned.

When the brief process was complete, a different warlock moved in T.J.'s place. While Dayna gawked, the unknown warlock stepped through the market's exit. He paused there.

He glanced at her, his expression alert.

Startled, Dayna jumped. One of her books slid from the stack in her arms. It thwacked to the ground in a puff of dust.

A little freaked out by what she'd just seen, she bent to retrieve it. Then she remembered that she was a witch, damn it.

A *real* witch would use magic to pick up a fallen book. And a real witch would make the maneuver look cool, too. Drawing in a fortifying breath, Dayna tried to remember the spell she'd muttered to bring her backpack closer this morning. Filled with hopefulness, she uttered the spell's magical phrasing.

In response, the fallen book nudged itself an inch sideways. Its cover scraped noisily across the pebbles and dirt on the sidewalk. Dayna focused, then repeated the phrasing.

Yes! Success at last. The book shot into the air.

Someone stepped in place beside her and grabbed it.

"If you're trying to get arrested," came a familiar voice, "pulling off irresponsible public magic is a good start."

Surprised, Dayna stared. She expected T.J., with an excuse for being himself one minute . . . and another warlock the next.

Instead, IAB Head Agent Leo Garmin stood in front of her. With a charming gesture, he offered her the book.

"Thanks." Still wondering about T.J., Dayna looked around. She saw no sign of her tracer or the warlock he'd morphed into. She turned her attention to Garmin. "See you around."

With no desire to delay her studying any further, she set her Converses in motion. Leo Garmin followed her. He materialized at the next junction in the redbrick sidewalk without taking a single step, then gave her a mocking IAB salute.

"Nice trick." It really was impressive. All the same, Dayna stopped in annoyance. "Are you stalking me now?"

"No, I'm warning you. That was unlicensed magic. You've got to watch that, Ms. Sterling. You might get in trouble."

"Okay. Thanks for the heads-up. I've got to run."

She started walking again. Ahead at the trolley stop, the two cowboy-boots-wearing tourists glanced her way.

"Wait." Leo Garmin's hand closed on her upper arm.

Then it swerved—forcibly—away.

He frowned. Drawing himself up, Garmin moved to restrain her again. This time Dayna's golden armlet warmed perceptibly before the IAB agent's touch ricocheted away from her.

His scowling gaze met hers. "How did you do that?"

"I just learned a new stalker deflector spell," Dayna fibbed, stopping to give him a sardonic grin. "I guess night school for witches is coming in handy already."

"I'm not stalking you." Humorlessly, Garmin peered at her armband. "I saw you leave the library and followed you."

"I hate to break it to you, but . . . that's stalking."

"I was working around the corner on an IAB case." Garmin rubbed his bald head, then put his hands on his hips in an exasperated pose. "A human murder. It happened last night."

"Oh. That's too bad." Sobered, Dayna examined him. Today, Leo Garmin appeared weary—but no less authoritative. She guessed that tracking down magical killers took its toll. "Unless things have changed a lot around here, one murder is practically a crime wave in Covenhaven. Do you know who did it yet?"

Tight-lipped, he shook his head. "That's why I'm here."

Jolted, Dayna frowned. "You don't think *I* did it?"

"No, I think your boyfriend did it."

"My . . . boyfriend?" *He must mean T.J.* A sense of unreality slammed into her. All at once, the gelato shop and Laundromat bordering the sidewalk seemed to recede in her vision; the clanging bell of the approaching trolley sounded hollow. "I just got here two days ago. And I'm not exactly a player, so—"

"Save it. I know you and T.J. McAllister are close."

"But he's not my *boyfriend*." *He's my bonded warlock. My kind of . . . sort of . . . magical husband.* "And he's not a murderer either." Shaken by Garmin's accusation, Dayna hugged her books more closely. "If this is your idea of a joke—"

"You'll notice I'm not laughing." Wearing his usual grim scowl, Garmin met her incredulous gaze. Then he appeared to yield a fraction. "Look," he said in a more conciliatory tone, "Agent McAllister's past is . . . complicated. We have reason to believe he's fallen on the wrong side of things. That's why I followed you—to warn you. To tell you to stay away from T.J."

Stay away from T.J.? The idea made every ounce of rebellion rise up inside her. She *needed* T.J. At least for now.

Dayna shook her head. "You can't be serious. Come on. He's an IAB agent. If you can't trust one of your own agents—"

"I'm not talking about trust. I'm talking about reality." Garmin gazed toward the bustling market. Dayna wondered if he'd glimpsed T.J.'s doppelganger there, too. "The reality is, Agent McAllister is a loner. He always has been. He doesn't confide in anyone. He doesn't trust easily either. When I recruited him, it was one hell of a fight just to convince him that I wouldn't—" Garmin broke off, gave her a strangely nostalgic look, then shook his head. "That doesn't matter. What's important now is that he's trusted you. It's all over you."

Dayna swore. He must be able to see her unusual aura, just like her mother had done. The realization made her feel naked.

"I have *got* to learn to read those things. Like, yesterday." With a beleaguered frown, she looked up at Garmin. "Yes, all right. T.J. and I have a . . . relationship." She felt no readier to confide the details of her bonding to the IAB than she had been to Margo. But it could not be smart to lie to the magical equivalent of the FBI. "But there's no way he's a killer! For one thing, I would have sensed those emotions in him. He can't hide anything from me."

Garmin was clearly unimpressed. "Knowing when someone is lying to you is a witchy talent. I'll grant you that. And maybe it feels new to a runaway like you. But however unfamiliar to *you,* typical witch abilities are not on the same level with—"

"Are you guys *required* to be patronizing, or something?"

"No." The head agent smirked. "It's strictly a perk."

"Fine. What I mean is, T.J. *literally* can't hide anything from me. I can feel every emotion he has. Including— presumably—the homicidal ones. I haven't sensed anything like that, so—"

"You're a clairvoyant?" Garmin's expression sharpened with intense interest. "Are you sure? True clairvoyance is rare."

"But useful, I'd imagine. Especially to the IAB. Right?"

"I can have a desk for you at the bureau in ten minutes."

"Wait. Don't start recruiting me yet." Laughing, Dayna held up both hands to ward off Garmin. "My clairvoyance only works with T.J. I can't explain it." She felt sorry she'd mentioned it at all, given how weird he was being about it. Garmin appeared ready to jump her and forcibly extract whatever memories she had of T.J. "Look, if it would help T.J., I'd be happy to come down to the IAB offices and make an official statement or something."

"Yes, fine. That would be helpful." Garmin verbally waved away her offer, plainly interested more in her experience of T.J.'s feelings than in her avowal of his innocence. "But you can *read* his emotions? All of them? How strongly?"

Instantly, Dayna flashed on the loving way T.J. had cradled her face after they'd been together that morning. She thought of the way he'd smiled at her—as though she were indescribably wonderful. His smile had sent a tingle all the way to her toes.

T.J. had warmed her heart. He had awakened her.

"Um, pretty strongly." It was an outrageous understatement, but it was all she had. "They're pretty strong emotions." Dayna realized how incriminating that might sound. She hastened to correct herself. "Not murderously strong! Just intense. *He's* intense. You know that. You've known him awhile, right?"

Garmin nodded. "More than ten years."

It occurred to Dayna that, despite his unforgiving demeanor, Garmin was probably trying to clear T.J.'s tarnished reputation, not condemn him. After all, they'd worked together at the bureau for a long time. They had to be friends.

On the other hand, Garmin *was* here to warn her away from T.J., in no uncertain terms. It seemed likely that Garmin knew something about her bonded partner that she didn't.

Confused by the implications of it all, Dayna did what she always did. She decided to escape the situation.

"Well, it's been real, Agent Garmin. But I'm in kind of a

hurry." She gestured to the trolley stop. "I've got a busy day ahead. So if that's all you wanted from me . . ."

"Actually, there's more. Especially now, there's more."

Cripes. What had she said? It had to be that stuff about being able to discern T.J.'s emotions. She should have known better than to blab about something that was connected to her bond with T.J. Telling people about it would only make that bond feel more real.

More lasting and unbreakable and essential.

Suddenly, Dayna felt twice as eager to run away.

"Let's put it all in my statement then. Later. Bye!"

She shrugged her backpack higher, hoisted her armful of books more securely, then headed for the trolley stop.

She made it three steps before Garmin appeared.

Literally. He crackled into being in front of her with blatant disregard for the public practicing of magic he'd warned her about earlier. He crossed his arms, his gaze forceful.

"Nope. I need more from you, Ms. Sterling. You can do this my way, or I can arrest you for unlicensed use of magic and bring you in to the IAB to determine your penalty. You choose."

"Umm . . . What's the usual penalty for unlicensed magic?"

"Imprisonment without parole."

She stared, openmouthed. "On the first offense?"

"At the IAB, we don't allow a second offense." Garmin adjusted his necktie, then the lapels of his suit. All signs of fatigue were gone now. "That's why the bureau is so successful."

The trolley bell clanged again. Had it only been seconds since she'd first heard it? Or had Garmin somehow magiked time into slowing while they talked? He was probably powerful enough to cast a time spell. With a sense of unreality that felt just as strong as before, Dayna stared as the trolley trundled toward the stop. The two tourists approached the curb expectantly.

"I've really got to go. I don't drive"—she didn't trust

herself to do it, given her inability to control things outside of herself—"and I have a *lot* of homework to do before class tonight. Can we continue this on the trolley?"

"The trolley?" Garmin made a face. "No. I don't do the trolley. Can't you just magik yourself wherever you need to go?"

Deadpan, Dayna looked at him. "Not legally."

"Very funny."

"Aha. You *do* have a sense of humor."

"Fine. Hold on to me." Careful not to grab her arm again, Agent Garmin focused on Dayna. He bent his knees and then . . . *whooshed* them both to the trolley stop. "There."

"Wow. Invasive, yet effective." Wobbling, Dayna righted herself. "Thanks. You IAB guys don't mess around."

One of the tourists gawked at them.

"After you," Garmin told the man. As the tourist turned, the agent casually brushed his shoulder. At Dayna's questioning look, Garmin leaned down. "Forgetfulness spell," he confided.

"Ah. Slick." She remembered T.J. using the same spell on the docent, Francine, at Dynamic Research Libraries. Then it had seemed kind. In Garmin's hands, that spell might feel different. Still . . . "After our talk, can I get one of those?"

The agent gave her a lingering look. Then a smile unexpectedly quirked his mouth. "Maybe. If you're very good."

"Define 'good.'"

"Cooperative."

"Yeah. Good luck with that. Especially if you want me to throw T.J. to the wolves. *Not* going to happen."

"Mmm." Garmin gave a noncommittal sound. "We'll see."

He and Dayna waited for both tourists to wheeze their way onto the trolley, shopping bags in tow. Garmin squinted at the HALLOW-E'EN FESTIVAL banner on the trolley's side. Dayna wondered what more the IAB could possibly want from her. Then they both boarded the trolley and creaked down the street.

* * *

That afternoon, T.J. sat in one of his magus's ultramodern chairs, with autumn sunshine streaming through the earth ship's rounded port windows. That warmth felt good. His magus's wolfhound sat at his feet. His magus herself sat across from him, watching as he toyed with the spicy cookie on his plate.

"This one is a molasses cookie with vanilla icing." A familiar expectant gleam lit her eyes. "When the weather cools off, all I want are sugar and cinnamon and lots of ginger."

The fragrances of those spices assaulted him. Eyes watering with the fumes, T.J. blinked. Taking his first bite of cookie was an act of extreme bravery. He chewed. "Mmm. Effective."

His magus burst out laughing. "*'Effective'?* You're something else, T.J. Just when I think I have you figured out—"

He swallowed heavily. "I found the vixen witch."

"Aha." She sobered. "That explains your agitated mood."

Maybe it did. Maybe it didn't. T.J. just hoped like hell that his magus couldn't see his completed bond with Dayna. He hadn't come to terms with that himself. He refused to now.

Ignoring his magus's too-perceptive remark, he continued his report. "She fits your prophesy and your spirit vision. She's powerful, alone, and indecisive. She's young. She's beautiful. She's part of a leading clique among the witches."

"In other words, she fits. That *is* good news." Still eyeing his molasses cookie, his magus leaned back in her chair. With an effortless motion, she pulled over a shaft of sunshine, then noticed T.J. watching. She shrugged. "I'm old. I get cold."

He nodded, instantly rejecting the idea of his magus's advancing age. The thought of losing her was unbearable. But like all Patayan—like all witchfolk—he knew his magus's time here was finite. Just like his faith in anything or anyone except her was finite. He'd never seen a reason to change that.

Although his bonding with Dayna seemed to be forcing him to. Bit by bit, T.J. felt himself weakening. *Wanting* . . .

His magus's voice cut short his brooding. "Will she help us, this vixen witch? Will she join the Patayan?"

T.J. nodded. "She hasn't agreed yet. She will."

"I see. Did you seduce her, then?"

"No!" Affronted, T.J. dropped his plate to the table with a clatter. The wolfhound lunged to its feet. The beast scarfed his forgotten cookie in a single bite. "I'm a warlock, not a whore."

His magus suppressed a grin. "And the difference is . . . ?"

"Minuscule," T.J. admitted with a grin he could not hide. He stood and then paced, filled with emotions on a scale he'd never experienced. *Agitated* was accurate. Damn it. "But my legacy magic is tempered by my better-controlled Patayan side."

His magus laughed again. "If this is control, I'd hate to see your version of abandon. It must be near madness."

T.J. frowned. He'd come close to that kind of abandon— that kind of passion—this morning with his bonded witch. It had done something to him. Their coming together had changed him.

"It feels like madness," he muttered. "I don't like it."

"Give it time." Leaving off the topic of his lapse in control— which must be obvious in his aura—his magus nodded at him. "Did you notice that your birthright mark is changing?"

Startled, T.J. glanced down at his arm. His golden Gila monster tattoo appeared more deeply etched now. It gleamed with a new richness that crept upward from the creature's claws.

"You've completed your bond," his magus observed. "Your birthright mark is entering maturity, becoming fully realized."

T.J. scoffed. "It can't be. I passed maturity long ago."

"You think you became a man when your parents died— when you were forced to care for yourself all those years ago." A current of sadness swept from his magus to him. Usually T.J. could not sense his wisewoman's emotions. He wondered why he could now. "But the true test of maturity is not caring for yourself," she said. "Real maturity means caring for someone else—sacrificing for someone else. *Giving* to someone else."

"I give." He fisted his hands. "I sacrifice."

"That's true. You've gone beyond all measures of loyalty—for your people's sake. Now it's time to claim some happiness for yourself." With a steady gaze that focused a few inches past his body, his magus examined him. She smiled. "It's time for you to trust the bond you've made—to trust your bonded witch."

"Later. After this crisis is past."

"All we have is now. This moment. Take it."

"I've already taken more than I meant to." Caught up in a memory of Dayna atop him, urging him to join with her, her face open and beautiful, T.J. smiled. He trailed his fingertips over his mouth, remembering how it had felt when she'd kissed him.

Sweet. Hot. Necessary. *Inevitable.*

"I feel more myself with her than with anyone. I *feel* . . . more." Conflicted, he gazed at his magus. "Is this a trick of our bonding? Is this what it's like for a human to be bewitched?"

"I don't know. Did you complete your bond willingly?"

He thought about the heat between him and Dayna, the need and whispers and urgent touches. He grinned. "Ravenously."

"Then it's not bewitchment you feel. It's more than that."

"A desire spell?" He scoffed. "I'm a grown warlock. I—"

"No." His magus's smile brightened the room. It softened and reassured something inside him, too. "It's love."

He swore. "I don't know what that means."

Another perceptive look. "You're afraid to know. Afraid that if you reach for it, it will disappear. But your body knows. *It* knows. It reaches. It needs. Your heart will follow."

"So I'm going to fuck my way into true love?"

"Be as crude as you want." With a serene expression, his magus conjured a clean plate. She gestured to the pile of spicy cookies beside her. Magically, she lifted one and transported it on the new plate past her hungry wolfhound to T.J. "We both know these are delaying tactics. We both know the truth."

"And that is?"

"That your heart has already followed the rest of you." His magus directed a canine biscuit at her dog. "Soon you'll be able to trust it. Then you'll shout your love from the rooftops."

T.J. laughed. "The day I yell out loud like a warlock from a freaking musical-theater production is the day the earth stops spinning." Still chuckling to himself, he picked up his cookie and finished it in two bites. He went to his magus, leaned down to envelop her in an arthritis-ointment-scented hug, then rose. He smiled at her. "I'll report when I know more. Be well."

He headed for the door. His magus's voice trailed him.

"I'm already well," she said in a contented tone. "You just initiated a hug all on your own. For the first time. This change in you is good, T.J. It's very, very good."

Hell. He wanted to disagree. He wanted to prove that he was still strong, still a rock, still impenetrable. But he couldn't. So T.J. only raised his hand in farewell, then slipped outside into the soul-warming sunshine, his birthright mark all but sizzling with enjoyment of the heat.

This change *was* good. It was very, very good.

And T.J. knew exactly how to get more of it.

Chapter Eighteen

After a long night of cusping-witch class, Dayna trod up the sidewalk to Deuce's apartment. Shrouded in shadows, she moved through the courtyard that centered the units in the complex, then edged along the border of bougainvillea and oleander. The plants' branches rustled in the cold wind. In one of the nearby apartments, a TV screen glowed through the blinds; from another, the heady aroma of chile verde wafted into the night.

Everyone was settling in for the evening—greeting their loved ones, sharing a meal, hugging hello. Those homey scenarios should have made her nostalgic for her life in Phoenix. They should have made her want to work harder to return there. Instead, they only exposed her "real" life for what it was—a hideout. In the human world, Dayna was a permanent expatriate. Even her closest friends didn't know the truth about her.

But what was the truth? That she was really a witch?

Ha. Tonight had proven that "truth" wrong all over again.

Although she'd experienced a few bursts of magical acumen during class, she'd endured twice as many moments of failure. Where the other cusping witches seemed to be experiencing surges in both magical ability and magical strength, Dayna was simply experiencing a series of surges—unpredictable, uncontrollable, and prone to embarrassing malfunctions . . . most of which had been caught and replayed on memory flickers during the breaks.

It had been just like old times—the old times she'd escaped from once but couldn't escape from now. Being in cusping-witch classes was like attending an involuntary three-week high school reunion. Everyone wanted to make a good impression. The former nerd wanted to wow everyone with her high-salaried high-tech job. The once chubby girl wanted to show off her newly svelte shape. The one-time band geek wanted everyone to hear about her Grammy nomination. Dayna hadn't achieved spectacular success—at least not in a form that witchfolk would recognize—but she'd still hoped she'd changed enough that she would fit in. That she'd somehow make a triumphant return to town and everyone who'd excluded her would welcome her back. But her hopes had evaporated with her first step into Covenhaven Academy.

With a bitter thrust of her temporary apartment key, she opened Deuce's front door. It banged against the interior wall, rattling Deuce's framed print on the other side—a piece of "artwork" that depicted a trio of bikini girls lathering up a replica of the Mustang he and T.J. had stolen her away from Phoenix in. The image didn't quite fit with Deuce's personality, but he seemed to like it. Besides, however heinous her roommate's "art" was, it wasn't up to her to destroy it.

Lunging sideways, Dayna tried to catch the frame before it rattled off the wall. Instead, an instant before she touched it, the picture went completely still. Then it slid upright. It was just as though an invisible Martha Stewart had entered the room, found that print crooked, and expertly straightened it.

Caught off guard, Dayna frowned. Then the truth hit her.

Deuce. He must have beaten her home tonight.

"Great. Even a turned human is better at magic than me." She slung her backpack on the floor and groused her way into the living room area, ready for a nice, restorative bitch session with Deuce. "It just figures. After the night I've had—"

She stopped, gawking, at the sight that greeted her.

T.J. lounged on the sofa, naked from the waist up. From the waist down, he wore a pair of witchmade pants that reminded her of track pants . . . only softer and (she imagined) more inviting to touch. He was lit by the glow of Deuce's big-screen TV, its images flickering across his features. His feet were bare, his hair was messy, and beard stubble darkened his jaw. His hand was poised halfway in the act of raising a beer to his lips.

Instead, seeing Dayna, he smiled.

Somehow, that smile had the power to make her heart skip a beat. *I see you*, it said. *And I'm so glad you're here.*

Helpless to resist, Dayna returned that smile. Widely.

T.J. made a simple gesture. His beer disappeared. The TV switched itself off. Maybe it was magic. Maybe just the remote. Either way, Dayna only had eyes for T.J.'s brawny chest, his exotic Patayan amulets, his muscles and smooth skin and aura of welcome. As though entranced by it, she moved toward him.

"Didn't Deuce tell you?" T.J. asked in a level tone. "Turned humans can't practice magic." He tsk-tsked. "That should really be part of your curriculum at cusping-witch school."

"He might have told me that. And it might be on the class curriculum, too." Still smiling, Dayna reached him. She put her hands on her tracer's shoulders and then straddled his lap, as comfortable in that position as a kitten in a patch of sunshine. Her knees framed his hips; her pelvis hovered just above his groin. Heat rushed between them, immediate and intense. "Suddenly I can't remember a single thing I've learned since coming here."

"Shame on you." Without the least bit of censure, T.J. reached for her. Fondly, he twined his fingers in her hair, then urged her closer. Their gazes met; their mouths hovered enticingly near, sharing the same breath. Warmth reached from him to her, along with a sense of joyfulness and desire. He searched her face, smiled once more, then tugged her down to meet him. "Maybe you need private lessons," he told her.

"That's what *I* said!" she began . . . but then he kissed her, and every rational thought evaporated from her brain.

Exhilarated, Dayna melted into his kiss. Her body leaned against his, her heart and mind easing their way into a union she knew would be good. Their mouths slid, angled, then reconnected; their hands sought and found sleek muscles and bare skin; appreciation rumbled from them both in matching moans.

Being with T.J. felt like coming home. It felt like those lighted windows and hello hugs—except those, Dayna hadn't been a part of. *This*, with T.J., was part of *her*. Even though she hadn't known him for long, she felt as though she had. She felt as though she always would. With him, she felt *whole*.

Contentedly, Dayna leaned back to study him. *Mmmm.* Her bonded tracer had a way with partial nudity. It agreed with his six-pack abs and gilded skin. It made her want more of him.

She trailed her fingertips over his shoulders, his arms, his chest. "Mmm. Are you volunteering for the job?" she asked.

"Yes." He groaned, restless and urgent. "God, *yes*."

Her smile blazed again. "To be my tutor, I mean."

"Anything you want." T.J. traced his hands over her back. Magically, her corduroy jacket peeled away. It dropped to the floor. "I'll teach you everything you need to know."

"Hmmm. I think I'd like that." Attempting a little magic of her own, Dayna wriggled atop him. He felt hard and full and perfect. She groaned with anticipation. "First you can teach me how to magik away my jeans. And your pants. And my shirt, and—"

A rush of cool air washed over her. Agog with disbelief, Dayna looked down at herself—her suddenly *naked* self.

"It's trickier with human-made clothes," T.J. said as he savored the view, "but I'm up for the challenge." With a hoarse sound of masculine pleasure, he brought his mouth to her pointed nipple. He nuzzled her. "I'll show you how to do it later."

Tipping her head back, Dayna nodded. "Yes. Yes, later."

Mindlessly, she grabbed T.J. and held him to her. Her thighs quivered. The whole world narrowed to the soft glide of his tongue, the faint rasp of his beard stubble, the pleasure that shot from her breasts to her middle, straight down to . . .

. . . to the place where T.J.'s pants prevented her from doing what she *really* wanted to be doing. Groaning in frustration, Dayna reached down. Her fingers closed on witchmade fabric first, then on *him* beneath it. A hot rush of approval swept from him to her, coupled with a surprising jolt of tenderness.

Leaning back, Dayna caught his gaze. "You're all I could think about today," she admitted. "I tried to study, but I kept remembering *this*." She caressed him through that soft witchmade fabric, thrilled with the way he hardened even further against her palm. She exhaled shakily. "I tried to focus on class tonight, but I kept wondering how it would feel to do *this*."

Awash in longing, she sank to her knees. With an unconscious magic that worked exactly as she'd hoped it would, she lowered T.J.'s pants. He sprang free instantly, hot and hard and beautifully formed. Dayna licked her lips in expectation.

A heartbeat later, she closed her mouth around him. He felt warm and smooth and indescribably wonderful. He pulsed with life and need and urgency, and as she swirled her tongue around him, she moaned her intentions to enjoy him fully— to make him feel her desire completely. This was going to be good. *So good.* Good for her and for him, because nothing was more intimate than this union between them, complete and delicate and full and new.

"Wait." Beneath her, T.J. jerked. A hoarse moan came from him, then a husky protest. "Stop. Dayna, you don't—"

"—know what I'm doing?" Pausing to give him a very personal kiss—one that made him shudder—Dayna wrapped her hand around his cock . . . the better to keep him with her. "I think if you'll give me a minute, you'll realize I know *exactly* what I'm doing."

Smiling, she enveloped him once more. She stretched her mouth wide, wonderfully wide, forgetting all about the nubbly carpet beneath her knees and the difficult night she'd had. Now there was only T.J., groaning and panting and grabbing her head with a touch that communicated apprehension and need at once.

"No." Shaking, he held her away. He stroked her cheek with his thumb, his desperate gaze full of questions. "You must know I want this, but warlocks . . . even Patayan . . . they don't—"

"They don't . . . what?" With difficulty, Dayna lifted her attention from his cock. She raised her eyebrows. "They don't like this?" She trailed her fingertips along the rigid length of him, loving the way he quaked at her touch. "I disagree. I think you like this a lot. I know *I* do. I want more." She leaned upward, kissed him, then smiled. "Give me what I want, T.J."

He seemed shaken. "It's forbidden. Like bonding magic."

Confused, she stared at him. "Bonding magic is forbidden?"

Reluctantly, T.J. nodded. "Yes. And so is . . ." He gestured to his still-erect cock, drawing her rapt attention—and inciting her interest—all over again. "What you were just doing."

Dayna scoffed. "You're kidding me."

He gave an agonized groan. "I wish I was."

He really meant it, she realized. "Oh." Wow. "I see. I guess I left Covenhaven before I learned about that policy." *Thank God.* In some ways, the witching world was completely whack. "Then that means you've never . . . ? With anyone?"

"Hell no." His denial was instant. "And I shouldn't have let you go as far as you did either. I don't know what's wrong with me." T.J.'s gaze veered guiltily to hers as though confessing a dark secret. "I never allow intimacy like that."

"*Never?* That's too bad. You're missing out."

"Maybe humans would think so, but—"

"No, *everyone* would think so. Seriously."

"I shouldn't have said anything." Uncomfortably, T.J. shifted. Dayna guessed that having a heart-to-heart while sporting a raging hard-on was awkward, to say the least.

"Come on," she urged. "Hold still. Let me show you."

With a suspicious glint to his gaze, T.J. stared at her. His chest heaved on an indrawn breath. He fisted his hands.

"I'll take your silence as a 'yes.'" Overwhelmed with tenderness for him, Dayna bent her head. She trailed her tongue along one side of his shaft, then the other. T.J.'s hands tightened in her hair. His next attempt to stop her ended on a strangled groan. "See? It's good, right? Mmm. So good . . ."

T.J. shook his head, anguish plain on his face. He nodded. "I—you can't— if you continue, I don't know what will happen."

"Mmm." She kissed the fat head of his cock, enjoying the way he trembled. "I have a pretty good idea. Trust me."

His whole body quivered. "It's a total loss of control."

"That's the plan." Slowly, she licked him. She sucked him into the warm wetness of her mouth again, luxuriating in the heat and texture and scent of him. She lifted her head and ran her mouth along him, smiling as she did. "Trust me, T.J."

"I can't." Struggle emanated from him. "I won't."

"Try it. For me." She caressed him with her palm, amazed that he could have any resistance left at all. She'd never seen a warlock so huge, so stiff, so ready. "Think of it as a favor. You know I love everything that's forbidden and dangerous."

For a heartbeat, T.J. was silent. Then laughter burst from him in an intoxicating wave. It was the first time, Dayna realized, she'd ever heard her tracer sound truly free.

"You want this because it's against the rules?" he asked.

"Well . . . not *just* because of that." With a naughty grin, Dayna traced a path upward from his flat belly. She swirled her fingers in his chest hair, then gave a gentle tug. "Also because I want to feel as close to you as possible. And this"—

she returned to his cock, kissing him before dragging her lips against him in a silent entreaty—"is how I want to do that."

"It's not safe. I've never lost control before. I—"

"I'll take my chances. You don't have to protect me."

He frowned. "I'm a guardian. I'll always protect you."

"Not from yourself." She gave him a stern look. "Okay?"

To her surprise, T.J. paused to think about that. Conflict still radiated from him. But then, slowly, he grabbed the sofa cushions beside him. He fisted his hands until the muscles in his arms grew taut and corded beneath his multiple tattoos. He planted his feet, drew in a deep breath, then nodded.

"Go ahead," he said in a gravelly voice. "I trust you."

At his roughly spoken words, Dayna felt oddly blessed. She had the sense that trust was a gift T.J. didn't give easily—or if Leo Garmin was right—ever before. That made her special to him.

"Since it's your first time," she said with a fond smile as she settled back on her knees, "I'll try to be gentle."

Then she lowered her head and took her tracer to a place he'd never been—but, if she was very, very lucky, would want to visit with her time and time again.

Sprawled on the sofa in a daze, T.J. wrapped his arm protectively around Dayna. She gave a lazy wiggle, then snuggled closer to him. Her mussed hair tickled his nose; the delectable curve of her ass fit against his groin as though she'd been born to spoon him. Short of breath and filmed in sweat, he sighed.

"I love the way you break the rules," he said.

"I knew you would." The teasing smile in her voice touched him clearly. "If only you'd give it half a chance."

"I still want to know what happened, though. I really can't remember." *Because he'd trusted her. He'd lost control.* That made today a day of firsts. Marveling at the realization, T.J.

kissed the top of his bonded witch's head. He squeezed her more tightly against him. "You're going to tell me sooner or later."

"What . . . happened?" With outrageous faked innocence, Dayna rolled over to face him. Her breasts pressed against his chest. She batted her eyelashes. "I'm sure I don't know what you mean. I guess . . . there was shaking. And moaning. And some begging. And I'm pretty sure Deuce's sofa will never be the same—"

United, their gazes traveled to the shredded cushions.

"—but as far as 'what happened' to you goes . . ."

"Yes?" T.J. urged in a growl. "What about it?"

". . . when you lost control . . ." Dayna pursed her lips. "Well, that's a delicious memory I'm keeping *all* for myself."

Her warm laughter drove him crazy. With another growl, T.J. pulled over a covering of shadows—just to prove he hadn't surrendered all his power to her—then flipped Dayna on her back.

He moved atop her in almost the same moment, savoring the surprise in her eyes almost as much as he relished what was coming next. He caught hold of her knees, tugged them apart, then settled himself on his belly between them. Wearing a wicked grin that probably matched his bonded witch's smile, T.J. trailed his hand over her stomach . . . then lower, between her thighs. The heat and scent and wetness there made him groan.

"If you're planning to coerce me into confessing," Dayna said pertly, "I have news for you. It won't work."

"That's what you think." Leisurely, T.J. caressed her. He watched her reaction . . . and was gratified when she moaned. "I'll give you one more chance. Tell me what happened when I lost control . . . and I'll go easy on you. I won't even make you beg."

She laughed. "Go ahead. Do your worst. I'm unbreakable."

On an indrawn breath, T.J. lowered his head. He spread her wide, then gently . . . softly . . . swept his tongue over her.

"Hey!" Dayna yelped, instantly quivering. "Wait. You're—"

"—enjoying myself. Mmmm." Closing his eyes, he lost himself to the slick, smooth feel of her—to the joy of making her feel every bit as good as he did right now. "You feel so amazing."

She squirmed, surprise evident in the way she planted a hand on his head. "Hold on. Doesn't this witchfolk ban go both ways? I mean, I realize we've only just gotten bonded, so this whole witch-warlock thing is pretty new to me, but it only seemed reasonable to assume that if *you* weren't supposed to enjoy what I did, then you're *really* not supposed to do what you, um—" She broke off, shaking beneath the next slow, circular movements of his mouth. "Um, are doing. Mmm. Right now. So—"

Momentarily, T.J. stopped. "I already broke one rule." He smiled at her. "What makes you think I won't break another one?"

"Uhh . . . Patayan honor?" Dayna asked feebly. She caught the look in his eye. "Uh-oh. But—but—it's forbidden! What about—"

"It's only forbidden because warlocks are susceptible to losing control during sex," T.J. told her. "They can't help it. They're notorious for it. That means they're liable to confess their magic to the wrong women. Sometimes to *many* wrong women."

"Warlock sluts," Dayna muttered. "Oh! That feels *so* good. I'm going to stop you in a second, but in the meantime—"

"In ancient times," T.J. said in his most scholarly tone, "those women were sometimes deliberately sent to discover the warlocks' witchfolk origins—and wipe them out." He pressed his mouth to Dayna, then trailed his tongue up, down . . . He almost forgot what he'd been saying. It required all his discipline to sound unaffected when he picked up his explanation again. "The warlocks' loose talk put entire communities at risk."

With a moan, T.J. decided he'd proved his point. Besides, he couldn't remember why he was telling her this. Instead, he thought about learning what Dayna liked most. So far, she liked a gentle caress here . . . a softer touch there . . . and a whole lot of his agile tongue, moving in *exactly* the right way to bring her closer . . . closer . . . to losing control herself.

"Ah. This isn't fair!" Typically, Dayna didn't surrender easily. She wriggled beneath him. "You *still* shouldn't be—"

"Witches don't have the same susceptibility," T.J. broke in, catching the trailing threads of his argument. "They can separate sex and love. And they can detect deception. That's why the coven elders ruled that *this*"—T.J. swirled his tongue over the most sensitive part of her, thrilled by the way she clutched his head closer, despite her objections—"is okay."

Dayna panted, tensing beneath him. "Smart elders," she managed. She fell silent. Then she appeared to remember she was debating with him. Weakly, she added, "But the coven elders who made that decision were all witches." Another pant. "I think—they might have had"—she arched upward—"ulterior motives."

"Maybe." T.J. lapped more slowly . . . more tauntingly. "And apparently, the truth still holds. I'm just as bad as those ancient warlocks were, because I just told you a closely guarded secret." Lifting his head with effort, he smiled at her. "I guess you're like those seductresses. You fucked my brains out."

"Not yet. But I will." Dayna gasped. "Just—please—don't—"

"Stop? I won't." He gave her another smile. "I promise."

For long moments, T.J. kept his promise. The room filled with Dayna's breathy cries. She rocked beneath him, making him hold tight to her hips as she finally, achingly, came undone beneath his mouth. She moaned and clutched him to her, then sank against the sofa's ruined cushions.

Beautiful and flushed, she lay there panting. Then Dayna opened her eyes. "You," she accused, "don't play fair."

"Tell me that later." T.J. could scarcely form the words. With a rough, rocking motion, he covered her body with his own. He kissed her hungrily, reveling in the way Dayna opened herself completely to him. "After I make us both crazy."

"Again?" she breathed. "But I . . . oh! *Ah. Mm-hmmm.*"

Her husky cry of assent made him want her even more. Wild with desire, T.J. thrust himself inside her. At the last moment, he'd have sworn he saw the swirling aurora borealis of Dayna's magic again . . . and his own magic, leaving him to join with it.

An instant later, Dayna arched her hips upward to meet him, and T.J. lost his mind completely. Whatever he'd seen was gone.

Chapter Nineteen

Dayna emerged from her bedroom the following morning with an unstoppable smile on her face. If this was what cusping felt like, it wasn't all bad. Sure, her thigh muscles felt quivery. Her knees felt wobbly. And her throat ached with the uninhibited cries T.J. had wrung from her over the course of the night. But she could cope with that. Just so long as she had a little pick-me-up to take the edge off. And maybe some breakfast to—

Something zoomed toward her. A plate, she realized at the last second. Dayna thought about ducking—her usual nonathlete's reaction whenever anything came at her quickly—but at the last second she whipped her hand upward. The plate smacked into it with a jolt. With an equally jarring reaction, she realized she'd actually caught it: a plate of waffles. The aromas of maple syrup, bananas, and—peanut butter?—reached up to her.

She was much faster with the flying glass of orange juice.

Catching it in her opposite hand, Dayna smiled. Hmm. Today was off to an excellent start already. Happily, she followed the sound of voices toward the tiny patio outside Deuce's kitchen. As she'd predicted, her roommate and her bonded Patayan guardian were already seated at the sun-splashed wrought-iron table.

"Good morning!" Smugly, she slid her breakfast into position. She helped herself to a seat next to T.J. "My magic is *awesome* this morning! I guess being bonded agrees with me, because I only have to think about something and . . . poof! It's there, magiked into existence. It's just like the books say."

"That's not magic, that's theft." With a dour look, Deuce stared at her plate. "That's my breakfast. I left it on the counter when I followed *him* out here a few minutes ago."

Deuce jerked his thumb toward T.J., who lounged in the sunniest seat, entirely naked . . . except for the low-slung, waist-wrapped striped beach towel that Deuce had obviously tossed his way. In the light of a new day, her tracer appeared even yummier than last night.

"Oh." Disappointed, Dayna looked at her waffles. "That explains why these waffles are covered in bananas, maple syrup, *and* peanut butter. I wondered why I would conjure up something like that. I don't even like peanut butter, so—"

"Exactly what," Deuce broke in, "did you do to him?"

"Huh?" Dayna chugged some juice. "What do you mean?" Deuce jabbed his chin at T.J. "He looks all googly eyed."

"Ah." Realizing what Deuce meant, Dayna smiled. She caught T.J.'s hand. "Yeah, well . . . That makes two of us."

T.J. smiled at her. His smile broadened as his gaze dipped to her golden armlet. Her armlet warmed itself in response.

Mmm. Being bonded was good. Humming to herself, Dayna examined her breakfast. Then she closed her eyes, recalled an incantation from a book she'd read yesterday, and . . . *"Voilà!"*

A duplicate breakfast appeared. Pleased, Dayna nudged her original plate toward Deuce, then dug in. She was *starving*.

"Ugh." In dismay, she let her fork clatter to her plate after one bite. "These waffles taste funny. Flat, somehow."

"It's the peanut butter," Deuce said. "Give it another—"

"It's not the peanut butter," T.J. disagreed. "It's the magic.

Specifically, the molecules. You didn't conjure new waffles—you rearranged Deuce's waffles. And his plate." Ignoring a stony-faced Deuce, T.J. pointed to a hairline crack as it crept across the new plate she'd conjured. "Even witchfolk can't create something out of nothing. Your results are weaker than usual, because your magic is so . . . inexpert." T.J. frowned. "Can't you see the pixilation? It's all over everything."

"Are you kidding me? I can't even see my own aura."

T.J.'s frown deepened. "You can't?"

"Nope." Dayna peered at her arm. Still no dice. Whatever her mother had seen was invisible to her. "Is it still there?"

"Yeah." Deuce nodded. "Even *I* can see it. It's a little weird looking, kind of raggedy around the edges, but—"

"But it's yours." T.J. shot a quelling glance at his partner. "You can learn to see it—it just takes practice and openness. I'll show you how."

"Okay." Neither *practice* nor *openness* sounded all that great to her. But she was here to learn. "I still think you're just annoyed because I didn't conjure *you* any waffles," Dayna teased. She gave T.J. a sunny smile. "Admit it. You were hoping I'd pamper you like a witchy version of June Cleaver."

"Not hardly. I like my women strong—and capable of wielding more than a vacuum." T.J. traced his fingertips over her arm. His touch made her shiver. For a minute, all they did was gaze at one another. "Besides, I'm perfectly capable of taking what I want, when I want it. Do you need a reminder of that?"

Spellbound, Dayna shook her head. "No. I remember."

She remembered him, making her writhe with desire and need. She remembered herself, taking more and more from him. And as she looked at T.J., she knew he remembered, too. The air between them felt thick and soft, warm and safe. It lulled her into releasing a contented sigh. She wove her fingers with T.J.'s.

"Oh, for fuck's sake," Deuce grumbled, staring up from his magically duplicated waffles. "Can you two get a grip, please?"

Dayna and T.J. smiled. "Get a grip? Well, I guess we—"

Another obscenity. "Okay, poor choice of words. What I mean is . . . Hello?" Deuce clapped. "Jesus, you're like two halves of a whole, all of a sudden. What happened last night?"

United, Dayna and T.J. gazed at him. "What *didn't* happen?"

They went back to mooning over each other. T.J. hugged Dayna close. Cooing, she nuzzled her tracer's jaw, amazed at his impressive overnight growth of beard stubble. T.J. rubbed his cheek. Appearing adorably self-conscious, he gave her a cryptic explanation involving Patayan and strong emotions and razors.

Evidently, feeling something strongly made him hairier.

"Kinky." Dayna laughed, then stroked T.J.'s bristly jaw again. "I guess I'd better buy razor blades in bulk. Because I plan to make you feel a lot of things, starting with *this* . . ."

Subtly, she dropped her hand to his lap. That towel had to go, she decided. And the sooner it did, the sooner she could—

"So," Deuce broke in. "Who's going to repair my sofa?"

Guiltily, Dayna started. What was the matter with her? She'd been on the verge of jumping T.J. right there, no matter who was watching. Freezing in place, she gazed through the patio door to the living room area beyond. Deuce's wrecked sofa looked as though a rabid coyote—or two—had chewed through it.

"I'm sorry, Deuce. I'll fix it, I promise. Right now."

"Oh, Dayna. That's okay." Deuce stared meaningfully at T.J., his tone laden with sarcasm. "*You* don't have to do that."

"Of course I do. Besides, it will be good practice for cuspingwitch class later." With an apologetic smile, Dayna set aside her pixilated waffles. "Prepare to be amazed."

* * *

With a very foreign-feeling sense of gratitude, T.J. watched Dayna slip past the open patio door. She stood in the distance, silhouetted in morning sunshine, and frowned at the sofa cushions that T.J. had destroyed in his abandon last night.

Mmm. That had been some night. And morning. And today was shaping up to be just as good between them. Maybe it was unwise to trust his bonded witch so quickly. But T.J. didn't regret it.

How could he? He'd never felt so free before. So whole.

It had been years, T.J. realized as he studied Dayna's newly certain magical maneuverings, since he'd felt this *good*.

"Wow." Beside him, Deuce watched Dayna, too, his expression shuttered. "Our little runaway has come a long way with her magic. She's gotten downright cocky." Balefully, he turned to T.J. "Or maybe she's just gotten a little cock. Is that it?"

"Hey. Watch yourself." Instantly tense, T.J. swerved his gaze to his partner. "First, it was a *lot* of cock. Second, I'm bonded with her. If it comes down to you or her, she wins."

"Hey, that's nice." Deuce's face hardened. Hurt feelings whooshed from him to T.J. in a bitter rush, chased by a hefty dose of cynicism. "You get a little witchy action, and all of a sudden you're a traitor to the rest of mankind. I should have expected as much. Jesus, T.J. That's so—"

His voice strangled to a stop. Wide-eyed, Deuce slammed against his chair. The wrought iron scraped across the patio.

Magic hummed. Deuce stiffened into position, his massive body pinned to his chair. An instant later, T.J. found himself standing over him, hands filled with a buzzing vortex of magic.

His partner's gaze shunted to that magic. He grunted.

Grunted, because he couldn't say more. Without conscious thought, T.J. had acted to defend his bonded witch. He'd shut up Deuce—literally—and now stood prepared to do even more.

T.J. didn't know what. And he didn't want to find out.

With effort, he relaxed his hands. Frowning, he kicked the chair. His motion released the spell he'd cast, setting Deuce free. With a gasp, his partner stared up at him. Accusingly.

"*Don't* call me a traitor," T.J. warned. "*Don't* forget I'm not part of mankind—I'm just watching out for it. Your lame-ass human fate isn't mine. And whatever else you do, *don't* fuck with Dayna. She's mine. I'm hers. That's it, now and later."

"Oh yeah? Does Dayna know that?" Wearing a pissed-off look, Deuce yanked his T-shirt collar as though fighting for breath. "All that 'now and later' bullshit you're spouting? Because from where I sit, that witch is using you to get off. Period."

"That's *your* experience with witches. Not mine."

The cynicism surrounding Deuce intensified. "All witches are the same. If you're too horny to realize that—" With a swearword, he broke off. "I'm your friend. I'm supposed to—"

"You're a dozer. You'll never understand—"

The magical world, T.J. meant to say. But he never had a chance to finish. His partner's doubt increased, fueled by an underlying fear and a protectiveness he'd never have admitted. Soaking up those emotions wasn't pretty. T.J. did it anyway.

"Screw you, T.J. I'm turned," Deuce said hotly. "Whether you like it or not, I'm your partner. Or did you convert to The Old Ways when I wasn't looking? Because the way things are changing around here, we're going to need a scorecard soon."

"I'm no *myrmidon*. And if you can't keep up—"

"I can keep up." Deuce swore. "And *I* can stay on target. I've been with Lily Abbot almost twenty-four/seven for the past few days, trying to find signs that she's the vixen witch you're looking for." He pointed toward Janus, where his mission to trail Lily had taken him. "Can you say the same thing?"

"I assigned myself Sumner and Francesca. Not Lily." T.J. scoured his partner with a hard look. "You deal with your work. Leave me to deal with mine. You're in no position to talk smack about what I'm doing. Without magic, you can't be expected to—"

"To what? To do *anything*?" Looking aggrieved, Deuce slammed his chair to the patio. He stood. "I can still *think*, dickwad. Which is more than I can say for you." He jabbed his finger at T.J. "When Dayna dumps you, don't come crying to me."

"Jesus, Deuce. Come on." Sorrowfully, T.J. shook his head. "You've got to let it go. Not all witches are like—"

"*Don't* say her name again." Deuce wasn't magical. At times like this, he was fearless enough to make up for it. His burly arms bulged with strength. His jaw jutted with belligerence. His heart and mind tightened with a willingness to make the world's magical inhabitants suffer the way he had. "I swear I'll spend the rest of my days making you sorry for it if you do."

"Hey." In ostensible surrender, T.J. held up his palms. They'd been friends too long for this. He grinned. "Don't let me slow down your revenge plans, pal. You'd be wasting your time on me. I don't care enough about anyone to matter. I never have."

For a long moment, his partner only glared at him. "Maybe that used to be true," Deuce said. "But it's not anymore."

Then he grabbed his keys and left . . . probably for Janus. If T.J. were smart, he would do the same thing.

Beaming from ear to ear, Dayna looked up. "Hey, Deuce! Check it out. I totally made the fabric mend itself—*without* creating a killer cottonseed tornado this time. See?"

Her roommate delivered her a scathing look. "Nice. Bye."

"Hey! Hang on." Troubled by the atmosphere of fury that clung to Deuce, Dayna chased him. "What's the matter?"

"Ask your boyfriend." Deuce slammed the door.

This time, Dayna was the one who saved Deuce's bikini-girls "artwork" from crashing to the floor. With a flash of magic, she straightened the picture. Proudly, she glanced up just as T.J. entered the room. His gaze arrowed to the sofa. He stopped.

"You have a talent for repairing things that are broken."

"Yeah, well . . ." That was a strange way to interpret the situation. "I've had a lot of practice fixing mistakes."

"It shows." T.J. frowned. "I didn't think you could do it."

"If that's your way of saying you're impressed, you need a better vocabulary."

T.J.'s expression softened. "You don't need me to believe in your magic. You need *you* to believe in it."

Touché. It wasn't like her to hunt for compliments anyway. Regrouping, Dayna nodded at the apartment's front door. "What's wrong with Deuce? He looked ready to kill someone just now."

T.J. exhaled. "Let's just say . . ." He swore. "The witch who turned Deuce did a hell of a head trip on him. He's not over it yet. I think seeing us together gets to him."

"Oh. Are you sure that's it?" Dayna wrinkled her nose in curiosity. "Because I thought Deuce and Lily Abbot were—"

T.J. stiffened. "What do you know about Lily Abbot?"

"Just that she and Deuce have been seeing one another." Taken aback by his intent tone, Dayna frowned. "And that when Deuce talks about her, he seems pretty head over heels for her."

"Impossible. Deuce would never fall for another witch."

"Well, you should clue him into that then." Smiling, Dayna crossed her arms. "Because I think he already has."

"Deuce is working a mission. He's helping me. So whatever you think you see . . ." Tersely, T.J. broke off. "It's a lot like magic. Whatever you think you see isn't necessarily there."

"But it's *partly* there," Dayna argued. "You just said so.

Magic is always based in truth. It can't come from nowhere. It leaves signs, like pixilation or an aura, right? So—"

He gave her a long look. "You can't see those either."

Ouch. That hurt. Sharply, Dayna lifted her chin. "Maybe not. But I can feel things just fine. And what I feel right now is *you*, keeping a secret from me." Frustratingly, that was *all* she could feel—the same warning tingle that told a witch there was deception in the air. She couldn't discern its exact source. Even with her correctly functioning witchy abilities, there was always a loophole. "What aren't you telling me?"

"Nothing you need to know." T.J. conjured a pair of canvas pants, then yanked a T-back tank top over his shoulders. His Patayan amulets jangled. His tattoos gleamed, enigmatic and enthralling. "I'm putting a charm on this place to keep it hidden. Can you handle learning the spell to release it?"

Garmin's warning clanged in her head.

"Why does it need to be hidden?" Dayna asked.

Impatiently, T.J. exhaled. "Can you learn it or not?"

"I guess I won't get in if I can't." Focusing intently, Dayna learned T.J.'s concealment charm. It used magic she'd never witnessed before. "I'll have to write this down in my notebook to make sure. What about Deuce? How will he get in?"

"This is an antiwitchfolk charm. It won't affect him."

"Then why bother hiding this place at all? If your charm won't affect humans, then—" Dayna stopped as the truth struck her. This charm would affect Garmin and the IAB. They were of magical nature—and they were after T.J., too. "Are you sure it's Deuce's apartment you want to hide? Or is it yourself?"

Palming his keys, T.J. looked up. The moment his gaze met hers, comprehension rolled from him to her in a prickly rush.

So did frustration. He didn't like her questioning him.

"I made a promise to the Patayan," he said in a gruff tone. "I'll do whatever it takes to keep it. Right now, this is it."

"Hiding?" Dayna asked. "Keeping secrets?"

T.J. compressed his mouth. His cheekbones stood out in bold relief, a visible sign of his Patayan birthright. Jaw tight, he shook his head. "It's better that you don't know."

"Don't know what?" Dayna thought about the human murder that Garmin had told her about. She thought about how troubled Garmin had seemed about it. There were a lot of things she still didn't understand about the new Coven-haven. "Did you *do* something, T.J.? Is there something I should know? Maybe I can—"

His exasperated exhale cut her off. Her tracer traversed the length of the living room, then stopped in front of her.

"Look at me." Roughly, T.J. cradled her cheek in his hand. He tilted her face upward. "Whatever you think you see in the coming days, you have to believe I'm on the right side of it."

We have reason to believe he's fallen on the wrong side of things, Garmin had told her. *Stay away from T.J.*

Wordlessly, Dayna gazed up at him. His face was still exotic to her, his features handsome and of undeniable witch-folk heritage. Everything she believed about T.J. was based on the feelings she intuited through her own witchy abilities. But those abilities had always failed her in the past.

Could she trust them now? Could she trust *him*?

How could she not?

"I don't know if I can do that," she said.

Briefly, T.J.'s hand tightened on her face. Disappointment flickered from him to her . . . then vanished, squashed beneath an abrupt wave of determination. "I hope you can," he said, stopping to give her a rough kiss, "because I'm too far gone to turn back now. Good luck in class. I've got to go."

Troubled, Dayna stared at the still-shuddering door to Deuce's apartment. She watched as the whole place went still, then ballooned outward. In a burst of magic that made her eardrums hurt, T.J.'s concealment spell fell over everything.

That did it, then. With trembling knees, she headed for her bedroom. Her gaze dropped to the unmade bed she and T.J. had shared, then to the clothes still scattered on the floor. Her open backpack lay in the same place she'd left it, beside the bureau; library books stood in a pile on the room's only chair, the topmost volume opened to a chapter on conjuring familiars.

Shaking her head, Dayna knelt beside her backpack. After a little rummaging, she pulled out an embossed business card.

It felt strange in her hand, laden with importance and imprinted with an identity she didn't particularly want to be associated with. With a sigh, she withdrew her cell phone, too. She carried them both to the bed, then sat on its messy sheets.

Before she could dial, a plaintive sound reached her. Going instantly still, Dayna listened, her cell phone held to her ear.

The noise came again. It sounded like . . . a meow?

Searching for its source, Dayna swiveled her head. She spotted a tentative movement near the closet. Its door stood open a few inches. There in the gap, a sleek tabby kitten stood watching her. Its paws were ungainly, its posture unsteady. Its dark gaze gleamed with intelligence . . . and uncertainty.

She could hardly believe her eyes.

She'd done it. Somehow, she'd conjured a familiar!

It must have happened yesterday, when she'd been trying to study, Dayna realized. She'd left her meeting with Garmin, her mind whirling with all he'd asked of her, then arrived home with her books . . . and apparently been successful with at least one element of her homework. How had she not realized it before?

Her (multiple) encounters with T.J. must have scared away the kitten. They'd gotten pretty loud. The poor creature had probably taken refuge in the closet almost immediately.

"Wow. Usually all my familiars run away," Dayna told the kitten in a soft voice. "You must be braver than all the ones who came before you." Moving as slowly as she could, Dayna sank to the floor. She motioned to the creature. "You must be very, very brave to answer my call. And to come out now to see me."

The kitten took a cautious step closer.

"That's it. Come here and let me look at you."

Another meow. She'd swear it sounded reproachful.

"I can't help it if you didn't like being conjured. You're here now, and you're mine." She wiggled her fingers. "Are you hungry? I'm pretty sure I can dredge up some waffles."

The kitten perked up. It padded a few inches closer.

"That's it," Dayna cooed. "Don't be afraid. Come here."

The moment she said the words, the kitten sat. Stubbornly.

Dayna almost laughed. It figured. She'd conjured herself a familiar with an attitude problem. That was so *her*.

Stricken by an idea, she squinted at the business card, then dialed her phone. She glanced deliberately away from her familiar, feigning disinterest. The phone rang. It connected. A male voice came instantly over the line, startling her.

"I didn't think you'd answer your own phone," she said.

Garmin sounded unfazed. "I've been expecting your call."

"Oh." Biting her lip, Dayna hesitated. An instant later, a small, soft weight bounded onto her lap. The kitten purred and rubbed against her knee. Its small body vibrated with the force of its joy. Taking that as a magical sign, she smiled. She spoke into her phone again. "I have something to tell you."

At quarter past six that evening, T.J. strode down the deserted hallway at Covenhaven Academy. The place smelled like floor wax and sneakers and cheap perfume. It vibrated with the aftereffects of beginner spells and teenage enchantment pranks. Ahead at a row of lockers, a rogue memory flicker bounced off a door, babbling its story with high-pitched feminine zeal.

With a frown, he dispatched it. The memory flicker fizzled.

In a spurt of acrid smoke, it flopped onto a locker that was embellished with a homecoming poster. It slid down, then died.

"Wow. Nice work," came a voice from ahead of him. Francesca Woodberry nodded from her languorous position at Professor Reynolds's classroom doorway. She leaned against the door with her arms full of witchcraft books and her gaze full of witchery, looking beautiful and spoiled. "I wish I could make all the annoyances in my life go up in a puff of smoke. You're amazing."

"You have annoyances?" Clad in a disguise fashioned of Professor Reynolds's likeness—based on the surveillance he'd done already—T.J. ambled toward her. He adopted the bookish demeanor Reynolds used. "I'm surprised anything dares to bother you."

Francesca laughed. "That's what I like about you, Professor. Your open adoration of me." She gave him a curious look, all her feminine powers on full display. She seemed to know better than to touch him outright. "It's a good thing I'm crazy about you. Otherwise, you'd have an unfair advantage."

He already did have an unfair advantage. The Patayan magic T.J. had added to his disguise made it impervious to witchy detection. His intrinsic magic couldn't block the deception he was using, but it muddled its signals just enough—just enough that when Francesca felt that witchy warning tingle, she would think it was because of the clandestine relationship she'd been carrying on with her professor. The witches in her cusping-witch class would believe the same thing. Francesca hadn't exactly been discreet in her zeal to be awarded *juweel* status. Everyone in the class knew about her dalliance with Professor Reynolds.

Just as importantly, T.J.'s disguise—like the disguise he'd employed with Sumner—would keep the IAB from learning more about his Patayan mission. He knew Garmin was keeping tabs on him.

This time, though, his boss hadn't employed foragers.

This time, Garmin had used Dayna. T.J. had detected the head agent's imprint on her yesterday, when they'd reconnected. It had been all he could do not to confront her—to demand, with warlock possessiveness, why she'd allowed another male's touch. But he'd resisted, knowing that waiting was a better strategy. And he'd withstood the unpleasant results of Garmin's contact today, when Dayna had questioned him. He hoped she would have enough faith in him not to fall for the IAB's scare tactics.

But for now, he had Francesca to deal with.

As Reynolds, T.J. chuckled. He hadn't planned to meet her alone tonight. He was here to test Sumner and Lily—the likeliest vixen witches in the class—and learn which of them possessed the strongest magic. He was sure it was Sumner. But he couldn't afford to overlook Lily . . . or Francesca.

As a recognized leader, she would be integral to any vixen pact that formed—including the vixen pact that might lure Sumner away from the Patayan's cause. In a sense, Francesca was T.J.'s competition for Sumner's allegiance. It would benefit him to know as much about her as possible.

At first, he'd believed Francesca might be the *juweel* he was looking for. She was a vixen. She was powerful. She was undeniably charismatic. But his magus's assertion that the vixen they needed would be isolated, unsure, and indecisive had eliminated Francesca from consideration.

The flirtatious witch in front of him was nothing if not socially adept, self-confident, and decisive. While shadowing her at Janus, T.J. had seen Francesca orchestrate complicated events, berate employees, cajole resort guests, and make decisions with ruthless certainty. Unless his magus was wrong . . .

But his magus couldn't be wrong. T.J. was sure of that.

As far as T.J. could tell, Francesca was not spending her time deliberating over which witchy alliances to make in the magical world. Most of her energies—and magic—seemed to be aimed at belittling other witches . . . and bewitching Professor Reynolds into making her the *juweel* of her class. Her naked ambition had made her easy to dupe with his disguise. All Francesca really saw was herself. In his eyes, she saw only her own reflection.

"So . . . it's getting late." Francesca tilted her head toward the classroom door. She licked her lips. "Shall we?"

Her invitation was even more blatant than Sumner's had been. When he'd first infiltrated the class, T.J. hadn't been surprised to learn that Professor Reynolds's integrity had lapsed during his tenure as cusping-witch class instructor. But he had been disappointed.

On the other hand, what warlock's integrity hadn't wavered once or twice? Especially when faced with an alluring witch and a half hour to kill before class?

Offering her a smile, T.J. raised his arm.

At his magical nudge, the classroom door whooshed open. Francesca squealed with delight, then hugged his arm with an enthusiasm such minor magic definitely didn't deserve.

"Ooh! I love it when you show how *powerful* you are!"

"You haven't seen anything yet," T.J. promised.

He put his hand to Francesca's back, guided her into the classroom, then shut the door firmly behind them.

An instant later, the lock engaged. For better or worse, T.J. was about to make a deal with the devil.

Chapter Twenty

Running typically late, Dayna ducked into class at the last minute. Witches were already in their seats, chatting and casting minor spells; Professor Reynolds was at the front of the room, discussing something with Francesca. Behind him, the whiteboard showed a syllabus written in a language Dayna didn't recognize, full of cryptic symbols. That probably meant it was a magical pop quiz. Great. Toting the pet carrier she'd spent the past half hour selecting at a downtown store, she headed for her usual seat in the back of the room. Or at least she tried to.

Two of the cashmere witches blocked her path. Dressed in skinny black pants and chic sweaters, Sumner and Lily leaned across the aisle between desks, their heads bent over a cell phone. They laughed and pointed to something on EnchantNet.

Dayna exhaled. "Excuse me."

They ignored her. In gossipy, privileged tones, they critiqued whatever they were reading. Without so much as a glance at Dayna, Sumner stretched her legs farther across the aisle. Her glossy boots formed a rude but efficient barrier.

"Excuse me," Dayna said more loudly.

Her voice carried. Several curious witches, including

Camille, turned her way—as though anticipating another Dayna Sterling–style gaffe. Or some misused magic. Or both.

Beneath their scrutiny, Dayna considered relenting. There was another aisle only steps away. She could easily avoid this confrontation. But there was something about the way Lily and Sumner blocked her path. It was as if they knew they could do whatever they wanted . . . and other witches would applaud them for it. Even now, the nearby witches—many of them dressed in copycat cashmere—leaned closer, eager to follow the unfolding drama.

Defying Francesca or her cohorts was social suicide. They knew it. So did Dayna. It didn't stop her.

"You're blocking the aisle. Would you mind moving, please?"

Languidly, Lily looked up. "Yes, we would mind."

Sharing a giggle with Sumner, she flicked her fingers over her cell phone. The device's smooth black screen looked exactly like the one the warlock agent, Luis, had used at the IAB.

"Well, don't say I didn't ask nicely first."

"We won't." Looking annoyed, Sumner glanced up. Her gaze traveled over Dayna's clothes, then landed on her new pet carrier. She smirked. "A kitten familiar. How . . . basic of you."

"I had one exactly like that," Lily said. "In third grade."

The witches surrounding them tittered. Dayna clenched her fist on her carrier's handle. Protectively, she turned the latched opening away from their derisive laughter. If she was lucky, her familiar wouldn't hear it. The kitten might be stubborn, headstrong, and quick to express her displeasure at whatever was happening around her . . . but so was Dayna. Sometimes a bad attitude was just a cover to hide softer feelings.

Feelings that could be easily hurt. Just like Dayna's were right now. She still didn't belong here. But she was done with trying to fit in. All that had brought her was humiliation.

At the realization, a buzz began at the base of her spine. It moved up her backbone, just like the warning sensation

Dayna had experienced when T.J. had come for her at DRL, then vibrated to her extremities. Like an able child, she felt powerful, ready to perform magic beyond all her abilities. Even before she heard the voice behind her, she knew whom it would belong to.

"Is there a problem here?" Francesca asked.

Dayna turned to face her witchy rival. The queen bee of Covenhaven stood with one hand on her cashmere-clad hip, looking undeniably stylish and indisputably commanding. Her pretty face was arranged in an expression of polite interest. But underneath all those external factors, Dayna sensed . . . something else.

It was *protectiveness*, she realized with a jolt. Francesca Woodberry actually felt protective toward her friends.

Even though she didn't know exactly what was happening—and even though Dayna hardly posed a terrifying threat—Francesca had instantly rushed to take Sumner's and Lily's side in the issue.

What must that be like? Dayna wondered with a sense of grudging awe. To have lifelong friends who stood by one another, no matter what? To be part of a friendship that was closer than sisterhood? To stand together, united, against all threats?

Dayna didn't know. She'd never experienced that kind of friendship or that kind of belonging. She'd abandoned her own best friend, Camille, years ago. When cusping-witch class was finished, she would likely abandon Camille all over again. She had to. Her life was in Phoenix; she'd lived too long as an unlinked witch to turn back now. Still, Dayna couldn't help yearning for that kind of friendship . . . however foolishly.

It was the naked yearning that finally pushed her.

"No, there's no problem." Drawing in a deep breath, Dayna focused on Sumner's shiny knee-high boots. Briefly, she closed her eyes. "Sumner was just on her way to the ladies' room."

"No, I wasn't." Sumner rolled her eyes. "Francesca, you—"

Suddenly, Sumner's eyes widened. She lurched from her seat by force, flailing her arms. Jarringly, her left foot took a step. Then her right. With a squeal, Sumner grabbed her boot.

It wobbled in her hands, then thunked another step forward. Sumner teetered behind it. Awkwardly forced by her enchanted footwear, she headed to the Covenhaven Academy lavatories.

Clumsily, she banged into a desk and stubbed her toe.

"You *bitch*!" Her gaze, malevolent and incredulous, veered to Dayna. "These are brand-new boots. What did you do to them?"

"I don't know." Dayna smiled. "It must have been an accident. I'm pretty bad at magic, remember?" She watched with satisfaction as Sumner took another staggering, disjointed step toward the door. "You've got the memory flickers to prove it."

"I'll erase them!" Sumner reeled down the aisle like a fashionably dressed drunk. Her pleading gaze flashed to Francesca, then to Dayna again. "I swear I will! I'm sorry!"

"Say something nice about my kitten, too."

Sumner's gaze swerved to Dayna's familiar. "It's a very nice kitten!" She jolted another step. "It's awesome! So furry!"

With fleeting interest, Francesca looked at Dayna's pet carrier. Upon glimpsing the now-meowing kitten inside, her gaze narrowed. Without looking at Sumner, she gave an impatient wave.

At the gesture, Dayna's enchantment fell away. Sumner wobbled once more, then straightened. She gave her boots a suspicious glare. Then her gaze lifted to Dayna.

If looks could kill, Dayna would have been underground.

In the silence, Professor Reynolds's voice boomed. "Take your seats, everyone. We have a lot of work to do tonight."

With a flurry of disappointment, the other witches turned their attention to their instructor. Francesca turned to Dayna. "Cool spell," she said. "You remind me of myself, Darla." Regally, Francesca took her seat beside Lily and Sumner. Dayna gawked after her in surprise. *Francesca Woodberry was impressed by her.* Could this night get any more surreal?

The curious thing about cusping witches, T.J. thought, was that they were so hungry for their instructor's approval. Even though they were reaching the apex of their powers and would soon command magic stronger than any warlock could manage, they remained eager for a kind word, a nod of appreciation, or a special accolade from him. The cusping witches, he'd realized, *needed* his attention. They were hardwired to get it. From his position at the front of the class, he could scarcely take a step without thirty pairs of eyes following his every move.

From each row of desks, hushed witches leaned into their hands, their gazes fixed on his face and body as they listened to his lesson for the night. Interest, fascination, and even sexual curiosity flowed from his "students" to him, moving in undulating waves that were impossible to block completely.

The same thing must be happening to instructors all across Covenhaven—and in witchfolk districts worldwide—as the IAB strove to educate this year's collective of cusping witches. There were over a thousand cusping witches in Covenhaven alone. T.J. wasn't sure if Garmin and his allies appreciated the magnitude of what they'd done when they'd stolen the education of cusping witches from the coven elders and bureaucratized it.

They must be realizing it now, for better or worse.

As he strode toward the middle of a row, intent on making a point about transmogrification spells, one brazen witch squeezed his ass. Startled, T.J. jumped. When he gazed down at the witch, she met his look with a provocative expression of her own, then slowly licked her lips. *You're fantastic*, she mouthed.

No wonder a weaker warlock like Reynolds had caved in to his primal instincts. Teaching a pack of hormonally surging, magic-wielding, ultrapowerful cusping witches was like running a psychological gauntlet. Naked. In a maze. With a hard-on.

Fortunately, T.J.'s IAB training came to the fore. Ignoring his warlock urgings for pleasure, he focused on sending out his own signals—signals of authority, expertise, and detachment. He remained unmoved by the witches' antics. He was here for a higher purpose: to learn, once and for all, which of these witches was the vixen witch he sought. The *juweel*.

To that end, he devised a series of tests. The first two involved complex spells; their results were inconclusive. The third involved interpretation of ancient incantations. Gesturing to the whiteboard, T.J. again used Reynolds's academic tone.

"Who can explain this series of incantations?"

Obediently, the witches turned their faces toward the board. Instantly, their expressions creased with confusion.

The kind-faced witch, Camille, raised her hand. "Is it in code?" she asked. "I don't recognize the dialect."

"It is not encoded," T.J. told her. "Anyone else?"

Lily Abbot rolled her eyes. "It's a trick. It's not real."

T.J. shook his head. "It's real. And very powerful."

Yawning, Sumner examined her manicure. Dayna squinted at the board, determination written on her face. In that moment, T.J. loved her for that—for her grit and willingness to try.

He simply loved *her*, he realized with a rush of giddy emotion. He loved his bonded witch wholly and unstoppably.

A second later, Dayna sighed. She looked away, clearly having given up. Disappointed, T.J. examined the rest of the class. A few witches scrolled through EnchantNet on their cell phones, searching for clues. Others copied down the words, frowning as they wrote the unfamiliar ancient symbols.

"How long are we going to spend on this?" Francesca gave him a bored look. "It's clear nobody knows the answer."

"This is the most important lesson for tonight," T.J. said. "We'll stay here as long as it takes."

Impatiently, Francesca exhaled. With an air of annoyance, she blurted the words of the first incantation. The old dialect rolled easily off her tongue, laden with augury and potency.

With a crack of magic, the room wavered, then surged. The sulfurous smell of magic tinged the air. The desks suddenly heaved, animating themselves. Beneath the arms and hands of the witches who occupied them, the desks bucked violently upward.

A chorus of squeals erupted. Books and possessions slid to the floor in a jumble. Wide-eyed witches clutched their desks. Their efforts only added to the mayhem; sensing their occupants' unease, the charmed desks shuddered in response and jumped more wildly. More books flew through the air, then collided and crashed to the floor. Several witches reeled out of their seats. They fled to the back of the room, near the darkened windows.

Francesca sat safely in her seat. With a smug gesture, she petted her desktop. Beneath her touch, the wood and metal sighed with contentment. Beside her, Lily and Sumner did the same.

Their responses were interesting, but not sufficient for his purposes. T.J. still couldn't tell which of them had stumbled upon that soothing tactic—or which of them was most powerful. Uttering a Patayan enchantment, he countered the desks' animation charm. At once, they went still. They landed with all four legs on the floor, creating a loud clatter. His students cried out. They stared, a few of them pointing.

"It's all right," T.J. said. "Come back to your desks."

Two witches near him gave their desks wary looks. One leaned toward the other. "Night school just got *intense*."

"It's probably just a trick, like Lily said," the other witch disagreed. "Nobody knows magic like a vixen witch does. We're lucky Francesca doesn't do that stuff all the time."

T.J. already knew that Francesca's, Lily's, and Sumner's status as a vixen trio was well known around Covenhaven. Hearing it discussed so casually still took him aback. On the other hand, most of these witches had known each other since they were able children. It was no surprise they accepted the vixen witches in their midst—and by all appearances, envied them, too.

"Francesca, that was impressive." As Reynolds, he turned to face her. "How did you know to enact the enchantment?"

The beautiful witch shrugged. "I didn't."

"Clearly"—T.J. pointed his arm at the desks—"you did."

"That was just an accident." Francesca traded a mischievous glance with her friends. "I pronounced the words phonetically. I had to. If I hadn't, you would have kept us here all night."

The class burst into laughter. A few witches sent admiring glances Francesca's way. Some of them leaned across the aisle to whisper their approval, embellishing their words with nods and smiles. Francesca accepted their praise with jaded equanimity.

From the back of the room, Dayna cleared her throat.

"Um . . . what do I do with this?" she asked.

Still distracted by Francesca's effortless absorption of the other witches' admiration, T.J. glanced upward.

Then he gawked. An enormous tiger stood beside Dayna, its eyes deadly and its fangs bared. Beside the creature's huge clawed paws lay the remnants of Dayna's pet carrier, its wire-mesh door and plastic sides twisted almost beyond recognition.

The desks hadn't been the only things to react to the magic in the room, T.J. realized. Dayna had reacted, too. While the other cusping witches had run for shelter, Dayna had altered her familiar into a form that could protect her. What was most amazing about the magic she'd used, though, was its appearance.

It was *unpixilated*.

Just as T.J. realized that unprecedented detail, the tiger lowered its head. It gave a rumbling growl. The threatening sound reverberated through the room. Fear whooshed from Dayna to T.J.; the class of witches collectively held its breath.

Terrified, Dayna stood stock still.

Her gaze met T.J.'s . . . then widened in recognition.

She'd seen him not as Reynolds, T.J. realized, but as himself. That shouldn't have been possible. But he had no time to contemplate the problem further. An instant later, the creature tensed and lunged toward the closest group of witches.

Horrified into immobility, Dayna stared as her former kitten familiar lunged. As though the creature were moving in slow motion, every detail stood out to her. She glimpsed the tiger's furry stripes, eerily reminiscent of her familiar's tabby coloring. She saw the ripple of feline muscle and a flash of claws. Helplessly, she looked at T.J.—because that's who he was, beyond all reason—and felt courage move from him to her.

"Only you can stop this," he said. "It's *your* familiar."

His words, hoarsely spoken but imbued with calm awareness, snapped her out of her paralysis.

"No!" Dayna dived forward, almost at the same instant as her familiar did. Blindly, she managed to grab two handfuls of rough-feeling, striped tiger fur. "Stop. Be still."

The tiger snarled. Twisting its spine, it leaped on its rear paws, towering over her. Dayna shrank back as its breath—bizarrely redolent of Kitten Chow—flowed over her in a hot rush. Its jaws snapped shut with an awful sound, inches above her staticky hair. Its eyes rolled back in its massive head.

Her familiar was afraid, Dayna realized. It was afraid because *she'd* been afraid—and she'd reacted to that fear by transforming her familiar into a protective form. Somehow. She still wasn't sure how she'd done it. Focusing on calming her breath, she made herself loosen her grip on the tiger's fur. She stroked the creature's heaving sides, murmuring comforting words. "It's all right," she crooned. "We're all right now."

At her touch, her familiar shuddered. A weird feline vocalization rumbled through the air. Not quite a roar, not quite a purr, it felt like a mixture of both. The creature sank to its haunches, its gaze wary. Its huge body still quivered.

"That's it." More boldly, Dayna petted the big cat. "You're very brave, but we're all right now. Shh. It's all right now."

A hush fell over the classroom, broken only by her familiar's panting breath and the scrape of its claws as it trembled. Dimly, she registered her classmates' awestruck faces and fearful postures. She peered upward. T.J. had morphed into Professor Reynolds again, but this time, Dayna wasn't fooled.

For whatever reason, her tracer was in disguise, just as he'd been at the Covenhaven farmers' market. She would not be the one to rip off that disguise . . . at least not tonight.

Another rumble came from her familiar. The creature seemed to shrink in her arms. It contracted, shifted . . . changed. As it did, the sulfur stink in the room grew stronger. Dayna swayed beneath the force of her magic, absorbed in its raw strength.

An instant later, she opened her arms. In place of the tiger she'd been cradling, her kitten sat alone on the classroom floor. It looked tiny, defenseless, and adorable again . . . but this time, the kitten's feline gaze held a secret. It meowed.

With a smile of relief, Dayna scooped up the kitten in her shaky arms. She glanced down at the wreckage of her new pet carrier, then shrugged. "I guess that one wasn't a good fit?"

Her fellow cusping witches laughed. Camille shot her a concerned look, then hurried over to help pick up the pieces of the ruined pet carrier. The other witches burst into motion, talking with each other; a few opportunistic witches showed memory flickers of the incident, destined for EnchantNet.

"That's enough." T.J.—as Professor Reynolds—clapped his hands. "Witches, take your seats. We have more work to do."

A groan of disappointment went up, but Dayna wasn't part of it. As the other witches returned to their places, scooping up their fallen books and purses and pencils, she cradled her kitten familiar. She gazed into its innocent-looking eyes.

"Very impressive," she murmured, "but how did we do that?"

The creature merely stared back at her. What had she expected? An explanation of how she'd achieved her own magic?

An instant later, the kitten leaped from her arms. Dayna jerked in readiness, fearing another unexpected transformation. But the kitten only pounced up to her shoulder, then climbed into the fleece hoodie she'd layered under her old corduroy jacket. It poked her, batted her hair with its paws to make itself comfortable, then nestled into position in her hood.

A contented purring sound came next.

A first-time metamorphosis could tire out anyone, Dayna decided with a smile. The only trouble was . . . exactly how had that transformation happened? She'd never accomplished such advanced magic before. She didn't know if she could ever do it again.

If she hoped to graduate from cusping-witch class, she knew she would have to try. She would have to achieve advanced magic *and* do a better job of controlling it, too. She was lucky her tiger familiar hadn't hurt anyone—including her.

The realization was sobering. With only two weeks left of cusping-witch classes, she would have to work harder than ever. Fortunately, Dayna had an ace up her sleeve: She had

T.J. on her side to help tutor her. If he couldn't explain how she'd morphed her familiar tonight, no one could.

The most startling event of Dayna's cusping-witch classes didn't happen that night. It didn't even happen the following night. Instead, it happened on the third day of the third week of night school, when she was least prepared and most surprised. .

She'd spent the preceding weeks in a haze of magical study, magical practice, and nearly nonstop sexual marathons with T.J. When Dayna wasn't casting remedial spells, she was lying beneath her bonded tracer, dreamy eyed and gasping for breath. When she wasn't getting to know her kitten familiar, sneaking past the concealment charm on Deuce's apartment to visit the library, or cramming for a magic test with Camille, she was learning about how various Patayan erogenous zones interacted with warlock seduction skills. When she wasn't attending class, she was jumping T.J.—in the shower, on the kitchen table, outside on the patio beneath the bougainvillea bracts and brilliant sunshine—and indulging in her witchiest instincts. When she wasn't focusing on learning to control her cusping magic, she was giving herself wholeheartedly to T.J. and the bond they shared.

And she loved it. She loved learning, loved feeling that she was improving, loved *giving* to someone outside herself. She loved seeing T.J. at the end of the day when they reunited at Deuce's protected apartment. She loved stepping into her tracer's burly arms and resting her head against the special nook on his shoulder that she'd claimed for herself. She loved talking with him, loved being with him, loved . . . *him*.

For the first time, Dayna began entertaining the idea of staying in Covenhaven . . . even after her classes were finished.

Beneath T.J.'s tutelage, her magic bloomed, too—even as

his, her tracer complained, mysteriously declined. Dayna didn't see the problem. If what she'd witnessed from him was a diminished form of magic, he was even stronger than she'd suspected.

"You're the strong one," T.J. insisted after the incident with her kitten-turned-tiger familiar. "*Unpixilated* magic is a matter of legend. And you did it. Try to remember how."

"I honestly don't know. I thought *you* would know."

He shook his head. "Not about this."

"Maybe you only imagined that you didn't see the pixilation," Dayna argued, unable to believe that her magic had been even more advanced than she'd guessed. "It can't be easy pretending to be an asshat like Professor Reynolds. You were stressed out, and your imagination ran away with you."

"I know what I saw."

"Then maybe it was a reverse magic pattern that you saw. You know, like the patterns that humans see in drifting clouds, a tiled floor, an abstract mural. They think they're creating patterns with their minds, but they're really seeing remnants of the items those molecules have been magiked into in the past."

"It wasn't that." T.J. growled and pulled her close for a kiss. "But I'm happy you're learning your magic so thoroughly."

After that, he continued to help train her, but despite her progress, it felt to Dayna as though she was never good enough. She improved. She mastered new spells. Most thrillingly, she actually made one of her Magic Marker weapons shoot tiny bullets. But time and again she caught T.J. watching her with disillusioned eyes. No matter how hard they worked, her magic never attained the levels it did in cusping-witch class.

T.J. was baffled by it.

"Don't worry," she told him. "I'm the queen of flukes."

"You did it once. You can do it again."

"Let it go, T.J. It's not as though I *want* to be magical."

He'd given her the same appalled look that the IAB agents at the bureau had done when she'd asked to be rid of her magic altogether. After that, they'd quit discussing the matter.

Night after night, her experience in cusping-witch class was similar. She achieved flashes of proficiency, but Dayna couldn't help feeling they were coincidences, brought on more by desperation than by any real witchy talent. Crushingly, T.J. seemed to agree with her analysis. By the time the final week of her IAB-mandated training arrived, she felt as unprepared as ever for the upcoming graduation and licensing test.

Morosely, Dayna loaded her backpack after class, trying to psych herself up for the grueling week ahead. Witches chatted all around her, confident and friendly. As usual, they appeared unbothered by the fact that there were still so many charms to learn, enchantments to cast, and transmogrifications to master.

That's when it happened. Francesca Woodberry, flanked by Lily and Sumner, sauntered up to Dayna's desk. Startled, Dayna stared at them. The appearance of Covenhaven's ultrapopular trio could not bode well for her. Unhappily reminded of how little progress she'd made toward being accepted as a witch, Dayna gave her final textbook a violent shove into her backpack.

She shouldered the unwieldy bundle. "Excuse me."

"Wow, that looks heavy." Francesca tsk-tsked, a smile on her face. "Lily, would you grab that for Dayna, please?"

"No thanks." Mulishly, Dayna slapped both hands on her backpack. Despite her grasp, the padded nylon straps peeled away from her shoulder. Wrenched by Lily's vixen magic, the whole thing sailed into the other witch's arms. "Hey! That's mine."

"Thanks." Obviously pleased by Lily's compliance, Francesca turned to Sumner. She gestured elegantly toward

Dayna's desk. "Sumner, would you please get Dayna's pet carrier?"

Unhappily, the curvaceous witch eyed the magically mended pet carrier. Inside, Dayna's kitten familiar meowed.

Sumner blanched.

"No! Thanks, but that won't be necessary." Dayna tried to snatch up her pet carrier. Sumner got there first. She levitated the carrier into her grasp, then held it at arm's length with an almost comical expression of dismay. Deprived of her belongings, Dayna confronted Francesca. "Look, this is about to get real ugly, real fast. Tell them to give me my things back."

"Ugly? I don't think that's going to happen . . . this time."

Reminded of her backfiring ugliness hex, Dayna felt herself flush. She put her hands on her hips. "Look, it's obvious we don't get along. So why don't you just leave me alone?"

A few of their classmates lingered at their desks, watching with overt curiosity. From the front of the room, T.J.— disguised as Professor Reynolds—observed them through narrowed, wary eyes.

Francesca chuckled. "I can't do that, Dayna."

"Why the hell not? Just point your feet toward the door and start moving." With a mocking tilt of her head, Dayna nodded in that direction. "Sumner can give you pointers on technique."

The other witch gave her an icy glare.

"Mmm, I'd rather not." As though considering the idea, Francesca pursed her movie-star lips. "So I'm not going to."

She began walking toward the hall, gesturing for Dayna to join her. With an exasperated sigh, Dayna did. Sumner and Lily followed, dutifully schlepping Dayna's belongings. They passed another Hallow-e'en Festival banner. Francesca smiled at her.

"I've been watching you in class these past few weeks," she said. "I think you're . . . special, Dayna. Very special."

Dayna scoffed. "You're special, too," she said with a heavy dose of sarcasm. "Can I have my stuff back now? As much fun as this little strolling quartet routine has been, I'd rather be—" She froze as something occurred to her. "Hey. You got my name right. You just called me Dayna."

"Of course I did. I've just decided—you're one of us now."

One of us. Suspiciously, Dayna stared at Francesca's guile-less profile. The other witch's words reverberated in her head, impossible to ignore or resist: *You're one of us now.*

Dayna had longed to hear those words her whole life. And now here they were, heralded by the star treatment from Sumner and Lily—however resentfully given—and officially made public by Francesca herself. At long last, *she was in.*

Against all her better judgment, Dayna couldn't help preening. Still feeling naked without her trusty backpack, she cocked her head. "What did you have in mind, Francesca?"

"We're having a little girls' spa day at Janus tomorrow afternoon to get ready for graduation." With a sense of warmth and kindliness that probably owed itself to a witchy charm, Francesca smiled at her. "I would love for you to join us."

There was only one thing to say. "Great. I'll be there."

Chapter Twenty-One

Pulling her hybrid subcompact into the curved entryway of the Janus Resort and Spa, Camille gave Dayna a dubious look.

"You're crazy for doing this, you know." Her hands tightened on the steering wheel. "Francesca has always been snooty to both of us. What makes you think she's changed?"

"She invited me here."

"So? That's it?" Anxiously, Camille scanned the resort's driveway. At the nearby valet stand, three uniformed—and male-modelesque—Janus employees jockeyed to reach their car first. "She *invited* you? You've never been that gullible, Dayna."

"Maybe I've changed—finally. Maybe I've grown into my witchiness." Dayna shrugged, unwilling to have her day spoiled by doubts. Francesca had *chosen her*. That was good enough. "Isn't this what you wanted? What everyone wanted? For me to grow into my magic? To change into the right kind of witch?"

Her friend sighed. "This is the kind of change that can hurt you. Don't you know that? This must be a trick."

"A trick?" Dayna laughed. "I never thought I'd see the day when Camille Levy sounded as cynical as bitchy Lily Abbot."

"It's so fancy here." Worriedly, Camille peered through the windshield at Janus's elaborate courtyard fountain, lavish landscaping, and well-dressed guests of the witchfolk and human variety. "We don't belong here. I feel like an impostor!"

"We're every bit as good as Francesca and Lily and Sumner and everyone else." As the Janus valets arrived at their car, one at each door, Dayna squeezed her friend's hand reassuringly. "Besides, I'm not about to enter Covenhaven's inner circle without you. Aren't you glad I brought you? This might be fun."

The valets opened their doors. A cool autumn breeze swept inside the car, bringing with it an unidentifiable but wonderful fragrance. Even the air smelled better at Francesca's resort.

Dayna felt pampered already. That sensation only grew as a valet helped her onto the walkway, then ushered her beneath the porte cochere. Camille, similarly escorted, joined her there.

"That's another thing." Self-consciously, her friend watched the valet drive away with her tiny car. "I doubt you were supposed to bring me with you. Francesca will take one look at me and call security. I'll be thrown out on my ear."

"She wouldn't dare." Brimming with anticipation, Dayna looked around. Tourists pattered to and fro, some carrying shopping bags from Sumner's gift shop, others toting bakery boxes from Lily's patisserie, and still others dressed in swimsuits. She recognized several cusping witches from class, too. Uniformed Janus employees moved among them like members of a semi-invisible but dignified army. "If *you* leave, *I* leave."

Camille's uneasy gaze met hers. "Is that a promise?"

"Absolutely. Are you kidding me?" One glance at Camille told Dayna this was no laughing matter. She gave her friend a warm smile. "Best friends stick together no matter what— and you'll always be my best friend. You know that, right?"

"Well . . . Once you've spent more time around Francesca, you might change your mind. I'm just a regular witch, with no special abilities or anything. I can't even afford cashmere."

"Hey. Stop right there. You're amazing! I'm so proud of everything you've done with your job and your husband and kids. Even Spencer!" At her mention of her Corgi, Camille laughed. "I might be your long-distance friend, but I'm still your friend." Dayna lowered her eyebrows with mock ferocity. "Got it?"

Silently, Camille nodded. For a long moment, she gazed in thought at the resort's tinkling fountain and the stone planters of flowers surrounding it. Then she heaved in a breath.

"If that's true, then why do you need Francesca, too?"

Camille's mournful tone jabbed right at Dayna's heart. Feeling responsible, Dayna vowed to do her best to fix things between them. No matter what it took, Camille was going to have the best girls' spa day ever in the history of Covenhaven.

"Because when Francesca invited me," Dayna confessed, tugging at her newest vintage T-shirt, then fiddling with the scarf Camille had lent her, "I started to feel *linked* again."

Clearly startled, Camille stared at her. "Dayna . . ."

"It's been a long time since I've felt like that," Dayna went on hastily. "It was . . ." She faltered, unable to describe it. "I thought I didn't need connection. I thought I was okay with being unlinked, as long as I was free. But I was never free. Not in the human world. Because I was always hiding—I was hiding *me*. So now, here in Covenhaven of all places—" Suddenly choked up, Dayna blinked. With a mighty effort, she sniffed to stop her tears. She offered up a big smile. "Now we're going to enjoy a day of all-out pampering like we've never seen! Woohoo!"

Camille's eyes gleamed with unshed tears. As game as ever, though, she pumped her fist in the air. "Pampering! Woohoo!"

With her best friend in tow, Dayna headed for Janus's

lobby. Her stomach whirled with nervousness—or maybe that was just hunger. Halfway there, still surrounded by privileged resort goers, she leaned closer to Camille. "Hey. Do you think they have Cap'n Crunch at a fancy place like this? Because Deuce finished the last box this morning, and I'm starving."

"If they don't, I'm sure Francesca can ask one of her flunkies to snap their fingers and conjure some."

"And popcorn, too. Like they have at the movies."

"They probably have gold-plated popcorn. Don't worry."

"Oh!" Entering the sweet-smelling, serenely decorated, and luxe lobby, Dayna grabbed Camille's arm. "And Skittles, too."

Beneath Janus's massive and ornate central chandelier, Camille stopped. Shaking her head, she gave Dayna a motherly look. "You're going to drop dead of a heart attack, eating junk like that. How are you supposed to get any vitamins?"

"By having my hostess provide them for free." Dayna spotted Francesca in the distance, chatting with two uniformed porters. She offered her a long-distance smile and a wave. "How else?"

"You're hopeless." Beside her, Camille waved, too. "First chance I get, I'm reporting you to your mother. I swear."

Dayna gasped. "You wouldn't!"

"I would." Camille stiffened as Francesca came closer. "At least have some fruit first, before the junk food. Humor me."

"All right. But then, the Cap'n Crunch."

The moment the words left her mouth, Dayna sensed that peculiar tingle again. It swept up her spine, alerting her to . . . something. Curiously, she glanced up at the skylights.

They dazzled her. Shaking her head, Dayna peered one story above her. That's where that weird sensation seemed to emanate from, but the staircase and mezzanine level appeared empty.

A few seconds later, Dayna forgot that tingling sensation altogether. Francesca entered their midst on a surge of ambient lobby music, charmed lighting, and personal verve, then swept them away to their first-ever magical girls' spa day.

Lounging on the mezzanine level that hugged the sky-high perimeter of the Janus lobby, T.J. frowned. He didn't like the resort or the kinds of people who stayed there. To step inside Francesca's domain was to enter into a lie. The place pretended to be formed of natural things, with fountains, cascades of water, green growing plants, and tumbled stone walls.

But to his Patayan eye, the fountains revealed themselves as intricately plumbed and made of poured concrete. The water smelled chemically treated and was forced to stream down prescribed pathways. The stone walls were fashioned of plaster with a veneer of crushed rock surfacing. Even the centerpiece of the lobby, a colossal slab of regional red rock, had been shaped and polished and treated with chemicals . . . all the better to improve its appearance. The potted cacti at its base only added insult to injury. Those plants didn't belong in the high country. He doubted the gardeners had put them there by choice.

"I hate this place." Sprawled on a smooth leather settee with both legs spread and his feet planted on the marble floor, T.J. gave Deuce an impatient look. "The sooner we're out of here, the better. Where's your damn bug anyway?"

His partner peered at the guests milling in the lobby. He transferred his gaze to the sweeping, architectural stairway they'd used to get upstairs, then put his hand to the discreet earpiece he wore. He listened. "It's still trailing Lily."

"Call it back. I don't trust that thing."

"Don't worry—I've been working with this bug. Its IAB programming isn't a factor anymore." As though remembering the way T.J. had freed the agency's tiny spy when it had been set to report on them, Deuce curled his fingers protectively over his earpiece. "Besides, the little guy is perfect for this job. I can't exactly trail Lily into the spa's massage rooms. He can."

T.J. gave a disgruntled sound. "They've been in there a long time now. What the hell are they doing?"

"Probably having a girl-on-girl massage spank party."

Jolted from his restlessness, T.J. stared. "What?"

"Kidding." Seated in similar fashion, Deuce gave a very human-style chortle. "Gotcha, didn't I? You can't be bored when you're picturing a naughty girl-on-girl party, now can you?"

"Is this how you always pass the time on tracer missions?"

"Sometimes. Hey, you're the one who leaves me behind with the getaway car half the time. It gets dull waiting for a grab."

T.J. shook his head. "One of those witches is yours, pal."

"You mean Lily?" Deuce's face turned pensive. "Nah. That's the other reason for using the bug this time. I think all those hours I was spending around her gave Lily the wrong idea about us. At this point, it's better to keep a low profile."

"You dog. Did you lead her on to get information?"

"No!" Deuce's frown deepened. "She's a witch, that's all. She doesn't respond well to being told 'no.' It's like the word doesn't even register. At this point, I figure it's better to keep my distance from Lily and the rest of . . . her kind."

"Whatever you say." Feeling fidgety—and unwilling to bicker with Deuce over his antiwitch prejudices—T.J. exhaled. He made a face as a party of giggly, overperfumed witches passed by on their way to the elevator bank. As a unit, they turned to give him and Deuce interested looks. "Jesus, cusping witches are horny as hell. Give me your earpiece. Let me listen awhile."

"No way. You're just worried because Dayna is in there."

Reminded of that, T.J. scowled more deeply. He'd been unhappily surprised to see his bonded witch arrive at Janus a short while ago, with her friend Camille accompanying her.

He didn't know why Dayna was here—or why she was suddenly so sociable with Francesca—but he intended to find out. Later.

"Dayna might interfere with my meeting with Sumner." The vixen witch had contacted him earlier with a request to come to Janus. He hadn't expected to be kept waiting like this. Given Sumner's high-handed view of Patayan—and compounds—he probably should have. "Dayna has seen through every disguise I've used so far. She'll know I'm here." In fact, he'd have sworn his bonded witch had sensed his presence when she'd arrived at the resort. She'd cast a curious glance up at the mezzanine level before greeting Francesca, then had distractedly turned away. "She'll ask questions."

"So answer them." Deuce listened through his earpiece, then grinned. "They're having naked mud baths now," he reported with an impish gleam in his eye. "That's awesome. Anyway, what's the problem? Didn't you tell Dayna about your Patayan mission?"

"I told her a little." Restlessly, T.J. aimed his gaze at the hand-raked Zen garden at the lobby's edge. He tried to carve a new pattern in the sand. Frustratingly, the grains didn't shift. "She knows about the coming confrontation and the *juweel*. I don't think she believed me." He'd confided as much to his magus. The wisewoman had advised patience and nothing more. "Dayna is sensitive about her weak magic. She turns every talk about magical skills into an evaluation of her own powers."

"Well, that's women for you." Prosaically, Deuce shrugged. "Somehow they turn every helpful comment into criticism."

"She says I believe her abilities aren't good enough."

"You *do* believe her abilities aren't good enough."

"I know, but that's because it's true. Her abilities *aren't* good enough yet. The truth shouldn't hurt her feelings."

"Dude, it's a good thing you don't date human women."

"Bite me." Delivering his partner a quelling look, T.J. gestured again. "I mean it. Give me your earpiece."

"If you want to know what's happening down there, morph yourself into a Patayan shaft of sunshine or a freaking legacy-witch pigeon and sneak in there yourself, why don't you?"

Giving up on his latest attempt to shift the Zen garden sand, T.J. growled in annoyance. "Because I can't," he admitted to Deuce. "My magic is getting more erratic by the day. I don't know if it's being bonded that's screwing with things—"

"Dayna's gone all Sampson-and-Delilah on your ass." His partner shook his head in sympathy. "I warned you, right? I hope the epic sex is worth it, buddy. That's all I'm saying."

"—or if it's co-opting Professor Reynolds's identity every night at cusping-witch class that's draining me somehow—"

"You're welcome for the IAB reassignment hack, by the way."

"—but the end result is that sometimes my magic is fine, and sometimes it's impossibly fucked up." Disconsolately, T.J. stared at his hands, with their scarred remnants of earlier magical endeavors. "When the conflict comes, I'll be useless."

Deuce went on staring at the humans and witches in the bustling lobby. For a few heartbeats, the only sounds between them were New Age music wafting from hidden speakers, the laughter of witches, warlocks, and tourists drifting upward, and chlorinated waters pouring over concrete and plaster fountains.

Just when T.J. had decided the situation really was hopeless—and so was he, if this went on—his partner spoke up.

"You're not wrecked forever." Deuce gave him a solemn look. "Whatever else goes wrong, you've got to believe that."

In his partner's earnest tone, T.J. couldn't help hearing a few echoes—echoes of Deuce's struggle to deal with being turned. He must have felt hopeless sometimes, too.

"All right, Oprah." T.J. glanced at him, feeling uncomfortably grateful. "Save the pep talk. We're working."

"If you're angling for a hug, you're way off base."

Grinning, T.J. flipped him the finger. "That's your dream, not mine. Sorry to disappoint." Then he sobered. "But seriously, thanks, Deuce. Thanks for watching my back. I mean it."

His partner smiled. Understanding flowed between them, the way it always did—eventually—when they disagreed. "You got it."

Still wearing that smile, Deuce put his hand to his earpiece again. "They're toweling off now. Hubba hubba."

"Your whole life is a potential porn movie."

"Hey, everybody needs something to live for."

Laughing, T.J. stood. "If they're done with the mud baths, that's my cue." He took out his cell phone, punched in a number, then waited. A witch answered. "It's time," he told her.

"I'll be right there," she said. "Hang tight."

Feeling almost too relaxed to stand up, Dayna nodded at the Janus spa attendant. The employee, a helpful witch, shut off the shower spray. All six deluxe nozzles surrounding Dayna in the granite-walled shower area switched off. Instantly, the attendant conjured up a thick terry cloth bath sheet.

Blissfully, Dayna wrapped herself in its preheated warmth. She could really get used to this treatment. Undoubtedly, human visitors to the Janus Resort and Spa were impressed by the conscientious service they received. They could not have known that legacy magic was behind the resort's famous attentiveness, just as talented witches and warlocks were responsible for the exemplary service at five-star hotels across the world.

"Thank you very much." Toasty warm and dry, Dayna accepted a plush terry cloth robe embroidered with the Janus logo.

The witch's gaze lingered on her golden armband. Dayna hadn't removed it since T.J. had given it to her. By now, it carried as much meaning as a wedding band did . . . maybe more. Feeling oddly protective of it, Dayna covered it with her robe.

The witch snapped her attention upward again. Politely, she suggested, "If you'll please follow me this way?"

"Of course." Heaving a contented sigh, Dayna followed the witch to the next room. Francesca, Lily, and Camille were already there, ensconced in matching mani-pedi lounge chairs. She and her friend had already been treated to a series of spa treatments, each one more outrageous than the last. First, foot massages and facials. Next, hot stone massages. After that, mud baths and relaxing aromatherapy. "So, what's next?" she asked.

"Manicures, pedicures, and a little fortification." From her lounge chair in the center, Francesca gave a lazy wave. From nowhere, another attendant appeared, bearing refreshments. "We have to keep up our strength, you know. Who wants a snack?"

"Me!" Camille blurted. "I do!"

She caught Dayna's eye and laughed, even as she helped herself to a beautifully arranged plate of strawberries and cream. She shrugged. "What can I say? I'm a mom. I don't get pampered very often. This is incredible, Francesca. Thank you."

"You're very welcome." With a benevolent smile, the vixen witch gestured for Dayna to take her place . . . in the lounge chair to her right. "Any friend of Dayna's is a friend of ours."

"Speaking of friends . . ." Hesitating beside the chair, Dayna looked around. "Where's Sumner? Isn't this her chair?"

"Not anymore," Francesca said. "Please, go ahead. Take it."

"Sumner got an emergency call from the gift shop." This came from Lily, who sprawled in a lounge chair to Francesca's left. Moist cotton pads covered her eyes; toe separators stuck out from her feet in preparation for her pedicure; an attendant crouched at the ready. "She left to deal with the problem."

"Oh. Well, in that case . . ." Dayna accepted the chair.

Beside her, Francesca smiled with pleasure. "How about those refreshments? We have fruit, as Camille has discovered"—her charm didn't waver as she indicated Dayna's best friend and her plate full of strawberries—"dark chocolate, spa cuisine—"

"Pastries," Lily added in a meaningful, peeved tone.

"—pastries, of course," Francesca continued, "plus all kinds of beverages: wine, tea, fruit smoothies, champagne—"

"Ohh! So I see. Yum." With relish, Dayna eyed the tray of drinks carried by still another hushed but dexterous Janus employee. On the tray sat several glasses of sparkling liquids. She spied one with an especially creative garnish and selected it. "I think I'll try this one. It looks delicious."

"Not that one." Francesca spoke sharply. Her gaze, frosty and firm, spun to the attendant. "You should be more careful."

"I'm sorry, Ms. Woodberry. It won't happen again."

"Indeed it won't." With a careless gesture, Francesca hexed her employee. As Dayna watched, wide eyed, the poor witch's ponytailed hair seemed to . . . melt away from her head, leaving her bald. Examining the effect, Francesca clucked her tongue. "Oh no. It seems you've violated the Janus appearance code."

Chuckling, she embellished her hex with a broad, swirling skull tattoo. Dayna and Camille gawked. The attendant stiffened in pain as a series of dark inked marks spread across her scalp.

"Tattoos are not allowed to be evident during work hours. You should know that. How many years have you worked here?"

The witch gulped back tears. "Eight years, Ms. Woodberry."

"Then that's long enough to understand our policies. Also,

with that bald head of yours, I don't think you'll be capable
of achieving an appropriately professional-looking hairstyle."

"I—I could wear a hat? Or get extensions? I need this job."

The attendant's face tightened with desperation. Still
frozen with her fancy drink in her hand, Dayna swallowed
hard.

"Francesca," she said in a conciliatory tone, "this is really
all my fault for choosing the wrong drink. I think—"

"You're dismissed," Francesca told the witch crisply. The
Janus employee's posture crumpled. Francesca merely gestured for another witch to escort her from the room. Then,
with the slightest crease across her forehead to show her concern, Francesca magically plucked the drink from Dayna's
hand. "This drink was meant for Sumner. But you couldn't
have known that, of course. You're free to choose another—
I promise, they're all excellent." Recovering her equanimity,
Francesca blinked. "Well. That's that then. All settled. I'm
sorry you had to see that."

"Me, too." Dayna exchanged an appalled gaze with
Camille. As though compelled, the two of them turned their
attention to the drinks waiting beside Francesca's and Lily's
chairs. Each of their glasses bore the distinct garnish that
Dayna's prohibited drink had. "What's so special about that
drink, anyway?"

Deadpan, Francesca lifted her glass. She took a seductive
sip. "It's a potion that makes cusping witches invincible."

Dayna laughed. "Fine. Don't tell me."

Lily quaffed her drink, too. "You're not ready for it yet," she
announced as she snapped her fingers for more. "You probably never will be, despite your little bursts of magic in class."

Wounded, Dayna stared at them. Could Francesca possibly
be telling the truth? She glanced at Camille. Her friend
shrugged and went back to her strawberries, unconcerned.

Maybe things like this happened all the time in Covenhaven.

"Seriously?" Dayna shifted her gaze to Francesca. "You've made a potion that makes cusping witches invincible? And you're offering it to witches over mani-pedis and backne treatments?"

"Only to a few *select* witches." Giving her a contemplative look, Francesca made a graceful gesture. The wall behind her turned transparent. Through it, witchy spa guests were visible, all of them enjoying the specially garnished drink. "For now."

At her wave, the wall became opaque again.

Like magic, Dayna *needed* that drink. She didn't care about being invincible; she wasn't even sure she believed in that part. Francesca probably wouldn't hesitate to stretch the truth if it enhanced her own reputation. But all at once, that drink became another link in the chain of becoming a true witch.

"How do you get selected?" she asked in a shaky voice.

She expected to hear another motherly rebuke from Camille. Instead, her friend sat as transfixed as she was, listening avidly to the discussion, barely noticing the diligent spa attendant who was applying petal pink polish to her toenails.

Francesca and Lily traded glances. Then Francesca turned to Dayna. She held up her drink. Solemnly, she said, "This potion could be dangerous in the wrong hands. I might already have trusted you too much. For all I know, you're a *myrmidon*."

"Me? A Follower?" Dayna blurted out. "You're kidding, right?"

"Do I look like I'm kidding?"

Dayna examined Francesca. Mutely, she shook her head.

"I hear the IAB has bugs everywhere now. I wouldn't want to get in trouble—or be tagged as a potential Follower myself." Idly, Francesca studied her pedicure-in-progress. She dismissed her attendant. "The bureau is watching, you know.

They're concerned about the rise of The Old Ways here in Covenhaven."

"I noticed—there's a definite revival of The Old Ways going on. But it doesn't include me," Dayna said. "I lived among humans for more than ten years! There's no way a Follower would hide out for that long, concealing their witchy gifts."

"That's probably true." Francesca lifted her gaze. "On the other hand, *your* 'gifts' are . . ." She broke off, smiling. "Let's just say, your grasp of magic hasn't always been the strongest."

Beside her, Lily snickered into her cocktail. "So you wouldn't have sacrificed much to hide it all those years."

"My magic is improving all the time." Dayna cast a covetous glance at that specially garnished drink. It looked delicious. "I'm a witch, first and last. I'm even bonded," she added with a burst of inspiration. "To a compound."

"A compound? Really?" At that, Francesca perked up. She gave Dayna a look of shimmering approval, filled with enviable charm and spirit. "Then you're definitely not a Follower."

"I'm not either!" Camille said, eager to join in.

Francesca smiled more widely. So did Lily.

"Well then," Francesca said as she lifted her glass for a toast. "Welcome to the club, witches. This is going to be fun."

Waiting in the resort's greenhouse, located at the very back of the Janus grounds, T.J. aimed a speculative glance at a potted orchid. All around him in the damp, warm space, water dripped from hidden irrigation systems. Condensation beaded on the greenhouse's walls, splintering the sunshine that fought its way through the glass. The air smelled richly of earth and moss.

With a gentle burst of concentration, he watched the orchid. Beneath his gaze, it spread its petals. The flower bent and reached toward him, its stem arched gracefully. That was more like it: working magic. Pleased, he stroked a petal.

Behind him, a door banged shut. Footsteps echoed.

The orchid shrank and shriveled, hunching toward the soil.

"I hope I didn't keep you waiting too long," Sumner said.

Already cloaked in his usual farmers' market disguise, T.J. turned. He stepped from the shadows he'd pulled. "I wouldn't be here if you had. I know what you need. I need it, too."

With an angry chuckle, Sumner approached him. She still looked vivacious, still moved with a sexy swagger, but now there was something new in her demeanor. Anger swept from her to T.J., tinged with an emotion he recognized well . . . but didn't want to.

Betrayal. It pained him to absorb any of it from her.

"Save the sweet talk, Neal," she said. "I don't care about your mission. I don't care about the Patayan. I don't even care about the Samhain Festival and graduating from cusping-witch school. All I care about is making an alliance I can trust."

"You can trust me."

Sumner's gaze narrowed. Her hips swiveled as she came closer, eyeing him with evident suspicion. She stopped beside the withered orchid and frowned. "I detect deception from you."

"You have reason to," T.J. said. "Do we have a deal?"

Another bitter laugh. "With a compound who admits he's lying to me? What do I look like, some kind of idiot?"

"You show me your faith. I'll show you mine."

She crossed her arms. "Why should I have to go first?"

"Because I never do." With a rough movement designed to tamp down his eagerness, T.J. stepped closer. He eyed Sumner's rigid posture. "Also because you want to do this. You need to."

Acquiescence flowed from her to him. As though hoping to deny it, Sumner closed her eyes. Her face tautened with emotion.

"My best friend betrayed me. She's trying to replace me! Do you know what that feels like?"

T.J. nodded. "I do."

His avowal was truer than Sumner knew. Even now, he took in much of her pain and disillusionment . . . her envy and anger.

"Join us," T.J. urged. "I don't care if you do it to help the Patayan or to exact revenge. The results are the same."

"And I'll make witchstory, like you said?" Sumner asked with raw need. "Everyone will remember my name? *Everyone?*"

"If you're the *juweel*, no one will be able to forget you."

"Then sign me up, Neal." Wearing a grim smile, Sumner offered him her handshake. "I'm ready to do whatever you want."

Chapter Twenty-Two

The moment Margo Sterling opened the door of Dayna's childhood home—a two-bedroom bungalow in the heart of Covenhaven's historical district—her face fell.

"Oh, Dayna. It's you."

"Surprise!" Wrapped in the scarf Camille had lent her in deference to the chilly weather, Dayna spread her arms wide. She waved her newly manicured fingers. Even after two additional days of classes, they still looked good. "Can I come in?"

"Of—of course." With a baffled frown, Margo opened the door. "We weren't expecting you. We were just about to—"

"Dayna! It's about time you visited us again, young lady." From behind her mother, Sam Sterling blustered his way forward. In a haze of aftershave and magical liveliness—plus a soft wooly sweater and jeans—he embraced her. Beaming, he held her by the shoulders to examine her. "Come in! Sit down! Stay awhile!"

Relieved that at least one parent seemed pleased to see her, Dayna stepped into the cozy living room. Her mother's traditional decorating taste was on full display, with knit throws over the plump sofa, generous armchairs, a fire in the fireplace, cushy rugs, low-lit lamps, and a burning wand of incense to offset the faint sulfurous scent in the air.

Dayna sniffed. "Conjuring up something, Mom?"

"Samhain decorations. I'm running late this year." Her mother cast an uncertain glance at her father, then perched herself beside him on the sofa. Her hands folded. Then unfolded. Then folded in her lap again. She smiled. "Didn't you notice the autumn wreath and jack-o'-lanterns on the front porch?"

"Sorry." Slinging her backpack to the floor, Dayna rummaged around in it. She pulled out two embossed envelopes. "I was a little distracted by these—your invitations to the cusping-witch graduation ceremony at Janus! On Hallow-e'en. Remember?"

The big event was almost here. Bright-eyed, Dayna held out the invitations. Her parents eyed them as though they might explode in her hands. They exchanged uneasy glances.

"They're magically imprinted." Dayna waggled the envelopes, putting on her most chichi expression. "You'll need them to get into the ceremony. It's exclusive. They had to limit invitations because of the at-capacity crowd—you wouldn't believe how many tourists are in town this week, in anticipation of the Hallow-e'en Festival. *Thousands*, Francesca told me. So . . . here!"

Sam and Margo didn't budge. Hurt, Dayna stared at them.

"Don't you want them?" she asked. "You said you would come to see me graduate. Everyone in town will be there."

"Are you sure you're going to pass the class?" her mother blurted out. "Remember, you can tell us if you're failing, Dayna. We'll still love you. No matter what, we'll always—"

Feeling crushed, Dayna let the envelopes sag.

"We heard from Camille that you were doing well in class," her father rushed to assure her. His voice was gentle. "But when you didn't come by to visit more often, we just assumed—"

"That I was *failing*?" Feeling tears burn at her eyelids,

Dayna tossed the envelopes on the coffee table. They skidded to a stop halfway across its polished surface, undoubtedly halted by a counterspell. She stood. "Well, this time you're wrong, Dad. I'm not failing. I'm doing pretty great, actually." Her voice cracked. Doggedly, Dayna kept going. "My magic is coming along well, I'm having fun hanging out with Camille again, *and* I'm making friends with all the cool witches in my class."

"Cool witches? Like who?" her mother asked sharply.

"Francesca Woodberry. Lily Abbot. Sumner Jacobs."

"We always liked Camille," her father said wistfully.

"Well, I have new friends now, Dad. They like me."

Falling silent, her mother stared at the abandoned invitations with palpable dread. It must have been Margo's spell that had stopped them from sliding all the way across the table.

The realization felt more hurtful than Dayna would have expected. She was a grown witch. Did she still care that much what her parents thought of her? What they thought of her magic?

Yes, she realized as Sam and Margo made no move to claim the two invitations she'd brought. She did care. A lot.

"Everything is going so well, in fact," Dayna went on, "that I've been thinking of staying here in Covenhaven. For good." She felt a familiar weight creep toward her shoulder. Without much thought, she reached for the comfort of her kitten familiar. It must have sensed her upset feelings and emerged from its habitual position inside her hoodie. "So if that's going to be a problem for you, I guess we'd better—"

"What's that?" Her father went still. "In your arms?"

Her mother gawked, her face ashen. For an instant, Dayna was afraid her familiar was morphing into a tiger again. But then she realized the truth. Her parents were obviously astonished that she'd achieved such (relatively) advanced magic.

"It's my familiar," she announced proudly, nuzzling the creature to her cheek. "She's almost two weeks old now."

"You've never managed a familiar before," Margo said.

"At least not one that stuck around this long," Sam added.

"I know, Dad. That's what I mean. I'm getting good at—"

"This is all because of that warlock, isn't it?" her mother demanded, looking wild-eyed. "The one you're *bonded* with."

Her accusation came at Dayna with surprising vehemence.

"Now, Margo." Her father patted her knee. "Take it easy."

She rounded on him. "*You* take it easy! I told you this would happen. This is ruining *everything*." Gulping back a sob, Margo shook her head. "I knew I should have intervened."

"It's a little late for that now," Sam said.

"Don't you think I know that?" Her mother gave Dayna a distressed look. "I did some research after we met in the library. I know what happened to you, Dayna. I know you're bonded. I know it's forever. I know it's increasing your magic, too. I *don't* know why you didn't share that with me, but—"

Margo's aggrieved tone was more than Dayna could stand.

"Um, maybe I didn't share my bonding with you because I thought you might have this reaction?" Taken aback by her parents' bizarre behavior, Dayna cradled her kitten familiar with one hand. With the other, she picked up her backpack. "Look, all I ever wanted was for you to be happy I was back in town. To be *proud* of me, for once." With stinging eyes, she stared at them. "I guess that's never going to happen, is it?" She sucked in a quivering breath. "I might as well give up."

In the stillness, the fire crackled. The incense sent up a curling tendril of smoke. The clock in the corner ticked away.

Blinking back tears, Dayna waited for her parents to tell her she was wrong. Wrong about them, wrong about their lack of faith in her, wrong about their willingness to believe she was a permanent magical screwup instead of a trueborn witch.

Her father broke the silence first. In a blatantly hopeful

tone, he asked, "Is there any chance you *will* give up and go back to Phoenix before graduation day?"

Stunned, Dayna stared at him. Her kitten familiar shivered in her arms, probably sensing her injured feelings.

Dayna lifted her chin. "No, Dad. It turns out, this time, I'm not giving up. At least not on my cusping-witch classes." She hefted her backpack higher, then tucked her kitten familiar securely in her hoodie. After a few seconds, it was settled in. "I've worked a long time for this. I've tried really hard. So . . . No. I'm not giving up." She gazed at her mother. "I'm sorry to disappoint you—again. I've got to go."

Blinded by emotions that felt almost as uncontrollable as her magic had been, Dayna turned. She charged past the end table, sighted the front door, and headed straight toward it.

"Dayna, wait." Her mother's voice came from behind her.

Hauling in a breath, Dayna stopped. She turned. A crackle of magical energy sparked from her feet. With a practiced gesture, she extinguished it. Her father's eyes widened.

Margo caught his reaction, too. She inhaled. "Sam, no—"

"Yes, Margo. It's time." Her father looked at her. "Dayna, sit down. We have something important to tell you."

Silhouetted on the mounded roof of her earth ship home, T.J.'s magus gazed toward the isolated lights of Covenhaven. The autumn breeze lifted her flowing witchmade garments, making it appear that she was about to take flight. On the ground below her, beside a sentinel saguaro, her wolfhound whined in concern.

"I was hoping you would come," she said without turning.

"I'm here." With what he hoped was a reassuring smile, T.J. stepped toward her. He navigated the dips and turns of the hard-packed earthen dwelling with easy Patayan movements, then embraced her. "But no cookies this time? What's up with that?"

Distractedly, his magus pulled away. "There is too much to be done. I can't waste time with hobbies." She drew a prism in the quiet night air, then pulled over a shaft of moonlight. With urgent eyes, she directed him to peer through it. "Look how many are gathering there. I've never seen so many humans in town."

Her earth magic had formed a viewing port. T.J. looked through it and discovered it functioned as a telescoping lens.

"So this is how you knew what I was up to as a teenager."

His magus didn't smile. "Do you see them? And the witches?"

"I see witches. Humans. Warlocks and Patayan." T.J. blinked and refocused his gaze. "Covenhaven has drawn them together for years. The enchanted red rocks, the canyon—"

"It's more than that this time. I sense more." With an apprehensive gesture, his magus made the prism vanish. "The conflict we've feared is coming closer. The dark forces are stronger. They're preparing for . . . something. I can't see what. By the time I can, it may be too late. We need the vixen."

"Then it's a good thing I've found her."

"You found the *juweel*?"

"She's agreed to help us." T.J. touched his magus, soaking up as much of her worry as he could. "I had to reveal myself to her. But she'll do whatever I ask."

His magus paced. "I don't know what to ask of her."

"You will when the time comes. You've prophesied it."

"You put too much faith in me, T.J." His magus's dark gaze met his. "You always have. I'm only one being."

"You're the one being I would give anything to protect."

His words, even harshly spoken, made her smile. "That's not true. There's another you would guard even more fiercely than me." She caught his protest, even before he made it. "Don't bother to deny it. I see it in you. Your birthright mark is mature. Your aura is at peace. Your bond is complete."

Beside her, T.J. stiffened. He didn't want to be open; not even to her. He didn't want to be readable, didn't want to be breakable. If his magus was right, it was too late not to be.

It was only fair, he realized. In his lessons with Dayna, he'd taught his bonded witch to let go of the defensive barrier she held between herself and everyone else. With words and magic and—on one memorable occasion, a shuddering sexual union—he'd coaxed Dayna into the bravery she needed to be truly open.

Her reward had been the ability—fleeting then, but growing stronger by the day—to see her own aura and to recognize magical pixilation. It had felt like a breakthrough . . . and it had been.

For both of them.

"Just promise me," his magus said in a tone of urgency. "If it comes to your bonded witch or me . . . you must save her."

Instantly, T.J. refused. "I'll protect you both."

The wisewoman smiled sadly. "That might not be possible."

"It will be." Fiercely, T.J. gazed toward Covenhaven. He didn't need his magus's prism to sense the dark forces at work there. His Patayan instincts clamored with alarm, honed by centuries of conflict and infallibly accurate. "Just as you prophesied, the *juweel* will step forward and end the conflict."

"I hope so." His magus embraced him again, her garments swirling with an upswing in the breeze. When she released him, her expression was somber. "If she does, you'll have to be ready, T.J.—ready to let *her* do her work. This is a mission you can't fulfill alone. You'll have to trust the *juweel*."

A prickle of unease snaked up his spine. All the warnings he'd received clanged through his head. Deuce, asking him to trust him, to treat him as a true partner. Garmin, demanding that he rely on the turned human when they worked together on IAB tracing assignments. Even Dayna, provocatively on her knees before him, urging him to yield to her forbidden kiss.

T.J. had found those requests nearly impossible to fulfill.

Would that change—would *he* change—if the looming conflict demanded it of him? Would he be able to step aside and trust the *juweel* completely?

He needed to tell his magus that he could. But the moment T.J. opened his mouth to assure her, his throat closed up. Raw pain clogged his voice, leaving him unable to speak at all.

He'd never lied to his magus. Apparently he still couldn't.

With a rough gesture—half nod, half shake of his head—T.J. left the dark mound the way he'd come—before his magus could press him any further . . . or see the truth in him any more clearly.

Seated on an armchair with her backpack at her feet, Dayna stared at her parents with utter confusion. On her lap, her kitten familiar gave an urgent meow, batting her with its paws.

"I'm a *what*?" Dayna asked.

"You're a leapling," her father repeated, looking nervous.

"I heard the word. I don't understand what it means."

"It's how we refer to someone who was born in a leap year," her mother explained in a hasty academic tone, "as opposed to a common year. Your birthday, February twenty-ninth, only occurs on the calendar every four years. That's because it's necessary to keep the calendar year synchronized with the astronomical or seasonal year. Otherwise, a certain amount of drift would occur in the—"

"Wait." Feeling a sense of unreality waiting to envelop her, Dayna shook her head. "*My* birthday is February twenty-eighth. You both know that. You were kind of, um, *there*, right?"

"Yes." Sam squeezed Margo's hand. They shared an enigmatic look. "We were there. The funny thing is, three other families were also there on the day you were born. At the

Covenhaven maternity ward. We saw them, and the hospital staff saw them—"

"And that means the InterAllied Bureau saw them, too." With an anxious look, her mother leaned forward. "I saw Leo Garmin—"

"Garmin?" Startled, Dayna stared at them. "How could he have been there when I was born? Leo Garmin doesn't look a day older than thirty-five right now—over thirty years later."

"He's a very powerful warlock. His age, measured in human terms, is irrelevant. The important thing is, Agent Garmin was new to the bureau then. He was assigned to monitor legacy witch births. Specifically, he was looking for . . . anomalies."

"I knew it," Dayna said. "I really *am* a freak."

Her parents frowned at her, seeming perplexed. "What?"

Dayna gave a shaky laugh. "What kind of anomalies?"

"Overlapping births, mostly." Margo breathed in deeply. Her next words tumbled out quickly. "Vixen births. The IAB tracks them. It's a recruitment technique, partly, but a control measure, too. Vixen witches are filled with The Old Ways' dark magic. If a fully formed pact were to come to power, it would be a serious threat to the IAB's authority. That's why they—"

"Wait. Hang on." Even more baffled now, Dayna put out her hand in a *stop* gesture. "What do The Old Ways have to do with me? Are you trying to tell me my own parents are *myrmidon*?"

"No." Intent and serious, her father shook his head. "We're getting off track here. Dayna, what we're trying to tell you, what we've been trying *not* to tell you, until tonight—"

"Is that you," her mother finished, "are a vixen witch."

Cloaked in darkness, T.J. rode an air current from the edge of Covenhaven to the sheltered hill where Deuce's apartment building stood. Below him, the apartments' lighted windows glowed as he neared them. Mesquite trees quivered in the autumn wind. A lone voice called out, flat with human intonation.

Reminded by that voice of the risk he was taking, T.J. let his sweeping airstream die. He sank to his feet just outside the complex's landscaped common area, then strode forward.

Moonlight illuminated his path—and the warning charms he'd set. After confirming that they'd been undisturbed, T.J. shrugged off his concealing shadows. He maneuvered the walkway leading to Deuce's apartment, then released the apartment's protective spell, still preoccupied with his magus's counsel.

Could he allow the *juweel* to work alone?

Could he stand aside and do nothing?

He never had before. But if that's what his magus needed . . .

The moment the apartment door cracked open, T.J.'s thoughts turned away from his mission. The air felt broken, laden with trouble. Something was wrong. It was only because he'd been inattentive that he hadn't noticed the aberration sooner. Cursing himself for that, T.J. stepped into the apartment.

A wave of sulfurous magic struck him. He recoiled. "Deuce?"

The place felt strangely quiet. It lacked the jovial aura that Deuce, even turned, brought with him. With his senses ready and his body humming with magic, T.J. moved farther inside.

His partner's bikini-girls print lay on the floor, its frame broken. The TV stood off-kilter on its metal stand, as though something had hit it. A knit cap lay on the floor beside a video game controller. Two beer bottles sat on the coffee table, primly perched on a pair of matching coasters.

Grimly, T.J. swept his gaze over the room. Nothing else seemed amiss. He moved to the kitchen. One of the cupboard doors stood partway open. Two half-filled cocktail glasses waited on the countertop beside a pink-tinged spill. He touched it. His fingers came away wet, coated with sweet-smelling liquid.

He tasted it. It was sweet . . . then intensely sour.

Making a face, T.J. glanced at the stemmed glasses, at the spill, at the glasses again . . . at the very *feminine* glasses.

"Dayna?" Heart pounding, T.J. turned. "Dayna?"

A groan came from the rear of the apartment. With an impatient airborne whoosh, T.J. moved in that direction.

His hulking partner lay in a heap in the hallway.

Not Dayna. Not his bonded witch. Deuce. *Deuce.*

Fear jolted through T.J. He dropped to his knees beside his partner, urgently checking his condition. At a glance, he could tell this was magic at work—dark magic. Deuce lay unconscious on the floor, his face squashed into the rug and his legs stretched out at awkward angles. His big hand curled on the bathroom door frame, as though he'd attempted to pull himself to his feet.

Alone and weakened by whatever . . . *this* was, he'd failed.

With a muttered swearword, T.J. lowered his head. Deuce's breath rattled weakly through his chest. His pulse felt slow. His skin felt clammy. His face looked as pale as death.

Swiftly, T.J. tried a legacy curative spell. Deuce didn't stir. Feeling increasingly desperate, T.J. attempted a Patayan healing incantation. His partner only moaned, his eyes moving behind his closed lids as though seeing a terrible dream.

With another vicious curse, T.J. got to his feet. He paced, uncertain what to do. If he'd had full command of his magic . . .

But he didn't. He didn't know how to save Deuce, or even if the spells he'd already tried should have worked. He'd been weakened by his bond with Dayna, by his maneuverings at cusping-witch class, and by his betrayal at Leo Garmin's hands. All those things conspired against his magic . . . just when he needed it most. Bleakly, T.J. stared down at his partner.

He had to get a healer for Deuce. But he didn't want to leave him alone, especially like this. His friend groaned again, hexed or spelled into immobility—but clearly able to feel pain.

Fisting his hands, T.J. paced further. Then, with his decision made, he paused beside Deuce. He focused his thoughts.

An instant later, his familiar appeared. A hawk surged into view, with a wide wingspan and a piercing cry. Hungrily, the bird fixed its predator's gaze on T.J.'s birthright mark tattoo— on his gilded Gila monster. It spread its wings in eagerness.

"No," T.J. told it. "I have other work for you."

The hawk gave a complaining cry, its gaze disgruntled. Despite the circumstances, T.J. almost laughed. This was what he got for being of compound birth. His witchfolk familiar and his Patayan identity were permanently at odds.

Neither trusted the other.

This time, T.J. would have to trust at least one.

He gave his familiar instructions to find a healer. The hawk gave an almost imperceptible nod, then flew through the window T.J. magically flung open. All that remained was to wait—and worry. If someone had hexed Deuce, T.J. wondered in that moment, had they also hexed Dayna . . . or taken her away from him?

Feeling numb with disbelief, Dayna gawked at her parents. She could not have heard them correctly. "Wait. I'm a *what*?"

"You're a vixen witch," her father confirmed. His face brightened with evident relief. "We didn't want you to know. It was too dangerous. So we bribed the hospital officials, forged the official documents, and told everyone—"

"Including the IAB," her mother put in.

"—that you were born on February twenty-eighth. It was

an impulsive decision, but once it was made, we could see that it was the right one. Especially after we saw how the other vixens in your pact were growing up—rebellious, headstrong, too powerful—"

"I'm a vixen?" Dayna repeated. *"Me?"*

"Yes." Her mother nodded. "That's why we had to protect you. We had to make sure you didn't start dabbling in The Old Ways' dark magic. We had to make sure the IAB didn't find out about you. They would have singled you out, watched you, taken you away for special training." Margo gave her a pleading look. "You're our only child, Dayna! We couldn't risk any of that."

"I don't see how it was a risk. You must have seen, as I grew up, that I wasn't a *real* vixen." Obdurately, Dayna stared at them. "You could have showed Leo Garmin how pathetic my magic was, and he would have forgotten all about me."

"That wasn't an option," her father said flatly.

"But *lying* to me was?" Dayna shook her head. "I don't believe it. This is all some kind of joke, right?"

"It's not a joke." Calmly, her mother folded her hands. "We're sorry. We'd hoped to never have to tell you this. But with your magic flourishing now, and with you about to be on display at graduation, we knew the IAB might notice you. So we decided to warn you about the dangers, and hope that—"

"But I'm *terrible* at magic!" Dayna shouted. "I've always been terrible at magic. How can I be a vixen witch if—"

She broke off as her parents exchanged guilty looks.

"You're not terrible at magic," Sam admitted.

Her mother cleared her throat. She shifted uncomfortably. "Actually, you're incredibly gifted. Just like all vixen witches are. But even vixens make beginner mistakes. So we simply . . ."

"Allowed your beginner mistakes to flourish," her father said. "Eventually, you came to believe you had no ability."

"Believe me," Margo said with an awkward laugh, "it was a great relief when you finally gave up on practicing magic and left for Phoenix. I was so worried until then! You're very stubborn, Dayna. It took a long time to discourage you."

"To discourage you enough," her father elaborated, "to make you quit magic altogether. But once you did, you were happier."

"*Happier?* I was unlinked. I was alone. I was terrible at the one gift I was supposed to have!" Feeling on the verge of . . . something, Dayna stared at them. "I was never happier."

"You seemed happy enough," her mother said blithely. "Everything was fine! The only trouble was, we forgot about your cusping. We didn't take into account what it might do to you."

"And we definitely didn't take into account the IAB," her father agreed. "That was a major *whoops!* on our part."

They traded glances, both of them chuckling anxiously.

Dayna didn't think any of this was funny. "So until T.J. dragged me back here, you were fine with doing this to me?" she asked. "With discouraging me from practicing magic . . . on purpose? With letting me believe I'd failed, over and over again?"

"It was the only way." Her father shrugged. "If we'd left you alone to learn naturally, you would have been casting spells with the talent and ease all vixens are born to enjoy, just like the other members of your pact. You would have stood out."

"You would have been discovered," her mother said. "We love you! The last thing we wanted was for you to be—"

She went on, but Dayna was in no mood to hear about parental devotion. Not then. Maybe not for a long while. "So I spent all those years believing I wasn't good enough—believing I couldn't even practice the simplest magic—and it was all a *lie*?"

Her parents blinked. "Well. We wouldn't quite put it *that* way," Sam said. "We had your best interests at heart, Dayna. If you'd seen what spoiled brats those other vixens turned out to be . . ." He gave an uneasy laugh. "It was for the best, really."

"I *have* seen how those other vixens turned out, Dad. I grew up with them, remember?" Feeling sick at heart, Dayna shook her head. "Francesca, Lily, and Sumner are the most powerful, most envied witches in town. They're accomplished, and beautiful—"

"Appearance charms." Her mother tsk-tsked. "Easy but fake."

"They're everything I've ever wanted to be! And now you're telling me I could have been *exactly* like them?" Distraught, Dayna reached for her backpack. As she did, her kitten familiar retreated to the safety of her hood. "I could have been linked all along. Instead, I was alone. I was apart from everyone." Sadly, she inhaled. "Even, it turns out, from the two of you. This is the meanest thing you ever could have done to me."

Her father looked away, his face lined with worry. Her mother pressed her lips together, giving her a defiant stare.

Dayna only stood there, feeling her whole life slide sideways. Her parents had lied to her. No one in the witch world had truly known her. And she'd been capable of superior magic all along . . . even as she'd struggled with the most basic spells.

A sigh flowed through the room, stirring the air.

"You can't tell anyone you know about this," Sam said. "Please, Dayna. For once, think before you act. It's important."

At his words, fresh magic sparked from Dayna's fingertips. Feeling its power flow through her, she stared at her hands with grim surprise. Maybe her stifled magic knew it was finally free.

Idly, she wondered exactly what it was capable of.

"Yes, Dayna," her mother urged. "Your father is right. I realize this news must come as a shock to you—"

"A shock?" Dayna gave a bitter laugh. "I'll say."

She raised her head and looked at her parents. Their gazes were still fixed, apprehensively, on the place where her magic had sparked a few seconds ago. In that moment, everything seemed plain to her. With new clarity, Dayna could see the lies, the mistakes . . . the deliberate deception that had led her here.

"Just don't do anything you'll regret," Margo begged.

"The only things I regret," Dayna told her parents as she straightened a little further, "are the things I *haven't* done. I think it's about time to get started on those."

In a flurry of shimmering magic, she left to do just that.

Chapter Twenty-Three

With his head bowed, T.J. stood in Deuce's dimly lit bedroom. On the rickety bed, his partner lay without moving. His big tracer's body appeared incongruously muscular and vigorous, even as he labored for breath. It was as though Deuce might sit up at any second, wipe the fever sweat from his brow, and go for a run. Or crack a joke. Or rescue another damn IAB bug.

T.J. wondered if Deuce would ever do any of those things again. He watched the healer, fighting an urge to shove aside the elderly Patayan and magik Deuce back to health himself.

"You were right—this *is* magic at work." Wearing an expression of concern, the healer gazed up from Deuce's body. His hands still moved, completing his spell. "But this is ancient magic, twisted and dark. It will take time to unravel."

"We don't have time. He's vulnerable." T.J. took in a deep breath, then admitted the worst. "He's human."

"Human?" The healer blinked, startled. "But his mind shows signs of growing magic." He pointed a trembling hand. "Even now, his mind is reshaping itself to form new magical connections."

T.J. compressed his mouth. "He's turned."

"That doesn't explain this. Although if he's turned, as you

say . . ." Lost in thought, the healer gave his patient a frown. "Maybe he sought out legacy magic, hoping to complete—"

"No. Deuce wanted nothing to do with magic."

"He may have said as much," the healer agreed. "But sometimes turned humans yearn for more. They yearn to be able—"

"Deuce never yearned for anything except revenge."

"Ah." With a nod of understanding, the healer shook out a healing charm. He applied it to Deuce's chest. "I see. He must be very strong to have withstood this, then. A weaker man would have sensed the presence of magic and grasped at it— all the better to gain his revenge on the witch who turned him."

Deuce groaned, a guttural sound that wanted to be words but could not be. His eyelids flickered with disturbing speed.

"Leave me be while I deal with this," the healer said.

T.J. planted his feet. "I'm not leaving him alone. Whatever you have to do, do it with me here."

"I'm not going to hurt him. You have to trust me."

"I've trusted you enough to bring you here." T.J. slanted a grateful look at the window through which his familiar had retreated. The hawk had done well. "That's as far as I go."

"Very well," the healer said. "But this won't be pretty."

Feeling distraught and rebellious, Dayna stepped off the Covenhaven trolley at the Janus Resort and Spa with her backpack in tow and her mind awhirl. She'd arrived at the resort half on autopilot, with no clear sense of where to go or what to do next. All she knew was that her life had just changed forever.

She couldn't confide in Camille about what had happened— about what her parents had done or about being a vixen. Her best friend, as wonderful as she was, would never understand. She couldn't go to T.J. or Deuce either. Technically, Sam and

Margo Sterling had broken the law; Dayna was upset, but she wasn't ready to report her own parents to two IAB tracers. At a loss, she'd wandered the Covenhaven historical district for an hour or so before realizing who she could turn to: Francesca.

Francesca had always told her the truth, however hurtfully. Ironically, that meant she could trust Francesca. Besides, Dayna had a link with her fellow vixens that surpassed all others.

Francesca had said it herself: *You're one of us now.*

How true that had been. Suddenly eager to tell Francesca the news that she was a vixen, too, Dayna headed toward the Janus lobby. The place looked awash in lights and festive Samhain decorations, filled with even more tourists and cusping witches than had been there earlier. From amid the crowd, one bald, suit-wearing warlock separated himself and came toward her.

Garmin. Exuding power and authority, he moved faster.

Not him. Not now. Reluctant to deal with him, Dayna swerved to the left, then ducked behind a group of uniformed porters.

She was too late. Garmin arrived there first, transported via whatever magical means he favored. He crossed his arms.

"Ms. Sterling. I thought we had an understanding."

"Look, I'm kind of in a hurry. So if you don't mind—"

"You're always in a hurry." With deceptive smoothness, the IAB agent stepped straight into her path. His shoulders loomed above her. His aura—which, she realized with a minor thrill, she could actually see tonight—gleamed with a metallic shimmer. "I'm afraid you're going to have to make time for me."

"Fine." Stopping short, Dayna stared up at him with an elaborate show of patience. "What do you want now?"

"I want the same thing I've always wanted—for you to stay away from T.J. McAllister." With menacing intensity,

Garmin moved closer. "But since you're unable or unwilling to do that—"

"Unwilling. You nailed it."

"Hmmm." Garmin arched his brow. "And yet *you* called *me*."

Well, that was true. Uncomfortably, Dayna shifted. Janus's New Age music wafted toward her, accompanied by the spicy scent of the clove cigarettes that cusping witches favored to hide their magic. Her kitten sank its claws in her shoulder, then peeked its head around. Its soft fur grazed her ear.

Garmin glanced at it, then smiled. "Your familiar?"

"Yes."

The agent waited for more. Stubbornly, she shut her mouth.

"You're not feeling chatty. I understand." Garmin's smile flashed, indescribably appealing. Under the circumstances, she should not have found him so charismatic. "All I need from you is one thing: McAllister's location. Then I'll leave you alone."

"You're the IAB. Can't you track him yourself?"

The agent's eyes narrowed. "No."

"Well then. Bureaucratic shortcomings aren't my problem." With a flip of her hair, Dayna turned toward the lobby. She fluttered her fingers. "Good night, Agent Garmin."

Without moving, he seized her. Dayna felt her arm lock in position; her leg froze up next, fixing her in place. Dismayed, she glanced over her shoulder. In the darkness, amid the laughter and frivolity of the Janus courtyard, Garmin waited.

"He's dangerous," he said. "Tell us how to find him."

Struggling against his warlock grasp, Dayna frowned.

"Tell us how to find him," Garmin repeated as he advanced closer, "and we'll make sure you pass your cusping class. We'll license you today. You'll be able to go home again. Tonight."

His voice rumbled over her, filled with everything she wanted to hear. Filled with escape. But this time Dayna couldn't run away from the challenges in Covenhaven . . . could she?

Amid all the turmoil she faced, the offer felt tempting.

"You can run," he said intently, again demonstrating his uncanny witchfolk clairvoyance. "You *can* run. Or . . ." Garmin stopped beside her, his polite demeanor giving no sign of the hold he kept on her. His expression brightened with interest. He tilted his head as though listening to something. "Or you can make sure your parents aren't prosecuted for breaking the law when they hid you. When they hid your vixen birthright."

Shocked by his insight, Dayna couldn't help jerking.

The agent detected that faint tremor. His voice pursued her, relentless and seductive. "I know what they did, but you can protect them. Agent McAllister is a big boy. His problems with the IAB are his to deal with, not yours. He's bitter about his suspension. I get that. But that's no reason for you to—"

"T.J. has been suspended? From the IAB?"

This time, Garmin did release her. His satisfied expression told Dayna everything. He knew he no longer needed magic to hold her there. "I suspended him weeks ago. He didn't tell you?"

Mutely, Dayna shook her head. She couldn't believe T.J. hadn't confided in her, especially about something so important.

This explained the subterfuge, the protective charm, the way T.J. had refused to confide more than scant details about the Patayan mission he'd been on. She wondered if the "conflict" he'd warned her about was real. If any of it was real.

Garmin chuckled. "I didn't think he would. I already told you—Agent McAllister doesn't trust easily . . . if at all."

"He trusted me." *Just not enough.* Drawing in a calming breath, Dayna regrouped. "And I trust him. I guess you'll just have to deal with your administrative issues on your own."

"You can't be serious." Garmin frowned. "You mean—"

"I mean find him yourself," Dayna said. She spotted Francesca nearby and, encouraged by the appearance of her fellow vixen, straightened in front of Garmin. "I'm done helping you."

With a plaintive meow, her kitten familiar retreated back to her hood. At the same moment, Francesca arrived.

Her vivacious smile lit the resort's courtyard. "Dayna! What a nice surprise. And Agent Garmin! I thought you'd already left for the night. What brings you back to Janus so soon?"

Back to Janus? Dayna wondered what he'd been doing there.

"Just some unfinished business." The agent nodded at Francesca, then at Dayna. "It's concluded now."

His intimation was clear. He would not give Dayna another chance to pass her class, get licensed, return to Phoenix early . . . or save her parents. How had he known about their lie?

Before she could figure it out, Garmin turned abruptly. An instant later, the warlock vanished into the crowd of tourists.

Francesca burst out laughing. "Wow! Those IAB types aren't big on small talk, are they?" She looped her arm in Dayna's, gave the departing agent a curious look, then smiled. When she gazed more closely at Dayna, her smile wavered. "Wait a minute. You're not here for a mani-pedi touchup, are you? Something is wrong. Really wrong. What happened?"

Awash in Francesca's comforting tone and empathetic look, Dayna realized she'd done the right thing by coming to Janus. Probably she and Francesca shared a vixen-witch connection—one that made her new friend unusually sensitive to Dayna's turmoil. With a hesitant smile, Dayna gestured toward the resort.

"Why don't I tell you over a drink?" she suggested with an overwhelming sense of relief. "This might take a while."

"Of course." Crooning with sympathy, Francesca ushered her

inside the resort. The crowds parted to let them pass, murmuring and smiling, obviously recognizing Francesca as a VIP. "Tonight, I think you need a very *special* cocktail. Let's go."

With his face cast in conjured shadows, the Patayan healer motioned for T.J. to come closer. Solemnly, he gazed at him.

"Are you all right?" the healer asked.

"I'm fine." Still reeling with the effects of absorbing the fear and pain in the room, T.J. straightened. Sweat beaded his brow; his fists clenched at his sides. "How is Deuce?"

"You shouldn't have helped me. It's weakened you. Let me—"

"Is he healed?" T.J. wavered. He flung his arm to the bureau to steady himself, then peered at the healer. "Is he?"

"It's difficult to say. I've never seen anything like this. This magic is . . . splintered. It's forcing his brain to make new connections—the same connections that allow us, as witchfolk, to practice magic." With his expression bleak, the healer watched as Deuce lay silent. "In humans, able magic has been latent for generations—imagine trying to achieve eons of evolution in just hours. The human mind was not designed to withstand the strain. He should not have survived even this long."

"I understand. What do we do now?"

"Now?" The healer blinked. "Now we wait."

T.J. swore. "There must be more. A potion, a spell—"

"More magic could be deadly. For whatever reason, Deuce has not tested these new connections of his. His ability to resist using this magic probably saved his life."

My pops was doing magic, T.J. suddenly remembered Jesse Obijuwa telling him after their basketball game. *He was doing tons of magic. Just like all those witches and warlocks in town.*

T.J. looked at the healer. "What if he hadn't resisted?"

"You mean if Deuce had tried using his rudimentary magic as it formed?" Wearily, the healer frowned. "It's difficult to say. An unprepared and unschooled mind—a mind still evolving—would produce fleeting magic, at best. But even that much success would have created a desire to try again."

T.J. was familiar with that desire. It was present in all able children, encouraging them to persist after failures.

"Deuce might have literally magiked himself to death," the healer said, "unable to stop practicing his new skills."

With eerie synchronicity, T.J. recalled the conversation he'd overheard on the night the IAB had found the second gardener's body. *There were certain . . . artifacts near the body,* the female IAB agent had told Garmin. *We have reason to believe the victim was trying to practice legacy magic himself.*

"Magic use isn't deadly," T.J. protested, half to himself. Dark currents whirled around him, restless and turbulent, as he paced the room. "Otherwise, witchfolk would not exist."

"That's true," the healer agreed. "But in humans? Magic use is too much for the mind to absorb, especially all at once."

Stopping beside Deuce's bed, T.J. stared down at his partner. It killed him to see his friend this way.

And if all they could do now was wait . . .

"Someone did this to him. They should be forced to pay."

Decisively, T.J. turned. The healer swept himself sideways, blocking his path. On the verge of shoving the elderly Patayan, T.J. checked himself. Was he so distraught he would attack an elder of his circle? A Patayan who deserved all his respect?

Almost. But not quite.

"Move," T.J. growled. "Please. I won't ask again."

"Revenge is not productive. It will only hurt you."

For a long moment, T.J. stared at the healer's wise expression. Then he flexed his hands. Magic crackled from them, wicked and ready—ready to punish someone for Deuce's condition.

"As long as it hurts them first, I don't care."

"You are bonded!" the healer cried as T.J. brushed past him. "Think of your bonded partner. Would she want you to damage yourself this way? To give over to your darker instincts?"

Roughly, T.J. stopped. The healer's gaze swept to his birthright mark tattoo—to the symbol of his bonding. Its usual glow looked dim. Its warmth, he realized dully, had retreated.

He wondered if that meant Dayna had been hexed, too.

"Seeking revenge will lessen you." The healer cast a wary glance at Deuce, checking his condition. "It will damage your bond. If you still want to leave, at least know that first."

Caught between loyalty to Deuce and loyalty to Dayna, T.J. stopped. Frustration roiled through him, hard and swift. The air currents he'd picked up increased in tempo, ruffling his hair.

With a savage gesture, he swept them away. They blew through the apartment, picking up debris and hurling fixtures before slamming into the wall. The items the current had carried fell to the floor in a resounding crash. Glass shattered.

"I'll stay." T.J. glowered toward the bedroom. "For Deuce."

Even as he said it, he couldn't help wondering . . .

Where was Dayna? And why the hell wasn't she there already?

Surrounded by cusping witches dressed in the chicest autumn resort wear, highlighted by the expertly conjured lighting at Janus's VIP lounge, and laughing as she cradled her third special cocktail of the night, Dayna gestured for the server.

"Barkeep? Another round!" she called tipsily.

At her side, Francesca gave the Janus bartender a subtle

nod of approval. Then she went back to the box of magical amulets she'd been working with, her expression relaxed.

"I can't believe those are *all* for cusping-witch graduation tomorrow." Dayna goggled at the pile. It easily contained thousands of golden graduation amulets. "And I *really* can't believe you're the one doing the grunt work of engraving them."

"Mmm. I enjoy it. It's nice mindless work." Francesca shrugged, focusing on the collection. At her direction, one of the amulets lifted from the pile. Francesca consulted a list at her elbow, then waved her fingers. Magically, a cusping witch's name engraved itself on the amulet. "Besides, it gives me more time to talk to *you*." She smiled. "Are you feeling better?"

"After three of these?" Grinning, Dayna lifted her cocktail—her specially garnished, exclusively offered, invincibility-endowing cocktail. "I'm feeling incredible!"

"Good. Then you're probably ready to tell me what happened." Wearing an expression of concern, Francesca left her preparations alone for a minute. "You seemed really upset."

"Well, I can't imagine why now!" Dayna took a gulp of her drink. Like a good margarita, her cocktail tasted sweet, sour, and delicious. She licked a spill on her glass. "I'm so glad you pushed all these drinks on me. You knew exactly what I needed."

"I could help you even more if you would tell me what's the matter. I'm only sorry I have to keep working on this engraving while we talk." Francesca gestured at the graduation amulets. "I'm afraid I bit off more than I could chew when I agreed to host the graduation ceremony *and* the Hallow-e'en Festival here at Janus. Back to back, on the same day, no less. Whew!"

Dayna scoffed breathily. And maybe a little drunkenly. "You can handle it. You're perfect at everything. And maybe"—she hinted with an elaborately confiding tip of her head—"so am I."

"Ooh, mysterious." Francesca smiled. "What do you mean?"

"Well . . ." Dayna paused as the server arrived with her fourth cocktail. She glanced up, startled to see the same witch who'd suffered Francesca's wrath for delivering the wrong drinks on their girls' spa day. Tonight, though, the employee appeared to have regained her full head of hair and her job. The realization loosened Dayna's lips at last. "I'm a vixen witch!"

Pleased and proud, she slammed back her drink. Then she licked her lips and watched Francesca's reaction. The other witch wavered in her vision, beautiful and serene and gifted.

"You're a vixen witch," Francesca repeated. "Yes, I know."

"You *know*?" Dayna blinked. "But how? *I* didn't even know."

Her fellow vixen shrugged. "I just knew. I realized it in cusping-witch class weeks ago. Vixen magic recognizes its like, you know, just as other forms of special magic do."

"Huh." Astonished and a little deflated, Dayna twirled her finger around the sticky rim of her cocktail glass. She pulled away her finger, then sucked its sweet-and-sour tip into her mouth while she considered the way her bond with T.J. had been formed. "I guess that's true. I hadn't thought about it before."

"Well, you've been among humans awhile." Francesca went back to engraving her pile of amulets. "That's understandable."

"I guess. But what's *not* understandable is the way my parents kept the news from me," Dayna complained. With a twinge of her old rebelliousness, she confided the whole sordid story to Francesca. "But now the secret is out. I'm a trueborn witch!"

"Of course you are." Smiling, Francesca continued engraving the piled-up amulets. "I never doubted it at all."

"You didn't?" Dayna peered at her. "Is that why you decided to be friends with me? Because you realized I was a vixen, too?"

"Oh, come on, Dayna." Francesca laughed, shaking her head. "I'm not *that* calculating! I wanted to be your friend because I like you, that's all. Lily and Sumner do, too. It just took us a little while to realize it. For that, I'm sorry."

Warmed by Francesca's apology and kind words, Dayna beamed at her. It felt good to be part of a close-knit group at last. It felt good to be on the inside, to be linked again, to be drinking special cocktails and brimming with powerful magic.

Which reminded her . . .

"Hey, I've got a few things I've been wanting to try out." Eagerly, Dayna nodded to the mezzanine level overhead. "Are you game to join me? And maybe make a *good* memory flicker of my magical exploits to post on EnchantNet, for once?"

Francesca looked intrigued. "What did you have in mind?"

"I think my vixen magic needs a test drive." Brimming with enthusiasm, Dayna set down her glass. "Right here, right now."

Chapter Twenty-Four

The Patayan healer had been gone for almost an hour by the time T.J. heard the first clatter at the apartment's front door. Poised beside Deuce's bed, staring watchfully at his friend, T.J. listened. A noisy bang burst the stillness . . . then giggles.

A feminine voice uttered a swearword.

Like a shot, T.J. swept himself to the front door. Just as he reached it, the door shuddered beneath the force of a kick.

Frowning, he yanked it open. Dayna stood illuminated in the glow of the moonlight, her jacket missing and her scarf askew. Her dark hair stuck out from her head. Her eyes looked bleary.

She'd never seemed more beautiful to him.

With a sense of undeniable relief, T.J. pulled her to him.

"You're here." Feeling overcome, he buried his face in her messy hair. He inhaled her scent. But instead of her usual sweetness, he detected the tang of liquor, the spiciness of cloves . . . and an aura of guardedness. With a deepening frown, T.J. looked down. "What happened to you? Where have you been?"

"Celebrating. Woo!" Unsteadily, Dayna threw her arms in the air. The motion made her wobble. She stepped on his foot.

She giggled, then swayed again. She sagged in his arms. "Yay!"

"Celebrating." He didn't care why. That could wait until later. He peered at her with concern. "Then you're all right?"

"Never better!" Dayna swerved into the apartment, crunching broken glass and papers underfoot. Unfazed by the destruction T.J.'s dark current had wrought, she stepped over a tipped-over chair. She dropped her backpack, then struggled with her hoodie. The complications of her zipper stymied her. "I feel great!"

Confused, T.J. watched as his bonded witch battled to undo the fastener. She yanked, frowned, then swore. She held up her arms like a child. "Help, please. I can't get this off."

"Leave it on. There's something I have to tell you. Deuce—"

"Deuce!" Dayna's face brightened, cheerful beneath her smudged eye makeup. "*He'll* help me if you won't. Hey, Deuce!"

She wandered toward the kitchen, peered inside, then gave the debris on the floor a cursory glance. Making another stab at removing her hoodie, Dayna yanked at it. Her kitten familiar meowed, trapped in a fold of the hood by her earlier efforts.

T.J. reached up to grab the creature. It purred.

"Hey." Dayna grinned unsteadily at him. "That's the first time you've ever touched my familiar. I think she likes you!"

"I'm sure she does." Setting down the creature, T.J. watched with abstract interest as the kitten padded through the open doorway. He didn't have time to waste on its whereabouts. If Dayna had been strong enough to conjure it, she would be able to retrieve it later. He shoved the door shut with a burst of magic, then followed Dayna. "Something happened to Deuce. He—"

"My familiar likes *you*, just the way my fellow vixens like *me*!" Dayna announced. "I'm in the cool-witches' club now, T.J. I had the special cocktails to prove it, and everything!"

He couldn't believe she was babbling about cocktails. Not now, while Deuce lay unmoving in the next room. Before T.J. could say anything though, Dayna swerved her way toward him.

Woozily, she flung her arms around his neck. Her boozy breath blasted him. "I would have had even more drinks, but that stupid dozer had to go and fall off the mezzanine at Janus tonight." Her luscious mouth turned down at the corners. "Just when I was about to do some totally amazing magic, too! Francesca was even going to flicker it for me. I don't know what's up with the gardeners in this town, but they sure are accident prone."

T.J. stilled. "Another human died tonight?"

Dayna gave a drunken nod. "That's why I cleared out. The human police swarmed the place. The IAB, too. The fall shouldn't have been fatal, they said, but the aneurysm definitely was."

An aneurysm. That's what had killed Henry Obijuwa. And the other gardener—the one whose death had put the IAB on alert—too.

T.J. grabbed her. "Someone attacked Deuce tonight. The healer is gone now, but Deuce still hasn't awakened. He—"

"What?" In the midst of unwinding her scarf, Dayna gawked at him. She stumbled, then righted herself. Comprehension rolled across her face in an awful wave. "Deuce is hurt?"

Without waiting for his answer, Dayna wheeled her way toward the bedroom. She thumped into the hallway wall, then righted herself and kept going. T.J. followed her. He found her standing beside his partner's bed, staring perplexedly at Deuce.

"Oh my God." Her face, ghostly and aghast, turned to T.J. Feebly, she waved her arm. "What's wrong with him?"

"He's hexed. Or spelled. Or something." Tight-mouthed,

T.J. looked at him. "He's been this way since I got here—hours ago."

"*Hours ago?* Oh, Deuce." Mournfully, Dayna sank to her knees beside the bed. She took Deuce's hand and stroked it. Anxiously, she fluffed the blankets, then tucked them more securely around Deuce's motionless body. Frowning, she glanced up. "Where is Lily? Does she know? I think she'd want to be here."

"Deuce ended things with Lily."

"Oh." Appearing concerned, Dayna squeezed Deuce's hand. Her gaze met T.J.'s. "I'm sorry. I guess that means—"

"*I'm* not sorry," Deuce croaked.

T.J. stiffened. With a surge of hopefulness, he dropped to his partner's side. Deuce flailed in the bed, then blinked. He opened his eyes. He smacked his lips together as though tasting something bad. He looked at Dayna's hand, then up at her, a shadow of his usual happy-go-lucky smile on his pale face.

"Because that witch was *pissed* when I broke it off," Deuce said. "That's it. No more witchy romances for me. I'm done."

"Deuce!" Dayna leaned nearer, smiling. "You're awake."

The tracer swore. "Looks that way. But I'd rather not be."

Frowning, T.J. looked at his bonded witch—at her hand, linked with Deuce's. Had she managed to awaken him somehow?

Before he could decide, he felt Deuce's gaze on him.

"I have a mother of a headache," his partner said. "And you're freaking me out there, pal. What's up with the funereal expression? Did somebody steal your Patayan mojo or what? You're actually wearing clothes. I know *that* doesn't make you happy."

"If it would make you feel better, I'll strip right now."

"No thanks." With a hoarse chuckle, Deuce held up his hands. He shook his head as though trying to clear it, then pushed himself up in bed with Dayna's help. "I've had all the surprise views of your Patayan . . . assets that I ever want. For the rest of my life. Just keep it zipped, okay?"

Swallowing against the lump in his throat, T.J. nodded.

"How do you feel?" Dayna hovered near Deuce, magically plumping his pillows. With concern, she lay her hand on his forehead. "You were out a long time. Do you know what happened?"

Deuce made a face. "Lily happened. She came over here to 'talk,' wearing sexy lingerie and toting a couple of beers—"

That explained the beer bottles on coasters, T.J. thought.

"—and telling me how I was being 'hasty,' not giving us a real shot at a relationship. Well, she has this way about her, you know? When she's trying, Lily can be kind of irresistible."

"Yeah." T.J. nodded. "All witches are like that."

With a rueful grin, Deuce kept going. He stretched his arms as he talked, then rotated his shoulders, obviously feeling better by the minute. "Anyway, in the end, I told Lily it wasn't going to work between us. We're from two different worlds, I said. With her being a witch and me being human, we were pretty well doomed, I told her. But she had a solution for that."

Deuce's expression turned forbidding. A wave of bitterness and regret swept from him to T.J., revealing everything.

"I'm pretty sure Lily dosed me with a conversion potion." Deuce pushed off the bedclothes, then swiveled to sit on the edge of the bed, his usual vitality returning. "She kept talking about how this Old Ways elixir she'd heard about was the best thing for 'awakening' nonmagical humans—dozers, like me."

"And you took it?" Dayna blurted. "Deuce, how could you?"

"I didn't know what I was doing." He rubbed his head. "Lily brought out a couple of cocktails from the kitchen and made a toast. 'Here's to moving on,' she said. She seemed resigned to splitting up. I thought I'd finally convinced her to see things my way. So I wasn't going to quibble at that point."

T.J. remembered the cocktail glasses. The spill. The sweet and sour flavor of the liquid he'd tasted. A conversion potion?

"She didn't tell me what it was until too late," Deuce said. "By then, everything was getting kind of foggy. I remember feeling weird. Powerful. Something stank, like burnt matches—"

"That's what magic smells like," T.J. said. Appalled that any witch would go to the lengths Lily had, he glanced at Dayna.

She refused to meet his eyes. Instead, she fussed over Deuce, her expression closed. He didn't have time to wonder why.

"The healer said you're lucky to have survived," T.J. told Deuce. "Apparently being thick-headed saved your ass this time."

"Oh yeah?" Deuce seemed pleased—and revitalized. "That's cool. Maybe someday being a pain in the ass will save yours."

"Real funny, you two." Obviously more sober now, Dayna put her hand on Deuce's shoulder. She peered into his eyes with evident concern. "But I've already seen one person die tonight, and I don't ever want to see another. I'm glad you're okay."

Deuce blinked. "Someone died tonight?"

"A human. At Janus." Dayna nodded, explaining in a shaky tone about the gardener who'd fallen from the mezzanine. "Apparently, it wasn't the fall that killed him, though—the poor man. The paramedics thought it was probably a brain aneurysm."

"It wasn't an aneurysm." T.J. stared at them, suddenly struck by the pattern of events they'd seen. "It was a failed conversion. Exactly like the one Deuce just survived. The difference is, those gardeners got dosed with the elixir and tried to use their new magic—like Henry Obijuwa did." For a moment, T.J. fell silent, remembering his friend. Then he gazed at Deuce. "Even dosed, you were too pigheaded to succumb."

"Hey, the last thing *I* want is magic." Deuce shuddered.

"Well, your aversion to the magical world probably saved your life." Gratified by that, T.J. gave him a somber nod. "Because it's looking like someone in Covenhaven is trying to convert humans into witches—and the results are deadly."

"You can't convert humans into witches," Dayna argued. "Surely that would have been covered in cusping-witch class."

T.J. shook his head. "Cusping-witch classes teach an IAB-approved curriculum. Those lessons barely scratch the surface of witchstory and culture and magical lore. Why do you think the bureau stole cusping-witch training from the covens?"

"I don't know . . . Because Leo Garmin is a control freak?"

"Because it serves the IAB to keep witchfolk ignorant."

With evident skepticism, Dayna frowned at him. But before T.J. could say more to defend his position, Deuce spoke up.

"The Followers believe conversion is possible *and* desirable. I read about it in the *Book of The Old Ways*."

Dayna frowned. "You read the *Book of The Old Ways*?"

Resistance flowed from Deuce in waves. Then, grudgingly, "I was looking for a way to get unturned."

For a moment, T.J. and Dayna fell silent. His bonded witch gave Deuce a sympathetic look. "So . . . there wasn't one?"

His partner shook his head. "No. But I did find out a lot of unsavory *myrmidon* facts in that book. And I know this much for sure: The Followers want witches to dominate. They're sick of being marginalized, and they blame people like me for it."

"*Myrmidon* want to live freely," T.J. said, "without fear of persecution and without hiding. They believe it's their right as witchfolk—as 'superior' witchfolk. But if this is an example of their methods . . ." He broke off, shaking his head. "I guess if there aren't any humans, there aren't any problems for them. If they increase their ranks by force, witchfolk *will* dominate."

"But the conversion elixir is deadly!" Dayna protested. "How would it help them to make new witches who instantly die?"

"Potions are mutable. They're probably still working on improving it. And judging by what we know already"—T.J. thought about what Jesse had told him about Henry's use of legacy magic—"the *myrmidon* are very close to a working conversion elixir."

"Besides, to a Follower, a dead converted witch is better than a living ignorant 'dozer,'" Deuce said grimly. "As a human, that position didn't exactly give me a warm and fuzzy feeling."

They stared at each other, the room growing colder.

"The Hallow-e'en Festival kicks off tomorrow, right after graduation." T.J. crossed his arms. "Soon there'll be thousands more humans at risk in Covenhaven. If that elixir gets out—"

"It could happen way too easily," Deuce said. "Concession stands, sales at the farmers' market, roving vendors . . ."

The Followers' plan unfolded in T.J.'s mind, easy to see now that the pieces were coming together. The annual festival, always so popular with residents and tourists alike, would act as a lure and a mechanism for conversion at once. After the Followers succeeded here in Covenhaven, they would spread their conversion attempts everywhere. It mattered little to them whether the humans they dosed with the elixir converted or died.

He was a Patayan guardian. He couldn't allow this to happen. Just as his magus's tocsin had foreseen, dark forces were here in Covenhaven. They had to be stopped. Whether they were led by Lily Abbot—which seemed likely, given her use of the elixir on Deuce—or another witch, they had to be defeated. The question now was, would Sumner Jacobs really join with him and the Patayan . . . even against a member of her own vixen pact?

Before T.J. could pose the question, Deuce stepped up beside him, clearly ready to take on whatever lay ahead.

Beside him, Dayna rubbed her arms, shivering. She glanced from T.J. to Deuce, then back again.

"Okay, I'm ready," she announced. "How do we stop them?"

Obviously taken aback by her pugnacious tone, Deuce stared. At his partner's incredulous expression, T.J. stifled a laugh.

"What's with you two?" Dayna asked. "Come on! We can't let the Followers run amok with that potion. I have a lot of human friends. I'd rather not see them forcibly 'converted.' So let's go!"

Filled with love for her—and admiration for her courage, however misguided it was—T.J. turned to his bonded witch. He made sure to soften his voice. "You don't realize what we're up against, Dayna. I can see that you're ready to fight, but—"

"Are you kidding me? I was *born* for this moment, T.J. I have awesome magic skills. You have no idea." Excitedly, Dayna faced him. Liquor still lingered on her breath. "*I* had no idea, until tonight, actually, but now I do. I'm pretty sure I can take on a bunch of The Old Ways zealots. How tough can they be?"

"They've already killed three people," Deuce pointed out.

"And you aren't ready for this," T.J. said gently. "You're not equipped for a battle. Your magic is not purposeful enough." He looked at Deuce. His partner gave him a nod. "We're going to fight the Followers. You're staying here, where it's safe."

Appearing crestfallen, Dayna stared at him, her eyes filled with tears. Then she sniffled. She jabbed her chin upward.

"That's where you're wrong, T.J. I'm going with you."

No. This was a terrible time for her rebellious, stubborn streak to kick in. What T.J. needed now was a powerful vixen witch like Sumner on his side—not an eager, cute-but-clumsy runaway witch who still couldn't conjure a decent cloaking spell. He didn't want to hurt her. But too much was at stake to let his feelings for his bonded witch dictate his actions.

"You need me," Dayna insisted. "I found out something—"

"No. You weaken my magic." T.J. frowned at her. He fisted his hands, then turned his back. "I need you to stay away."

With patent disbelief, Dayna followed him to the doorway. She pointed her finger at him. "You're the one who trained me! You know how much my magic is improving. I can see your aura!"

"Not for much longer, you can't. I'm leaving. Stay here, where you'll be safe. Wait here for me." Stoically, T.J. looked at Deuce. "Are you sure you're ready for this? A half hour ago, you were practically comatose. And before that, you were still—"

"A turned human. I know." Deuce's eyes glimmered with humor, but his face looked taut with determination. "And that's why I'm going. Being turned gives me twice as much reason to send those motherfuckers a message. As long as I'm around to stop them, nobody else is getting turned against their will."

"Or killed," T.J. reminded him. "That potion is lethal."

"No. You're both crazy!" With her hands on her hips, Dayna confronted them. She eyed Deuce first. "You should go to the hospital, get some treatment, and sleep it off. In that order. And you," she told T.J. "*You* should believe in me for once. I'm telling you, I found out something important tonight."

"And I want to know all about it." Mustering up as much patience as he could, T.J. gave her a smile. He leaned nearer, cupped her cheek in his hand, then kissed her with as much love as he could. "Later. Right now, I need to know you're safe."

"I'll be safe with you," Dayna insisted, her blue eyes unrelenting. She squeezed his hand. "I belong with you."

"Forever." T.J. kissed her again. "Now and later."

"If that's true, then take me with you. Show me that you believe in me." Dayna stared mutinously at him. "At least *you* must, T.J., even if no one else does."

He shook his head. "You're asking too much."

Tears shimmered in her eyes. "*Believing in me* is too much?"

"You don't understand." It bothered him that Dayna felt hurt, but he didn't have time to charm her into feeling better. "That's not what I mean. But thanks to my IAB work—"

"Which you didn't bother to tell me you'd been suspended from," Dayna pointed out in an accusatory tone. "Why, T.J.?"

"—I know where the largest contingent of Followers is likely to be," he continued doggedly. He didn't know how Dayna had found out about his suspension. Probably from Garmin. Right now, it didn't matter. "That's where Deuce and I are headed."

Resolutely, T.J. gathered his supplies. He magiked a few things into existence, then took a sample of the potion from the kitchen. "You could still help," he said to Dayna as he moved from one room to the next, the idea occurring to him even as he caught sight of her waiting there. "You could take a message to my magus for me. She needs to know what's happening."

Pausing, he explained how to find the wisewoman's home. As he spoke, Deuce arrived beside him, equipped and ready to go.

"Do you understand?" T.J. asked Dayna. "Will you do it?"

"Mmm. I don't think so." Dayna folded her arms, her face filled with emotions he could not read. "I've decided that I can do more to fight against those Followers with my fellow vixen witches. As soon as we form a quad pact, we'll be unstoppable."

He frowned. "As soon as you do what?"

"Form a quad vixen pact. With my fellow vixen witches."

Stunned, T.J. gawked at Dayna. Then, as though awakening from a bad dream, he remembered the things she'd said while she'd stumbled tipsily around Deuce's apartment earlier.

My familiar likes you, just the way my fellow vixens like me. I'm in the cool-witches club now.

I have awesome magic skills. You have no idea.

I found out something important tonight.

T.J. didn't know how it could be true. But he believed it was. Dayna was a vixen witch. And he'd never even guessed it.

"Surprised? Shocked?" With something akin to triumph—tinged with undeniable sadness—Dayna watched him. "I thought so. Too bad you blew off my offer to help you, isn't it? I hope your supervixen *juweel* can do the job, because I'm out of here."

He'd thought she hadn't even registered his talk about finding the *juweel* for his magus. He'd thought her interest had ended at feeling competitive with the chosen vixen's magic.

He hadn't even bothered to tell her the *juweel* was Sumner.

Too astonished to speak, T.J. watched as Dayna turned away from him. With wounded grandeur, she flung her scarf around her neck, then marched to the door.

"Dayna, wait!" Deuce called. "Don't leave like this."

His partner shafted him a warning look. T.J. knew he had to move, had to speak, had to stop Dayna from leaving him. But if what she wanted from him was faith . . . He still couldn't offer that. Feeling like the rock his magus had so often accused him of being, T.J. stood steady as Dayna wrenched open the door.

A group of IAB agents stood on the other side.

Dressed in the magical equivalent of riot gear, they wielded powerful governing charms. Magic whirled around them, visible in the dark. Their leader gave a signal.

They surged inside the apartment.

Startled, Dayna stepped back. The agents strode past her. Each paused long enough to give her a knowing look, a nod, or a brief word of acknowledgment. At the rear of the group of agents, Leo Garmin entered the apartment with a smug expression.

"Thanks for your help, Ms. Sterling," he said. "You led us straight to Agent McAllister. And his fellow conspirator, Agent Bailey." He glanced at the agents. "Restrain them."

Chapter Twenty-Five

Disbelieving, T.J. made ready to fight. Beside him, Deuce did the same. But even as T.J. inhaled a preparatory breath, getting ready to resist arrest, the awful truth struck him.

Dayna had betrayed him.

The witch who knew him best, the witch who claimed to love him most, the witch who'd lain with him and laughed with him and brought him closer to vulnerability than anyone ever had, *his bonded witch,* the witch he'd trusted . . . had turned him in.

At the realization of her treachery, T.J. nearly did turn to stone. Except stones couldn't hurt . . . and he did. The pain of her betrayal doubled him over. Exactly as it had in Garmin's office, his heart faltered, then squeezed in agony. He groaned.

Two agents hexed him into immobility. Another added magical bonds to restrain him. T.J. couldn't move. Dimly, he heard Deuce punch someone. He heard a gust of exhaled air, felt the floor vibrate as an IAB agent hit the ground. He saw more agents swarm inside the apartment, moving past Dayna with their magic ready.

His bonded witch only stood, unmoving, beside Garmin.

"This concludes things between us," Garmin told her curtly. He watched with feigned regret as Deuce was restrained—and as T.J. was hit with another hex. "Thank you again."

Dayna gave Garmin an unreadable look. If T.J. had been able to detect her emotions—if he'd been capable of doing anything except reeling beneath the pain of her betrayal—he might have deciphered it. As it was, he only buckled in anguish.

"I've decided to forget about your parents' . . . indiscretion." Garmin smiled. "You're free to go, Ms. Sterling. Unless you have more information to offer me?"

In the pause that followed his question, T.J. felt his heart spasm. It clenched in his chest like a painful fist.

"I should tell you about the Followers," came Dayna's tentative voice. "About their conversion plans."

"We already know about that. It's being handled."

"Then I guess . . . there's nothing to keep me here."

T.J. wasn't sure if he heard Dayna's voice or imagined it. Sweating and shaking, he lurched in the IAB agents' grasp. From between two of them, he saw Dayna sling her backpack over her shoulder, exactly as though she were preparing to run again.

He needed the strength to call her back. He wasn't sure if he'd be able to trace her again—if he'd be able to bring her in.

Somehow, T.J. found it. Barely. "Dayna."

Her name scraped through his chest, stealing his breath. All the same, his bonded witch heard it. Already in motion, she turned her head to look at him. Through the hazy grip of his betrayal, T.J. glimpsed her pale face, her hurt eyes.

"Don't go," he rasped. "I need you."

That stopped her. Filled with hopefulness, T.J. waited.

"Why?" Dayna clenched her backpack, her knuckles white on its straps. "Do you need me because you love me? Or because I'm a kickass vixen witch who's going to rule the world?"

Yes. Both. No. Love. In that moment, T.J. didn't know

which was true. He could barely think. Beneath a fresh onslaught of pain, he closed his eyes, trying to find the answer she needed.

An IAB agent gave him a jostling shove in the other direction. "Get moving, half-breed. We don't have all night."

With an unwanted jolt of clarity, T.J. remembered that he had defied his IAB suspension. That was a punishable offense. Depending on how lenient Garmin felt, his punishment might be severe. It paled beside the threat of losing Dayna.

His gaze met hers. Desperately, T.J. tried to form words.

"If you can't tell me that," Dayna said with tears in her eyes, "at least tell me this: Do you trust me, T.J.? Because I swear—I didn't do this to you. I don't know how it happened."

She nodded at the burly agents. One of them snickered.

T.J. couldn't believe it had come down to this. He had a chance to trust her—to put all his faith in his bonded witch—and he couldn't move. Couldn't think. Couldn't speak.

Beside him, Deuce jabbed him. "Jesus, T.J. Tell her you trust her. Before it's too late."

Garmin watched, his aura muted and his gaze shuttered.

T.J. looked at Dayna again. But by then, it *was* too late.

All he saw was her lithe form, slipping away through the doorway to Deuce's apartment . . . escaping from him all over again.

This time, he wouldn't be able to track her down and bring her back. This time, Dayna—as a vixen witch—would know how to elude him for good. If she didn't, she would learn quickly.

Almost as quickly as he'd learned to love her.

A heartbeat later, T.J.'s chest clenched again. Doubled over with pain, he gritted his teeth, holding back a moan.

He gasped . . . and everything went dark.

* * *

Stepping onto the front stoop outside Deuce's apartment, Dayna felt her whole body sag. Weak and trembling, she fell against the hard stucco wall outside the front door, still hearing reverberations of the IAB agents' activities inside.

The autumn air bit into her skin. The cold Samhain wind coursed through the oleander and bougainvillea, stirring their branches. Overhead, the moon cast just enough light that she could see the grass in the courtyard, trampled carelessly by the IAB agents' boots. It would be weeks before the turf recovered.

It would be even longer before she felt . . . anything again.

T.J. didn't trust her. He didn't believe in her. And he hadn't even been able to give her a warlock's charming lie to pretend he did. He couldn't love her. If he ever had, he didn't now.

Obviously, T.J. believed she'd set Garmin and his agents on him and Deuce. He believed she'd turned him in.

The idea was laughable. She hadn't even known about his suspension until tonight. But with tears welling in her eyes and her heart filled with what felt like a stony ache, Dayna didn't feel much like laughing. She'd thought T.J. was the one person she could count on in the magical world. It was a bad end to a bad night to realize that she could count on him least of all.

At her feet, a noise caught her attention. A meow.

With a muffled sob, Dayna spotted her kitten familiar. She scooped it into her arms, her backpack swaying clumsily with the movement, then cradled it gently to her cheek. It purred.

Beside her, the apartment door opened. Leo Garmin emerged, then shut the door on the chaos and curse words behind him.

With easy familiarity, Garmin nodded at her familiar. "The kitten suits you. You should keep it."

She frowned. "Of course I'll keep it. It's mine."

"Actually . . . it's mine. I conjured it. When we took our

trolley ride, I planted it in your backpack. Then I spelled you to make you believe it was yours."

It was *his*? She hadn't even conjured her own familiar?

Dayna opened her mouth to argue. She'd been so proud of that kitten familiar—and the burgeoning magic she'd thought she'd used to conjure it. But what Garmin was saying made sense.

Feeling newly defeated, Dayna slumped against the wall.

"It's clearly imprinted on you." The agent gave the kitten a contemplative look. "Besides, it's done its work now."

"What work?" Protectively, Dayna tucked the kitten in its habitual spot in her hoodie. "I don't know what you mean."

He shrugged. "You couldn't be expected to. Although your magic *has* improved greatly." Garmin gazed at her with flattering interest, his face enigmatic. "I've never met an untried vixen."

"You can forget you ever met me. I'm going to do the same for you." Shocked out of her misery, Dayna straightened to confront him. "Exactly what work did my familiar do for you?"

"It led me to Agent McAllister, of course. I knew you were with him. You admitted as much to me when we met. After that, all I needed was an in." Garmin gave her a disturbingly astute look. "Your desperation to do well with magic provided it."

She frowned. "I was never desperate enough to turn in T.J."

"You didn't have to be. The kitten was enchanted to react to Agent McAllister's touch. As soon as he touched your familiar tonight, it brought a message to me." Garmin smiled. "I didn't think it would take so long, though. I guess I underestimated Agent McAllister's animosity toward kittens?"

"You underestimated a lot of things. Including me."

At that, Garmin laughed outright. "You led me straight to what I wanted. I think I can cope with my disappointment."

"Can you cope with being wrong about T.J.?" Dayna asked. "Because you are. He's not on the wrong side of anything."

"So you said when you phoned me. You should have used a persuasion spell along with your lie. It might have worked." He eyed her with interest. "I have a soft spot for innocents."

Dayna quirked her lips. "Then you won't be interested in me. After tonight, I doubt I'll ever feel innocent again."

Garmin laughed at that, too, but Dayna turned away.

With his amusement still ringing in her ears, she left at least one of her most regrettable mistakes behind her for good. No matter what Garmin had done to her, she had her big chance now to save the day for the people of Covenhaven. With T.J. and Deuce in custody, it was up to her to stop the Followers.

But first, she needed some help. When it came to saving the world, there was no way Dayna could do it alone.

Bereft and forlorn, Dayna arrived at Janus well after midnight. The resort's landscape lighting was dimmed; the valets were inside, with no cars idling beside the fountain to deliver new arrivals. Even the usual ambient music had been turned off for the night, leaving only the ghostly wail of the canyon wind to accompany her descent from the last running trolley.

"Thank you," she told the driver with a sad wave. "I'm sorry to keep you working so late. You've been very helpful."

"Not a problem, ma'am. Enjoy your stay in Covenhaven."

At that, Dayna gave a bitter laugh. When she'd arrived in town—by force, in T.J.'s grasp—she'd expected to encounter magical disappointments. She hadn't expected heartbreak.

On the other hand, she realized as the trolley trundled away behind her, she hadn't expected a group of evil Followers to be plotting to take over all of human and witchkind either. And that was happening, too. So she'd just have to roll with it.

Drawing in a deep breath, Dayna headed for the lobby.

After only a few steps, though, she stopped. She could sense activity inside Janus. She could *feel* the magic whirling through the place. She was even aware of the cusping witches who'd gathered there, all their magical skills surging in readiness.

Maybe if she connected them all, it occurred to her, she could convince them to help. Maybe the key to defeating the Followers was linking all the other witches more strongly than ever—relying on witches who weren't *myrmidon* and didn't want to awaken humans against their will. Maybe that would work.

Maybe it wouldn't. Dayna didn't know. In that moment, she felt too overwhelmed to try. Despite her vaunted research and organizational skills, she wasn't up for the task. Even if she had been, she didn't have the necessary magic to defeat the Followers on her own. T.J. had made that abundantly clear.

Shaken by his lack of faith, still hurt by her parents' deception, and troubled by everything she'd seen tonight, Dayna stared into the waters of the Janus fountain.

Maybe she should run. She could be gone before morning . . .

"Dayna!" Lily Abbot appeared beneath the porte cochere, shivering in the chilly night, her expression welcoming. "What are you doing out here? Francesca sent me to come and get you."

"Francesca?"

"She sensed you were here." As though such clairvoyance were an everyday occurrence, Lily wrapped a pashmina around Dayna's shoulders. She hurried her inside the luxurious warmth of the resort's lobby. "We're all in the ballroom, making final preparations for graduation and the Hallow-e'en Festival."

Lily hustled in that direction, clearly expecting Dayna to follow her. Instead, Dayna lingered in the curiously deserted lobby. She stared at her fellow vixen's departing figure.

All at once, Dayna felt woozy again—not intoxicated and giddy, the way she had while slurping down Francesca's special-blend cocktails earlier—but dizzy. Uneasy. *Really* strange.

Baffled by the sensation, Dayna struggled against it. She blinked. Then she remembered at least part of what was wrong tonight. "Lily. Your conversion elixir almost killed Deuce."

"What?" Lily turned to her, her beautiful face punctuated by an expression of childlike surprise. "What elixir?"

"He told us what you did." Struck by a wave of vertigo, Dayna grabbed the concierge desk. It wavered in her vision. So did Lily. The vixen witch stepped toward her. With effort, Dayna clutched her borrowed pashmina, trembling beneath an onslaught of shivering. "He told us about the potion. He told us—"

"Then Deuce is awake?" Lily asked. "He's all right?"

Was that relief on her face? Dayna wasn't sure.

Nausea hit her. The lobby went dark, as though shutters had dropped in front of her eyes. The room flickered, then tilted.

"Dayna?" came Lily's muffled voice. "Are you okay?"

"I—" Dimly, Dayna felt her hand slide off the concierge desk. The lamp on top of it fell and shattered. Her pashmina slipped from her shoulders, down . . . down . . . down. "I don't—"

I don't know, she meant to say. But suddenly she couldn't speak. Her mind refused to participate in the effort. Her mouth moved, but none of the words she wanted emerged. She groaned.

"Hold on. I've got you." Lily was there, warm and surprisingly sturdy. Apparently creating artisanal baked goods made a witch stronger than usual. "There. Is that better?"

Dayna fought to open her eyes. Her throat tightened, then began to close up. The feeling made her panic. Wide-eyed, Dayna grabbed Lily's sweater. Soft witchmade cash-

mere met her grasp. She needed to hold on. She needed to
fight against . . . this.

Lily chuckled. "I doubt Deuce told you *everything*."

Dayna thought she might have imagined those words.
She couldn't be sure. The lights overhead tilted; Lily's face
loomed over hers, filled with concern. Then everything
went black.

With his back against the cold wall of an enchanted IAB
holding room, T.J. closed his eyes. Blissful darkness pulled at
him. He welcomed it. It promised relief from the squeezing
hand that gripped his chest. Each heartbeat brought new pain.
Drawing in a breath was agony; thinking about losing Dayna
was worse.

With a fierce scowl, he let himself drift. Chaotic images
chased through his head, coupled with events he didn't want
to remember and feelings he didn't want to feel. In the darkness, he saw Dayna, staring at him with accusing eyes. He
saw Dayna, standing beside Garmin as though *he* were the
warlock she trusted. He saw Dayna, leaving him without a
backward glance.

"Hey." Deuce's voice shattered the stillness, interrupting
T.J.'s dark escape. His partner snapped his fingers. "What do
you call a witch who won't put out on the first date?"

Not this again. Eyes still closed, T.J. ignored him.

"You *don't* call her. Get it?" Deuce elbowed him. "You
don't call her, because she won't get freaky with you." He
laughed.

Desolately, T.J. turned his face away. The wall felt rough
against his cheek. For an instant, he attributed the sensation
to magical pixilation. Hopefulness fluttered to life inside him.

Then reason returned, hard and cold. Garmin would never
place them in a holding room that was so easy to escape from.

"Not going for that one? Okay." Still on the floor where

he'd been since T.J. had awakened to find a cadre of IAB agents locking them in, Deuce sighed. "How about this: What do you call a warlock who acts like a complete asshole, even to the extent of locking up his two best freaking agents?" In a flurry of motion, Deuce got to his feet. He moved under the autoshadowing memory flicker affixed to the ceiling, then punched his fist toward it. "You call him Leo Garmin! That's right! King Asshat of the InterAllied Bureau. I hope you hear this, you jerk—"

"Knock it off." Blearily, T.J. opened his eyes. "Garmin's charges won't stick to you. This is all on me. So shut up."

"Oh. You're awake then." Eyes narrowed, Deuce whirled around. "Howdy." Hé stalked closer. "I've only been wiping your forehead and holding your fucking hand for the past hour while you did your best impression of a heart attack victim. Very convincing. Really scared the shit out of me. Nice work."

"Sorry." T.J. gave a halfhearted wave. "It's a Patayan thing. I don't think it's fatal. It just feels like it is."

Deuce's gaze softened. "Is it because of Dayna?"

T.J.'s throat closed up. His heart clenched. He nodded.

"Aww." Deuce shook his head. "Good. Maybe that will teach you not to make such a boneheaded move again, you idiot!"

His scathing tone washed over T.J. He closed his eyes.

But Deuce wasn't finished. "You can wallow in misery all you want, but the plain truth is, you made Dayna leave."

Scowling in response, T.J. lifted his middle finger.

"Hell, you practically pushed her out the door," Deuce went on, his tirade unabated. "She begged you to let her come with us to fight the Followers, but what did you do? You shot her down. It was like kicking a puppy. A hot, sexy, capable vixen puppy."

T.J. opened his eyes again. "It was necessary."

"Why? So you could feel like a big shot and save the day?"

His partner paced across the room, oblivious now to its security features. "You heard Dayna. She's a vixen witch! Not a bad asset to have on our side in the big showdown. You should have trusted her. Maybe then she would have told you about being a vixen before it was too late."

"She betrayed me!" T.J. roared, fully alert now. "She turned me in." He sobered long enough to glare at Deuce. "In case you haven't noticed, she turned you in, too, jackass."

Prudishly, his partner crossed his arms. "She didn't do it. She told you that. Am I the only one with eyes and ears around here?" He stared at T.J. in blatant disgust. "I heard Dayna swear she was innocent. I heard her beg you to trust her."

"I *did* trust her." T.J. winced as his heart gave another spasm. He panted for breath. "Now it's killing me. Happy?"

"Not until we find a way to stop the Followers."

"Your concern for my welfare is really touching."

This time, Deuce flipped him the finger. "We finally know what's happening in this town. Just like your magus said, it's not good. *Really* not good. And we're stuck in here." He wheeled around, ruffling his hair in frustration. "Do you think Garmin is on top of this thing with the Followers, like he said?"

T.J. shook his head. "I don't trust him."

"Oooh. Big surprise there. The lone wolf is suspicious."

T.J. ignored Deuce's sarcasm. "Think about it. We should be in a regular holding cell, with regular agents watching us." He gestured at the holding room with its various IAB enchantments. He nodded in the direction of the guards outside the door. "Instead, we're secreted in a magically enhanced back room with Garmin's private foragers on the watch. This goes way beyond flouting an IAB suspension."

"You think Garmin is corrupt?"

"I think everyone is corrupt." With a ragged exhalation, T.J. leaned his head against the wall again. "But I'm magically useless and you're . . . *chronically* magically useless. Unless that changes between now and tomorrow morning, we're screwed."

Deuce frowned. "I don't accept that."

"Too bad." T.J. closed his eyes, surrendering to the darkness again. "Because I do. It's over, Deuce. We're done."

Chapter Twenty-Six

Dayna awakened in the Janus lobby. Muzzy-headed and confused, she squinted at the glittering chandelier overhead. She patted her hands. A sleek leather settee met her palms.

It looked as though Lily had moved her to a more comfortable spot. Dayna couldn't remember exactly what had happened. She had a vague recollection of hurrying inside the resort's lobby, following Lily . . . confronting her. *Deuce.*

She sat up. Her head swam. Voices surged toward her.

"You *can't* put her in the penthouse." Sumner's petulant tone came first. "You promised *me* that suite, Francesca!"

"Don't be such a baby, Sumner." This, from Lily. "We have more important things to worry about right now."

"Lily is right," Francesca said. "If we don't hurry—"

"Of *course* she's right!" Sumner interrupted in a caustic voice. "That's just great. Not only have I been replaced by a *nobody* like Dayna Sterling, but now Lily is runner-up, not me."

Runner-up for what? Dayna wondered fuzzily. She was used to being the subject of Sumner's insults—but the rest of what Sumner had said didn't make sense. Confused, she peered toward the other end of the lobby. Near the concierge desk, her fellow vixen witches stood with rigid posture, clearly arguing.

"This isn't the time for your competitive streak to raise its ugly head, Sumner." Francesca turned her face toward Dayna. She smiled. "The important thing is, Dayna is our friend now. She needs us. I'm not going to send her out into the night all alone. What if she keels over on the trolley? Or in a taxi?" Francesca shook her head, her expression filled with certainty. "Dayna is taking the penthouse suite, and that's that."

"But Francesca!" Sumner wailed. "You *can't* give her the—"

"I just did." On a wave of unassailable charm, Francesca moved across the lobby. Murmuring with concern, she sat beside Dayna on the settee. "How are you? Are you feeling better?"

Dayna frowned. "I think so. What happened?"

"Lily says you passed out. You still look pretty pale. Fortunately, she was here to take care of you. And when the two of you didn't come back to the ballroom right away, I knew something must have happened. Sumner and I came at a run."

Behind Francesca, Sumner crossed her arms. She glared.

It didn't take T.J.'s special blend of Patayan sensitivity to recognize the animosity flowing from Sumner to Dayna. The realization bothered her, but Dayna had more important issues to deal with tonight. Biting her lip, she leaned toward Francesca.

"I have to tell you something. But it's sensitive."

Led by Dayna's pointed gaze, Francesca glanced over her shoulder. Now Lily waited beside Sumner, too, wearing a peevish expression. Both the vixen witches' auras shimmered darkly.

"We still have a lot to do before tomorrow," Lily reminded Francesca with a look at her watch. "We'd better get back."

"Thanks, Lily." Pursing her lips in displeasure, Francesca

turned to Dayna again. "We don't have any secrets between us vixens. Whatever you have to say, you can say to all of us."

Doubtfully, Dayna glanced at the vixen duo behind her.

"But tonight . . . I'm afraid your news *is* going to have to wait." Francesca gave a weary exhale. Even frazzled, she looked beautiful and in command. "Lily is right. We are *way* behind on the preparations for tomorrow. The festival and graduation will be here before we know it. I'm going to have to pull an all-nighter just to get ready. This event could make or break Janus. I really can't afford to blow it."

Uncertainly, Dayna hesitated. She didn't want to blurt out the whole scheme that T.J. had laid out about the Followers' conversion plans—at least not in front of Lily and Sumner. It was still possible that Lily had masterminded the whole thing.

After all, she was the one who'd dosed Deuce tonight.

I doubt Deuce told you everything.

And Dayna didn't trust Sumner. Not even a little bit. But she couldn't wait too long to deal with the Followers. If T.J. was right, they'd set their conversion plans in motion tomorrow.

Maybe Francesca, with her influence, could help get T.J. and Deuce released from the IAB? It was clear she knew Garmin . . .

"Besides, you look positively ghastly," Francesca told her, "and I'm *not* saying that to be mean. I'm saying it as a friend." Warmly, she urged Dayna to her feet. "You've been through a lot today. You had a big shock earlier. Plus, you're probably still feeling the effects of the cocktails you drank. After a good night's sleep, you'll feel *so* much better, I promise."

"Well . . ." Gazing into Francesca's face, Dayna wavered. It was nice to know that someone cared about her well-being. The night had definitely taken its toll on her. Finding out she was a vixen, seeing that gardener die, worrying about Deuce, arguing with T.J., being tricked by Garmin, *losing T.J.* . . . "You do have a point. I *am* pretty wiped out." If she explained the Followers' conversion scheme in this state, it would sound like something out of a Scooby Doo cartoon. Francesca was right—she did need a chance to rest and regroup. "Maybe just a short nap. But after that, I've really got to talk to you. It's important."

"I'll put in a request for a wake-up call in an hour. Whatever you want." With easy agility, Francesca walked Dayna to the elevator bank. She magiked a key card, then inserted it in the private express elevator slot. Silently, the doors whooshed open. "After you're feeling better, if you still want to talk, I'll be down in the ballroom. I'm sure I'll be there all night."

"Okay." Suddenly overcome by a wave of fatigue, Dayna yawned. She was *so* tired. Maybe her earlier dizzy spell was still affecting her. "I'll tell you all about it then."

If she was lucky, Sumner and Lily would be busy elsewhere.

"Sounds good. If you need anything—anything at all—just call me, okay?" Francesca beamed at her, as though accepting a luxury penthouse suite for the night were a tremendous personal favor. She slipped a card in Dayna's hand. It tingled as it struck her palm, imprinted with Francesca's charismatic witchy identity. "You can reach me here anytime, day or night."

"Thanks, Francesca. This is really kind of you."

"I could tell you needed a friend tonight." Francesca gave her a hug. "Just don't give that card to anyone else," she warned. "That's my special line, for close friends only."

Warmed by the glow of Francesca's friendship, Dayna nodded. When the queen bee of Covenhaven decided to appoint you a member of the in crowd, she definitely went all the way. If Dayna hadn't felt so heartbroken just then, she would have been jubilant. As it was, she could only offer Francesca a wan smile. She'd wanted to fit in. Now, beyond a doubt, she finally did.

"Now shoo!" Waving her arms, Francesca urged her into the

elevator. Its sleek paneled walls hugged Dayna close, leaving her feeling cosseted and cared for. Francesca pulled out a second gold keycard, then gave it to Sumner. "Sumner, why don't you show Dayna which way the penthouse suite is?"

It wasn't a suggestion; Sumner's irate expression said that she realized as much. Her aura turned from dim to murky.

Then she smiled. Ruthlessly. "All right. Let's go, Dayna."

Dayna took a step back as the vixen witch entered the elevator. With enviable poise, Sumner inserted the keycard, then pressed the *P* button. Soundlessly, the doors began to slide closed. Suddenly alarmed, Dayna stuck her hand between them.

They bounced apart.

"That's all right, Sumner. I've got it from here."

"Nonsense." With relish, Sumner pressed the *P* button again. She wiggled her fingers in a cheerful wave to her fellow vixens. "I'll make sure you get *properly* settled in. Here we go!"

The doors closed all the way. Feeling a distinct sense of menace infiltrate the elevator's tiny space, Dayna watched as the numbers lit up. The car set itself in motion, taking her to the penthouse suite.

When the elevator reached the penthouse level, the doors slid open again. Sumner stared resentfully at the luxurious hallway that lay beyond the elevator bank. She didn't move.

Warily, Dayna looked at her. "Thanks, Sumner. Good night."

Sumner's expression remained fixed and sullen . . . except for the tiniest wobble of her chin. Was übercool Sumner Jacobs actually about to cry? Dayna could hardly believe it.

"Listen, Sumner . . ." Awkwardly, Dayna gestured toward the penthouse. "I didn't come here for any of this. If it helps, I'm really not trying to wreck your plans. This night has *not* gone the way I wanted it to. I found out some major news, and then I broke up with my"—she paused, unsure what to call her bonded warlock/Patayan guardian—"boyfriend, and then I had that weird dizzy spell, and now I don't know *what* to believe anymore. So—"

"It wasn't a dizzy spell. Lily hexed you."

Surprised, Dayna stared at her. "Come on," she blurted out. "That can't be true." Lily had obviously done the wrong thing when she'd dosed Deuce. But Dayna still believed that might have been an accident. Lily had honestly cared about Deuce; if she'd stolen that conversion potion in a misguided attempt to keep them together . . . Well, what witch hadn't done something crazy in the name of love? "Why in the world would Lily—"

"You'd better watch your back. Lily is devious. She goes after whatever she wants full force. And she never loses."

Dayna thought about Deuce—about almost losing him tonight. She thought about what Lily had said to her earlier, as she'd collapsed in the lobby. *I doubt Deuce told you everything.*

"I don't have anything Lily would want," Dayna argued.

"That's where you're wrong." Sumner's eyes glittered with a peculiar brightness. "From where I sit, you have *everything.*"

"Then I need a seat near you, because I can't see it."

Her joke didn't faze Sumner. Feeling goose bumps prickle along her skin, Dayna rubbed her hands over her arms. "Well, thanks again." She made an awkward grab at the keycard. "If I could just have the keycard, I'll be on my way to—"

"Oh, this?" Sumner held up the keycard. "Sure. You can have it." She tossed it toward the penthouse. It skidded to a stop on the glossy marble floor, then clinked against the suite's double doors. "You can have it now, and later, and later!"

Laughing, she swept her hands toward the keycard. A peculiar popping sound erupted. Dayna turned to see what it was.

At the same moment, Sumner shoved her. Dayna fell into

the hallway, wobbling in surprise. She stepped on something hard and slick. It skated along beneath her foot, nearly making her fall.

She looked down. A keycard.

Sumner had spelled them into multiplying. The floor was already littered with them. Even as Dayna watched, the keycard she'd stepped on split itself in two. Each of the halves divided as well. She had no idea which card was the original.

"Enjoy the penthouse suite!" Nastily, Sumner waved.

The elevator doors closed on her laughter. Dayna had the crazy thought that Sumner would be a perfect partner for Leo Garmin. They were both equally maniacal. Then she dropped to her knees and scrambled to pick up the keycards before they filled the hallway to the penthouse suite and buried her completely.

Frowning with fatigue, Dayna inserted a keycard into the electronic lock on the penthouse door. Unlike the fifty-two other keycards she'd already tried over the past half hour, this one actually worked. The lock clicked open.

"Finally." Weak with weariness and heartache, she opened the door. She'd already been upset when she'd arrived at Janus. Downstairs with Francesca, Lily, and Sumner, she'd battled to remain upright under a weird wave of exhaustion. The last thing she'd wanted after that was to battle with Sumner's spiteful keycard trick. But she'd persevered. Now she was in.

She stepped inside. Magically, the remaining keycards swept along in her wake, skittering like eager puppies. Great. Sumner had given her an irritating, thousand-piece magical entourage.

Francesca might have befriended her. Lily might be warming up to her. But Sumner? Sumner was obviously still a holdout.

Well, Dayna didn't like Sumner much either. With an impatient gesture, she magiked the keycards toward the foyer wall. They piled up like a golden plastic snowdrift, shining beneath the penthouse's automatically brightening lighting.

Trudging farther inside the suite, Dayna realized the place was bigger than her apartment in Phoenix. Inhaling deeply, she glanced at the lavish furnishings, the huge flat-screen TV, the remote-controlled sound system, the full bar, the dining table that seated twenty and boasted a direct line to an on-call butler . . . Shaking her head, she looked out the windows at the darkened view. In the daytime, she realized, this suite would overlook the canyon and red rocks, making it twice as desirable.

There was probably more—Dayna spotted double doorways to each side of the main penthouse, undoubtedly leading to a pair of bedrooms—but for right now, she had all she needed. With a sigh of relief, she dropped her backpack beside a leather sofa.

She dragged off her scarf, then her hoodie. With concern, she realized that her kitten familiar wasn't with her. Sometime during the night, it must have slipped away. She hoped it hadn't gone to be reunited with Garmin. It deserved better than that.

The thought of Garmin reminded her that she still had a lot to do—and not much time to do it in. Frowning, Dayna kicked off her Converses. She pulled off her socks. Barefoot, she headed toward the nearest bedroom. But ironically, now that she'd reached the penthouse, she wasn't tired anymore.

First, she decided, a hot shower to revive her. That would help get her thoughts in order. After that, a call to Francesca.

No matter how busy Francesca was, she needed to know what was happening tomorrow—especially since it was happening here on Janus's grounds. And no matter what Francesca had said about vixen solidarity, the news of the

Followers' scheme was not something Dayna could explain with Lily and Sumner around.

She still didn't trust them. When she turned the corner to the bedroom, she realized she had a very good reason not to.

The bedroom was filled with boxes—boxes, crates, and entire shrink-wrapped pallets, all of them stacked haphazardly around the room and each filled with ingredients for witching potions.

A couple of boxes containing potion ingredients would not have been out of the ordinary, Dayna told herself as she sorted through them. Most witches kept such supplies on hand. Even her own mother did. But *dozens* of boxes—containing myriad vials of banned ingredients—were definitely suspicious. So was the fact that they were here, arrayed in a penthouse suite instead of a storeroom somewhere on a service level twenty floors down.

Even more awake now, Dayna sat on the floor and dragged over another box. The first one she'd glimpsed had been open already. After noticing its contraband contents, she'd felt no compunction about tearing open a second box—then a third, a fourth . . . a tenth. At first, she'd hoped she'd been mistaken about the boxes' contents. But after opening most of them, she'd realized there was only one conclusion that made sense. Someone had been stockpiling banned ingredients in this penthouse suite.

Methodically, as only a researcher like her would have done, Dayna considered the contents of the nearest boxes. Some of the banned ingredients caused forgetfulness. Some boosted magic. Some suppressed caring and promoted ruthlessness; others amplified focus or increased mental agility. All the ingredients were on hand in quantities far too vast for ordinary use.

With dawning horror, Dayna stared at the multiple open

boxes surrounding her. These were ingredients, she realized, for Francesca's witchy invincibility potion. Taken together and served to witchfolk, they would make up the specially garnished, exclusively offered "cocktail" that Dayna had enjoyed earlier.

Taken together and given to *humans*, however . . .

They would make up a deadly conversion potion.

Dayna was sure of it. No wonder Sumner hadn't wanted anyone else to stay in her penthouse suite! She'd discovered a lethal side use for Francesca's cocktail. For all Dayna knew, Sumner had been dosing humans with it, trying to awaken them.

Francesca would be appalled. Obviously, Sumner had been keen to keep her activities a secret, and with good reason. She'd probably thought her keycard trick would be enough to keep Dayna from entering the penthouse suite. Given Dayna's usual lack of magic, it was a reasonable assumption. Sumner had been able to do as Francesca had asked—without arousing suspicion *and* without surrendering the penthouse suite and its secret cache.

Or so she'd thought.

Unhappily alert, Dayna stared at the opened boxes and their poisonous contents. Everyone knew Francesca wasn't an Old Ways sympathizer. She'd made that clear on their girls' spa day, when she'd questioned Dayna about her potential *myrmidon* beliefs. So of course Sumner would have to hide the truth about herself.

Sumner was a Follower. Francesca wasn't.

This was where their vixen friendship fell apart. This was where Dayna found the link to the Followers that she'd needed—right in the midst of Covenhaven's most popular witchy trio.

There were enough banned potion ingredients there to dose everyone who came to graduation and the Hallow-e'en Festival tomorrow. Dayna didn't have a second to waste. Getting to her feet, she pulled out the card Francesca had given her.

Again, it tingled in her palm as she stared at it. She hadn't wanted to use it to deliver this kind of bad news. But she didn't have much choice. With her heart pounding, Dayna picked up her cell phone and dialed Francesca.

"I thought you were planning to sleep." Wearing a frown that did little to mar her perfect appearance, Francesca entered the penthouse suite. "What's this all about?"

Nervously clenching her fists, Dayna opened her mouth to explain. Then she thought better of it. "I'll show you."

With a bewildered Francesca on her heels, Dayna strode to the bedroom. She flung out her arm, indicating the boxes.

"These are all full of banned potion ingredients." She named them, in order from most forbidden to most toxic, ticking off each one on her fingers. "There's no legitimate use these ingredients can be put to." Gravely, Dayna turned to Francesca. "Someone is using your penthouse suite to make lethal potions for a mass conversion attempt. And I'm pretty sure I know who."

"At the moment, it looks like it's *you*." Francesca appeared amused. She waved her arm, then laughed. "Oh, don't be so somber, Dayna! I'd wondered where Lily and Sumner had stashed all this stuff. These boxes will be out of here by morning. Just use the other bedroom. I've got to get back downstairs."

Confused by Francesca's blasé tone, Dayna blinked. She stepped nearer as her fellow vixen turned to leave. "Wait. Don't you want to know who is getting ready to use these ingredients?"

"Well . . . I imagine it's someone who wants to make sure that witchfolk will be able to live openly, in a world free of discrimination." With her usual ease and confidence,

Francesca stopped in the doorway. She gave Dayna a smile. "I imagine it's someone who has the future of witchkind at heart. Someone who is willing to risk everything to make sure that ignorant dozers won't hold us back any longer from the destiny we deserve."

Feeling chilled, Dayna stared. "Someone . . . like you?"

"Of course." Warmly, Francesca trailed her fingers over the nearest open box. She lifted a shimmering vial. "I was fated for this. From the time I was just an able child, everyone told me how special I was. Once I read the *Book of The Old Ways*, I knew what I was meant to do. It was only a matter of how and when."

"You *were* always special," Dayna agreed, her mind racing. Her heart thumped faster. She hadn't expected *this*. And compared with Francesca, she was completely outmatched in magic. She struggled to remain calm. "Everyone in Covenhaven could see it."

"You're special, too." With a generous smile, Francesca nodded at her. "You're a vixen, like me. You're clever, like me. You're rebellious, stubborn, and—suddenly—very gifted. Like me."

"Not—not really," Dayna stuttered. *Francesca expected her to help with her scheme,* she realized in shock. "My magic is still pretty balky. Especially when I'm not in class. So—"

Francesca laughed. "Are you really *that* innocent? Your magic was better in class because of your proximity to your fellow vixens. Remember when your kitten familiar morphed into a tiger? That was just one example. I can't believe you didn't know that." Shaking her head, Francesca gave her another amused, knowing look. "Our magic is amplified when it's together. Once we complete our quad vixen pact—you, me, Sumner, and Lily—we'll be *so* powerful. It's been centuries since witchfolk have experienced a quad vixen pact. It ought to be quite a show!"

Fighting not to reveal her fear, Dayna looked past the boxes of ingredients, past the penthouse itself, all the way to the view outside. "Somebody should have clued me in then. I'm not exactly prepared for a once-in-a-century show tomorrow." She mustered up a shaky laugh. "Exactly what did you have in mind?"

"Oh, please." Francesca gave her a playful look. "You're the smarty-pants of the group. You must have guessed."

"Nope." Dayna shrugged. "I've been out of the witchy loop for a while though, remember? I'm still catching up."

"I'll give you the condensed version then." Francesca moved languidly across the room, then sat on the bed. She patted the mattress, motioning for Dayna to join her, slumber-party-style.

Trembling, Dayna did. If she didn't play this right, Francesca could reduce her to dust with a snap of her fingers. No one would know where she'd gone. Her parents would hang on, always hoping she'd merely run away again. T.J. would . . . brood, caught up in the darkness that always loomed around him.

T.J. Silently, Dayna gave an anguished groan. She wished T.J. were here now. He would know what to do. He would have the magic to defeat Francesca. As it was, she had only herself to rely on. And she'd *never* been good enough for the magical world.

"Okay. Here's the thing." Eagerly, Francesca tucked a hank of long dark hair behind her ear. She appeared to be settling in for a sisterly gossip session. "For a long time, we Followers have been looking for a way to shake up the status quo." She broke off, then gave Dayna a shrewd look. "By the way, bravo on the way you answered my *'myrmidon'* questions on our girls' spa day! You saw the IAB bug hovering in the corner, too, right?"

She hadn't. Mutely, Dayna nodded. "Of course."

"Anyway, we've been trying to find a way to make sure that

witchfolk are given the respect they deserve. There's no good reason we should be persecuted and marginalized while humans rule the world." Francesca made a face. "For too long, witchfolk have allowed their traditions to be eroded. Even otherwise good witchfolk have been abandoning their time-honored ways, using human-made devices instead of magic. Seriously, Botox? iPhones? Satellite GPS? Who needs them?" Aggrieved, Francesca flung out her hands. She shook her head. "If we keep adopting the dozers' technology this way, witchfolk culture will disappear altogether. I say, if you have magic, use it."

"And if you don't . . . ?"

"*Get it.* Exactly." Like the proud parent of an able child, Francesca beamed at Dayna. "So that's what we're going to do. We're going to give magic to all the dozers—with *my* conversion elixir. The latest version works even better than before. Once those humans see what they're capable of, they'll be sold." She snapped her fingers. "Like that. And *voilà*! Once we're all witches and loyal Followers, there'll be no more harassment, no more discrimination . . . no more battles to fight."

"It all sounds"—appalled, Dayna hesitated—"too easy."

"Oh, it won't be easy. Believe me. Without a huge collective of powerful cusping witches, a mass conversion like this wouldn't even be possible." Confidingly, Francesca put her hand on Dayna's forearm. Magical tremors sparked between them. "But once the IAB rounded up all the cusping witches, it became a *lot* more manageable. The trick is, *I* know how to use them."

"Use the cusping witches? How?"

"Wow." Francesca shook her head, trailing her hand away from Dayna's arm. "You really are innocent. You'd better stay away from my boyfriend, okay?" She laughed in a girl-to-girl way. "He's kind of a freak for the naïve type."

She meant Leo Garmin. Shocked, Dayna gave a weak chuckle.

"Cusping witches are especially open to becoming linked. It's part of our cusping process—part of being at the height of our magical abilities," Francesca said. "In the old days, linking was designed to make sure we bonded in close-knit groups instead of competing with each other. Funny, right? That biology has to ensure a way for witches to get along? It's crazy."

Obviously, Francesca had never been shunned by the other witches in her school, in her neighborhood . . . in her town. She had no idea how painful it had been for Dayna to be ostracized.

"Makes sense to me," she said. "Everyone likes positive feedback. Everyone likes to feel appreciated and rewarded."

"Right. Like with cusping-witch classes—our hard work should be recognized. Which is where the IAB's graduation amulets come in. But you *must* have already guessed about them, right?"

Dayna murmured a denial. She gave Francesca what she hoped was an inquisitive—but not terrified—look. "What about them?"

"Seriously." For the first time, Francesca seemed perturbed. "You were right there when I was engraving them."

"I know, but—" Frantically, Dayna tried to think up an excuse for her lack of witchy acumen. "I was kind of freaked out, remember? Tonight was not my best-ever night."

Francesca narrowed her eyes. Then her expression softened.

"All right, you're right. Sorry! I must be getting paranoid after all this plotting with Lily and Sumner." She gave Dayna a camaraderie-filled poke to the shoulder. "And now, with *you*! Who would have believed it, right? The two of us, best friends?"

"It's . . . unbelievable, all right."

Francesca sighed. "Well, it's actually inevitable, is what it is. We're vixens. We're sisters, forever."

Years ago, Dayna would have given anything to hear those words. To be accepted. To be linked. To truly belong in the witching world. Now she could scarcely contain her fear. She didn't want to belong in a world ruled by witches who got their way by force. Witches who dominated through fear and prejudice.

Witches like Francesca.

It was clear that Francesca couldn't conceive of any other way to be—couldn't imagine that anyone, especially some-one like Dayna, would disagree with her. Francesca hadn't even questioned her assumption that Dayna was a Follower, like her. Apparently, Francesca was arrogant enough to be-lieve *everyone* wanted to be like her—including unawakened humans.

". . . so that's how I'm going to spread my magic," Francesca was saying. "Once I've given a piece of myself to every cusp-ing witch who graduates, there'll be no possibility of failure. My magic will be enhanced a thousandfold! The Old Ways will be here for good, bringing enlightenment to everyone." She smiled broadly. "And *we'll* form a fully united quad vixen pact to rule over all of it—you, me, Lily, and Sumner. We'll be unstoppable."

With a rush of despair, Dayna realized she'd said much the same thing to T.J. tonight. Only then she'd been plan-ning on defeating the Followers—not helping them take over the world.

But that's exactly what she was—accidentally—about to do tomorrow, if she didn't stop this. Dayna had missed some of Francesca's chatter, but overall, her plan seemed clear.

Francesca intended to spread her magic among the cusp-ing witches who drank her invincibility-endowing "cocktail." That would ensure that witchfolk would be at their strongest tomorrow. Then she would give the same cocktail—now functioning as a conversion elixir—to unsuspecting humans all over Covenhaven, trusting in the combined powers of the newly linked cusping witches to make the conversion process work.

The humans would never survive their forced magical "endowment." At least the unturned humans wouldn't.

And if that happened . . .

Dayna felt frozen in place, totally unable to move.

"Hey." Francesca frowned. "Are you all right? You look really pale again. Maybe you should take that nap after all."

"Um, maybe I should." Grasping at that opportunity, Dayna nodded. "It's going to be a big day tomorrow."

"You can say that again." Seeming pleased, Francesca stood. She gave Dayna a fond look. "Hey, I'm sorry to keep you in the dark for so long. Sumner and Lily insisted you would freak out if you heard about the plan beforehand, so I was just going to make you form a vixen pact with us by force. But now that you're in on everything . . . It will be so much better!"

Cheerfully, Francesca hugged her. Stiffly, Dayna pantomimed a return hug. She doubted it felt very convincing, but Francesca didn't appear to notice. Her self-absorption seemed to make her oblivious to everyone else's feelings . . . including Dayna's.

"So, I'll see you tomorrow at graduation. 'Night!"

With a triumphant sparkle of magic, Francesca left.

Dayna just stood there, afraid and alone. There were only a few hours remaining until the graduation ceremony. Somehow, she had to stop Francesca and the Followers. But with T.J. and Deuce locked away, Leo Garmin and the IAB not to be trusted, and her own magic seriously unreliable, what could she possibly do?

Chapter Twenty-Seven

Groggily, T.J. felt himself being gripped by unknown hands. He felt himself being lifted in strong arms, then carried . . .

Jolted awake, he swung his fist. It connected.

Whoever was holding him grunted, then dropped him. T.J. fell, hitting something hard beneath him. The floor.

"Ouch! What the hell, T.J.? I'm trying to help you."

Deuce. Through bleary eyes, T.J. looked up. His partner stood over him, an injured expression on his face, squinting through a shaft of sunlight. Somehow, T.J. had gotten moved into the center of the IAB holding room. Somehow, he had—

"Sunlight." He croaked the words, belatedly feeling its healing warmth on his skin. "That's sunlight."

"No shit, Sherlock. It's coming through that window over there. I was trying to move you closer to it when you decked me." Grumpily, Deuce gestured at the floor. "I've been rotating you like a roast on a rotisserie ever since dawn, trying to get you into the optimal spot for your Patayan mojo to kick in."

T.J. sat up. Easily. His chest felt better, his arms didn't hurt . . . even his mind felt clearer. "How long has it been?"

"Long enough that you almost look like yourself again.

That's too bad for you, dude, but I'm kind of happy about it." Purposefully, Deuce hunkered down. "I've got to take a piss. And I'll be damned if I'll use that bucket our forager guards left in here. So how about busting us out of this place?"

"You want to escape so you can piss in peace?"

With a serious expression, Deuce nodded.

T.J. cocked his head. He considered his legs, his hands, his heart . . . *No, not his heart.* That still hurt too much. Determinedly veering away from that region, he calculated his magical strength. Experimentally, he focused on the bucket.

It burst into flames, then melted. The floor sizzled.

Deuce smacked his fist in his hand. "Is that a yes?"

"I might be wrecked, but I'm not pissing in a bucket either." T.J. stood, then nodded. "That's definitely a yes."

T.J. called the flood first.

Using his Patayan earth magic, he focused on all the water in the IAB building. He moved it toward him, pulling it with ancient magic, making it gush from the faucets and spurt from the taps in the sprinkler system. It flowed from the toilet tanks and raced up the stairs, inexorably drawn by his command.

He knew the moment it reached the door. A roaring torrent could be heard; the water combined and surged forward. The forager guards outside yelped in surprise. Their footsteps sloshed and splashed as they shouted and tried to maneuver.

That's when T.J. unleashed the wind.

Again using his earth magic—much to Deuce's delight—he called up a harsh airstream. It mixed with the inundation of water, then lifted it with blinding energy. Driven hard, the water pelted against the door. Some of it gushed underneath.

"Seriously? Water?" Deuce gave T.J. a wry look. "I've been

dying to shake the snake for the past hour and *that's* what you come up with? Water? You're trying my patience here."

"Hang on. This is where the legacy magic comes in."

Drawing on the other side of his compound nature, T.J. focused on the holding room's door. The door wasn't pixilated—so it hadn't been magically formed—but that didn't mean it wasn't vulnerable to his magic . . . especially now, with the forager guards busy battling the unexpected wind and water.

Drawing in a deep breath, T.J. aimed a burst of legacy magic at the door. It peeled away in sheets, exposing its hollow core and all the layers of laminate and veneer it was made of. With hardly any effort, a gaping hole emerged in the doorway.

"See? Shoddy human workmanship comes in handy." T.J. gave his friend a grin. "No offense, but that door couldn't hold back a gentle breeze."

As though demonstrating that fact, the wind and water rushed in, bombarding the floor and fixtures—and T.J. and Deuce. Forager guards shouted. One of them pointed, his arm dripping with water. Barely visible in the watery torrent, he tried to send a burst of restrictive magic at T.J.

Easily, T.J. countered it.

Deuce planted his feet in readiness to fight. "If you could have done that all along, why the hell didn't you?"

T.J. didn't answer. Feeling revitalized, he kicked one of the guards. The forager landed with a splash. T.J. shook the water from his hair, then motioned for Deuce to move forward.

Drenched, they ran through the opening in the door. T.J. cleared the way with magic; Deuce swung his burly arms, landing more than a few good punches. Apparently, Garmin hadn't thought their escape was likely—he'd assigned them only four guards.

Standing over those four guards' inert bodies a few minutes later, T.J. magiked some bonds to restrain them. "These won't hold for long, but it should be enough to give us a head start."

Deuce nodded, his whole body as soaked as T.J.'s was. Reminded of the ongoing water and wind, T.J. stopped the flood. At his direction, the wind died. The water receded, drawn back to its usual holding places. The drip-drip-drip of multiple streamlets sounded loud in the sudden stillness.

"Nicely done," Leo Garmin said. "I should have expected as much. A minute later, and I would have missed all the fun."

T.J. turned. His former supervisor stood at the end of the hall, his suit unaffected by the wind and water. Garmin strode toward him, his feet magically pushing aside the puddles.

"You can't hold me," T.J. told him. "You got lucky last night. I won't let the same thing happen again today."

"Then we're at an impasse. Because I can't allow you to leave." Garmin compressed his lips, cast a glance at Deuce, then appeared to come to a decision. "I need your help, T.J."

At that, T.J. gave a bitter laugh. "You've got a funny way of showing it. You're beyond my help, you corrupt bastard."

"Bastard? Yes." Garmin sighed. "Corrupt? I don't think so. Everything I've done, I've done for a good reason. If you—"

"Save the homily. I'm leaving. Come on, Deuce."

Frowning, his partner stepped to his side. He nodded.

They made it halfway to the stairs before Garmin spoke.

"I was wrong to suspend you, T.J. I made a mistake," the head agent called out. "But you have to listen to me. You owe me that much, at least." He paused. "I saved you once, didn't I?"

Damn it. That was true. Fisting his hands, T.J. stopped. Reluctantly, he turned. "You have three minutes. Start talking."

"Oh Christ, T.J.!" Deuce shifted. "Let's just go."

Garmin ignored his turned human agent. "Have you ever done something stupid for the sake of a witch?" he asked T.J.

T.J. narrowed his eyes. "Two minutes, fifty-five seconds."

"Fine. I can see you're going to need the short version. I'm in over my head, T.J. Things have gotten out of hand. I thought

I could handle Francesca myself, but now—" Garmin broke off, exhaling. "She's obsessed with The Old Ways. She'll stop at nothing to grow the witchfolk population in Covenhaven. It's my fault. I'm the one who gave her the *Book of The Old Ways* in the first place. I'm the one who mentored her. But now—"

"You're involved with Francesca Woodberry," T.J. said.

It wasn't a question—it was a confirmation of something he'd suspected for a while now. Leo Garmin had been in charge of monitoring Covenhaven's vixen witches for years. No warlock could have been expected to watch over the most alluring and powerful of all witches and emerge unaffected by the experience.

"Who cares about who he's dating?" Obviously stunned, Deuce gawked at Garmin. "*You're* a Follower? *You?*"

With a shuttered expression, Garmin nodded. Tightly, he said, "I usually keep my beliefs separate from my work, but—"

"Wait. Isn't that kind of like the Pope being a Satanist?"

"That clumsy analogy only shows your ignorance," Garmin disagreed. "Under my direction, the InterAllied Bureau is coming to recognize the truth: that witchfolk *should* dominate the world. It's only right. We should live openly. And what better way to do that than to make *everyone* a witch or warlock? I agree with the *myrmidon* conversion plan in theory, of course, but—"

"One minute left." Losing patience, T.J. frowned. Among their other unpleasant beliefs, the Followers didn't embrace compounds like him. He was hardly in the mood to listen to a *myrmidon* diatribe. "You just admitted you've been using bureau resources to support the Followers' agenda. You've been directly undermining the IAB's mission in the magical world. That's a subversive act, Leo. Tell me why I shouldn't lay you out right now, then drag you to the coven elders for judgment."

At his mention of the coven elders, Garmin quailed. He held out his hands. "Because I'm coming to you for *help*, T.J.

I was willing to go along with Francesca at first, but not this far. That witch has to be stopped. Her conversion elixir is deadly."

"Come on. That's a minor drawback, right?" Deuce glowered. "Lily Abbot doesn't have a problem with it. Why should you?"

"You should have brought in Francesca yourself," T.J. said. "You're head of the IAB. You have the authority to stop her."

"I can't." Garmin shook his bald head. "The Followers have *myrmidon* inside the bureau—*myrmidon* who are increasingly loyal to Francesca's plans. I don't know whom to trust. That's why I need you! I only suspended you as a favor to Francesca—"

T.J. scowled, remembering the betrayal he'd suffered.

"—to keep you out of her way. But I regretted it almost instantly, I swear. I've been trying to track you ever since." Urgently, Garmin stepped closer. "I've done too much for that witch. I rounded up all the cusping witches for her—"

"*That's* part of this scheme, too?" Deuce asked.

"—I instituted mandatory magic training for her, I set the graduation and the Hallow-e'en Festival at Janus for her . . . It goes on and on." Looking beleaguered, Garmin stared at his forager guards, still unconscious on the floor. "I loved her enough not to turn her in. I'd hoped she'd get bored and move on. I'd hoped I could change her mind. But I couldn't."

"That's a sad story." T.J. crossed his arms. "Time's up."

He gestured for Deuce to follow him, then headed for the bureau's emergency stairs. Behind him, Garmin's voice rang out.

"It was *my* familiar that found you last night," he confessed. "I used your bonded witch. Dayna didn't know."

T.J. longed to believe it. Grudgingly, he stopped.

Deuce stopped, too. His gaze shifted to T.J. He nodded.

As though sensing that T.J.'s openness might not last, Garmin spoke quickly. "If you try to surprise Francesca, you'll lose. She has a vixen pact behind her. Their power will astonish even you. That's why I kept you locked up

overnight—so I could make sure you brought in Francesca
the right way."

"Nice try," T.J. gritted out. "But I'll take my chances."

"Do you know what a quad vixen pact is capable of?"

"A quad—" T.J. stopped, abruptly remembering. Dayna
was the fourth member of Francesca's vixen pact. Would his
bonded witch really join in Francesca's scheme? "There won't
be a quad vixen pact. They'll form a vixen trio, at worst.
Sumner will join me."

He'd already made sure Francesca would see nothing amiss
if Sumner left her side for a while. The persuasion spell he'd
used when he'd met Francesca—as Professor Reynolds—
would ensure that.

"I hope you're right," Garmin said. "Otherwise, you're
walking into a trap. If you would only listen to me, you
could—"

"I've already listened to you." Darkly, T.J. pulled a current
of wind. It swirled around him, indicative of his restless
mood. "I shouldn't have. For all I know, this is a trap, too. It
feels like one." He cast an impatient glance at Deuce, then at
his former supervisor. "If your warning is right, I have a fight
ahead of me. I'm done talking. Let's go, Deuce."

But his partner didn't move. Uneasily, he frowned at T.J.
"He might have a point. Sumner doesn't seem very reliable to
me. And Dayna was pretty hurt when she left last night. She
might—"

"Shut it." T.J. slanted him a warning look. "This is not the
time for your antiwitch phobia to kick in."

"Or maybe it is," Garmin rushed to say. "Agent Bailey is
right to be suspicious of vixen witches. They're dangerous. I
know that more than anyone. That's why the only way to succeed is for you to trust me." Eyes shining, Garmin came
closer. "At the right moment, I'll sneak you out of here
myself, under the guise of questioning you. No one will be
the wiser. We'll go together to the graduation ceremony. You

can stop Francesca there, at Janus. We'll catch the hidden
Followers among the IAB flat footed; they'll have no time to
react—and neither will Francesca. Everyone will believe
you're still in custody." Garmin looked around at the wreckage T.J. had wrought. "We'll have to set this place right
again, throw a few forgetfulness spells on my foragers . . .
But it's definitely manageable."

"You know . . ." T.J. considered it. "That makes sense."

"Yes." Garmin's face brightened. "Then you're in?"

"No." T.J.'s frown deepened. "You deliberately misled me.
And thanks to Deuce"—he gave his partner a nod to acknowledge his attempts to get T.J. the healing sunlight he
needed—"I feel pretty good. My own magic will take me out
of here—and it will be enough to defeat the Followers, too.
Especially now that you've given me some inside information. I'm still leaving."

"Don't do it, T.J. I swear, you can trust me now."

T.J. gave Garmin a hard look. "I wish that were true."

But after all that had happened . . . it wasn't.

At least T.J. wouldn't have to turn in Garmin to the coven
elders. Maybe later he would, but not now. Judging by the re-
morse flowing from his former supervisor to him, Garmin no
longer had the heart to help the Followers succeed with
Francesca's destructive forced conversion plans.

Deuce cleared his throat. "Uh, you might want to consider
this a little more closely, dude. You had a chance to trust
Dayna last night, and you didn't. I'm pretty sure you regretted it afterward. Maybe this is your chance to have a do-over."

Unhappily remembering that, T.J. turned to Deuce. His
partner had a point. His magus had already told him that this
was one mission he could not complete alone. For the first
time ever, she'd warned, he would have to trust someone else.

But she'd told T.J. he would have to trust the *juweel*. The
wisewoman had warned him that he'd have to step aside and
let the chosen vixen witch do her work to save humankind . . .

and witchkind. Besides, giving Garmin a second chance was not in the same league as giving Dayna a second chance.

When he saw his bonded witch again . . .

"I don't want a do-over." Decisively, T.J. straightened. "I trust *myself*, first and last. That's it."

He flexed his Patayan magic, unleashed a minor magical earthquake, then bolted for the exit. Deuce ran, too. Behind them, Garmin yelled. The wall crumbled. Garmin went abruptly silent, even as an aftershock rumbled through the building.

T.J. couldn't stop. He had to find Francesca. Now.

Unhappily clenching the steering wheel of Deuce's Mustang, Dayna jolted over one of the rough reservation roads outside Covenhaven. She knew how to drive; she simply didn't like to do it. Apparently, navigating a two-thousand-pound steel cage with wheels hadn't gotten any less nerve-racking in the years since she'd tried it. But that didn't matter now. She had to get to T.J.'s Patayan magus and alert the wise-woman to the Followers' scheme—and to T.J.'s and Deuce's incarceration by the IAB.

It was clear now that Francesca would *not* be using her influence to persuade Leo Garmin to let T.J. and Deuce go. And Dayna didn't see how *she* could get them released herself. The best she could do was enlist the help of some Patayan guardians. Maybe they would know how to free T.J. and Deuce.

Sneaking out of Janus this morning had been no problem. Francesca's trust in Dayna had seemed complete; she hadn't even spelled the penthouse suite to keep Dayna inside it. So after a sleepless night of pacing and planning and researching via EnchantNet—and making her best attempt at sabotaging the potion ingredients—Dayna had struck on her plan to visit T.J.'s magus.

The earth ship that the magus called home was difficult to find. It was even more difficult to approach. Fortunately, T.J. had warned her about that. Following his instructions, Dayna navigated past the sentinel saguaros. She moved slowly, keeping her gaze fixed on the mound of red-tinged earth in front of her.

The mound almost seemed to move, as though it were breathing. Surely that was her overwrought imagination at work.

"I'd hoped T.J. would be the one to bring you here."

At the sound of that serene voice, Dayna whirled around. An elderly wisewoman wearing witchmade garments stood a few feet away from her, holding a just-picked gourd in her hand. At her feet, a huge gray wolfhound eyed Dayna through mistrustful eyes.

"I've been wanting to meet that boy's bonded witch. But if you're here on your own, this is not a social call." The magus aimed her chin toward the earth ship. Like magic, Dayna glimpsed the hidden entrance. "Come inside and tell me about it."

Harried and a little hoarse, Dayna concluded her account of the Followers' plan to awaken humans by force—to dose them with the conversion elixir en masse and create a world ruled by witchfolk. She made sure to leave out nothing. Urgently, she told the magus about Deuce's dosing at Lily's hands, about T.J. and Deuce being captured by the IAB, about her own potential role in Francesca's scheme. Finally, still grasping the cup of tea the magus had thoughtfully given her, Dayna exhaled.

"So that's it. And I need help!" she said. "I'm on my own, and I'm *not* equipped for this. Until recently, I lived among humans. I didn't even practice magic. I might be a vixen, but—"

"There's something you haven't told me." Keeping her

voice soft, the magus lifted her gaze to Dayna's face. "About T.J."

"T.J.?" Confused, Dayna frowned. "I think I told you everything. He doesn't know I'm here, of course. I haven't tried going to the IAB yet. Leo Garmin is not to be trusted. He—"

"Have you noticed that your armband has fallen off?"

Stricken, Dayna stared at her arm. It was true. The golden armband that T.J. had given her—the armband that matched his birthright mark tattoo and made them a bonded pair—was gone.

It won't come off, Deuce had told her gravely, weeks ago. *Not unless something really drastic happens.* She guessed a complete breakdown in trust was a sufficiently drastic event.

Bereft, Dayna turned to the magus. "What does this mean for T.J.?" she asked. "If my armband is gone, is T.J.'s birthright mark tattoo gone, too?" With an erratic movement, she set down her teacup. "Someone once told me that, for a Patayan, removing a birthright mark tattoo is like removing a piece of your soul."

Lost in concern, she gazed at the earth ship's modern interior. If she'd somehow cost T.J. his *soul*, she would never—

"That's interesting." The magus gave Dayna a warmhearted smile. "Your first thought was for T.J.'s well-being instead of your own. Maybe the bond between you has strength yet."

"No." Forcibly snapping herself out of her worries, Dayna shook her head. "It doesn't. I'd be an idiot to hope for that."

"*I* hope for that. Do you think *I'm* an idiot?"

Not for the first time, Dayna cursed her stupid habit of blurting out whatever she thought. The magus was too caring to be treated that way. "No. I'm so sorry. It's just that—"

"He hurt you. I can see that. I can feel it."

Dayna nodded. Her throat tightened. "T.J. didn't believe in me. Just when I needed it most! He only looked at me. And even though I begged—*I begged!*—T.J. wouldn't tell me what

I needed to hear." She elaborated, describing the scene between them at Deuce's apartment before and after the IAB had taken T.J. into custody. "It was humiliating. It was . . . heartbreaking. I could tell he knew I needed his faith in me, but he stayed silent."

"More than likely, he could not speak."

"Or wouldn't speak," Dayna scoffed. "You know T.J." But she'd already soaked up too much of the magus's empathy. She sat up straighter. "That's a problem for another day. The plan is set for the Followers to do their conversion *today*, and I—"

"Did T.J. believe you had betrayed him?"

"Yes." Startled by the magus's insight, Dayna stared. Then, with difficulty, she regrouped. "But the Followers are going—"

"We'll get to the *myrmidon*. But first . . . I can see that you don't understand what's happened." The magus gazed kindly at Dayna, one hand petting her loyal wolfhound. "For a Patayan, any betrayal causes physical pain—devastating physical pain. In the most extreme cases, it's debilitating. We are guardians. We must trust those we protect. But if that trust is shattered . . ."

Dayna remembered the effort it had required for T.J. to call out to her when she'd been leaving Deuce's apartment. He *had* seemed in pain then. At the time, she'd attributed T.J.'s harsh tone to his lack of faith in her. But if he'd actually felt betrayed, then he truly might not have been able to speak.

"You're wrong." Dayna shook her head, afraid to hope that she'd misunderstood him. "T.J. never really trusted me."

"He became bonded with you. That's the ultimate trust."

Oh God. The magus might be right. Filled with remembrances, Dayna thought about when she'd coaxed T.J. into letting her give him that intimate, forbidden kiss. *Go ahead. I trust you.*

She'd never meant to betray his trust. And she hadn't—at least not when she'd allowed him to be taken into IAB custody, Dayna realized. That had been an accident. But later, when she'd begged T.J. for an affirmation he'd been physically incapable of giving—when she'd refused to accept his belief in her without his spoken promise to back it up—then she'd betrayed him.

And she could never take it back.

"You must go to him," the magus said. "There's still time."

Jolted by the wisewoman's urgings, Dayna looked up. "T.J. is at the IAB headquarters. I'll never reach him. My magic is weak. It's erratic! I've never been able to depend on it."

"It's not your magic you must depend on. It's yourself."

Dayna gave her a sad smile. "You sound just like T.J."

"Good." The magus grinned back at her, her face bright with pleasure and pride. "Then some of my teachings have sunk in."

But Dayna still wasn't ready. "Isn't there someone who can help me? Another Patayan? A guardian who's equipped to cope with dangerous situations? Someone with extra-strong magic?"

"Magic is not what's needed here."

Frustrated and afraid, Dayna bit back a hasty retort. She should have known a wisewoman would have cryptic advice to offer. "I can't deal with the Followers alone. I need help."

The magus shook her head. "T.J. is the only Patayan with the strength and skill to handle such a threat. I know that he's found the *juweel*. Maybe if you can reach her—"

"He didn't tell me who the *juweel* is."

"I'm sorry. He didn't confide her name to me either." The magus sighed. "I trusted him to enlist her help. But now that T.J. is in the custody of the IAB, and likely injured, too . . ."

The magus trailed off, but her silence spoke volumes. Dayna had gotten T.J. arrested—and she'd been the one to injure him, too. Now it was up to her to make things right. Somehow . . .

Chapter Twenty-Eight

By the time Dayna arrived at the IAB headquarters, all of Covenhaven's touristy downtown was in chaos. Peering through the Mustang's windshield, she maneuvered the vehicle as close as she dared to. Yellow police tape cordoned off the block where the bureau's headquarters was located. Human officers stood beside their crookedly parked police cruisers and directed traffic past the area. They motioned with curt gestures for her to detour.

Beyond them, several of the downtown buildings sagged at weird angles. Tendrils of smoke lifted into the air. Debris littered the street. Firefighters still labored to extinguish a minor blaze near the café that sold ostrich burgers and pie.

Awkwardly, Dayna parked the Mustang. She got out and ran to the nearest officer, her heart pounding. "What happened here?"

"You'll have to move along, ma'am. It's not safe to stay."

"Not safe? Why not?" To Dayna's witchy gaze, the IAB headquarters sagged atop the nearby buildings, still magically hidden behind their decorative false fronts. "Was anyone hurt?" She grabbed the officer's arm. *"What happened?"*

The officer's gaze dropped to Dayna's hand. "You'll want

to move your hand, ma'am," the woman said. "And leave the area."

"I can't leave the area! I know someone who works in that building." Dayna pointed to the shop closest to the IAB.

The officer's demeanor softened. "Family and friends are gathering over there." She nodded to a clump of onlookers—humans and witchfolk alike. "We'll keep you updated when we have news."

"Thank you." Anxiously, Dayna crossed the street. She reached the nearest bystander. "What happened here?"

"Earthquake," a warlock said. "Pretty bad one. Luckily, it happened just after dawn. Most of the shops weren't open yet."

The IAB must have been open, though, Dayna knew. *T.J.* . . .

"It's pretty surreal," a witch told her. "An earthquake in Arizona. Sometimes we feel the big ones from California, though."

Only half listening, Dayna focused on the IAB building. If she tried, she hoped, she could detect the presence of magical beings there, the same way she'd done at Janus last night.

But no auras met her gaze. No witchy clairvoyance arose to help her. The IAB headquarters appeared deserted. Without her golden armband to augment her bond with T.J., she couldn't be sure he wasn't nearby. But knowing him . . . She hoped he and Deuce had already gone, escaped from the IAB under their own power.

Now more than ever, it looked as though stopping the Followers was up to her—alone. Worried and fearful, Dayna raced back to Deuce's Mustang. It was time for her last-ditch plan.

Grim-faced and determined, T.J. let the airstream he'd been riding die out. He dropped to the frost-tinged autumn soil and released Deuce. His partner tripped, then righted himself.

"Don't *ever* do that again." Deuce glared at him. To his left, the red-rock canyon gouged the earth. To his right, less than a mile from their location, the Janus Resort sprawled in all its artificial glory. "I would have preferred a damn broom to that!" Deuce yelled. "What the hell were you thinking?"

"That your car was gone and we needed to get here quickly."

"Yeah. Thanks for the sympathy on my missing car, by the way." Dolefully, Deuce shook his head. "I built that Mustang with my bare hands. I can't believe it's gone."

"We'll mourn your loss later. Let's go."

With Deuce swearing beside him, T.J. set off toward Janus. He hadn't dared to bring them any closer—not when he'd used his warlock ability to ride the air currents to take them there. If someone had seen them arriving warlock-style, they'd have sounded an alarm—an alarm that would have spoiled everything. It had been risky enough to transport Deuce that way; T.J. would not have done it if he'd had a better option available.

From the top of the next rise, he scanned the resort just below them. The elegantly manicured grounds had been given over to the Hallow-e'en Festival activities. Enormous tents perched atop the chemically nurtured grass, surrounded by vendors' booths and even a few carnival-style rides. Pumpkins and Indian corn dotted the resort's walkways in faux-rustic seasonal displays; entertainers from clowns to jugglers wandered past.

Tourists thronged the place, drawn by the festival ambience. Several TV news satellite vans parked along one edge of the overflowing parking lot. T.J. squinted, spotting their occupants milling among the visitors with cameras in hand.

Several of the humans were in costume. Children laughed and ran between the Hallow-e'en tents with their faces painted, caramel apples on sticks wobbling in their hands. A band played on an improvised bandstand, its music wafting toward T.J.

It would not be easy to find Francesca among these

crowds—or to catch her by surprise. Garmin had been right about that. It was possible that the vixen witch already knew about T.J.'s and Deuce's escape from the IAB. She might be arming herself against them even now, summoning her fellow vixens to help her.

"This is risky," he warned Deuce. "It might not go well."

"I know. I'm in." His partner inhaled, flexing his muscles in readiness. His gaze landed on T.J., then shifted to his arm. "I'm always in. Besides, I think we just got a lucky break."

Frowning, T.J. stared at him. "What do you mean?"

"I mean your birthright mark tattoo is gone." Deuce pointed at his biceps. "It's disappeared. See? Weird, right?"

T.J. looked. At the sight of his bare biceps, his heart twisted. He thought of his bonded witch and wondered where she was. Would Dayna really join Francesca's pact? Or could T.J. somehow convince her to join with him . . . even without their bond?

"That's good news, right?" Deuce asked. "You didn't want to be bonded in the first place. Now I guess you're not. Maybe this means your magic will get stronger and more predictable again."

"Maybe." Feeling bereft, T.J. stared at his arm. His bond with Dayna was gone. *She* was gone. Without her, he hardly cared what happened to him. "This is all the better for our mission. Come on. We have to find Sumner first. If my magus is right—"

"And she's never wrong," Deuce chimed in.

"—all we have to do is alert the *juweel*, then stand back and let her do her stuff. She'll end the conflict herself."

Decisively, T.J. started down the hill. After a few steps, he realized Deuce was not behind him. Confused, he glanced back.

Deuce gawked at him. "You're supposed to get Sumner to save the day? That's your mission? To let the *juweel* work *alone*?"

With a hard look, T.J. nodded. "Yes."

"But you've never let anyone else take the lead," Deuce argued. "You won't even let *me* help you."

"Yeah." Tightly, T.J. motioned him downward. "So?"

"So I didn't know that until now." Swearing, Deuce scrambled after him. "Because *you* didn't tell me." He gazed at the resort as they rapidly approached it. "We are *so* screwed."

With her tires squealing, Dayna pulled into the entryway at Janus. Her hands hurt from gripping the steering wheel; her heart ached from worrying about what had happened to T.J. and Deuce—and from wondering how in the world she was going to meet the challenge ahead. The only thing she knew for certain was that she could not do it alone. If there was one lesson she'd learned from spending all those years unlinked, it was that witches needed one another. *Everyone* needed one another. Remaining alone in the world was just asking for trouble.

Determinedly, she left Deuce's Mustang with one of the valets. She hurried inside the resort, marveling at the crowds that had gathered. Everywhere she looked, human tourists mingled with warlocks and witches, blind to their companions' true magical natures . . . and oblivious to the threat looming before them. She saw several of her cusping-witch classmates, too, all of them streaming toward the ballroom in formal attire.

Whoops. She'd almost forgotten—ostensibly, the reason everyone was here today was for graduation, then the Samhain Festival. With her heart pounding, Dayna ducked into an alcove.

The murmur of conversations swirled around her, combining with Janus's New Age background music to create a low hum of activity. Within moments, Dayna had magiked herself into a silver cocktail dress and heels. Simultaneously proud of the improved magic that allowed her to accomplish the task and irked that she had to hobble herself with fancy clothes, she stuffed her human-made jeans, T-shirt, and sneakers into her backpack.

When she emerged in the lobby, everything glittered and shone. The place had been impressively prepped and polished by Janus's conscientious witchfolk staff. A festive vibe filled the air as witchfolk continued to move toward the ballroom. The room had been enchanted, Dayna knew, to conceal the witchy activities that would be going on inside it today. No human would be the wiser about what she and her fellow witches would be doing—at least not until the newly empowered cusping witches poured out to forcibly convert the dozers outside at the festival.

Given Francesca's charisma and influence, Dayna doubted any of her classmates—or any of the hundreds of other cusping witches who'd gathered in Covenhaven—would be able to resist the Followers' scheme. They'd be emboldened by Francesca's special invincibility-endowing cocktail, fired up by her enthusiasm, willing to do whatever was asked of them. That was the power—and the downside—of being linked. Once one witch went astray, it was nearly impossible to prevent others from joining her.

For what felt like the millionth time, Dayna wished T.J. were there. She missed him. She still loved him. But as she stepped inside the ballroom for the pregraduation reception, she resolutely set thoughts of her bonded tracer aside. She had a plan to carry out, and she had little time to do it in.

Deliberately, Dayna sought out Camille. She found her best friend chatting with several students from cusping-witch class, all of them gathered in a remote corner of the ballroom. Even as Dayna approached, more witches joined their group, most of them offering Camille self-conscious smiles. These witches were not popular or gifted, like Francesca, Sumner, and Lily. These witches possessed lackluster spells at best. These witches were ambivalent about practicing magic; they were not A students or teachers' pets. But they *were* free spirits, like Dayna.

And that was why she needed them now.

She reached Camille and hugged her, doing her best to appear carefree. "Hi! You look beautiful. Thanks for your help."

Her friend smiled. "Well, I did get almost everyone here, just like you asked me on the phone. But I still don't know why you wanted me to. Are you hoping for a last-minute study session? They still haven't told us what the test will be, but—"

"No, it's nothing like that." The licensing test was the least of her worries now. But seeing Camille, Dayna was struck by a sudden wave of longing. She wished she were here for a real graduation celebration . . . not to thwart the Followers' plans to take over the world. With effort, she focused. "I can't tell you *exactly* what I need." If she did, Dayna knew, a gifted witch like Francesca would instantly detect her deception. Nervously, she bit her lip. "But I promise it's for a worthwhile cause."

"Okay." Camille shrugged. "That's good enough for me."

"Seriously." Dayna frowned. "I mean it. This is important."

"I get it." A few witches who'd been standing near Camille overheard her. They nodded, too. "Just tell us what you need."

"But . . . I'm not kidding. I'm going to have to ask you all to trust me." Dayna gestured to include the surrounding witches. "I can't tell you why until later. But I'm hoping that, on my signal, you'll do whatever *I* do. No questions asked."

They all gazed silently back at her. A few witches on the fringes of the group nodded; others glanced over their shoulders as though afraid of being overheard plotting together. Then one witch—one very *un*exceptional witch whom Dayna recognized from class—stepped forward. She offered her handshake.

"Whatever you want, Dayna," she said. "I'll do it."

"Me, too," another witch told her. "I trust you. We'll help spread the word to the other cusping witches. *Discreetly.*"

"But . . ." Dayna gawked as several more witches came forward, all of them pledging their help. "You barely know me! You—"

"We know you. You're the witch who defied Francesca."

"Yeah. You're the witch who ran away . . . and came back," an awkward-looking witch said. "That was really brave of you."

"You were *terrible* at magic," another witch said. "But you kept trying. You worked really hard. That inspired me."

"Me, too!" said a chorus of cusping witches. "Totally."

Dumbfounded, Dayna accepted their vows of cooperation.

"You know what?" she said. "With all of us together, I think we actually have a shot at succeeding. Just watch for my signal"—improvising, she demonstrated one—"and be ready. Okay?"

All the witches nodded. Stepping to the center of the group, Camille hugged her. "See? No matter what you think, you *do* belong here with us. I'm so proud of you, Dayna."

Overcome with emotion, Dayna blinked back tears. "Thanks. I don't know what magic you pulled to make everyone agree, but—"

"It wasn't me," her best friend argued. "It was you. But you can tell me I'm right about your inspirational mojo later. Right now, I think there's someone here who wants to see you."

With a gentle grasp on Dayna's shoulders, Camille turned her around. Coming toward her through the crowd, Dayna glimpsed Sam and Margo Sterling, dressed in their nicest clothes. Their faces looked anxious—until they spotted Dayna. Then they smiled.

Drawing in a deep breath, Dayna went to meet her parents.

* * *

When T.J. saw the group of witches clustered in the corner of the ballroom, he expected to find Francesca or Lily or Sumner holding court among them. All the witches in the group gazed toward its center with shining faces, their expressions filled with admiration and agreement. He'd only ever glimpsed similar emotions on the faces of the cusping witches in class when they'd been congratulating Francesca or her vixens.

Well, that meant he was in luck. Motioning for Deuce to follow him, T.J. headed in that direction. Partway there, the crowd shifted. A few witches nodded, then stepped away. Their departures revealed the witch at the crowd's center: *Dayna*.

Struck by her beauty and bravery and determination, T.J. stopped. While time seemed to slow around him, he stared.

He'd never seen his bonded witch appear more at ease than she did just then. He'd never seen her appear more *her*. As though lit from within, Dayna smiled and hugged Camille. She nodded at the witches surrounding her. Then, appearing incongruously tough for a witch dressed all in shimmery silver, Dayna glanced across the room. She went to meet someone.

In that moment, T.J. knew she'd come here to fight. This time, Dayna would not run away. He'd known and loved his bonded witch long enough to recognize the signs of impending rebellion in her. Even without his support, Dayna meant to join the battle against the Followers. Even without his help, Dayna had finally come into her own as a cusping witch.

Bowled over by her courage and certainty, T.J. watched as Dayna greeted an older couple. Her parents, he guessed with a peculiar pang; he hadn't met them, but the family resemblance was obvious. Wounded to know that he might never meet them—might never be allowed in Dayna's life again—he glanced down.

His birthright mark was still gone. But even without that

proof of his bond with Dayna, T.J. knew he would give anything for her. For Dayna, he would fight to his last breath.

The realization had scarcely left him before T.J. suddenly
felt called to defend it. A weird prickling sensation gripped
him. For an instant, he felt paralyzed, unable to speak.

"Mmm. You look nice all cleaned up." Making a sensuous
sound of appreciation, Sumner Jacobs stopped beside him.
She trailed her hand over the suit he'd magiked. "I approve."

"Sumner." Drawing in a deep breath, T.J. turned to face her.
The seductive blond witch gazed hungrily at him, clad in a
clingy red dress and little else. "I've been looking for you."

"Apparently you've been looking in all the wrong places."
Eyes narrowed, Sumner gazed in Dayna's direction. A spark
of pure dislike flashed across her face. As quickly as it arose,
it disappeared. "Besides, if you can't find me in this dress,
you're blind." She gave Deuce a sexy smile. "Who's your
friend?"

"Someone who doesn't dabble in witches," Deuce said.

"Funny." Dismissing his turned human partner, Sumner
turned back to T.J. "I guess you're here to close on our deal?"

T.J. gave a curt nod. "It's time. Can I trust you?"

Sumner smiled again. "Given what you told me, I don't see
where you have much choice about that. You have to trust me.
As *juweel*, I hold all the cards here. Wouldn't you say so?"

Deuce shot her a venomous look. "Fuck this. Be a lone
wolf one more time, T.J.," he urged. "Maybe your magus was
wrong."

Aggrieved, T.J. shook his head. His magus wasn't wrong.

"You're right," he told Sumner. "Do you know what to do?"

In an undeniable rush, uncertainty passed from the vixen
witch to him. Surprised by it, T.J. frowned. Then it vanished.

"Of course I do." Sumner smiled again. She gave a celebratory shimmy, making her slinky red dress move in all the
most attention-getting places. "Get your cultural archivists
ready, boys. Tonight, this witch is going down in witchstory."

* * *

"I'm so glad you're here." Weak with relief, Dayna beamed at her parents. "It wouldn't have been the same without you."

"Then you're not angry?" her mother asked. "I know we took you by surprise yesterday, but surely there's still hope that we can talk things out and smooth everything over."

"Of course, Mom. We'll get through this." Dayna hugged her. Since she'd crossed the ballroom to meet them, her mother and father had apologized at least a dozen times. "I didn't exactly react well. There's been a lot going on. But I'm sorry, too."

Her father exhaled. "You know how proud of you we are, right? This is a big deal!" He gestured at the ballroom. "Have you had your magic licensing test yet? Or is it coming later?"

"I'm not sure. Some of my classmates heard a rumor that the IAB is going to issue a group test." More than likely, Dayna thought darkly, that "test" would involve drinking Francesca's cocktail and awakening the unsuspecting humans outside. Even now, she saw that almost every witch and warlock in the room was quaffing the specially garnished drink. "I'm sure I'll be fine."

"Well, you certainly look nice. Is that a new dress?"

"We hardly knew you had legs. You're in jeans so often."

With a wry twist of her lips, Dayna looked down at herself, then made a joke of her own. When she glanced up again, her gaze fell on a spot across the room. *Francesca.* The übervixen witch of Covenhaven was circulating among the crowd, appearing just as charming and captivating as ever. Maybe even more so.

At the sight of her, Dayna sobered. In a heartbeat, the odds against her success seemed to skyrocket. Who was *she* to take on the most powerful and influential witch in town? She was just a witch who ran away when the going got tough. All she had was hopefulness, resolve, and a dollop of shaky magic on her side. She hadn't even been able to find T.J. and Deuce in time!

At the thought of her bonded partner, Dayna suddenly felt more miserable than ever. She wished T.J. were there. She wished he could see all she'd learned—not only to cast a spell or magik some new clothes, but also to lead other witches. To fight back against discouragement and fear. To believe in herself at last.

This time, the runaway witch was staying to fight. It was too bad, Dayna thought with a frown, she'd be fighting alone.

"Uh-oh." Her mother pointed to the stage at the other end of the ballroom. "It looks as though they're getting started."

While an IAB official cleared her throat at the microphone, Dayna gave her parents another hug. She watched with trepidation as Sam and Margo took their places in the audience. Things could get dangerous today. She hoped they'd be all right.

There was only one way to ensure that: Dayna had to confront Francesca. Determinedly, she headed toward her fellow vixen witch. If she couldn't convince Francesca to abandon her scheme, she would have to rely on her sabotage of the elixir ingredients. If that didn't work . . . It would be time for plan B.

Waiting in the wings in the ballroom's backstage area, T.J. glanced down. He'd disguised himself as Professor Reynolds again, and although he'd sworn to allow Sumner to complete her mission as *juweel*, he hadn't agreed to step aside completely. As Reynolds, T.J. knew, he could stay nearby as the graduation ceremony continued. He could watch the proceedings . . . and wait.

As the current speaker droned on, presenting the latest in a long series of cusping-witch graduating classes, T.J. paced. He peered through a gap in the stage curtains, looking for

Deuce. His partner prowled the perimeter of the ballroom, alert for any signs of trouble. Near Deuce's present position, the table full of graduation amulets stood, still piled with awards. There would be a long wait until the commencement was finished.

In recognition of that fact, a cadre of Janus staff members circulated discreetly among the attendees. They offered frothy refreshments from their trays, bowing in thanks as the audience members helpfully passed drinks from hand to hand down the rows. From outside the ballroom, the faint strains of human tourists and Covenhaven residents enjoying the Hallow-e'en Festival could be heard, reminding T.J. of the critical nature of his mission.

Irresistibly compelled, he sent his gaze in the other direction . . . toward Dayna. When he saw her, his heart expanded. He wanted to go to her. But until this was over . . .

He shifted his gaze a little farther, and saw that Dayna was seated between Francesca and Lily. His heart froze. As long as Dayna was near the other vixen witches, she was still in danger. But for now, all T.J. could do was wait—and hope for a chance to send his bonded witch a message.

His opportunity came when Reynolds's class was announced. Putting on his most professorial air, T.J. strode onstage.

Tense in her seat, Dayna watched as the graduation ceremony continued. So far, she'd been stuck beside Francesca, Lily, and Sumner the whole time. Her attempts to subtly convince the vixen witches to abandon their conversion scheme were failing. As Francesca shushed her for the third time, Dayna glanced away . . .

. . . only to see that even more witches and warlocks in the audience held one of Francesca's cocktails in their hands.

With dismay, Dayna saw that most of the cusping witches

grasped celebratory cocktails, too. Their graduation amulets were all but ignored as, smiling, they toasted one another's success.

The sight horrified her. Were *all* of them Followers?

Onstage, Professor Reynolds moved to the microphone. That meant it was almost her class's turn. Distractedly, Dayna transferred her gaze to the graduation ceremony . . . then stopped in surprise.

T.J. stood onstage. He was all right! He was . . . *perfect*.

With absolute witchy clarity, Dayna recognized her bonded tracer beneath his disguise. Then, feeling alarmed, she glanced at Francesca. The vixen witch didn't seem to recognize T.J.

Relieved—and trapped beside her unwanted new friends— Dayna waited as each cusping witch in her class was called onstage in turn. The licensing tests appeared to have been forgotten.

Instead, each witch received a license to practice magic from the IAB official who presided over the proceedings. Then they received a congratulatory handshake from their instructor. Finally, Dayna saw, they crossed the stage to receive an amulet.

One by one, the witches accepted their amulets. Then they trod offstage, flushed and proud, to be greeted by the Janus employee stationed at the edge of the stairs with Francesca's special cocktails. Appalled, Dayna watched as yet another witch giddily slurped her drink. It seemed that Francesca had hit upon a foolproof way to spread and amplify her magic among all the cusping witches in their collective . . . and eventually, with disastrous results, to take it to the unaware humans outside.

"Dayna Sterling." As Reynolds, T.J. called her name.

Her parents whooped in celebration. With a nervous smile, Dayna approached the stage. As she neared T.J., his true nature became even clearer to her. She saw his familiar dark eyes, his cleft chin, his strong Patayan stance, his dazzling warlock charm. She saw his courage, his determination . . . his love?

Gasping in surprise, Dayna stumbled as she moved to accept her handshake from him. T.J. reached out to steady her. "I can't give you much," he said in her ear, his voice stealthy and low. "But I can give you my trust—and I can give you this. I don't know what you have planned, but maybe this will help."

Urgently, T.J. spoke the phrasings of an ancient Patayan incantation. Dayna had never heard it before, but she recognized at least one of the words. Rapidly, she translated: *peace*.

With her heart in her throat, she nodded at him.

Her return to her seat was an anxious blur. Shaking her head, Dayna refused the Janus employee's offer of a cocktail. Deep in thought, she clutched her graduation amulet, the fact that she'd actually succeeded at magic leaving her numb.

How could she use the incantation T.J. had given her?

Distractedly, she watched as Francesca rose to accept her expected award as class *juweel*. With her usual poise, Francesca launched into an eloquent speech. She targeted the mood of the audience perfectly. All around Dayna, cocktail-carrying witches shouted their approval of her words. Some of them waved their graduation amulets, too. The fragile golden talismans shimmered under the ballroom's multiple chandeliers, catching the light.

Wincing at their brightness, Dayna blinked. When her vision cleared, she glimpsed Deuce, moving through the ballroom with clear antagonism and watchful eyes. Startled, she looked again.

At her glance, Deuce brightened. He nodded at the table of amulets. Its supply was almost depleted. He nodded at Francesca. Clearly, Deuce was trying to send her a message. But what?

Confused, Dayna frowned. She didn't know what he meant.

Even as Dayna struggled to figure out Deuce's silent communication, Francesca continued her speech. Increasingly, the witchfolk in the audience applauded. Phrasings from the *Book of The Old Ways* caught Dayna's ear, worrying her even further.

In only a matter of minutes, Francesca would complete her forced conversion plan—and it looked as though everyone in the ballroom would cheer her for it. At the realization, Dayna felt alone in the witching world all over again, still separated from whatever forces united other magical beings.

She'd hoped never to experience that kind of alienation again. But seeing the witchfolk crowd applaud and cheer reminded Dayna of every moment she'd felt left out—every moment she or her magic hadn't measured up. Stubbornly, she tried to distract herself by parsing T.J.'s incantation. That didn't work. She tried to reason out Deuce's pantomimed message. Nothing.

Despairing, Dayna glanced up. Lily and Sumner were onstage now, standing beside Francesca. The vixens smiled at the crowd's approval, accepting it as their due. And it was. It always had been. Francesca's lips moved. Dayna couldn't hear her.

"Go on, Dayna!" One row back, Camille nudged her. "That's you! Francesca just called your name."

Dimly, Dayna realized that Francesca was urging her to join the vixens onstage. This was it—the moment when they formed their quad vixen pact and set out to rule the world.

With a jerky motion, Dayna stood. T.J.'s face swam in her vision; Deuce still desperately gestured toward her, pointing at the amulets. But all Dayna could focus on was Francesca.

Francesca wanted *her*. Francesca was holding out her hand to *her*, waiting for Dayna to take her rightful place among the vixen witches. It was the most public declaration of belonging Dayna could ever have hoped for. Beyond any doubt, Francesca's actions proved that Dayna belonged in the magical world.

I should just accept this, Dayna thought, and took her first step toward becoming a trueborn witch.

Chapter Twenty-Nine

But the moment Dayna reached the stage, the spotlight blinded her. Dazzled, she stopped and blinked to clear her head. An instant later, T.J. was there. As Professor Reynolds, he took her elbow as though helping her join her fellow vixen witches.

Beyond him, Francesca smiled, encouraging Dayna to come closer. Even Sumner and Lily reached their hands out in welcome. But at T.J.'s touch, something in Dayna's righted itself.

"It's you," he said. "*You're* the *juweel*."

"No. I can't be the *juweel*!" Shaking her head, she glanced at him. Her panic increased. "I'm not good enough. I can't—"

"You can. Do what you have to do." Confidently, T.J. squeezed her hand. He released her. "I'll be waiting for you."

"No! Help me! I need your help. I can't do this alone."

At her plea, T.J. seemed pained. "Yes, you can. Do it."

A murmur rose from the crowd. Francesca leaned toward her microphone. With a flourish, she introduced Dayna again.

"But I don't know what to do!" Dayna cried in a hoarse whisper. Fear threatened to engulf her. The audience was waiting, Francesca was waiting, her parents were watching . . .

Deuce was watching. *Deuce.* All at once, Dayna realized

the message he'd been trying to send her. As a turned human, Deuce had done something none of the witchfolk—who'd always taken magic for granted—had thought to do. He'd detected magic someplace unexpected: in the graduation amulets.

Astonished, Dayna stared at the table. It was empty.

It was empty because Francesca had almost completed her conversion plan. She hadn't distributed her magic using her special cocktails, Dayna realized. Francesca had put pieces of her powerful vixen magic in the graduation amulets—the same amulets currently clutched in the hands of a thousand cusping witches, each of them overflowing with newly realized ability.

Suddenly, it all made sense. Francesca had appointed *herself* as the conduit for the dark magic she wanted to practice. She'd made sure *she* would be the heroine of the day—the indisputable queen of Covenhaven. But by doing so, Francesca had exposed herself in a way she never would have otherwise. She'd left herself open, thinking she really *was* invincible.

Instead, Dayna understood as she looked at her fellow vixen witch, Francesca's bitchy arrogance would be her downfall.

Drawing in a deep breath, Dayna held out her hand. Smiling, she walked toward the vixens with her head held high.

Frowning, T.J. watched as Dayna approached Francesca and her fellow vixen witches. He'd realized—finally—what he should have known all along: Dayna was the *juweel* he'd been seeking.

Now all that remained was trusting her.

Standing by as his bonded witch held out her hand to Francesca was the hardest thing he'd ever done. From the corner of his eye, T.J. saw Deuce watching him, his face taut. No doubt his partner feared that T.J. couldn't help intervening.

This time, though, T.J. believed. He believed in Dayna.

Beautiful and accomplished, Dayna reached her fellow vixens. Francesca murmured something to her; Dayna nodded.

She couldn't be forming the quad vixen pact . . . could she?

T.J. refused to believe it. Quietly shedding his disguise as Professor Reynolds, he fisted his hands. Far from him, Dayna lifted her arm, clearly preparing to link hands with Francesca.

At the last instant, though, Dayna wrapped her fingers around her graduation amulet instead. She turned to the cusping witches in her class. In an unmistakable signal, she raised her amulet high. The symbol of having finally overcome all her witchy struggles gleamed beneath the ballroom's bright lights.

With a hoarse incantation—one T.J. recognized—Dayna hurled her amulet to the floor. Noisily, it smashed in pieces.

To his amazement, at least two thirds of the cusping witches rose and smashed their amulets, too. Defiantly, they repeated the incantation Dayna had used—T.J.'s Patayan spell.

Their actions broke Francesca's hold on the cusping witches. Their voices rang out, overriding Sumner's outraged shriek and Francesca's desperate call.

Francesca tried to regain control of the witches, but it was too late. The combination of T.J.'s Patayan incantation and Dayna's ability to make the other witches link with *her* was too powerful to be countered—even with the vixens' Old Ways magic. Proudly, T.J. watched as Dayna stared in amazement at the crowd of witches she'd led and inspired and guided . . . all by herself.

A heartbeat later, all hell broke loose.

Shocked into stillness, Dayna stared at the mêlée surrounding her. The Followers in the audience—and among the cusping witches—bolted for the ballroom's exits. Hoping that meant she'd succeeded in ruining their plans, Dayna watched as IAB agents swarmed through those same exits, then took the Followers into custody with governing charms. Farther away, Deuce punched a warlock Follower who was sneaking past him. T.J. passed by in a blur of Patayan and legacy magic. Camille—to her astonishment—laid out a Follower with a well-placed kick. Proudly, she brushed back her hair and grinned.

Amid the mayhem, Dayna turned. Lily shouted something, then ran into the crowd—amazingly, it seemed, coming to Deuce's defense in his struggle with another Follower. Sumner cast Dayna a snarling look, then snatched the amulet from Francesca's hand. Leaving a visibly weakened Francesca behind, Sumner disappeared.

A flare of magic whooshed past Dayna. Newly alert, she tensed and prepared to fight back. But the battle was over almost as quickly as it had begun. Garmin appeared—bandaged but otherwise as in command as ever—and led his private IAB agents onstage. With blunt efficiency, the agents immobilized everyone whom Garmin identified as one of Francesca's Followers.

Hollow-eyed and pale, Francesca spit a hex at Garmin.

It had no effect. Her failure seemed to make the vixen witch twice as infuriated. It was obvious that Francesca hadn't had much experience with overcoming disappointment. With a frantic expression, she wheeled around, looking for an outlet for her rage. Her gaze landed on Dayna. Crazily, she smiled.

"That was so stupid of you. You turned down a chance to be one of *us*," Francesca said. "You could have had it all."

Dayna shrugged. "I already have everything I need."

Francesca gave a derisive laugh. "A loser like you would think so. But you don't know what you're missing."

Bitterly, Francesca cast a transmogrification spell. Dayna

sidestepped it easily. Strangely, she found no satisfaction in seeing her old witchy rival stripped of her powers.

"I guess you shouldn't have spread yourself so thinly," Dayna said. "You're too weak to make me feel bad anymore, Francesca. Besides, I'm not missing a thing. It turns out I have something you'll never have."

"What's that?" Francesca asked meanly. She tried another spell. "A half-breed boyfriend and a hideous haircut?"

"No." Dayna smiled. "I have real friends—friends who believe in me no matter what." Still astounded by that, Dayna broadened her smile. "*And* I have an awesome, kickass magical *compound* boyfriend. I'm going to find him right now."

Panting and battered, T.J. raised his head. The battle against the Followers—brief and intense as it had been—had wrecked the Janus ballroom. Overturned chairs littered the room; shattered chandelier crystals and broken glasses crunched underfoot; that hated sulfurous magic smell hung in the air.

Excited and chattering, the graduation attendees and their guests milled around the ballroom. Some of them cast repair spells. Others turned in avid circles, magically recording the event with memory flickers. Deuce sat across the room with Lily at his side, deep in conversation. Francesca cursed and swatted at the IAB agents as they hauled her away, ineffectually trying to hex a despairing-looking Garmin. Just as T.J.'s magus had foreseen, dark forces had come to Covenhaven.

But his bonded witch had bravely defeated them.

With thoughts of Dayna foremost in his mind, T.J. straightened. He peered over the heads of the witchfolk gathered in the ballroom, but he couldn't catch sight of her. Determined, T.J. used his earth magic to draw in a shaft of sunlight.

It roved over the ballroom, then came to rest on one rebellious dark-haired witch. She stood on her tiptoes, searching.

With his heart feeling newly full, T.J. headed in Dayna's direction. She hadn't seen him yet, but that didn't change his plans. Putting on his most single-minded expression, T.J. sneaked a pair of handcuffs from a nearby IAB agent's belt.

A short distance away, Dayna swiveled—her kitten familiar placidly grooming itself at her feet—dressed all in silver and looking like the magical answer to all his hopes and dreams. Still searching, she pursed her mouth, inspiring an urgent need to kiss her. Soon, T.J. would have his chance.

With his path lit by his conjured sunlight, he continued toward Dayna. His stolen handcuffs clinked at his side. If he was right—and T.J. fervently hoped so—these handcuffs would function the same way his magical bonds had done before.

Filled with raw anticipation, he unsnapped his restraints.

Standing close enough that his breath caressed her hair, T.J. stopped beside Dayna. The mayhem still continued around them, but he didn't care. His thoughts were filled with only one thing: making Dayna his own again . . . now and forever.

With a final flourish, T.J. conjured a field of wildflowers. Under his direction, the flowers popped up across the ballroom, following in the same path his footsteps had. Next T.J. made a few magical blooms spring up near Dayna's feet.

With a startled exclamation, Dayna looked down. Then she spun around, spotting him at last. Her smile broadened, more beautiful than the wildflowers and twice as magical.

With an answering grin, T.J. brandished his handcuffs. "Did you really think I wouldn't track you down and bring you in?"

"Well . . . Not for a minute. You're an excellent tracer."

"I'm even better at loving you. That's why I'm here."

"Okay then. I surrender. Make it official." Solemnly, she raised both her wrists. "You know I'm yours . . . now and forever."

Caught beneath her enchanting smile, T.J. dropped his

handcuffs. He didn't need them anymore. Instead, he pulled Dayna into his arms, then brought his mouth to hers. Amid the chaos of the ballroom, his senses filled with sulfur and noise, T.J. kissed his bonded witch with all the passion in his heart.

Dayna leaned back. "I love you, too." Leaning companionably against him, she whispered his name—his true name—in his ear.

Startled, T.J. reared back. "How did you do that?"

"I can't explain it." Happily, Dayna shrugged. "It just came to me—sort of like Garmin's clairvoyance. It's a good name, though. I don't know why you keep it a secret from everyone."

T.J. grumbled in disagreement . . . but he couldn't resist smiling. It was good to hear her call him by his true name.

"My ability to do that is probably similar to your ability to magik these wildflowers." Nodding at the floor, Dayna pointed. "Did you notice they're unpixilated?"

T.J. stared. To his surprise, the flowers were solid.

"Apparently, we're awesome apart . . . but we're *incredible* together." Dayna gave him an earnest look. "I'm so sorry, T.J. I promise I'll never doubt you again. I never meant to hurt you."

Urgently, T.J. kissed her again. "I'm sorry, too."

"The thing is, there was a lot I didn't know, and—" Dayna broke off and peered at her arm. "Hey. My arm prickles."

"Mine, too." Curiously, T.J. looked down. Then he looked at Dayna's arm. Just below her shoulder, something was happening.

"It's a tattoo!" Dayna stared at it. As they watched, a golden Gila monster formed above her biceps. With a distinct flourish, it ended its creation with a showy glow. "Look!"

"It's my birthright mark tattoo." Awestruck, T.J. watched as an identical symbol came to life on his arm. The golden Gila monster offered a swish of its tail, then settled into place, satisfied at last. "I think this means we're bonded forever."

"Sounds good to me." Dayna kissed him again. Teasingly, she said his true name—again and again and again. "I love you."

Feeling exactly the same way, T.J. smiled. "Life in a fully realized bonded pair isn't easy," he warned. "First, there's all the unstoppable love. Then there's the new and improved magic. Then there's the legendary, mind-blowing sex to reckon with—"

"Lead me to it." With an eager growl, Dayna rose on her tiptoes. This time, the words she whispered in T.J.'s ear had nothing to do with his true name . . . and everything to do with driving him crazy. Drawing back, his bonded witch arched her brow in a naughty way. "Are you up for it? I'm a fully licensed bonded witch now. I'm going to be a lot to handle."

"I'm a compound Patayan and warlock, fully in love and ready for action." With a lingering kiss, T.J. pulled Dayna closer. Outside, the Covenhaven Hallow-e'en Festival continued in all its noisy frivolity, its attendees blissfully unaware of how close they'd come to having their lives changed forever. "I'm pretty sure you just saved the world. I think you should be rewarded for that." T.J. gave Dayna his most wicked grin. "It turns out, I'm perfectly equipped for that job. So let's go."

With a satisfied smile, Dayna accepted his hand. Branded by their matching tattoos, she and T.J. headed for the door. This time they were bonded by choice and effort instead of magical fate. This time, they were ready to take on the world they'd saved. This time, they had a lot of love to guide the way . . .

. . . and a little bit of magic, too. Now and forever.

Dear Reader,

I'm so excited to bring you *My Favorite Witch*! This was a different kind of story for me, and it's taken my writing in a few new directions. I really appreciate your coming along for the ride. I did my best to bring you a world you would enjoy and characters you could believe in . . . and I had a lot of fun along the way! I truly hope you did too.

Don't forget to visit my Web site at www.lisaplumley.com, where you can read free first-chapter excerpts from all my books, sign up for my reader newsletter or new-book reminder service, catch sneak previews of my upcoming books, request special reader freebies, and more. I'm also on Facebook, MySpace, and Twitter, so please "friend" me on the service of your choice. The links are available on lisaplumley.com.

As always, I'd love to hear from you! You can send e-mail to lisa@lisaplumley.com or write to me c/o P.O. Box 7105, Chandler, AZ 85246-7105. In the meantime, I'll be hard at work on my next Zebra Books contemporary romance. I hope you'll be on the lookout for it!

Best Wishes,
Lisa Plumley